# DEBBIE MACOMBER

## Orchard Valley Grooms

**MIRA**

Recycling programs for this product may not exist in your area.

ISBN-13: 978-0-7783-2798-1

ORCHARD VALLEY GROOMS

Copyright © 2010 by MIRA Books.

The publisher acknowledges the copyright holder of the individual works as follows:

VALERIE
Copyright © 1992 by Debbie Macomber.

STEPHANIE
Copyright © 1992 by Debbie Macomber.

For questions and comments about the quality of this book please contact us at Customer_eCare@Harlequin.ca.

www.MIRABooks.com

**Printed in U.S.A.**

# CONTENTS

# VALERIE

To Dr. John T. and Kelly Dykstra
with grateful appreciation for their continued
support of the American Heart Association

# One

"Norah? Is that you?" Valerie Bloomfield's voice rose expectantly. She'd been trying to reach her sister for the past hour with no success.

"Valerie, where are you?"

"I'm on a layover in Chicago." She glanced around the departure lounge and surveyed the other passengers. "How's Dad?"

Norah hesitated, and that slight pause sent Valerie's worry escalating into panic. "Norah…" she began.

"He's doing as well as can be expected."

"Did you tell him I'm on my way?" Valerie had been in the middle of a business meeting in New York when she received the message. Her youngest sister had called the Houston office, and they'd passed on the news of her father's heart attack. Valerie had left immediately, catching the first available flight. Unfortunately that meant going to Oregon via Chicago.

"Dad knows you're coming."

"Were you able to get hold of Steff?"

Norah's sigh signaled her frustration. "Yes, but it took forever and my Italian is nonexistent. She's planning to catch whatever she can out of Rome, but she has to get there first—she's in some little village right now. It might take her a couple of days. The connection was bad and I couldn't understand everything she said. Apparently there's some sort of transportation strike. But she's doing her best...."

Valerie's sympathies went out to Stephanie, the middle Bloomfield sister. She must be frantic, stuck halfway across the world and desperate to find a way home.

"When will you get here?" Norah asked anxiously.

"The plane's scheduled to land at six-ten."

"Do you want me to meet you? I could—"

"No," Valerie interrupted. She didn't think it was a good idea for Norah to leave their father. "I've already ordered a car. It shouldn't take me more than forty minutes once I land, so don't worry about me."

"But the hospital's an hour's drive from the airport. You shouldn't even try to make it in less."

It generally did take an hour, but Valerie had every intention of getting there a lot sooner. "I should be at the hospital somewhere around seven," she said evasively.

"I'll see you then." Norah sounded resigned.

"Don't worry, kid, everything's going to be all right."

"Just be careful, will you?" Norah pleaded. "You being in an accident won't help Dad any."

"I'll be careful," Valerie promised, smiling at her sister's words. Trust Norah to take the practical approach. After a brief farewell, Valerie closed her cell phone and slipped it into her purse.

Half an hour later, she boarded her plane. She'd only brought a carry-on bag, unwilling to waste precious time waiting for luggage to be unloaded. Shutting her eyes, she leaned back in her seat as the plane taxied down the runway.

Her father was dying. Her dear father… His hold on life was precarious, and the burning need to get to him as quickly as possible drove her like nothing she'd ever experienced.

She was exhausted but sleep was out of the question. Valerie bent down for her purse, rummaging through it until she found the antacid tablets. She popped one in her mouth and chewed it with a vengeance.

No sooner had she swallowed the chalky tablet than she reached for a roll of the hard candies she always had with her. Four years earlier she'd quit smoking, and sucking on hard candy had helped her through the worst of the nicotine withdrawal. If she'd ever needed a cigarette, it was now. Her nerves were stretched to the breaking point.

Please, she prayed, not her father, too. Valerie was only beginning to come to grips with her mother's death. Grace Bloomfield had died of cancer almost four years ago, and the grief had shaken Valerie's well-ordered life. She'd buried her anguish in work; the biggest strides in her career with CHIPS, a Texas-based computer software company, had come in the past few years. She'd quickly climbed up the corporate ladder, until she was the youngest executive on the management team.

Her father had reacted similarly to Grace's death. Working too many hours, driving himself too hard. Norah had tried to tell her, but Valerie hadn't paid attention. She should've done something, anything, to get their father to slow down, to relax and enjoy life. He should have retired years before; he could be traveling, seeing exotic places, meeting with old friends and making new ones. In the years since her mother's death, Valerie had convinced her father to leave Orchard Valley only once and that had been a two-week trip to Italy to visit Steffie.

And now he was fighting for his life in a hospital.

Valerie hadn't said anything to him because…well, because they were so much alike. David Bloomfield was working out his grief the same way she was. Valerie couldn't very well criticize him for something she was doing herself.

Before she knew it, she'd chomped her way through two rolls of candy and another of antacid tablets.

When the plane landed, Valerie was the first one off, scurrying with her bag down the concourse to the rental car agency. Within fifteen minutes, she was on the freeway heading east toward Orchard Valley.

Heading toward home.

Norah was right; it took Valerie longer than forty minutes to reach Orchard Valley Hospital. She got there in forty-five. She took the first available parking space, unconcerned about whether the rental car would be towed. What did concern her was seeing her father.

Norah was standing in the hospital lobby when Valerie walked through the double glass doors. Her sister, looking drawn and pale, was visibly relieved by her presence. "Oh, Valerie," she said, covering her mouth with one hand. "Oh, Valerie… I'm so glad you're here."

"Dad?" Valerie's throat closed up. If her cantankerous father had had the audacity to die before she arrived, she'd never forgive him. The thought made her realize how much this ordeal had drained her.

"He's resting comfortably…for now."

Valerie hugged her sister. Norah looked dreadful, her stylish shoulder-length blond hair brushed away from her face as if her hands had swept it behind her ears countless times. Her blue eyes, normally so clear and bright, were red-rimmed from tears and lack of sleep.

Valerie hadn't had much rest herself, but she was still running on adrenaline. She wouldn't collapse until after she'd had a chance to see her father.

"What exactly happened?" she asked as they hurried to the elevator. Their shoes made a sharp, clicking sound against the polished linoleum floor, a sound that reminded Valerie of similar visits a few years ago, when her mother was dying. She remembered similar nighttime walks down these silent corridors. She hadn't been to this hospital since. The memories overwhelmed her now, tearing at the facade of her poise.

"After dinner last night, Dad went out onto the porch," Norah began, her voice quavering.

As far back as Valerie could remember, after the evening meal her parents had adjourned for coffee to the sweeping front porch of their large colonial home. They'd sat together on the old wicker chairs, sometimes holding hands and whispering like teenagers. Valerie was never sure what they discussed, but she'd learned early on not to interrupt them. In the winters, they'd sat in front of the basalt fireplace in her father's den, but during spring, summer and the early part of autumn, it was the porch.

"I should've known something was wrong," Norah continued. "Dad hasn't sat on the porch much since Mom's been gone. After dinner he goes right into his office and does his bookkeeping."

The guilt Valerie experienced was crushing. Norah had repeatedly told her how hard their father was working. She should have listened, should have demanded he hire an assistant, take a vacation, *something.* As the oldest, she felt responsible.

His heart was weak and had been since a bout of rheumatic fever in his thirties. By all accounts he should've died then, but a young nurse's devotion had pulled him through. The nurse was Grace Johnson, who became David's wife, and Valerie, Stephanie and Norah's mother.

"I brought him a cup of coffee," Norah went on, "and he looked up at me and smiled. He…he seemed to think I was Mom."

"Was he in terrible pain?"

Norah bit her lower lip. "Yes, he must have been. He was so pale… Only he was too proud to admit it. I asked him what was wrong, but he wouldn't answer. He just kept saying he was ready."

"Ready for what?"

Norah glanced away. "Ready to die."

"Die!" Valerie cried. "That's ridiculous! If there was ever a man who had something to live for, it's Dad. Good grief, he's worked hard all his life! Now, it's time to reap the fruits of his labors, to enjoy his family, to travel, to—"

"You don't need to convince me," Norah said quietly as they reached the third floor and stepped out of the elevator. The Coronary Care nurses' station was directly in front of them. Norah walked to the counter.

"Betty, would you tell Dr. Winston my sister's arrived?"

"Right away," the other woman replied. She appeared to be gentle, compassionate—and practical. No-nonsense. Valerie recognized those traits because Betty shared them with Norah. And with their mother…

Valerie had to suppress a sudden smile at the memory of her youngest sister lining up dolls in her bed and sticking thermometers in their mouths. She'd fussed over them like an anxious mother, bandaging their limbs and offering comfort and reassurance.

Norah came by this temperament naturally, Valerie supposed, since their mother had been the same. Although she'd given up her hospital job when she married David

Bloomfield, Grace continued to nurture those around her. It had been her gift. It was Norah's gift, too.

"Who's Dr. Winston?" Valerie asked. She'd never heard of him before; he must be a recent addition to the hospital staff. But the last thing their father needed at a time like this was some hayseed family practitioner. He should be in a major hospital with the best heart surgeon available!

"Dr. Winston's been wonderful," Norah returned, her eyes lighting up briefly. "If it hadn't been for Colby, we would've lost Dad in the first twelve hours."

"Colby?" The doctor was named after a cheese? This didn't sound promising.

"I don't know what I would've done without him," Norah said. "I wasn't sure what to do at first. I could tell Dad was in a lot of pain, but I knew he'd object if I called for an aid car. He'd argue with me and that would've made matters even worse if it was his heart like I suspected."

"So you phoned Dr. Winston?"

"Yes. Luckily I was able to get hold of him, and he drove out, pretending to drop in out of the blue. He knew the minute he saw Dad that it was a heart attack. He immediately gave him a couple of aspirin. Then he sat down on the porch and had a cup of coffee with him."

"He drank coffee while our father was having a *heart attack?*" Valerie wasn't finding this doctor too impressive.

"I believe it was what saved Dad's life," Norah said, her eyes flashing a protest. "Dr. Winston convinced Dad to go to the hospital voluntarily. It wasn't until he'd been admitted that he suffered the worst of the attack. If he'd been at home arguing, no one could've done anything to save him."

"Oh." That took some of the heat out of Valerie's argument. She suspected she was looking for someone to blame—in an attempt to ease her own guilt for having ignored Norah's concerns about their father.

The door Betty had walked through opened, and a tall dark-haired man came toward them, his expression serious. Valerie couldn't help noticing how attractive he was. In fact, the man had movie-star good looks, but good looks with nothing soft or insipid about them.

"Hello," he said, his voice deep and resonant. "I'm Dr. Winston." He held out his hand.

"Valerie Bloomfield," she responded briskly, placing her hand in his. She'd always been taught that it was impolite to stare, but she couldn't stop herself. Her father's physician didn't look much older than her own thirty-one years. "Excuse me," she said, not glancing at Norah, who would, she suspected, immediately leap to Dr. Winston's defense. "I don't mean to be rude—but how old are you?"

"Valerie," Norah groaned under her breath.

"I just want to know how long he's been practicing medicine. Good grief, Norah, this is our *father*."

"It's quite all right," Dr. Winston said, smiling at Norah. "If David was my father I'd have a few questions myself. I'm thirty-six."

Valerie found it hard to believe, but she couldn't very

well insist on seeing his birth certificate. Besides, her
thoughts were muddled and she was exhausted. Now
wasn't the time to question his qualifications. "How's
my father?" she asked instead.

"He's resting."

"When will I be able to see him?"

"I'd rather you didn't go in right away."

"What do you mean?" Valerie snapped. "I've flown
across the country to be with my father. He needs me!
Why shouldn't I be able to go to him?"

"It's not a good idea just now. He's sleeping for the
first time in nearly twenty hours and I don't want
anything to disturb him."

"I think you should wait," Norah seconded, as if she
feared Valerie might be on the verge of making a scene.

Valerie sighed; her sister was right. "Of course I'll
wait. It's just that I'm anxious."

"I understand," Dr. Winston said. But he spoke
without emotion. He led them to a room not far from
the nurses' station. Two well-worn couches faced each
other, and several outdated magazines littered the coffee
table that stood between them. There was a coffeepot
in one corner, with powdered creamer and an ample
supply of disposable cups.

Norah sat first, raising both hands to her mouth in an
effort to hide a yawn.

"How long have you been here?" Valerie asked, realizing even before she asked that Norah had stayed at
the hospital all night. Her youngest sister was exhausted.

"Listen, kid, you go on home and get some sleep. I'll hold down the fort for a while."

Norah grinned sheepishly. "I used to hate it when you called me kid, but I don't anymore."

"Why not?" Valerie asked softly, resisting the urge to brush a stray curl from her sister's forehead. She wasn't the maternal type, but she felt protective toward Norah, wanting to ease her burden.

"You can call me kid anytime you like because that's exactly the way I feel, like a child whose world's been turned upside down. I'm scared, Val, really scared. We almost lost him—we still could."

Valerie nodded, hugging her briefly. Norah had suffered through the worst of the nightmare alone, not knowing from one minute to the next if their father was going to live or die.

"Valerie's right," Dr. Winston added. "There's nothing you can do here. Go home and rest. I promise I'll call you if there's any change."

"Okay." Norah rubbed her eyes. "I'll take a shower and try to sleep for a couple of hours. That's all I need. Two, maybe three hours."

Valerie wondered if Norah was too tired to drive; Dr. Winston must have had the same concern.

"We'll phone for a cab from the nurses' station. I don't want you driving like this." He placed his arm around Norah's shoulders, apparently intending to walk her to the elevator. As they left, he turned to Valerie. "I'll be back in a few minutes."

While he was away, Valerie poured herself a cup of coffee. The pot had obviously been sitting there for hours; the coffee was black and thick and strong, just the way she needed it.

The urge for a cigarette was nearly overwhelming, so when Dr. Winston returned to the room she looked up at him and automatically asked, "Do you have any hard candy?"

"I beg your pardon?"

"Mints, anything like that." She was pacing the room, holding her coffee cup in both hands.

"I'm afraid not. Would you like me to see if I could get you some?"

Valerie dismissed his offer with a shake of her head. He was polite to a fault. The first thing she'd done had been to insult him, question his competence, and he'd taken it all in stride.

"Please, tell me about my father."

They sat, and for the next fifteen minutes, Dr. Winston explained what had happened to her father's heart. He did his best to describe it in layman's terms, but much of what he said was beyond Valerie's comprehension. She'd never been comfortable with medical matters. Her mother and Norah had always dealt with those. For her part, Valerie hated anything to do with hospitals or doctors. She detested being sick herself, and knew her father felt the same way.

"There's one underlying problem that needs to be dealt with, however."

"Yes?" Valerie asked, hating the way her voice betrayed her fear. Any show of weakness distressed her. If she'd ever needed to be strong, it was now, for everyone's sake, including her own. She was the oldest, and the others would rely on her.

"Your father's lost his will to live."

"That's ridiculous," she said, battling the urge to argue with him. "My father's life is brimming over, it's so full. Why, he's—"

"Lost without your mother," Dr. Winston finished simply.

Valerie bolted to her feet and resumed pacing. What Dr. Winston said was absolutely true; she had to admit it. Her father had been crushed under the load of grief, and while Valerie and her two sisters struggled to regain their own balance, their father had been slowly destroyed by his loss.

"What can we do?" she asked, trying to swallow her fears and her guilt.

"Support him, give him your love. The only thing keeping him alive now is his desire to see all three of his daughters before he dies."

"But… Okay, then don't let him know I'm here." It was the obvious solution. And if that was what it took to keep him alive, she was willing to play a little game of hide-and-seek. Norah could make up a series of excuses. No, forget Norah, Valerie mused bleakly. Her youngest sister couldn't tell a lie without blushing.

"How well do you lie?" she asked, thinking fast.

Dr. Winston blinked. "I beg your pardon?"

"We can't let my father know I've arrived. And that means lying to him."

"Miss Bloomfield—"

"Ms."

"Whatever," he said, sounding impatient with her for the first time. "We aren't going to be able to fool your father. Norah talked to him shortly after you phoned from…where was it? Chicago? He knows you caught a flight out of New York. No one's going to make him believe something more important came up that's kept you from him."

"Steffie!" Valerie cried. "When Norah spoke to her, she said there was a transportation strike."

"Yes, but these are only stop-gap measures. Your father feels there's nothing left to live for. He talks about your mother constantly, almost as though he's waiting to join her. We need something concrete that'll give him the will to fight, to hold on to life."

Again Valerie knew the doctor was right, but her confused brain was having trouble assimilating the most basic details, let alone a situation as complex as this.

"He's all we have," she whispered despondently. "Surely he realizes that."

"Yes, but at the same time, he believes you have one another."

"We have nothing in common," Valerie told him. "Steffie's a crazy woman who flies off to Europe to study the Italian Renaissance, and Norah's main goal in life is to become another Clara Barton. We don't even *look* alike." Valerie was grasping at weak excuses, and she knew it. Anything she could think of to enlist Dr. Winston's help in keeping her father alive...

"That has nothing to do with me, Valerie," he told her gently. "However, I'll do everything I can to see that your father regains his health and lives to a ripe old age."

Blinking away tears, Valerie nodded, reminding herself once again that she was the oldest of David Bloomfield's daughters. In a crisis everyone looked to her; she was the one who needed a cool, decisive head, who couldn't let her emotions dictate her reactions.

But it was different this time.

The man in that hospital bed, barely holding on to life, was her father, the man she idolized and loved beyond reason. Her emotions were so close to the surface that the force of them frightened her.

"I'd—I'd like to see him as soon as possible. Please." She'd grovel if necessary. She *had* to be with her father. "I won't make the least bit of noise, I promise." She certainly didn't want to disturb his rest. Somehow, though, she had to reassure herself that he was still alive. She'd never been more frightened.

Dr. Winston hesitated. "Wait here, I'll go and check on him."

He returned a few minutes later. "David's awake and asking for you."

Valerie was so eager that she nearly vaulted out of the room, but Dr. Winston stopped her. "Before you go to your father, let me prepare you for what you're going to see." He spent the next five minutes explaining the different medical devices used to monitor his patient's heart. He explained how the small electrodes on her father's chest detected the electrical impulses that signal the heart's activity. He warned her about the tubes going in and out of his body.

But nothing he said could have prepared Valerie for what she saw. Her father was connected to a frightening number of tubes, machines and devices. His face was ashen, so pale and bloodless that his skin seemed iridescent. His eyes, which had always sparked with vitality, revealed no emotion, only a weariness that was soul-deep.

"Oh, Daddy," Valerie whispered, fighting tears. She locked her fingers around his hand, careful not to disturb the intravenous needle.

"Valerie…so pleased you're here…at last."

"Where else would I be?" she asked, managing a smile. With the back of her other hand, she brushed a tear from her cheek.

"She's beautiful, isn't she?" her father said, apparently talking to Dr. Winston, who hovered in the doorway. "Only…what did you do to your hair?"

"Do you like it?" Valerie asked, rallying somewhat, surprised he'd even noticed that she'd changed the style. "I had it cut." The new look was short and tousled.

"She's got the temper to go with that red hair, you know."

Her father was speaking to Colby Winston again.

"My hair isn't even close to being red," she argued, annoyed by the doctor's effort not to grin. "It's auburn."

"Looks like you haven't combed it in a month," her father mumbled.

"Dad, I'll have you know I paid good money for this."

"In that case, you should demand a refund." His voice was weak, and speaking had clearly depleted him of what little energy he possessed.

"Dad," Valerie said, trying to disguise her concern. "Instead of complaining about my hair, you should rest."

He didn't respond, merely closed his eyes and sighed audibly.

"I'm going to leave you for a little while," Valerie said. "But I'll be right outside, so if you want to tell me how much you like my hair and beg my forgiveness, then all you need to do is ring for the nurse." Dr. Winston had told her earlier that she'd be allowed to visit her father five minutes out of every hour, depending on how well he was doing.

David's smile was barely discernible.

"Rest now, Daddy. I'm here."

Dr. Winston's hand was at her elbow directing her out of the glass-enclosed cubicle.

"Doc?" Her father's voice had a sense of urgency.

"What is it, David?"

"She's the one I was telling you about. You remember what I said, don't you?"

"Yes. Now don't you worry about a thing."

"Her hair doesn't usually look like a rag doll's."

"Daddy!" Valerie had no idea what was taking place between the two men but she wasn't going to stand idly by and let them insult her.

"This way," Colby Winston said, leading her from the Coronary Care Unit.

"What was *that* all about?" Valerie asked the instant they were out of earshot.

"I'm not sure I know what you mean," he said without meeting her eyes.

Valerie wasn't fooled. There was definitely something going on, and she wanted to know what. She'd been in business far too long to allow questionable remarks to slip past her unchallenged.

"What did Dad mean, I'm 'the one'?"

Dr. Winston still refused to look at her. "While we—your father and I—were talking earlier, he voiced a few concerns about his daughters."

"Yes?" Valerie said. Making an effort to appear nonchalant and relaxed, she walked over to the coffeepot and lifted it to him in silent invitation.

Dr. Winston shook his head and Valerie refilled her own paper cup. "So, what did Dad have to say about us girls?" she asked.

"He's very proud of all three of you."

"Naturally. We're his children. What I'd like to know is what he meant when he said I was 'the one.'"

"Yes, well…" He walked away from her and stood gazing out the window into the night sky.

"Come on, Dr. Winston, I'm a mature woman and this is my father. I'm sure if I insisted he'd tell me." They both knew that coercing her father was out of the question; nevertheless, it was an effective ploy. Dr. Winston went to the coffeepot and filled a cup, even though he'd declined one moments earlier.

"It seems he's the most worried about you."

"Me?" Valerie blurted. Of the three girls, she was the most financially secure. She was established in an excellent career and living on her own. For heaven's sake, she was the only one with investments! "That makes no sense at all."

"Yes, well…"

"Why is he worried about me? Furthermore, why didn't he talk to *me* instead of discussing it with you?"

"There are any number of reasons—"

"Just tell me what he said," Valerie interrupted impatiently.

"Your father seems to think—"

"Yes?" she prompted.

"That you should be married."

Valerie couldn't restrain her laughter. It shot out of her, like bubbles from a champagne bottle.

"In fact," Colby continued grimly, "your father seems to think you should be married to me."

# Two

"Married to you?" Valerie echoed, her laughter fading. Dr. Colby Winston! She'd never heard anything so preposterous. She had no intention of marrying *anyone* within the foreseeable future. There was simply no room for a man in her life. She wasn't a romantic; even when she was younger and in college, she hadn't dated much. Her father knew all that, and he'd never seemed particularly worried about it. This latest revelation shocked her nearly as much as Norah's call.

"I see no reason to be too concerned," Colby said, his voice compassionate as though he understood that his announcement had unsettled her. She was usually more proficient at controlling her emotions.

"This sort of delusion isn't unheard of in heart patients," he went on. "As I said, I certainly don't think you have anything to worry about."

"You mean your patients generally try to marry you off?"

"No." He smoothed his tie as if he needed something to do. "Your father fully expects to die. It's what he wants, but he'd feel better about leaving the three of you behind if at least one of you was married. Your father and I are friends, and I guess it's only natural that he'd attempt to match me up with one of his daughters."

"It should've been Norah. She seems more your type."

His smile was fleeting. "Perhaps, but it's your name he repeatedly mentions."

"Then apparently I'm the one," Valerie said, not realizing what she was saying until the words had left her mouth. "I mean—" She stopped abruptly.

"I know exactly what you mean," Colby assured her. "But I'm sure we don't have to take any of this seriously."

"Oh, I agree. That would be foolish in the extreme."

"Maybe your father feels you should marry first because you're the oldest," Colby ventured.

"Maybe," Valerie agreed. But something inside her suggested that wasn't the sole reason. She tucked her arms around her waist and inhaled deeply, hoping to breathe in a bit of calm and sense.

"I wouldn't have said anything," Colby said, "but I thought it was best to air this. If he mentions marriage again, my feeling is we should go along with him, at least for now."

"Go along with him? You've got to be kidding." Valerie could hardly believe her ears.

Colby shrugged. "You know your father better than I do," he muttered. "He's as stubborn as they come. Don't lie, but if he brings up the subject of…marriage, take the route of least resistance, then try to channel the conversation in a different direction."

"I'm not going to give my father any false hope. Or you either." She added the last part coyly and was rewarded when she saw him swallow tightly. An angry spark momentarily leaped into his dark eyes, but was soon quelled.

Sitting down, Valerie rummaged through her purse for a roll of antacid tablets. Her stomach ached and she was weary to her very bones.

Colby ignored her, although he made no move to go. The preoccupied look on his face suggested that he had something else to say; he seemed to be searching for words.

Valerie considered what Colby had told her. If she ever decided to marry—*if*—she'd settle down with someone who had the same drive, the same will to succeed, as she did. A man who knew where he was going, who'd set his sights high. Not some well-meaning small-town doctor.

She'd marry a man like Rowdy Cassidy.

The name sprang into her mind with a suddenness that shocked her.

Until that moment, Valerie didn't fully grasp how much she admired her employer. Rowdy had started his computer software business out of a friend's garage fifteen years earlier. He'd built the company into one of the most successful in the country. Although he'd earned more money than he could possibly spend in a lifetime, he continued to work ten- and twelve-hour days, demanding as much of his staff as he did of himself.

"It might, uh, help matters if you were involved with someone," Colby said in a casual voice. Valerie found his nonchalant tone a bit exaggerated, which for some reason made her suspect that he *wasn't* "involved with someone."

"I'm not in a relationship at the moment, but I might be soon," she told him. Valerie and Rowdy—a couple. Odd that she'd never thought of him in romantic terms before. He'd be the perfect husband for her. She liked him and respected him, as a man and a professional. Rowdy had hand-picked her for his management team because he believed in her abilities.

In retrospect, she realized Rowdy had sought out her company on several occasions. But she'd been so absorbed in proving herself worthy of his faith that she hadn't guessed he might have any personal feelings for her.

For months she'd been blind to what was right in front of her. Not that she was entirely to blame, though. Rowdy wasn't exactly a heartthrob kind of guy. Oh, he was handsome enough, with his rugged cowboy looks, but his brusque, outspoken manner didn't encourage romantic aspirations. As far as she knew, he'd never dated anyone seriously, at least not in the years she'd worked for him.

For that matter, Valerie wasn't any expert on falling

in love, either. She'd dismissed the possibility of romance in her own life; it was fine for her sisters and school-friends, but not for her. There'd always been too much she wanted to do, too much to strive for. Too much to achieve before settling down in a permanent relationship.

"I'm afraid I don't understand," Colby said, breaking into her thoughts. At her blank look, he elaborated. "You said you weren't involved with someone *yet,* but you will be soon. I may be overstepping my bounds here, but I wouldn't advise you to invent a phony relationship. Your father would see through that in a minute."

"I agree. I wouldn't even attempt anything so foolish. But there's a man I work with, and, well, it seems natural for the two of us to…get involved."

Dr. Winston looked so relieved that she might've been offended if she hadn't been warmed by the newly risen hope of a romance with Rowdy Cassidy.

"I've given your father something to help him rest," Colby went on. "He should sleep through the night without a problem, so if you want to drive home and join your sister—"

"No," Valerie interrupted quickly. "I won't leave Dad. I understand that I can't see him yet, but I want to be here…in case anything happens. It's important to me."

"That's fine."

Valerie was grateful. "Thank you."

He nodded, then yawned, revealing for the first time his own fatigue. "I've left orders that I'm to be contacted the minute there's any change in his condition."

"I can't thank you enough for everything you've done."

"No thanks necessary. I'll talk to you in the morning."

Valerie smiled and sat down to leaf through a six-month-old news magazine. She'd just finished reading the letters to the editor when the nurse appeared, carrying a pillow and a blanket.

"Dr. Winston thought you might need these," she said, setting the bundle down next to Valerie.

It was a thoughtful thing to do, she mused later as she rested her head against the pillow and tucked the thin blanket around her shoulders. She felt a twinge of guilt, especially since she'd already decided to call in the country's top heart surgeon first thing in the morning.

By noon, it was unlikely that her father would still be a patient of Dr. Colby Winston's.

He liked her, Colby realized. He'd been prepared not to. Valerie Bloomfield was everything her father had claimed. Professional, astute and lovely. But when it came to relationships, she was precisely the type of woman Colby made a point of avoiding.

He liked his women soft and feminine. He was looking for a wife, and David Bloomfield had somehow intuited that, or he wouldn't have dragged his eldest daughter into almost every conversation. But Colby didn't have a business executive in mind. He needed a helpmate, a woman who understood the never-ending demands of a doctor's work. A woman who'd understand the long hours, the emotional stress, the intrusions into his private life.

What he didn't need was a career-obsessed executive. Perhaps he was outdated in his thinking. He certainly acknowledged that a woman had every right to pursue her own profession, to choose her own calling in life, but Colby was looking for a woman who'd make that calling *him*. Well, not just him but *them*—their marriage, their family, their home.

He had to admit it sounded selfish and egocentric to expect his wife to wrap her life around his. Nevertheless that was exactly what he wanted.

His own career was all-consuming; there weren't enough hours in the day to do everything that needed to be done. When he got home at night he wanted someone there to greet him, to offer comfort, serenity.

Sherry Waterman fit the bill perfectly. They'd been dating off and on for almost a year. Lately, it seemed, more off than on. Colby wasn't sure why he'd allowed his relationship with Sherry to taper off. He hadn't talked to her in nearly two weeks now—maybe longer. But he knew she'd be an ideal wife for him, and for that matter so would Norah Bloomfield. Yet he couldn't picture spending the rest of his life with either of them.

If he was going to analyze his lack of interest in both Sherry and Norah, then he might as well examine what he found so attractive about Valerie. Not the briefcase she carried with her like a second purse. Certainly not the way she popped antacid tablets, or the way she dressed in a sexless gray suit that disguised every feminine curve of her slender frame.

What appealed to him most was the contrast he sensed in her. Outwardly she appeared calm and collected, asking intelligent questions with the composure of someone inquiring about commonplace statistics instead of her father's chances of survival.

Colby hadn't been fooled. He noted how she gnawed on her lower lip even while her gaze steadily met his. Valerie had been badly shaken by her father's ordeal. There were depths of emotion in this woman, a real capacity for feeling that was—or so he guessed—usually kept hidden.

He also noticed the love in her eyes when he took her to see her father. He'd watched her struggle to keep her emotions at bay. Her fingers had trembled when they reached for her father's hand and her face had grown gentle. There was a strong bond between those two.

It hadn't been necessary to repeat David's comment about their marrying, and Colby wasn't sure why he had.

He suspected he'd been hoping to discover if she was involved with someone. Knowing that she was, or rather that she was about to be, should have reassured him. But it hadn't. If anything, he was more curious than ever.

Norah's arrival stirred Valerie into wakefulness early the following morning. She hadn't slept much, too exhausted and keyed up to let herself relax. Toward dawn she'd drifted into an uneasy slumber.

"How's Dad?" Norah asked, handing Valerie a white sack that contained breakfast.

"The same. I haven't been in to see him, but I've talked to the CCU staff several times." She'd paced the hospital corridor most of the night and as a result had received intermittent reports.

"He's been like this from the first, as though he's balancing on the edge of a cliff. He could fall either way."

"He'll live," Valerie said fervently, as if her determination would be enough to keep him alive.

"I hope you're right."

"I am," Valerie returned, forcing her voice to remain confident.

"Oh, before I forget," Norah said, sitting opposite Valerie, "there were two messages on the answering machine when I got home last night. The first was from Mr. Cassidy at CHIPS. He's your boss, isn't he?"

Valerie nodded, opening the bag her sister had brought. She removed a warm croissant and a cup of fresh coffee. The last time she could remember eating had been at O'Hare, and although her pizza had looked decent, she'd been too upset to feel very hungry.

"What'd Rowdy have to say?"

"Just that he'd heard about Dad's heart attack. He asked if there was anything he could do."

Valerie smiled to herself, pleased that Rowdy had taken a few minutes out of his busy schedule to call. It seemed to confirm her thoughts of the night before; she was increasingly convinced that his interest in her was more than business.

"Who else phoned?" she asked, purposely turning

her mind from Rowdy. There'd be plenty of time later to mull over her recent revelation.

"Steff."

"How's she doing?" Valerie asked before biting into the flaky croissant.

"Not very well, I'm afraid." Norah's shoulders slumped forward slightly. "She sounded desperate."

"I take it she hasn't left Italy yet?"

"She can't. Apparently the whole country's at a standstill. Like I told you, she's trapped in this tiny village a hundred miles outside Rome. She'd gone there to spend a few days with a friend's family."

"Why doesn't she rent a car?"

"Seems everyone else thought of the same thing. There's not a car to be had."

"What about her friends?"

"From what I understand, the people she's with don't have a car. She and her friend got a ride there from someone else, and everyone she knows is away on spring break. She's very upset. I called her back, but she was out, so I left a message." Norah shook her head in frustration.

"What did you tell her?"

"That you'd arrived. That I'm on leave from my job as long as necessary. And…that Dad's condition is stable." It was a small lie, but necessary, Valerie agreed, for their sister's peace of mind.

"I'll try to give her a call later," Valerie said, sipping the rapidly cooling coffee. She glanced at her watch and calculated the time difference between Oregon and Texas. If she phoned now she might be able to catch Rowdy. If he was in the office, she'd ask him to locate the best heart surgeon in the state. No, on the West Coast.

She knew there were restrictions against using cell phones in hospitals, so she lined up at the pay phone, which didn't afford her much privacy. But that couldn't be helped. To her relief, she was immediately connected with her boss.

"Valerie," he said, his big voice booming over the wire. "Good to hear from you. How's your father?"

"We don't know yet. It could go either way."

"I'm sorry to hear that." Rowdy sounded genuinely concerned and again her heart warmed toward him. "If there's anything I can do, let me know."

"There is," Valerie said, lowering her voice in an effort not to be overheard. She looked around to make sure no staff members were within earshot. "I need the name and phone number of the best heart surgeon on the West Coast. Dad's too ill to be transferred to another hospital just yet, but the one here in Orchard Valley is small. I can't be sure he's getting the best possible care. I want to make other arrangements as soon as I can."

"Of course, I'll get right on it."

Not for the first time, Valerie felt a twinge of conscience. Colby Winston obviously cared about her father. If she hurt his professional pride by going behind his back, then she'd apologize. For now, though, her primary concern had to be her father, and if that meant offending a family friend, well, too bad. It couldn't be avoided.

"How can I reach you at the hospital?" Rowdy asked.

"It's easier if I call you back. In an hour or so?"

"Sure thing."

"I really appreciate this," Valerie told him.

A few minutes later, she strolled into the waiting room, where she'd left Norah. Colby had joined her and it struck Valerie a second time how perfect Norah would be for him.

Valerie should've been pleased by the idea. Excited, too. But she wasn't and she didn't know why.

Norah smiled at something Colby was saying, and Valerie realized with a small pang that her youngest sister was half in love with him already. If she could see it, then surely her father had, too. He was probably confusing the two of them in his mind, Valerie reasoned, which was certainly understandable under the circumstances.

"Dad's doing about the same," Norah said when she became aware that Valerie had entered the room. "Colby was just in to see him."

"Good morning," he greeted her, smiling briefly.

"Morning." Feeling guilty, she couldn't meet his eyes.

"You can take turns visiting your father if you'd like, but you can only stay five minutes, and I'd prefer that you waited an hour between visits."

"Fine," Valerie murmured. "Since I was with him last night, do you want to go first?" she asked Norah.

"All right."

Valerie assumed that Dr. Winston would go with her sister, but he stayed behind, pouring himself a cup of coffee from the freshly brewed pot. His back was to Valerie.

"Your father's going to require open-heart surgery," he said once he'd turned around to face her. "Right now his heart's too weak to withstand the additional stress, but we're fast approaching a crisis point, and you and your sisters need to prepare yourselves."

"Here?" Valerie challenged. "And who'd perform the surgery?"

"I will— I *am* a qualified cardiovascular surgeon. And Orchard Valley has one of the best heart units in the state," Colby said in a reassuring voice.

"I don't want *one* of the best, I want the *very* best! This is my *father* we're talking about." Valerie knew she sounded unreasonable, even rude, but her concern about David overrode all other considerations, including her embarrassment at misjudging Dr. Winston. Why had Norah never mentioned that the man was a heart surgeon? Still, it didn't matter; her father deserved the best-equipped facility and the best-trained specialist around. She spoke in a calmer voice. "If he needs surgery, then he'll have it, but not here. Not when there's a better hospital and more experienced..."

"Heart surgeons?" Colby finished for her.

She stiffened, wanting to avoid a confrontation and knowing it was impossible. "Exactly."

"You're welcome to a second opinion, Valerie. I'd be happy to review my credentials with you, as well."

Her arms cradled her middle. Her breakfast seemed to lie like a deadweight in her stomach.

Colby had begun to speak again. "Norah—"

"You already mentioned the possibility of open-heart surgery to Norah?" she flared, disliking the fact that he'd talked to her sister first.

He nodded. "Just now. While you were out."

That hurt her pride. She, after all, was the oldest, the decision maker, the strong one.

"If you'd like to talk to another specialist, I can recommend several."

"That won't be necessary," Valerie returned stiffly, feeling like a traitor. "I'm having a friend get me the names of the top heart surgeons on the West Coast."

A vacuum of silence followed her words.

"I understand."

She glanced toward him, surprised not to hear any resentment in his voice.

"It isn't that we don't appreciate everything you've done," she rushed to explain. "Norah's told me several times that if it weren't for you, we'd have lost Dad that first night. I'm grateful, more than you'll ever know, but I want to stack the odds in Dad's favor, and if that means bringing in another surgeon, I'll do it."

Her impassioned words were met with a cool but not unfriendly smile. "If David were my father I'd do the same. Don't worry, Valerie, you haven't offended me."

She was so relieved that she nearly sagged onto the sofa.

"Let me know who you want to call in and I'll be happy to confer with him."

"Thank you," she whispered. "Dad and Norah are right," she added, almost to herself.

"About what?" Colby asked on his way out the door.

She looked up, realizing he'd heard her. "You really are wonderful."

Their eyes met and in those few seconds an odd understanding passed between them. It wasn't a look lovers would exchange, she thought, but one close friends would.

Norah came back from the five-minute visit with their father, pale and clearly distressed. Slowly she lowered herself onto the sofa, her hands clasped tightly together.

"Dad's not doing well this morning?" Valerie ventured.

Norah nodded. "He's so weak…he's talking about dying and…" She paused, her light blue eyes glassy with tears.

"He isn't going to die," Valerie said vehemently, clenching her fists at her sides. She *refused* to let him die.

"He'd prefer if you and Steff and I were married, but that can't be helped now, he says. He told me he's sorry he won't be around to enjoy his grandchildren, but—"

"Norah," Valerie admonished briskly, "you didn't honestly listen to that garbage, did you? We can't allow him to talk like that."

"He seems to think you should marry Dr. Winston."

Valerie frowned. "So I heard. That just goes to show

you how illogical he's become. If anyone should marry Colby Winston, it's you."

Norah lowered her eyes and an attractive shade of pink flowed into her cheeks. "Every female employee in the hospital's in love with Dr. Winston. Even the married women have a crush on him. He's so strong, yet he's gentle and caring. I—I don't know what I would've done the last couple of days without Colby."

"You really care about him, don't you?" Valerie asked, fighting down an unexpected sense of disappointment.

"I'm not in love with him—not exactly. I admire him the way everyone else does, and if he ever asked me out, I'd accept without thinking twice, but he hasn't."

Valerie was sure she would. She paced the small room, wondering what had prompted this sudden need for movement—her father's apparent death wish or Norah's feelings for Colby Winston.

"I've been busy this morning myself," she said, not looking at her sister. "I asked Rowdy Cassidy if he'd get us the name of the top heart surgeon on the West Coast. Dad has to have the finest medical—"

Norah's head shot up. "You *what?*"

"Listen, if you're concerned about offending Colby, I've already spoken to him and he agrees we should get a second opinion."

"But Colby teaches at Portland University. He's the best there is!"

"For Orchard Valley." Of that Valerie was confident, but there was a whole world Norah knew little or nothing about. Her sister's entire universe revolved around Orchard Valley and their five-hundred-acre apple orchard ten miles outside town.

"Colby's one of the best cardiovascular surgeons in the state." Norah didn't bother to disguise her irritation. "Do you know what you've done?" she demanded. "You've just insulted one of this country's most—"

"I didn't insult him," Valerie insisted, interrupting her sister's tirade. "I made sure of that. Furthermore, you never even let me know he was a heart surgeon— I thought he was just a G.P. And even if he's considered good here in Orchard Valley, Dad needs absolutely the best one available anywhere. Shouldn't you be concerning yourself with his problems and not worrying about offending your doctor boyfriend?"

Norah's eyes widened with shock and hurt. She stood and without a word walked out of the room, leaving Valerie swamped in remorse. She hadn't meant to snap at her sister, nor had she wanted to sound so overbearing. Referring to Colby as Norah's boyfriend had been childish and petty, which proved how badly her nerves were frayed.

An hour passed and Valerie hurried down to the lobby to call Rowdy on her cell phone.

"It's Valerie," she said breathlessly when he answered.

"Listen, you're in luck. There's an up-and-coming heart surgeon working out of Portland University. Apparently he's developed an innovative surgical technique. I've talked to three of the top heart specialists in the country and they all highly recommend him."

"Great." She groped through her purse until she found a pen and a notebook, which she positioned against the lobby wall. "Ready."

"His name is Dr. Colby Winston."

Valerie dropped her arm. "Dr. Colby Winston," she repeated.

"I've got his phone number here."

"Thanks, Rowdy," she said, pride and shame clogging her throat, "but I've already got it."

She hadn't been home for twenty-four hours and she'd already managed to alienate her sister, insult a family friend and at the same time disparage a highly regarded doctor.

"Just great, Valerie," she muttered to herself. "Can things get any worse?"

# Three

"Steffie?" David Bloomfield's eyes fluttered open and he gazed up at Valerie.

"She'll be here as soon as she can," Valerie reassured him. It was now early evening, and during every previous visit that day, he'd been asleep, his heart's activity reported on the monitor.

How weak he sounded, she thought, as though death was only hours away. Her own heart clamored with dread and fear; she wanted to shout at him to fight, to hang on…

It wasn't that easy or straightforward—as Valerie knew. In the past two days she'd learned more about the functions of the heart than she'd ever imagined. In more ways than one… She'd learned that the symbolic heart, the center of human emotion, grew larger with the sorrows as well as the joys of love. And the physical heart was subject to its own stresses and risks.

Colby had strived to make the explanation as un-complicated as possible. Simply put, her father was experiencing heart failure; his heart was pumping blood less efficiently than it should. The decreased strength of the muscles then resulted in distended blood vessels that leaked fluid into his lungs, which interfered with his breathing. Each hour he was growing weaker and closer to death.

"Can't...hold out much longer."

"Of course you can," Valerie insisted, railing against discouragement and defeat. "You're going to live long enough to be a problem to your children. Isn't that what you've always said? You've still got years and years. Good years, with a houseful of grandchildren."

Her father's smile was fleeting. "Go home, sweet-heart," he whispered. "You haven't even been to the house yet."

"There's nothing there for me without you." She rubbed her thumb soothingly across the back of his hand, avoiding the IV needle. "Get well, Daddy, *please* get well. We all need you."

His eyes drifted shut, and the oppressive need to give in to the weakness of tears nearly overcame her. She blinked furiously in an effort not to cry, succeeding despite the enormous lump in her throat.

Valerie was grateful her features were outwardly composed when Colby entered the cubicle a few minutes later. He read over the clipboard that outlined her father's progress, then made a brief notation.

"He'll sleep now," he said, guiding her out of the room.

"What's happening?" she asked once they'd left the Coronary Care Unit. "Why is he so much weaker than before? It's like watching his life ebb away. Surely you can do something?" She heard the note of hysteria in her own voice and didn't care. Perhaps she was being selfish in wanting him to live when he so clearly wanted to be released from life. But she loved him so desperately. She *needed* him, and so did Steffie and Norah.

"We're doing everything we can," Colby assured her.

"I know—but it's not enough."

"Valerie, trust me, I love that crotchety old man myself. I don't want to lose him, either." He led the way to the elevator. "Come on, I'll buy you some dinner."

When she declined, he said, "Well, at least a cup of coffee."

She was on the verge of pointing out that there was coffee in the waiting room, then hesitated. He was right. She needed a break, even if it was only ten minutes in the hospital cafeteria.

They rode the elevator down to the basement and walked into the large, open room, which was mostly empty now. Colby reached for a serving tray and slid it along the counter, collecting a green dinner salad, a cellophane-wrapped turkey sandwich and coffee. Valerie surveyed the cottage cheese salad with the limp pineapple and instead grabbed a bottle of cranberry juice. She wasn't at all hungry, although she'd eaten very little in the past few days.

He withdrew his wallet and paid the cashier, then carried the tray to a table at the back of the room, near the window.

He chose one far removed from any of the occupied tables, and that started Valerie's heart pounding with a renewed sense of anxiety. Colby had brought her here to face the inevitable.

"I'm going to lose my father, aren't I?" she asked outright, determined to confront the truth head-on.

Colby looked up, his dark eyes filled with surprise. "Not if I can help it. What makes you ask?"

She slumped against the back of the chair, so relieved that it was all she could do not to weep openly. "I thought that was why you brought me here—what you intended to tell me." With trembling hands, she picked up the bottle of juice and removed the top.

"We aren't going to lose him." He spoke with such fierce conviction that she realized his will to keep her father alive was as strong as her own.

"How long have you known my dad?" she asked, leaning forward and resting her elbows on the table.

"A few years now."

Valerie vaguely recalled hearing Colby's name mentioned once or twice, but she couldn't remember when or for what reason. With her hectic work schedule she'd been home only intermittently. Her last visit had been nearly six months ago, although she phoned weekly.

"We met soon after your mother died," Colby explained. "Your father made a generous donation to the hospital in her name."

Valerie knew that David's contribution had been large enough for the hospital to begin construction of a new wing. The irony of the situation struck her for the first time, and she drew in a deep, painful breath. The new wing housed the Coronary Care Unit.

"By the way," she said, feeling obliged to apologize—or at least acknowledge his reputation. "I understand that I was, uh, mistaken earlier in what I assumed about your skills. I'm sorry about that."

"Don't worry." He shrugged. "It happens all the time. But back to your dad—he and I play chess once a week."

"You ever beat him?"

Colby grinned. "Occasionally, but not often."

Valerie was good at chess herself, which was hardly surprising since her father had taught her to play. One day, perhaps, when all of this was over, she'd challenge Colby to a game. Odd how easy it was to assume they'd continue to know each other….

"He's very proud of you," Colby said casually as he unwrapped his sandwich.

Valerie suppressed a sudden urge to giggle. "So…he mentioned me *before* his attack."

"At every opportunity." He frowned as he said it. He was, no doubt, thoroughly sick of the subject.

Valerie settled back and crossed her arms, enjoying herself. "In other words, Dad's preoccupation with matching the two of us up isn't something new."

Colby paused, averting his gaze. "Let's put it this way. He wasn't quite as blatant about it as he's been the past few days."

"You must've been curious about me."

"A little."

"And?" she said. "What do you think?"

Colby lifted his shoulders, as if to say she hadn't impressed him. Or was he saying she hadn't disappointed him?

"That doesn't tell me a thing," she complained.

"You're everything your father said and more," he muttered, obviously hoping to satisfy her and at the same time put an end to the conversation.

Valerie knew it was sheer vanity to be so pleased. Still, although he might have intended his remark as a compliment, she didn't read any admiration in his eyes. If Dr. Colby Winston was attracted to her, he concealed it well. She hated to admit how much that wounded her pride. The truth was, she wanted him to be fascinated with her. She wanted him to feel enthralled, enchanted, impressed—the way she was with him. Because, despite herself, and despite their awkward beginning, despite the prospect of a relationship with Rowdy Cassidy, she couldn't get Colby out of her mind.

In a strictly objective way, Valerie knew she was slim and attractive. No matter what her father said about her hair, it was styled in an exuberant tangle of russet curls that highlighted her cheekbones and unusual gray-green eyes. Those eyes were her greatest asset in the looks department, although her mouth tended to be expressive. Being tall, almost five eight, was a plus, too. Norah was barely five three, and the entire world seemed to tower above her sister. When Valerie wore heels, there wasn't a man in her field she couldn't meet at eye level, which she considered a definite advantage.

"You don't like me, do you?" she asked bluntly.

Her question clearly took him aback, and he didn't immediately respond. "I don't dislike you," he finally said.

"I make you nervous?"

"Not exactly."

"Then what is it?" she prodded. "Don't worry. I'm not planning to fall in love with you. As I said before, there's someone else on the horizon. I'm just…curious."

"About what?"

"How you feel about me."

His mouth tightened, and Valerie could tell he wasn't accustomed to dealing with a woman as direct as she was. Most men weren't. Valerie didn't believe in suggestion or subtlety. The shortest distance between any two points was a straight line. She'd learned that in high-school geometry and it had worked equally well in life.

"I think you're very good at what you do."

He was sidestepping her question and doing a relatively competent job of it, but she wasn't fooled. "Which is?" she pressed.

"Functioning in a male-dominated field."

"Are you implying I've sacrificed my femininity?" She couldn't help sounding a bit sarcastic.

His lips tightened again. "You're good at putting words in someone's mouth, too, aren't you?"

"Sometimes," she agreed, "but only when it suits my purposes."

"No doubt."

"You're not sure how you feel about me, are you?"

"On the contrary, I knew the minute we met."

She cocked an eyebrow, waiting for him to finish. "Well?" she asked when he didn't supply the answer.

"You're bright and attractive."

"Thank you." It wasn't what she'd hoped to hear. He'd revealed no emotion toward her. She'd rarely met a man who was so…she searched for the right word. *Staid,* she decided. *Stoical.* He seemed to close himself up whenever he was around her, almost as though he felt he needed protection.

Valerie knew she could be overpowering and opinionated, but she wasn't cold or hard. Just straightforward. They were alike in that way, both sensible, seasoned professionals. It was common ground between them, yet Colby seemed determined to ignore their similarities.

He'd been kind to her, she reminded herself. But she sensed that he would have behaved in the same compassionate manner regardless of who she was. Valerie understood that, even applauded it.

So why was she looking for something that wasn't there?

She shook herself mentally. "All right, Dr. Winston," she began in a brisk voice. "Tell me about my father."

* * *

Norah was asleep on the sofa when Valerie returned from the cafeteria. She spread the blanket over her sister, wondering why Norah wasn't at home. Norah stirred, her eyes fluttering open.

"Hello, Sleeping Beauty," Valerie said, smiling tenderly.

"Where were you?" Norah asked, sitting up. She swept tangled hair away from her face, and Valerie saw that her soft blue eyes were puffy, as though she'd recently been crying.

"Down in the cafeteria with Colby."

Norah blinked, looking mildly surprised.

"He hadn't had dinner yet and asked me along so we could talk."

"I feel bad about what happened this morning," Norah said. "I was upset about Dad and angry with you for going behind Colby's back. But then I realized I should have explained things better—you know, told you about his qualifications." She sighed. "I was angry that you hadn't talked to me first."

"If I had, I might have saved myself a lot of trouble," Valerie agreed. "Don't worry about it, sis—I would've been upset, too."

"If there was ever a time we need to stick together, it's now. We can't allow a quarrel to come between us."

Valerie nodded. Norah looked small and lost, and Valerie crossed the room to sit down beside her, placing a protective arm around her sister's shoulders.

"I wish Steffie was here," Norah murmured.

Valerie did, too, but in some ways perhaps it was best that their sister hadn't arrived yet. Her absence might well be the only thing keeping their father alive.

"What did you and Colby talk about?" Norah asked, pressing her head against Valerie's shoulder.

"Dad, and what's going to happen."

"Does Colby know?"

"No, but it looks like he may not have the option of waiting until Dad's lungs clear before performing open-heart surgery."

"But his chances of survival would be practically nil if Colby went ahead with it now!"

Valerie had felt the same alarm when Colby described the procedure to her. He'd drawn a detailed diagram on a napkin and answered a multitude of questions. Although the surgery would be risky, it seemed to be the only alternative available to them. Valerie had understood and accepted Colby's reasoning, even though her father's chances were slim. She prayed the surgery could be delayed, but that was looking less promising every hour.

"The likelihood that he'll survive is a whole lot better with the operation than without," Valerie reminded her sister. "Still, he said he'd defer it as long as he could."

"Yes, but…oh, Val, it's so scary to think of what our lives would be like without Dad."

"I know." She stroked her sister's hair, offering what reassurance and comfort she could.

"Isn't Colby wonderful?" Norah asked after a while.

Valerie smiled to herself, then nodded. He'd made the surgery, with all its risks, seem the logical thing to do. For the first time since her arrival, she felt hopeful for her father's chances. She held on to that small surge of confidence with both hands. Colby had been patient, answering her questions, giving her reassurance and hope when she'd felt none.

"Now can you understand why everyone likes him so much?" Norah asked, her voice soft.

"Yes." She'd intentionally baited him, determined to find out how he really felt about *her.* She'd looked for some reaction, some sign, but he'd given her nothing.

The more reserved he was, the more challenged she felt. Valerie doubted he ever raised his voice or lost his cool, composed air. Even when she'd pressured him, he'd shown almost no emotion. Yet Valerie couldn't shake the conviction that he was a man of deep feeling—and strong passion.

Colby was smiling; he'd been smiling ever since he'd left the hospital. He wasn't sure what had prompted him to invite Valerie down to the cafeteria. But he suspected it was because…well, because he enjoyed being with her. He'd never known a woman who was so willing to speak her feelings. She was direct and honest and, damn it all, *interesting.* It wasn't that he found Sherry—or for that matter, Norah—boring. He enjoyed their company in an entirely different way.

But Valerie kept him on his toes. She didn't take

anything at face value, but challenged and confronted until she was satisfied. He admired that. In fact, he admired *her*. But that wasn't the end of it. This was a woman he could grow to love.

He'd gone off the deep end, he told himself. Worked too many hours without a real break. He'd listened to David Bloomfield once too often. There could never be anything between him and Valerie. She wasn't what he needed in a woman; not only that, she'd never be content with life in Orchard Valley again.

He knew that as well as she did.

The next morning, with Norah at the hospital, Valerie felt comfortable about leaving for the first time since her arrival from New York. She desperately needed a change of clothes. She was still wearing the business suit she'd had on when she'd received Norah's message two—no, three—days earlier.

She drove to the family home, down the mile-long driveway that led to the colonial house. She took a moment to glance at the hundreds of neat rows of apple trees, all in fragrant blossom. Then she hauled her suitcase up to her old bedroom, showered and changed into a pair of jeans and a soft blue sweater.

When Valerie returned to the hospital she felt a thousand times better. Norah was still asleep, curled up on the sofa, her knees tucked under her chin. She was so blonde and delicate that Valerie had an almost over-powering recollection of their mother. She came to an abrupt stop. The words of greeting froze on her lips and she turned into the hallway.

Quietly she fought back the tears. She'd barely managed to compose herself before she saw Colby striding intently down the wide corridor, heading straight toward her, his face taut.

"Have you got a moment?" he asked stiffly.

"Sure," Valerie said, puzzled by his obvious tension. "Is something wrong? Is it Dad?"

"No, this is between you and me." Colby actually seemed angry. Furious, even, although he hadn't raised his voice. This was certainly the most emotion she'd seen in him.

He marched toward the elevator, with Valerie following, and then down the narrow passageway to the back entrance of the hospital and the employee parking lot. He was several yards ahead of her.

"Where are we going?" she demanded. His pace was too swift for her to keep stride with him.

"Outside."

"In case you hadn't noticed, we already are."

"I don't want anyone to hear this."

"Hear *what?*" she practically shrieked, losing her patience.

Colby whirled around to confront her. "I want to know *exactly* what you said to your father."

Valerie was confused. "About what?"

"Us." The simple little word resonated with anger, contempt, disgust.

Well, so much for her assumption that Colby Winston felt any attraction for her.

"Us?" she repeated. "Don't be ridiculous. There isn't any us."

"That's precisely my point," he snapped. "Perhaps you can tell me why your father suddenly announced that you were falling in love with me—and that he expected me to *do* something about it."

"He *what?*" she exploded.

"You heard me. What in the name of heaven did you say?"

"Nothing." Except for the time she'd seen him yesterday evening, her father had been asleep. At least, his eyes had been closed and his breathing was shallow but regular.

"He knew we'd talked in the cafeteria," Colby informed her coolly.

"He did?"

"He mentioned it himself."

"Maybe Norah—"

"Norah, nothing. It came straight from the horse's mouth. That and a whole lot more."

Valerie frowned, staring down at the ground in an effort to think.

"Valerie!"

"I…thought he was asleep."

"What did you say?" he demanded a second time.

She was flustered now, which happened so rarely that it unnerved her even more. "Uh…just that we'd spoken the other night and I…"

"Go on," he insisted, his jaw muscles tightening.

"I, uh, have this tendency to talk when I'm upset. I don't mind telling you Dad's condition has really scared me. So if he's asleep, like he's been most of today, I sit by his side and tell him the things I've been thinking about."

"Which included me?"

Reluctantly, she nodded. Rarely could she recall being more embarrassed. Color burned in her cheeks.

"Valerie, what did you say to him?" Colby asked for the third time. His voice was quiet but his face had sharpened with tension.

She closed her eyes. She didn't remember everything she'd mumbled, but what she did recall made her cringe. She'd rambled on during those five-minute stretches, saying whatever came into her mind, and most of her thoughts seemed to concern Colby. Not for a second had she believed her father was awake enough to understand a word of it.

"I told him how impressed I was with you," she began hesitantly. "Although I don't know you well, I sense a strength in you. I told him how grateful I was to you because I've felt so helpless the last couple of days."

She chanced a look in his direction but his expression was impassive. Not knowing what else to do, she continued. "In any family crisis there's always one person who has to be strong, and everyone else leans on that person for support. I'm the oldest and I feel responsible for the others. But when I saw my father that first time, I just…couldn't cope. It's even harder for Norah.

I realized that the strong one in this situation is you. I told Dad that…and some other things."

"What other things?"

It wasn't getting any better. "That I…found myself attracted to you. Not physically," she rushed to explain, conscious that she was lying. "I'm attracted to the emotional stability I sense in you. Only I didn't say all that to Dad because I didn't think he could hear me anyway.

"Was that so terrible?" she asked, when Colby remained silent.

"No," he finally admitted in a hoarse voice.

"What did Dad say to you?" she asked curiously.

Colby's gaze touched hers, then withdrew. "That you'd fallen head over heels in love with me. And that's a quote."

"What?" Valerie said incredulously. "No wonder you were so upset!"

"Upset's not the word for it. I'm worried about how this is going to affect David's recovery, especially since he seems to have all kinds of expectations now—expectations that are going to be disappointed. Eventually he'll just have to realize you're not the kind of woman I intend to marry."

"Believe me, Dr. Winston, you have nothing to worry about," she murmured, annoyed now. "If I *was* going to fall in love, it would be with a man who was a little more sensitive to my pride."

"I apologize," he said, shrugging indifferently. "Your father unfortunately read too much into your…remarks. I'm afraid you'll have to say something to him."

"Me?"

"You're the one who started this."

"Why can't we just let the whole thing drop? By tomorrow he'll have forgotten I said anything."

"That's not likely," Colby said in a grim voice. "He asked me to bring a preacher so we could be married at his bedside."

Valerie couldn't help it, she burst out laughing. It was as though all the tension, all the waiting and frustration, had broken free inside her. She laughed until the tears streamed down her face and her sides ached, and even then she couldn't stop. Clutching her stomach, she wiped the moisture from her cheeks.

"Colby, darling," she said between giggles. "What shall I wear to the ceremony?"

Colby apparently didn't find her antics humorous.

"I'll want children, of course," she told him when she'd managed to stop giggling. "Nine or ten, and I'll name the little darlings after you. There'll be little cheeses running around our happy home—Cheddar and Parmesan and—"

"I have absolutely no intention of marrying you."

"Of course you don't right *now,* but that'll all change." She enjoyed teasing him, and the laughter was a welcome release after the tension of the past few days.

"You're not serious, are you?"

Valerie sighed deeply. "If you want me to say something to Dad, I will."

"I think that would be best."

"I'm really not so bad, you know," she felt obliged

to tell him. She was disappointed in his reaction, although she'd never admit it. If she was going to make a fool of herself over a man, she didn't need to travel halfway across the country to do so!

"We don't have a thing in common and shouldn't pretend we do."

"Well, but— "

"Let's leave it at that, Valerie."

His attitude hurt. "Fine. I'm not interested in you, either," she muttered. Without another word, she turned around and marched back into the hospital.

The man had his nerve. He made a relationship with her sound about as attractive as one with a…a porcupine! Colby acted as though she'd purposely set a trap for him, and she resented that.

Norah was awake when she got back to the waiting room. Her younger sister looked up, smiling, as Valerie hurried in and began to pace.

"What's wrong?" Norah asked, pouring herself a cup of coffee. She gestured toward the pot, but Valerie shook her head.

"Have you ever noticed how opinionated and high-handed Colby Winston can be?" she asked, still pacing furiously.

"Dr. Winston?" Norah repeated. "Not in the least. I've never known him to be rude, not even when someone deserved it."

Valerie impatiently pushed the sleeves of her sweater past her elbows. "I don't think I've ever met a man who irritated me more."

"I thought you liked him."

"I thought I did, too," she answered darkly.

"Steffie phoned," Norah said, cutting off Valerie's irritation as effectively as if she'd flipped a light switch. "She got through to the nurses' station here when she couldn't reach either of us at the house or on our cells."

"Where is she?" Valerie asked. "Is the transportation strike over?"

"No," Norah replied. "She's still trapped in whatever that town is. If she was in one of the big cities she wouldn't be having nearly as much trouble. She asked about Dad, and I told her everything's about the same. She sounded like she was close to tears."

"Poor Steffie."

"She said she'd give everything she owns to find a way home." Norah sighed. "If something doesn't break soon, I think Steff's going to hike over the Alps."

She'd do it, too; Valerie didn't doubt that for a moment.

"I was with Dad earlier," Norah said, changing the subject again. "He was more alert than before."

Valerie frowned, well aware of the reason. Her dear, manipulative father seemed to think he was about to get his wish. Little did he realize she had no intention of marrying Dr. Colby Winston. Or that Colby was no more interested in her than she was in him.

# *Four*

David Bloomfield's condition didn't change throughout the day that followed. Valerie saw Colby intermittently. He was in surgery most of the afternoon and came by, still wearing his surgical gown, to check on her father early that evening. Valerie happened to be there at the time, and she recognized the weariness in Colby's face. Without saying anything to her father, she trailed Colby out of the room.

"What about a cup of coffee?" she suggested, and when he hesitated, she added lightly, "I thought you might like to know how I warded off the preacher."

He grinned, then rubbed a hand across his eyes. "All right," he said, glancing at his watch. "Give me fifteen minutes and I'll meet you in the cafeteria."

Valerie headed downstairs with her briefcase and her laptop. That afternoon she'd had her assistant e-mail the contents of several files to her. Even if she had to be out of the office while her father was ill, there were still matters that required her attention. She'd spent much of the afternoon answering e-mails. Working out of the hospital waiting room wasn't ideal, but she'd managed.

She was at a table in the cafeteria, reading over some notes on her laptop, when Colby arrived. As he pulled out a chair, she straightened, shut down the computer and closed it.

After a somewhat perfunctory greeting, Colby reached for the sugar canister in the middle of the table and methodically poured out a teaspoon, briskly stirring it into his coffee. "I wanted to apologize," he began.

His words took her by surprise. "For what?"

"I was out of line, coming down on you the way I did about the marriage business. I should've realized your father was stretching whatever you said out of proportion. I took my irritation out on you."

She dismissed his apology with a shake of her head. "It was understandable. As far as I'm concerned, it's forgotten."

His eyes met hers as though he couldn't quite believe her. "You spoke to him?" he asked abruptly.

Valerie nodded, trying to conceal her amusement. "My poor father was distraught, or at least he tried to persuade me he was. But—" she sighed expressively "—he'll get over it just as I will." She fluttered her eyelashes melodramatically, teasing Colby just a little.

His eyes shot to hers, and a slow grin moved across his face, relaxing his features. "Disappointed, were you?"

"Oh, yes. I've always dreamed of a traditional white wedding gown—one that matches the sheets on my father's hospital bed." She smiled and relaxed, too, feeling at ease with him now. She'd been angry, but that was over, and she had to admit she actually liked this man. She certainly admired him.

Colby sipped his coffee, and once again she noted the lines of fatigue that marked his eyes and mouth.

"Rough day?"

He nodded. "I lost a patient. Joanne Murphy. She died this afternoon in surgery. We knew there was a risk, but…" He shrugged heavily. "No matter how often it happens, I never get used to it."

"I'm so sorry, Colby." Her hand slid over to his in a gesture of friendship and support.

His fingers gripped hers as if to absorb the comfort and consolation she offered. At the feel of his hand closing over hers, Valerie felt a thrill of happiness, and even more inexplicably, a sense of *rightness*. She didn't know how else to describe it. Yet almost immediately, the doubts and uncertainties flowed into her mind.

They were friends, nothing more, she reminded herself. And very recent friends at that. Neither of them was looking for anything else. Neither of them *wanted* anything else. But if that was really the case, why would she experience this deep ache of longing? For one impulsive moment she yearned to throw herself into his arms, rest her head against his shoulder and immerse herself in his strength. Lend him hers.

Valerie decided she had to ignore these uncharacteristic sensations. She withdrew her hand, hoping he wouldn't notice its trembling.

"I'd better get back before Norah wonders where I am," she said firmly. Valerie knew she was a woman who needed to be in control, who looked at a problem from all angles and worked toward the most favorable solution. But Colby Winston wasn't a problem to be solved. He was a man who left her feeling vulnerable and confused.

She was already on her feet, briefcase in one hand, laptop in the other, when Colby spoke. "Don't leave... not yet." His voice was low, hesitant.

Valerie stared at him, unsure whether to stay or go.

"Oh, never mind." Colby shook his head, eyes suddenly guarded. "Actually, I should be leaving myself," he said quickly, bounding to his feet. He drank down several gulps of coffee, then strode out of the cafeteria, with Valerie close behind.

"Colby." She stopped him in front of the elevator. "What is it you don't like about me?" The question was out before she had time to analyze the wisdom of asking.

"I do like you," he answered, frowning.

"But you wouldn't want to marry someone like me?"

"No," he agreed calmly. "I wouldn't want to marry someone like you."

"Because?" Valerie wasn't sure why she continued to probe, why it was necessary for her to understand his reasons. She only knew that she felt a compelling urge to ask.

"You have a brilliant future ahead of you," he said, not meeting her eyes. "Your father's proud of your accomplishments, and rightly so. I admire your drive, your ambition, your ability."

"But." She said it before he could. There had to be a *but* in there somewhere.

"But," he said with the slightest hint of a smile. "I'm not interested in getting involved with an up-and-coming female executive. When I commit myself to a woman and a relationship, I want someone who's more…traditional. Someone who'll consider making our home and rearing our children her career."

"I see." He was wise to acknowledge that she wasn't the type who'd be content to sit quietly by the fireplace and spin her own yarn. No, Valerie would soon figure out how to have that yarn mass-produced, then see about franchising it into a profit-making enterprise. Business was in her blood, the same way medicine was in his.

"I don't mean to offend you," he said.

"You haven't," she assured him, and it was the truth.

The elevator arrived and they stepped inside together. Neither spoke as Colby pushed the appropriate button. The doors silently glided shut.

Valerie wished they weren't alone. It seemed so intimate, so private, just the two of them standing there.

"Valerie, listen…"

"It's okay," she said, smiling up at him. "Really. I asked, didn't I? That's how I am. You were honest with me, and I appreciate that. It's true I'm attracted to you, but that's probably fairly common in our circumstances, since you saved my father's life and all. Being attracted doesn't mean I'm in love with you."

"I know, it's just that—" He broke off hastily, his eyes probing hers. "Oh, what the hell," he murmured, the words so low that Valerie had to strain to hear him. Then his hands were taking hold of her shoulders and drawing her toward him. His mouth unerringly found hers and without conscious intent, she responded to his kiss, feeling none of the awkwardness she experienced with other men. The kiss was much like the man. Warm, deliberate, devastating.

She heard a soft moan from the back of her throat.

His head shifted restlessly before he released her. He dropped his arms, looking completely shocked. Valerie didn't know what had distressed him most—the fact that he'd kissed her or that he'd enjoyed it.

"Valerie, I…" Her name was a whisper.

Just then the elevator doors opened, and Colby cast an accusing glare at the nurse who entered. Grabbing Valerie's hand, he jerked her onto the floor before the elevator doors closed again.

"This isn't CCU," she protested, glancing around. Good grief, they were on the maternity floor. Down the hall, a row of newborns was on display behind a glass partition.

But Colby didn't give her a chance to get a closer look. Still holding her hand, he led her to the stairwell. He held open the door, then released her and dashed up the steps. He was halfway up the first flight before he seemed to realize she was no longer beside him. He turned back impatiently.

"Colby," she objected. "If you want to run up the stairs, fine, but you're in better physical condition than I am. I sit at a desk most of the day, remember?"

"I didn't mean for that to happen."

"What, racing up the stairs?"

"No, kissing you!"

"It was nice enough, as kisses go," she said, out of breath from the exertion, "but don't worry, you won't have to marry me because of a simple kiss." The only way she could deal with this experience was to deny how strongly it affected her, push aside these unfamiliar, unwelcome feelings. She suspected that was how Colby felt, too.

"Our kiss may have been a lot of things, but simple wasn't one of them," he muttered.

"You're worrying too much about something that really isn't important."

His eyes held such a quizzical expression that Valerie continued talking. "You're tired, and so am I," she said, making excuses for them both. "We're under a great deal of stress. You've had a long, discouraging day and your guard slipped a little," she went on. "My being so pushy didn't help, either. You kissed me, but it isn't the end of the world."

"It won't happen again." He spoke with absolute certainty.

Pride stiffened Valerie's shoulders. "That's probably

for the best." Colby was right. Her personality was all wrong for someone like him. A doctor's work was emotionally demanding and physically draining; she couldn't blame him for seeking a wife who'd create a warm cocoon of domesticity for him. A home filled with comfort and love and peace. Valerie couldn't fault his preference. She wished him well and determined to put the kiss out of her mind.

The next afternoon, Valerie went downtown. The streets of Orchard Valley greeted her like a long-lost friend. She felt heartened by the sight of the flower-filled baskets that hung from every streetlight.

The clock outside the Wells Fargo Bank was still ten minutes slow, even after thirty years. When Valerie was thirteen, a watchmaker from somewhere out East had been hired to repair the grand old clock. He spent most of a day working on it, then declared the problem fixed. Two days after he'd left town, the clock was back to running ten minutes late and no one bothered to have it repaired again, although it came up on the town council agenda at least once a year.

The barbershop with its classic red-and-white striped pole whirling round and round was as cheery as ever. Mr. Stein, the barber, sat in one of his leather chairs reading the *Orchard Valley Clarion,* waiting for his next customer. Valerie walked past, and when he glanced over the top of the paper, she smiled and waved. He grinned and returned the gesture.

The sense of homecoming was acute, lifting her spirits. She passed the newspaper office, two doors down from the barbershop; looking in the window, she noted the activity inside as the staff prepared the next edition of the *Orchard Valley Clarion*. She hadn't gone more than a few steps when she heard someone call her name.

She turned to find Charles Tomaselli, the paper's editor, directly behind her. "Valerie, hello. I wondered how long it'd take before I ran into you. How's your dad doing?"

"About the same," she answered.

"I'm sorry to hear that." He buried his hands in his pants pockets and matched his pace to hers. "I haven't seen Stephanie around."

"She's still in Italy."

Although he gave no outward indication of his feelings, Valerie sensed his irritation. "She didn't make the effort to come home even when her father's so ill? I'd have thought she'd want to be with him."

"She's trying as hard as she can," Valerie said, defending her sister. "But she's stuck in a small town a hundred miles outside of Rome—because of that transportation strike. But if there's a way out, Steffie'll find it."

Charles nodded, and Valerie had the odd impression that he regretted bringing up the subject of her sister. "If you get the chance, will you tell your father something for me?"

"Of course."

"Let him know Commissioner O'Dell called me

after last week's article on the farm labor issue. That'll cheer him up."

"The farm labor issue?" Valerie repeated, wanting to be sure she understood him correctly.

Charles grinned almost boyishly, his dark eyes sparkling with pleasure. "That's right. I don't know if you're aware of this, but your father would make one heck of an investigative reporter. Tell him I said that, too. He'll know what I mean."

"Sure," Valerie agreed, wishing she knew more about the article and her father's role in it.

"Nice seeing you again," Charles said, turning to head back to the newspaper office. He hesitated. "When you see Stephanie, tell her hello from me," he said over his shoulder.

"Of course. I'll be happy to." Thoughtfully, Valerie watched him walk away. Charles not only edited the *Clarion,* he wrote a regular column and most of the major features, like the farm labor story he'd just mentioned. Considering his talent and energy, she was surprised he'd stayed on with a small-town paper; he could have gone to work for one of the big dailies long before now. But then, these days, with major newspapers folding, maybe he'd been smart not to leave.

She found it interesting that he'd asked about Steffie. Several years ago, Valerie had suspected there was something romantic developing between them. Steffie had been a college student at the time and Charles had just moved to Orchard Valley. She remembered Steffie poring over every article, every column, exclaiming over Charles's skill, his style, his wit. To Valerie, it had definitely sounded like romance in the making. His comments about Stephanie now suggested it hadn't been entirely one-sided, either.

But then, romance was hardly a subject she knew much about. So if there *was* something between Steffie and Charles, it was their business and she was staying out of it. She knew just enough about relationships to make a mess of them. A good example of that was how she'd bungled things with Colby.

She felt a twinge of regret. Since their kiss, he'd been avoiding her. Or at least she assumed he was. Until then, he'd made a point of coming by and chatting with her when he could. They'd always been brief visits, but their times together had broken up the monotony of the long hours she'd spent at the hospital. She hadn't realized how much those short interludes meant to her until they stopped.

Norah was the one who'd sent Valerie on the errand into town. Some flimsy excuse about picking up some photos from a roll of film their father had left for developing. He was admittedly old-fashioned when it came to cameras and photography; Valerie had wanted to buy him a digital camera last Christmas but he'd insisted that he preferred his forty-year-old Nikon, which had served him well all these years. Asking her to collect the pictures now was a blatant attempt to get her out of the hospital, not that Valerie minded. She was beginning to feel desperate for fresh air and sunshine.

Although most of the orchards were miles out of town, she could've sworn that when she inhaled deeply she caught a whiff of apple blossoms.

Spring was her favorite time of year. But although she'd been home intermittently over the past decade, she'd never spent more than a day or two and had never visited during April or May. She wondered if she'd been unconsciously avoiding Orchard Valley during those months, knowing that the charm and the appeal of her home would be at their strongest then. Perhaps she'd feared she might never want to leave if she came while the white and pink blossoms perfumed the air.

Not wanting to examine her thoughts too closely, Valerie continued down the street, past the feed store and the local café until she arrived at her destination. Al's Pharmacy.

Al's was a typical small-town drugstore, where you could buy anything from cards and gifts to aspirin and strawberry jam. At one end of the pharmacy Al operated a state-run liquor store and in the opposite corner was a small post office. The soda fountain, which specialized in chocolate malts, was situated at the front. It had been there since the fifties, the kind of thing rarely seen outside of small towns anymore. Valerie had lost count of the number of times she'd stopped in after school with her friends. She wondered if "going to Al's for a chocolate malt" remained as popular with local teenagers these days as it had been when she was growing up. She suspected it did.

"Valerie Bloomfield," the aging pharmacist called to her from behind the counter. "I thought that was you. How's your dad doing?"

"The same."

"Norah phoned and said you were on your way. I put those snapshots aside for you and just wrote it up on the bill. You tell your dad I'm counting on him to go fishing with me come July, and I won't take no for an answer."

"I'll tell him," Valerie promised.

She took the package and wandered outside. Curiosity got the better of her, though, and she paused on the sidewalk to open the envelope. Inside was an array of snapshots her father had taken that spring.

Valerie's heart constricted at the number of photos he had of her mother's grave site. In each, a profusion of flowers adorned the headstone. There were a couple of pictures of Norah, as well. The first showed her sitting in a chair by the fireplace, a plaid blanket around her knees and an open book on her lap. The second was taken outside, probably in late March. The wind had whipped Norah's blond hair about her face, and she was laughing into the sun. In both photographs her resemblance to their mother was uncanny.

Grief and pity tore at Valerie's heart as she imagined her father taking those pictures. He was so lost and lonely without his Grace, and the photographs told her that in an unmistakable and poignant way.

Her thoughts oppressive, Valerie walked aimlessly for a few minutes. When she saw that she was near the community park, she strolled in, past the swimming pool, now drained and empty, and followed the stone walkway that meandered through the manicured lawns. As she reached the children's playground, a breeze caught the swings, rocking them back and forth.

Memories of her childhood crowded her mind, and she sat in one of the old swings, almost wishing she could be a little girl again. It would've been easy to close her eyes, pretending she was eight years old. She allowed herself a minute to remember Sunday afternoons spent in this very park, with David pushing her and a tiny Stephanie on these swings, catching them at the bottom of the slide. But she was thirty-one now and her father, whom she adored, was in a hospital room, fighting for each breath he drew.

She refused to even consider the possibility of losing him. Was she being selfish? She didn't know. Her father had said he was ready to die, ready to relinquish his life.

She dragged the toe of her shoe along the ground, slowing the swing to a halt. When the time came to let go of her father, Valerie prayed she could do it with acceptance and strength. When death came to him, she wanted it to be as a friend, not an enemy with a score to settle. *But don't let him die yet. Please, not yet.*

As she drove back to the hospital, past the strip

malls that marked the highway, she caught sight of a recent addition. A movie theater, a six-plex. It astonished her that little Orchard Valley could have six movies all playing at once, especially in the era of DVDs and movies you could download from the Internet. She supposed that in a small town, going to the movies was still a major social event. The downtown theater she remembered so well from her teenage years still operated, but to a limited audience; according to Norah the features were second-run and often second-rate.

Orchard Valley had its share of national fast-food restaurants now, too, many of them situated along the highway. But as far as Valerie was concerned, hamburgers didn't get any better than those at The Burger Shack, a locally owned diner.

The summer she was sixteen, Valerie had worked there as a waitress, serving customers for minimum wage, thinking she was the luckiest girl in town to have landed such a wonderful job. How times had changed! How much *she'd* changed.

As she neared the hospital, Valerie felt a surge of reluctance. For nearly a week now, she'd practically lived on the CCU floor with only brief visits home to shower and change clothes. It had been a strange week, outside ordinary time somehow. Four years ago, when her mother was dying, she'd experienced something similar. But then her father and both her sisters had been there to share it. Now there were only two—Norah and her. And Colby…

She pulled into the parking lot and found a vacant spot, then walked toward the main entrance, sorry to leave the sunshine.

The minute she entered the lobby, Norah sprang up from the sofa she'd been sitting on. "I didn't think you'd ever get back," she said breathlessly. "What took you so long?"

"I stopped at the park. What's the matter?"

"Steffie called from Rome. She's flying home by way of Tokyo. I know it sounds crazy, but it was the most direct flight she could get. She's hoping to arrive sometime tomorrow night. She wasn't sure exactly when, but she said she'd let us know as soon as possible."

"How'd she make it to Rome?"

"I asked her that, but she didn't have time to explain. I told Dad she'd probably be here by tomorrow night."

Valerie felt herself relax. Until now, she hadn't realized just how tense she'd been over Steffie's situation.

"Colby wants to see you," Norah informed her next.

"Did he say why?"

Norah shook her head, frowning a little. "You two didn't have an argument, did you?"

"No. What makes you ask?"

Norah shrugged vaguely. "Just the way he looked when he asked for you."

"Looked?"

"Oh, I don't know." Norah was clearly regretting that she'd said anything. "It's like he was eager to see you, but then relieved when I told him you'd gone into town.

That might seem absurd, but I can't think of any other way of describing it."

"I'll catch him later." For some reason, Valerie wasn't quite ready to see him yet.

"I'm sure he'll stop by this evening."

"How's Dad doing?" Valerie asked as they headed for the elevator.

"Not so good. His breathing is more labored and the swelling in his extremities isn't any better. That's not a good sign. Colby's doing everything he can to drain his lungs, but nothing seems to work. In the meantime, Dad's growing weaker by the hour."

"He misses Mom even more than we knew," Valerie whispered, thinking about the snapshots she'd picked up at Al's Pharmacy. She wondered how often he'd visited their mother's grave. How often he turned to speak to the woman he'd spent a lifetime with, remembering too late that she was gone.

"What will we do if anything happens to Dad?" Norah asked quietly.

A few days earlier, Valerie would've rejected that possibility, adamantly claiming their father wasn't going to die. She'd stubbornly refused to consider it. She wasn't as unyielding now.

"I don't know," she admitted, "but we'll manage. We'll have to."

They were seated in the waiting room when Colby arrived. Valerie glanced up from a business publication she was reading and knew instantly that something was wrong. Terribly wrong. His eyes, dark and troubled, met hers. Without being conscious of it, she stood, the magazine slipping unnoticed to the floor.

"Colby?" His name became an urgent plea. "What is it?"

He sat down on the sofa and reached for Valerie's hands, gripping them tightly with his own. His gaze slid from her to Norah. "Your father's suffered a second heart attack."

"No," Norah breathed.

"And?" Valerie's own heart felt as though it were in danger of failing just then. It pounded wildly, sending bursts of fear through her body.

"We can't delay the surgery any longer."

Norah was on her feet, tears streaking her face. "You can't do the surgery now! His chances of survival are practically nil. We both know that."

"He doesn't have *any* chance if we don't." Although he was speaking to Norah, it was Valerie's gaze he held, Valerie's eyes he looked into—as if to say he'd do anything to have spared her this.

# *Five*

Colby had been with her father in the operating room for almost six hours, but to Valerie, it felt like six years.

While she waited, she recalled the happy times with her father and, especially as she entered adolescence, the not-so-happy ones. Her will had often clashed with his, and they'd engaged in one verbal battle after another. Valerie had found her father stubborn, high-handed and irrational.

Her mother had repeatedly told Valerie the reason she didn't get along with her father was that the two of them were so much alike. At the time Valerie had considered her mother's remark an insult. Furthermore, it made no sense. If they were alike, then they should be friends instead of adversaries.

It wasn't until her mother became ill that Valerie grew close to her father. In their love and concern for Grace, they'd set aside their differences; not a cross word had passed between them since.

Valerie couldn't say which of them had changed, but she figured they'd both made progress. All she knew was that she loved her father with a fierceness that left her terrified whenever she thought about losing him.

The passage of time lost all meaning as she paced, back and forth, across the waiting room floor. It wasn't the waiting room she was so familiar with, since Surgery was on the hospital's ground level; a small brick patio, bordered with a waist-high hedge, opened off glass doors. Every now and then, Valerie or Norah would wander outside to breathe in the cool air, to savor the peace and tranquility of the night. There'd been no other patients in surgery that evening, no other families waiting for news.

Somehow word got out about her father's crisis. Pastor Wallen from the Community Church stopped by and prayed with Valerie and Norah. Charles Tomaselli was there for an hour, as well. Various friends, including Al Russell from the pharmacy, came, too.

At midnight, an exhausted Norah had curled up on the sofa and fallen into a troubled sleep. Valerie envied her sister's ability to rest, but found no such respite from her own fears.

Pacing and sucking on hard candy to relieve her nerves were the only methods she had of dealing with the terrible tension. She stared out the window at the bright moonlit night, then turned suddenly when she heard a soft footfall behind her. Colby stood there, still wearing his surgical greens.

Valerie's eyes flew to his, but she could read nothing. "He made it."

She nearly slumped to the floor with relief. Tears welled up, but she blinked them back. "Thank God," she whispered, raising both hands to her mouth.

"I nearly lost him once," Colby said hoarsely, shaking his head. How exhausted he looked, Valerie noted. "I didn't think there was anything more we could do. It seemed like a miracle when his heart restarted. In some ways, it was. Only so much of what happens on the operating table is in my hands."

"I'm sure it *was* a miracle," Valerie whispered, hardly able to speak. She walked to the sofa on unsteady legs and bent to wake Norah. Her sister woke instantly—her training as a nurse, no doubt—and Valerie told her, "Dad made it through the operation."

"The danger's not over yet," Colby cautioned. "Not by a long shot. I wish I could tell you otherwise, but I can't. If he survives the night—"

"But he survived the surgery," Norah said, her voice raised with hope. "I didn't think that was possible. Surely that was his biggest hurdle?"

"Yes," Colby agreed, "but his condition is critical."

"I know," Norah answered, but a faint light began to glow in her eyes. From the little Norah had said, Valerie realized her sister hadn't expected their father to live through the ordeal. Now that he had, she was given the first glimmer of promise.

"I'll be back in a few minutes," Colby said, rubbing

his eyes in an oddly vulnerable gesture. He must be running on pure adrenaline, Valerie thought. He'd been in surgery earlier in the day and he'd lost a patient; he'd feared he was about to lose another one. He still could. He didn't need to say it aloud for Valerie to know.

Colby didn't think her father would live until morning.

"I wish Steffie was here," Norah said after Colby had left.

Valerie nodded. "I do, too."

Colby had been gone a few minutes when a male nurse appeared. He knew Norah and greeted her warmly, then told them they could each see their father, but for only a moment.

Valerie went first. She'd assumed she was emotionally prepared, but the sight of her father destroyed any self-control she might have attained. Seeing him lying there so close to death affected her far more acutely than she'd expected.

Hurriedly she turned and left, feeling as though she could barely breathe. She walked past Norah without a word. She stumbled onto the patio, hugging her middle with both arms, dragging in one deep breath after another in a futile effort to compose herself.

The tears, which she'd managed to resist all evening, broke through in a flood of fear and anger. It was *unfair.* It was so unfair. How could she lose her father so soon after her mother?

She didn't often give in to tears, but now they came as a release. Huge sobs shook her body. Slowly, she lowered herself onto a concrete bench, then rocked back and forth as the hot, unstoppable tears continued to fall.

A hand at her back felt warm and comforting. "Go ahead and let it out," Colby whispered.

He sat beside her, his arm around her shoulders, and gradually drew her to him. She had no strength or will to refuse. Nestling her face against his jacket, Valerie sobbed loudly, openly. Colby rubbed his cheek along her hair and whispered indistinguishable, soothing words. His arms were strong and safe, and she desperately needed him and he was there.

When there were no more tears left to shed, a deep shudder racked her body. She straightened and used her sleeve to wipe her damp face.

"Feel better?" Colby asked, his hand on her hair.

Valerie nodded, embarrassed now that he'd found her like this. "Norah?"

"She's talking to Mark Collins. One of the nurses who assisted me in surgery."

"I…thought I was prepared…didn't know I'd fall apart like this."

"You've been under a lot of stress."

"We all have." She edged away from him, and taking the cue, he dropped his arm. She offered him a trembling smile, her gaze avoiding his.

"I wish I could guarantee that your father's going to make it through this," he said, his voice heavy. "But I can't do that, Valerie."

"I know." Spontaneously, as though he'd silently

willed it, she raised her eyes to his. His hands grasped her shoulders, tightening as he urged her closer. His eyes seemed to darken as his mouth made a slow descent toward hers, stopping a mere fraction from her lips.

Valerie closed her eyes, and his warm breath caressed her face. She inhaled the pungent scent of surgical soap and something else, something that was ineffably him.

"We shouldn't be doing this," he whispered.

It certainly wasn't what she'd expected him to say. "I…know," she said, but she was beyond listening to common sense. She needed Colby. His warmth, his comfort, his touch. And she wouldn't be denied.

"Please," she whispered.

The driving force of his kiss parted her lips, and Valerie was instantly caught in a whirlwind of sensation. Her hands reached for him, sliding up his solid chest, her fingers locking at the base of his neck.

He moaned, and she did, too. There was no resistance in Valerie, none. She surrendered herself to his kiss, to his need and her own.

With what seemed like reluctance, he broke away and slipped his mouth from hers.

She felt cold when he lifted his face. Opening her eyes, she glanced toward the waiting room, grateful to see that it was empty. They were alone in the shadows of the hedge, but a few seconds earlier it wouldn't have mattered if they'd been standing in the middle of the bustling emergency room.

"I shouldn't have let that happen. We both—"

Valerie placed her finger over his lips, silencing him. "Don't say it. Please." Her hands cupped his face and she gazed into his eyes, dark now with desire. "I need you. Right or wrong, I need you. Just hold me."

A faint quiver went through her as he brought her back into his arms. Closing her eyes again, Valerie surrendered to the strength and safety she felt in his embrace.

He kissed her forehead lightly. His breath was uneven, and she found pleasure in knowing that he was no less affected by their encounter than she was.

As she'd already told him, Valerie didn't want to question the right or wrong of it now. Neither of them was in any real danger of falling in love. Colby had explained the reasons a relationship between them was unfeasible. And she agreed with him. But their calm, rational words didn't take into account what she was experiencing. This excitement, this weightless sense of release and longing. She didn't want it to end. Apparently Colby didn't, either, because he made no move to let her go.

"You shouldn't feel so good in my arms," he told her.

"I'm sorry." But she wasn't, not really. Soon they'd both regret this, but she'd save all the remorse for another day.

While she was in Colby's embrace, she didn't have to think about the future. She didn't have to worry about facing the world without anyone to guide and support her. For the first time since she'd come home to Orchard Valley, Valerie didn't feel inadequate or alone.

True, Norah was with her and Steffie was due to arrive soon. The three of them had each other, yet Valerie couldn't quite escape the old roles; she was the one they'd always depended on for encouragement, guidance, a sense of strength. Only Valerie didn't feel strong. She felt shaken, knocked off balance. She felt completely helpless....

"Norah's looking for you," Colby said.

Valerie sighed and grudgingly broke away from him. She peered into the waiting room and noticed her younger sister. Norah's eyes found her at the same time. She didn't do a good job of concealing her shock.

Valerie stood and turned to Colby. "Thank you."

He remained sitting on the concrete bench and sent her a smile full of private meaning.

Norah met her at the door, eyes shifting from Valerie to Colby. "Is everything all right?"

Valerie nodded. "Dad's holding his own at the moment."

"I didn't mean Dad. I meant with you."

"Of course," Valerie answered, forcing a casual tone. "I...just needed a good cry, and Colby lent me his shoulder."

Norah slipped her arm around Valerie's waist. "His shoulder, you say?" she asked, with more than a hint of a smile. "It looked like more than that to me."

It was the following night, and once again Valerie and Norah had taken up residence in the waiting room.

Several small groups of people were scattered about the area, either silent or speaking quietly.

"Dad's been asleep for nearly twenty hours." Valerie voiced her concern to Norah, who was far more knowledgeable about what was and wasn't usual after this kind of surgery. "Isn't that too long? I realize the anesthesia has a lot to do with it, but I can't help worrying."

"He's been awake for brief periods off and on today," Norah said. "He's doing very well, all things considered."

Her father wasn't Valerie's only concern. It was now after nine in the evening, and she'd been waiting since morning for some word from Steffie, who was supposed to be arriving sometime that day. But no one had heard from her, and Valerie felt anxious.

"Dad tried to talk the last time I was with him," Norah told her.

"What did he say?"

She shrugged. "It didn't make any sense. He looked up at me and grinned as if he'd heard the funniest joke in years and said 'six kids.'"

"Six kids?"

"I don't get it, either," Norah murmured. "I'm going to ask Colby about it when I see him, but we keep missing each other."

Valerie sat down and thumbed through the frayed pages of a two-year-old women's magazine. It was a summer issue dedicated to homes and gardens, which only went to prove how desperate she was for reading material that would take her mind off her fears.

She glanced at photographs of bright glossy kitchens and "country" bedrooms, wicker-furnished porches and "minimal" living rooms—all of them attractive, none of them quite real. None of them *home*.

And she knew with sudden certainty that home was *here*. Here in Orchard Valley at the family house. In the upstairs bedroom at the end of the hallway. Home was curling up with a good book by the fireplace in her father's den, and it was eating meals around the big oak table in the dining room her mother had loved.

That was home. She *lived* in her Houston condo in an exclusive neighborhood. She'd had a decorator choose the color scheme and select the furniture, since she didn't have the time for either task. A housekeeper came in twice a week to clean. The condo was a place to sleep. An address where she could pick up her mail. But it wasn't a place of memories and it wasn't home.

She read an article in the same magazine about herb gardens. Gardening had always been her mother's hobby, but every now and then Valerie had helped her weed. The times they'd spent working in the garden were among the fondest memories she had of her mother.

Perhaps in an attempt to recapture some of that simple happiness, Valerie had bought several large plants for her condo. But the housekeeper was the one who watered and fertilized them, since Valerie traveled so much.

Neither a home, at least not like the one she'd been raised in, nor a garden seemed to be in her future. Colby had recognized that from the beginning. Just as well, although it hadn't warded off the magnetic attraction between them.

Valerie's mind wandered to their exchange the night before. Their kissing was undoubtedly a mistake, but it was understandable and certainly forgivable. Both were emotionally drained, their resistance to each other almost nonexistent. Yet Valerie couldn't bring herself to regret the time she'd spent in Colby's arms.

It hurt a bit that he was avoiding her, because it told her he didn't share her feelings. In those moments with Colby, Valerie had experienced something extraordinary. She'd always considered romantic love a highly overrated commodity. Dr. Colby Winston was the first man who'd given her reason to reevaluate that opinion—despite the fact that a relationship between them had no possible future.

Just when she was beginning to think he planned never to seek her out again, Colby surprised her. Norah had gone to talk with the nurse who'd been assigned to care for their father, and Valerie sat alone in the SICU waiting room, shuffling through her thoughts. Colby was on her mind just then—not that he was ever far from it.

She happened to glance up as he walked in. He was wearing a dark gray suit; she didn't think she'd ever seen a handsomer man. Not even Rowdy Cassidy...

Their eyes met and held. "Hello," she said, with a breathless quality to her voice. Over the course of her career, Valerie had made presentations before large audiences. Her voice carried well, yet with Colby she felt like a first-grader asked to stand before the class and confess a wrong.

"Valerie." He paused and cleared his throat, then began again, sounding stilted and formal. "I've tied up everything here and I'm addressing a seminar this evening at the university. However, I have time for a bite to eat before I leave. Would you join me?"

"I'd be happy to," she answered.

"I thought we should eat someplace other than the cafeteria." His voice was more relaxed now. "There's an Italian restaurant near here that serves excellent food."

"Great." Valerie brightened until she realized he hadn't chosen the restaurant because he had a craving for spaghetti. He wanted to talk to her somewhere away from the hospital. Somewhere he could be assured none of his peers would be listening.

After leaving a message for Norah, they left the hospital in his car, a late-model maroon sedan. Sitting beside him, watching his strong, well-shaped hands on the steering wheel, gave Valerie a sense of intimacy, a feeling of familiarity.

The restaurant, a fairly new place she'd never visited before, was elegantly decorated in black and silver. The lighting, low and discreet, created a welcoming ambience.

"You didn't need to pay for my dinner to apologize, you know," Valerie said, reading over her menu. She quickly decided on a bowl of minestrone soup and fettuccine with fresh asparagus. No wine, because it would send her to sleep.

"Apologize?" Colby repeated.

Valerie lowered her menu and, crossing her arms, leaned toward him. "Not apologize exactly. You brought me here to tell me you're sorry about what happened last night, didn't you? I mean, it's fairly obvious, since you've been avoiding me all day. But don't worry about it," she said off-handedly, "I understand."

He scowled and set aside his menu. "Sometimes I forget how direct you can be."

"I'd rather have everything out in the open. There's no need to concern yourself with…what happened. I—needed you, and you were there for me."

His scowl intensified. "In other words, any man would have suited your purposes?"

"No," she said. "Only you. What we shared was very…sweet. I'll always be grateful to you for letting me cry."

"It's not the crying that concerns me."

"The kissing was very special, too," she said softly.

"Yes, I suppose it was. But it might be best to forget that, uh, particular part of last night."

The waitress approached with pad and pen in hand. They placed their orders, then Valerie resumed the conversation. "Maybe you can forget the kissing," she said in a mild tone, "but I don't think it'll be possible for me."

Colby's gaze left hers. "Personally, I don't think I'll be able to forget it, either," he said.

They both fell silent but a faint smile curved her lips as she savored his words. He'd tried to dismiss the attraction between them and couldn't. Neither could she.

"It doesn't change anything," he told her, his voice calm and resolute.

He'd meant everything he'd said earlier; that much Valerie understood. She couldn't change who she was. Easy as it would be to fall in love with him, Valerie knew she'd never be truly happy as a homemaker. She had too much ambition, too many dreams. A business career was what she wanted, where her skills lay, and she couldn't relinquish that any more than Colby could give up his medical practice.

"Your father's doing remarkably well," Colby told her in an obvious attempt to change the subject.

Valerie was delighted. Norah had told her repeatedly what excellent progress their father was making, and it was thrilling to have it confirmed.

"I've got him listed as critical at the moment," Colby went on, "but I have a feeling he's going to surprise us all and live to be a hundred."

Valerie beamed Colby a happy smile, hardly able to speak for the emotion clogging her throat. "We owe you so much, Colby."

He shrugged off her thanks and seemed grateful that the waitress appeared just then to deliver the first course of their meal.

The soup was delicious, but after a few spoonfuls Valerie was finished, her appetite gone. She managed only a taste of her fettucine. Colby glanced over, frowning, when she pushed the plate aside.

"Is something wrong?"

She shook her head. "No."

"You hardly touched your meal."

"I know."

"What's wrong?" he pressed.

Valerie lowered her eyes. "I was just trying to decide how I was going to leave you, Colby, and not cry." She hadn't meant to sound quite so serious; she'd meant to sound wryly amused.

Her words silenced him. His eyes met hers, and when he spoke, his voice revealed his sincerity. "You'd be very easy to love."

"But." She said the dreaded word for him.

"But we both know it wouldn't work."

"You're right," she said convincingly. Why wouldn't her heart listen?

"Valerie." Her father smiled weakly as she entered the cubicle in SICU. His hand reached for hers, brought it to his lips. "I wondered when I'd see you."

"I…went out for dinner."

"All by yourself?"

"No." But she didn't want to tell him she'd been with Colby.

Besides, there were other things to discuss. Norah had told Valerie the most unbelievable story. Apparently while Valerie was out for dinner, their father had told

Norah about a vision he'd had. A vision? Valerie didn't know what to make of that, any more than Norah did.

"What's all this Norah was telling me?" she asked.

Once again her father smiled, only this time it was brighter and there was a sparkle in his tired eyes. "I died, you know. Ask Colby if you don't believe me."

Vaguely Valerie remembered Colby saying something about her father's heart stopping and restarting, and considering it a miracle. "I know we're very fortunate to have you with us."

"More fortunate than you realize. Now, I don't want you getting all excited the way your sister did, but I don't expect you will. I had what those television reporters call a near-death experience."

"The long dark tunnel with the light at the end?" Valerie had certainly heard about the phenomenon.

"Nope," he said, shaking his head. "I was in a garden."

"The Garden of Eden?" she asked lightly.

"Might've been. I couldn't say."

He hadn't been aware that she was joking. "I didn't notice the trees so much, but there might've been an apple. What I did notice was the pretty woman tending the roses."

"Mom?" Valerie breathed the question, hardly knowing where it came from.

David smiled and shut his eyes. "We had a good, long talk, your mother and I. She convinced me it wasn't my time to die, that there's still plenty for me to do on this earth. I wasn't pleased to hear it because I've been thinking for some time now that I'd rather be with her."

"Daddy, I don't—"

"Shush now, because I have a lot to tell you and I'm getting weaker."

"All right."

"Your mother loves you and is very proud of everything you've accomplished, but she said you should take time to enjoy life before it passes you by."

That sounded like something her mother would say.

"She also told me I was an old fool to try and match you up with Colby."

"But—" She snapped her mouth closed, unwilling to say more.

"Grace feels my pushing the two of you to marry was ridiculous. Said I should apologize for that."

Valerie remained silent.

"There's more," David continued, "lots more. Grace wanted to be sure she gave me plenty of reasons to come back to this world."

"I'm very glad she convinced you."

Her father's eyes drifted shut, but he opened them again with apparent effort. "She talked to me about Stephanie and Norah, too."

"Good, Daddy," she said softly, patting his hand. "You can tell me all about it next time."

"Want to explain now…"

"Shh, sleep."

"You're all going to get married. Your mother assured me all three of you would."

"Of course we will. Eventually."

"Soon. Very…soon."

"I'm glad," she whispered, although she wasn't sure he heard her.

So her father had gone through a near-death experience. Valerie didn't know how much credence to put in what he was saying. Marriage was the farthest thing from her mind at the moment. Obviously, marrying Colby was out of the question. And—without even noticing—she'd lost interest in the idea of a relationship with Rowdy Cassidy.

"She gave me twelve reasons to live," her father announced sleepily. "Twelve very good reasons."

Valerie recalled that Norah had said something about the number six. She couldn't imagine why her father was speaking in figures all of a sudden.

"Twelve reasons," Valerie echoed, then leaned forward to kiss his cheek.

Her father's eyes fluttered open and he grinned boyishly. "Yup, my grandchildren. You, my darling Valerie, are going to give me three. All within the next few years."

# Six

"When's the last time you spoke to your father?" Colby asked Valerie when she arrived at the hospital the next morning, carrying an armful of apple blossoms for the nurses' station. He seemed to be waiting for her, and none too patiently.

She sighed, realizing what must have happened. "I take it Dad told you about his experience in the Garden of Eden?"

"It was the Garden of Eden?"

"Figuratively, I suppose."

"So you know, then," Colby muttered. A hint of a frown flickered across his expression.

"Look at it this way—at least Dad's given up his matchmaking efforts." Valerie had assumed Colby would be happy about that, so his reaction puzzled her.

His scowl deepened. "He apologized for even making the suggestion."

"See, what'd I tell you?" Valerie said, her mouth quirking with a smile. "We're both in the clear."

Apparently, this wasn't what Colby wanted to hear, either. "He also claimed you'd be married before the end of the summer—and that you'd present him with three grandchildren."

"In the next few years. It looks like I'm going to be busy, doesn't it?" Valerie hadn't taken her father's announcement too seriously; he'd had some kind of pleasant hallucination, and if it made him feel better, if it gave him a reason for living, then that was fine. She'd go along with it, although she wouldn't actively encourage him.

Besides, it was highly unlikely she'd marry anytime soon, and even if she did, she had no intention of leaping into this motherhood business. Marriage would be enough of an adjustment. She enjoyed children, and naturally assumed she'd eventually want a family, but definitely not in the first year or two following her marriage.

"Did he say *who* you're supposed to marry?"

"No. He wouldn't tell Norah, either, although he seemed to enjoy letting her know she's going to have six kids. Three boys and three girls, if you can believe it. You don't really buy any of this, do you?"

His mouth twisted into a wry grin. "That would be ridiculous, only... Never mind," he finished abruptly.

"No, tell me."

He shrugged, clearly regretting that he'd said anything. "Another patient of mine, an older woman, had a near-death experience. It was all rather...strange."

"She came back thinking she knew who her children would marry and how many grandchildren she was going to have?" Valerie asked sarcastically.

"No." Colby threw her an annoyed glance.

"What happened then?" She was curious now, unable to disguise her interest.

"She seemed to know certain things about the future. She—predicted, I guess is the word—certain political events. She wasn't entirely sure how she knew, she just did."

"So what was that all about?"

Colby obviously wasn't comfortable outlining the details of his patient's experience. "She didn't have any more than an eighth-grade education, and she'd never taken much interest in history or politics. But after that near-death phenomenon, she was suddenly able to discuss complicated world problems with genuine insight and skill. She didn't understand it herself, and I didn't have any medical explanation to offer her. The whole thing was as much a mystery to me as it was to her."

Until then, Valerie had to admit, she'd found her father's experience somewhat...entertaining. She'd been willing to tolerate it, since whatever had happened had been very real to David. This "dreamtime" with her mother had given his life a new purpose, and she was grateful for that, if nothing else.

"What are you saying?" she asked Colby.

"I don't actually know."

Suddenly none of this seemed quite as amusing. "Dad insists I'll be married before the end of the summer."

"He told me the same thing," Colby said. "About you, I mean." He paused. "Is it likely? I mean, is there someone back in Texas you've been seeing on a regular basis?" He clasped his hands behind his back and strolled slowly down the corridor. "Someone other than this person you were hoping to start dating soon?"

She puffed out her cheeks, debating how much to tell him about Rowdy Cassidy. "Not really, but..."

"Go on," he urged.

"My boss, Rowdy Cassidy." She shifted the spray of apple blossoms, conscious of their heady aroma in the antiseptic-smelling hospital corridor.

"The owner of CHIPS?"

Valerie nodded. "I've never gone out on a formal date with him, although until recently we saw each other nearly every day. We've often traveled together, and attend business dinners together. It wasn't until I got here and Dad started talking about you and me marrying that—well, Rowdy seems the natural choice for me. He's as dedicated to his career as I am and...we get along well."

"He's a wealthy man. Prominent in his field."

"Yes."

Colby clenched his jaw as though he disapproved.

"Do you know something about Rowdy that I don't?"

"I've never met the man. Everything I know about him I've read online or in the papers. But from all outward

appearances, the two of you should be an ideal couple."
His words were indifferent. Then without saying anything else, he turned and walked away from her.

"Colby," Valerie called, once she'd recovered from her
initial surprise. She hurried after him. "What's wrong?
You're acting like I've done something to offend you."

"I'm not angry," he said, his voice low. His gaze held
hers with a disturbing intensity. "I remember what you
said yesterday about wondering how we were going to
say goodbye. I was just thinking the same thing. I don't
know how I'm going to be able to stand by and watch
you marry another man."

To her the solution was simple. He could marry
her himself. But…they'd both already decided that
wouldn't work.

"What about you?" she asked, needing to know. "Is
there someone special you've been seeing?"

"Yes."

Her heart felt as if it had done a nosedive, colliding
with her stomach. Her face must have revealed her
shock because he elaborated.

"Sherry Waterman. I thought Norah might have mentioned her."

"A nurse?" she guessed.

Colby nodded. "Sherry has her nursing degree and
she's also trained as a midwife. That's what she's been
doing for the past five years. She's good with children and
she enjoys weaving and gardening." His voice was brisk
and matter-of-fact as he listed Sherry's qualifications.

"She...sounds exactly right for you." The aching admission was torn from her throat. Although it was painful to think of Colby with another woman, Valerie knew he'd chosen well in Sherry Waterman. Domestic, talented, perfect in all the ways Valerie wasn't.

"We've been dating for the last year."

"A year," Valerie repeated slowly, surprised he hadn't proposed to Sherry long before now. "You shouldn't keep her waiting then."

"I keep telling myself the same thing."

His words hurt, although Valerie pretended otherwise. "I'm delighted for you, Colby."

"Rowdy Cassidy will make you a good husband." His eyes probed hers.

Valerie smiled and nodded, then they both turned and walked in opposite directions. And although she was tempted, she didn't look back.

Valerie's cell phone vibrated, and she took the call in the hospital lobby.

"Valerie, it's Rowdy. Thought I'd check and see how everything's going with your father. No one's heard from you in a while."

When had she last reported into CHIPS headquarters? Two days before, she calculated. Two whole days! Valerie found that hard to believe. Until recently, her job had been all-consuming, but it wasn't that way now. She'd completely overlooked her work responsibilities, forgotten everything that had once been so important.

It seemed impossible that she could have allowed so much time to slip past.

"My father had open-heart surgery."

"How's he doing now?"

"Fabulously well. His recovery in the last twenty-four hours has been remarkable." She didn't tell him that much of the improvement was a result of a change in attitude. Since his "conversation in the garden" with Grace, David Bloomfield's will to live was stronger than ever. If there was anything to worry about now, it was the fact that Steffie hadn't arrived yet and no one had heard from her. Valerie had spent part of the morning calling the airlines to find out which flight she was on, to no avail.

"We miss you around here," Rowdy said in that casual way of his. Valerie could picture him sitting in his office, leaning back in his plush leather chair, cowboy boots propped on the mahogany desk. She couldn't remember ever seeing Rowdy without his boots and hat. She always thought of him as the Texan of frontier legend, the man who tackled life with robust energy, who considered no problem insurmountable. He worked hard, played hard and lived hard.

"I miss CHIPS, too."

"Any idea when you'll be back?"

"I'm sorry, no, but if you need me because of the Old West Bank deal—"

"No, no," Rowdy said, breaking in. "We're handling that from our end, so don't you worry about a thing. I just wanted you to know I miss you."

The personal pronoun didn't escape Valerie's notice. Rowdy *was* attracted to her. "My father wanted me to thank you for the flowers," she said. "Th-they got here yesterday morning." She'd hardly been aware of it at the time, although the nurses had all exclaimed over the lavish bouquets. Now, she felt flustered and nervous with him, something that had never happened before. Their relationship was moving into new territory, and Valerie found the ground unstable and a bit frightening.

"Actually the flowers were for you. I thought you needed something to brighten up your day."

"It was very thoughtful of you."

"It's the least I could do for my favorite executive. You hurry back, you hear?"

"I will. And, Rowdy, thanks for calling." She closed her cell phone and let her breath rush out in a deep sigh.

Norah was already in the waiting room when Valerie returned there. "That was Rowdy Cassidy," she explained unnecessarily.

"Are you in love with him?" Norah asked without preamble. "I thought you and Dr. Winston might be hitting it off, but…"

"Colby's involved with Sherry Waterman." Valerie kept her voice steady, making a strenuous effort to feign disinterest.

One glance at Norah told her she hadn't succeeded. "You'll recall that I never bothered to mention Sherry. There's a reason."

"Oh?" Valerie shrugged. "I wondered…I mean, even

Colby seemed to think you had, or rather that you should have." She'd wanted to ask her sister, but had hesitated, almost preferring not to know.

"Those two have been dating for a year. If Colby was serious about Sherry he would've asked her to marry him before now. Even Sherry's given up on them, although Colby doesn't seem to have figured that out yet. The last I heard, she was seeing someone else. Not that I blame her," Norah was quick to add. "It must be the most frustrating thing in the world to be crazy about a guy and have him lukewarm toward you."

"I'm sure it must be."

"You still haven't answered me," Norah pressed. "What about Rowdy? Are you in love with him?"

Valerie shrugged again, uncomfortable with the subject of her boss, unsure of her own feelings toward him. "Yes and no."

"You're beginning to sound like Colby. I think he loves everything Sherry represents. She's a nurturing, kind-hearted woman. She fits the image of what Colby wants in a wife."

"Then what's stopping him?"

Norah gnawed on her lower lip for a moment. "My guess is that she bores him. Don't get me wrong, Sherry's not a boring person. Actually when I think about it, Sherry and I are a lot alike. She's a homebody like me, and little things mean a lot to her. She doesn't need an active social life or fancy clothes. Given the choice between a stay-at-home date with a rented movie or dining in a world-class restaurant, she'd opt for the movie."

"I see."

"You're much better suited to Colby."

"Me?" Valerie asked, her voice rising in astonishment. Hadn't Norah just finished describing the kind of woman Colby wanted—a woman completely unlike Valerie?

"I've seen the looks the two of you exchange," Norah continued thoughtfully. "I'm not blind, you know. I can feel the attraction between you. It's mutual—and it's hot."

"Really," Valerie said, becoming preoccupied with the crease in her wool trousers.

"Yes, really!"

"Yes, well, I'll admit we're attracted to each other, but nothing's going to come of it." She glanced at her watch, wanting an excuse to leave. "I'm going to stop in and see Dad."

Norah's smile seemed all-knowing. "Okay."

David Bloomfield's color was better, and he grinned happily when he saw his eldest daughter.

"Hello, Dad," she said in a cheerful voice as she leaned over to kiss his cheek.

"Valerie," he whispered, holding out his hand to her. "Listen, sweetheart, you're spending too much time at the hospital. Take the day and get out in the sunshine. You're beginning to look pale."

"But…"

"It'll do you good. No more sleeping on some dilapidated couch in the waiting room, either."

She'd slept in her own bed in her own room for the first time the night before. In the morning, she'd been astonished at how well rested she felt. And she'd indulged in a long, hot shower, followed by a good breakfast—cooked by Norah.

The crews were just beginning to spray the apple trees under the direction of Dale Howard, the orchard manager. She'd heard the familiar sounds of men working in the orchards. It brought back memories of years past, of racing down the long, even rows, and climbing onto the low limbs of the trees, sitting there like a princess surveying her magical kingdom. Orchard Valley *was* magical, a town set apart.

For Valerie, coming home was like escaping to the past. The people were friendly, the neighbors neighborly, and problems were shared. It was a little piece of heaven.

"I wasn't at the hospital last night," she told him, pulling herself out of her musings. She loved Orchard Valley more than any place on earth, but she'd never be satisfied living here. There wasn't enough challenge, not enough to tax her mind. No, Houston was her future and she accepted that with only one regret. Colby.

"So I heard," her father answered. "I saw Colby earlier."

Valerie watched his expression, hoping for— what?—some sign, some indication of her father's thoughts. And of Colby's…

There was none.

"Well? What did the good doctor have to say?"

"Nothing much."

"Did he mention me?" she couldn't prevent herself from asking.

"Nope, can't say he did. Does that disappoint you?"

"Of course not."

"Is there any reason he *should* mention you?"

Valerie was sorry she'd brought up the subject. "Not that I know of."

Her answers seemed to make him smile. "So you like my doctor?"

"He's been wonderful to you," Valerie said.

"I wasn't talking about me," David told her gruffly. "I'm referring to *you*. You're attracted to him, aren't you, Valerie? You were never very good at hiding your feelings."

"I've never met a man who appeals to me more," Valerie said truthfully. There was no point in trying to deceive her father. He knew her all too well, and he understood her better than anyone, sometimes better than she understood herself.

"He feels the same way?" The question was calm, as though he were speaking to a child.

Valerie lowered her eyes before shaking her head. "It'd never work, and we both know it."

She expected an argument from her father, was even looking for one. She wanted him to tell her she was wrong, that love *could* work when two people were committed to each other. That it wouldn't matter how dissimilar they were, how differently they viewed life. That nothing mattered but the love they shared...

Her father, however, didn't respond.

Discouraged, Valerie said goodbye and returned to the waiting room. On her way, she saw that Norah sat talking to another doctor at the end of the hallway. She was grateful her sister had left, because she needed time alone to think.

If she wanted evidence that people with very different personalities could fall in love and make the relationship work, she need look no further than her own parents. The story of how they'd met and fallen in love was like a fairy tale, one that, as a child, she'd never tired of hearing.

Her father had gone to university and obtained his degree in business administration. Armed with his dreams, he'd built a financial empire and became a millionaire within a few years. Then he'd collapsed with rheumatic fever, nearly losing his life. While he was in the hospital recuperating, he'd met a young nurse. David knew the moment he met Grace Johnson that he was going to love her. It never occurred to him that she'd refuse his marriage proposal.

Several months of relentless pursuit later, he'd convinced Grace to marry him. Despite the fact that she was deeply in love with David, Grace had been afraid. She was a preacher's daughter who'd lived a simple life. David was a business tycoon who'd taken automation technology to new industry heights. Grace's fears about a marriage to David Bloomfield were warranted. But over the years, love had proven even the most hardened skeptics wrong, and the two had lived and loved together until her mother's death a few years before.

Her own romance wasn't going to have a fairy-tale ending, the way her parents' had. Her father knew it, too, otherwise he would've been the first to encourage her.

Her father, however, had said nothing.

Valerie was working in the den on her laptop, putting files in order, when she saw the red car hurtle down the driveway. She thought, for one hopeful moment, that it might be Colby, but then remembered he drove a maroon Buick. Still, she hastened to answer the door.

It was Charles Tomaselli, looking tired and frustrated.

"Have you heard from Stephanie?" he demanded without so much as a greeting.

Her sister's absence had been weighing on Valerie's mind, too. She'd done everything she could think of; she'd even placed a call to the American Embassy in Rome, with no results.

"I haven't heard a word. I don't know what could've happened to her."

"How late *is* she?"

Valerie had to think for a moment. In the past week, she'd lost all track of time. "Norah was the last person to speak to Steffie," she explained. "Let me see—that was just before Dad's surgery. Steffie thought she'd be home within twenty-four hours."

"That was forty-eight hours ago."

He didn't need to remind her, Valerie thought irritably. "She's coming by way of Tokyo."

"Tokyo? She's flying to Oregon via *Japan?*" Charles snapped.

"I gather she didn't have much choice."

"Don't you think you should be making some inquiries?" he asked gruffly.

"I already have. Tell me who else I should call and I'll be happy to do so."

Charles settled down on the top porch step, resting both elbows on his knees. "I have to tell you, Valerie, I'm worried. She should've been here before now."

"I know."

"I have some friends, some connections," Charles said absently, "and I've checked with them. But they can't find any trace of her on the flights scheduled out of Rome. If she isn't here by tomorrow afternoon, I don't think you have any alternative but to contact the authorities."

Valerie swallowed tightly, then nodded. She could slap Steff silly for putting them through all this worry.

"She's okay, Charles," Valerie said after a moment.

"What makes you so sure?" He turned to look up at her.

"I...don't know, I just am."

Charles stood agilely, his gaze leveled on the long narrow driveway that led in from the road. "I hope you're right, Valerie. I hope you're right."

Valerie hoped so, too. And she wondered if his concern for Stephanie meant as much as she thought it did.

* * *

Norah came back from the hospital a half hour later, talkative and lively. "I can't get over how much Dad's improved in such a short time."

Valerie took the shrimp salad she'd prepared for their dinner from the refrigerator. Salads were her specialty. That, and folding napkins. She could do both without a hitch.

For the first time since her arrival, Valerie had spent most of the day away from the hospital. When her father had suggested she leave, she'd initially felt a bit annoyed. But as she revisited the life that had once been hers in this quiet community, she accepted the wisdom of his advice. She *had* needed to get out, to breathe in the serenity she found in Orchard Valley and exhale the fear that had choked her from the moment she'd received Norah's frantic message. Then, after her walk, she'd come back to the house, and because she'd never been idle in her life, she'd set up a communications center in her father's den.

"I'm going back to work, starting tomorrow," Norah announced between bites of lettuce, shrimp and slices of hard-boiled egg. "The hospital's understaffed, but then when isn't it? I'll still be able to see Dad, maybe even more often than before. You don't mind, do you?"

"Of course I don't mind. You do whatever you think best."

"You're not going to leave, are you?" Norah asked, rushing the words. "I wouldn't do this if the hospital didn't need me so badly."

"I realize that."

Norah took another forkful of salad. "You're quiet tonight. Is anything wrong?"

"Not really." She didn't want to worry Norah about Steffie's disappearance.

"Colby asked about you."

She felt her stomach churn with contradictory emotions. Part of her was thrilled that he'd even mentioned her, yet she experienced a growing sense of apprehension.

"He wanted to know where you were."

"Did you tell him?"

"Of course," Norah answered blithely. "He said he thought it was a good idea for you to get out of the hospital more. You've practically been living there ever since you arrived." She slowly chewed another bite of her salad. "He asked me what I knew about Rowdy Cassidy," she said.

Valerie put down her fork, her appetite having fled. "What did you tell him?"

"The truth. That I've never met the man, but Dad seems to think he's wonderful. You probably weren't aware of this, but Dad's been following CHIPS ever since you started working there. He thinks Rowdy's a genius. Funny, though—I got the impression that wasn't what Colby wanted to hear."

"The shrimp was on sale at Vern's Market," Valerie said, changing the subject abruptly, not wanting to talk about Colby. Not now when she felt so vulnerable, so conscious of the attraction between them. "Vern said he cooked it himself this morning."

"You don't want to talk about Colby?"

Valerie grinned. Her sister hadn't graduated magna cum laude for nothing.

"You're not going anyplace tonight, are you?" Norah asked next.

"I thought I'd drive in to the hospital and visit Dad, but other than that, no. Do you need me to do something?"

Norah shrugged. "I may be wrong, but I think Colby wanted to talk to you. I have a feeling he might call."

Norah was right.

When Valerie returned from her trip to the hospital, her sister had left a note taped to her bedroom door.

COLBY PHONED. SAID HE'D TALK TO YOU IN THE MORNING.

Valerie read the message with mixed feelings. Thrill and dread went at it for round two, again evenly matched. She determined to forget everything—love, Colby, the future—for tonight. The morning would be soon enough to resume her worries. She craved the forgetfulness of sleep, the escape from thought and feeling.

Valerie had assumed she'd fall asleep with the same ease she had the previous night. For a solid hour she beat her pillow, tossed and turned in an effort to find a comfortable position. Finally giving up, she reached for the light on the bedside table and read until her eyes closed and the business journal slipped from her fingers.

But Valerie's exhausted sleep wasn't the restful

oblivion she'd longed for. Colby wandered into her dreams like an uninvited guest.

He looked handsome, dressed in the suit he'd worn the night he'd taken her to the Italian restaurant.

"You're not going to be able to forget me, are you?"

In her dream, Valerie said nothing, but only because she had no argument. She merely stared at him, adoring every feature, every movement.

A noise disturbed her, distracting her from Colby. Irritated, she looked over her shoulder to see what it was and when she looked back, he was gone. She cried out in frustration, the sound of her own voice jerking her awake. She was sitting upright in the bed, heart pounding furiously.

It took her another moment to realize there was some sort of commotion going on downstairs. She climbed out of bed and grabbed her robe.

From the top of the stairs, she saw Norah, laughing and crying at once. A battered suitcase stood on the floor, along with a leather coat and an umbrella.

"Steffie!" Valerie cried excitedly, racing down the stairs. Her sister was home.

# *Seven*

Colby picked up the clipboard at the foot of David Bloomfield's bed, scanning the notations the nursing staff had written through the night. Although his eyes were lowered, he couldn't help being aware of David Bloomfield's cocky grin.

"You must be feeling more like your old self this morning," he observed genially.

David's smile widened. "I'm feeling more chipper each and every day. How much longer do you intend to keep me prisoner here? I'm itching to get home."

"Another week," Colby answered, replacing the clipboard. "Perhaps less, depending on how well you do."

"A week!" David protested. "Are you sure you aren't holding me up just so you'll have an excuse to visit with Valerie?"

Colby's hackles rose, and he was about to defend his

medical judgment when he realized the old man was baiting him—and enjoying it.

"I'm going to have you transferred out of the Surgical Intensive Care Unit this morning," Colby continued, "but first I want you up and walking."

"I've been up."

Colby glanced back at the chart, surprised to see no indication of the activity.

"I just didn't let anyone know. I felt a bit dizzy, so I only walked around the bed. Not much of a trip, but it tired me out plenty."

"You're not to get out of this bed again unless there's someone with you, understand?" He used his sternest voice.

"All right, all right," David agreed. Stroking his chin, he studied Colby. "She's pretty as a picture, that oldest daughter of mine. Isn't she, Doc?"

Colby ignored both the comment and the question. "I'll have one of the physio staff come down in a few minutes and we'll see how well you do with your exercises. I imagine that by this afternoon you'll have conquered the hallway."

"From what I hear, that Rowdy Cassidy's been calling her two, three times a day."

Colby stiffened at the mention of the other man's name. He'd tried to tell himself that Valerie would be happier married to Cassidy. They shared the same attitudes, beliefs and ambitions; together they'd take the business world by storm. Rowdy was exactly the type of dynamic personality who'd help Valerie fulfill her goals and dreams. She'd never be content as a physician's wife, he told himself again. Nevertheless, he was having trouble accepting the obvious.

He'd never thought of himself as romantic. His career had consumed his life from the time he was a high-school sophomore. His much-loved grandfather had died of heart disease, and it was then that Colby had decided to become a doctor. Everything else had been subordinated to that goal. Only in the past year or so had he felt the desire to marry and start a family.

He'd acted upon that desire with methodical thoroughness, mentally tabulating a list of his wants and needs. He'd looked around at the single women in Orchard Valley and decided to date Sherry Waterman. If things didn't work out with Sherry, Norah Bloomfield was next on his list, although he was concerned about their age difference.

Things *had* worked out with Sherry, at least in the beginning. He'd found her refreshing and genuine and fun. Problems crept up later, when he discovered that she was entirely predictable. Involved with a woman who embodied every trait he wanted in his life's partner, he'd been…bored. He wasn't sure anymore that he needed someone quite so even-tempered and domestic.

According to the schedule he'd set for himself, he should have been married by now.

He wasn't.

To irritate him further, the only woman he'd been

strongly attracted to in the past year was Valerie Bloomfield, and anyone with a lick of sense could see they weren't the least bit compatible.

For months, long before his heart attack, David Bloomfield had found excuses to drag his oldest daughter's name into their conversations. By the time he met Valerie, Colby was thoroughly sick of hearing about her. He hadn't even expected to *like* her. Instead, his heart and his head had been spinning out of control from that first moment.

It was time to put an end to such nonsense, before either of them took this attraction business too seriously.

"Cassidy would be a good match for a woman like Valerie," he said as offhandedly as he could. The last thing he wanted was for Valerie's father to know how attracted he was to her, although he suspected David already knew. The old man seemed to have a sixth sense about things like this.

"Rowdy will, at that," David returned matter-of-factly. "I should know, too." The cocky grin was back in place.

Colby's chest tightened, his anger simmering just beneath the surface. David hadn't referred to his dream lately, the one he'd termed his near-death experience. But from bits and pieces of conversation, Colby had learned that David was still predicting Valerie's wedding. It made sense that the man he expected her to marry was Rowdy Cassidy.

All the better. He—

"Stephanie's home," David said conversationally, cutting into Colby's thoughts. "I saw her briefly this morning. What a lovely sight she was to these tired old eyes."

Colby nodded, finding it difficult to dispel the image of Valerie married to her employer. Well, he'd better get used to the idea, because it was likely to happen soon. And because he refused to deliberately ruin his life by marrying the wrong woman.

He'd call Sherry this afternoon, Colby decided with renewed determination, and ask her out to dinner. One thing was certain; he intended to steer clear of Valerie Bloomfield, regardless of how hard that was.

So much for the best laid plans, Colby mused as he left the Surgical Intensive Care Unit. Valerie was standing in the corridor waiting for him. As always, when he saw her, his heart was gladdened. An old-fashioned expression, perhaps, but he didn't know how else to describe what he felt when he was with Valerie.

He remembered the time he'd sought her out after losing Joanna Murphy. Just being with her had taken the sharp edge off the pain of that unexpected death, had helped him deal with the frustration, the sense of powerlessness. When she'd suggested coffee, his first inclination had been to refuse, but he'd found he couldn't. Sharing his concerns with her had, in some indefinable way, comforted him.

It seemed to him that their conversation had helped her, too, in coming to terms with her father's illness.

They'd helped each other. In thinking about those moments together, Colby understood why he couldn't simply dismiss his fascination with her as sexual attraction. That was part of it, all right. But more than any woman he'd ever known, Valerie Bloomfield was his equal. In intelligence, in emotional strength, in commitment to those she loved.

Every time Colby had been with her since, he experienced an elation, a small joy that left him feeling bewildered. Left him wanting to be with her even more. Yet he knew he couldn't afford to pursue a relationship that had no chance of lasting.

"You wanted to see me?" Valerie asked, her eyes meeting his expectantly.

He frowned and shook his head. "No."

"Norah left a note for me last night, saying you'd phoned."

"Oh, that. It was nothing." He wanted to kick himself for that phone call now. He'd been looking for a reason to talk to her. His day had been long and tiring, and his defenses down, so he'd made up an excuse to hear the sound of her voice.

"I just wanted to tell you I'm transferring your father from SICU this morning," he went on quickly. "His progress has been nothing short of remarkable. If it continues like this, he'll be out of the hospital inside a week."

Valerie's eyes sparkled with relief. "That's wonderful news! It seems everything's happening at once. I don't know if you heard, but Steffie got home last night."

"So I understand." Colby watched her closely. Although she said nothing else, he realized that something was troubling Valerie. Her brow had furrowed, ever so briefly, when she mentioned her sister's name. Colby suspected she wasn't aware of the tiny, telltale action.

"Something going on with your sister?"

Her eyes widened in surprise. "Yes, just now. She was sitting in the waiting room reading a copy of the *Clarion* when she jumped to her feet, demanding to know if I'd read it. Before I could say anything, she dashed out, taking the paper with her. I can't remember ever seeing Steffie so angry. I'm not sure what got into her, but I'm guessing it has to do with Charles Tomaselli."

"I'm sure she'll tell you eventually."

"I'm sure she will, too, although I have a feeling this is connected to an article he wrote with Dad's help. I just don't understand what she found so offensive. I read it and I didn't see any problem. Those two can't seem to get along. They never could. It's always surprised me, because she seemed to be so keen on him and I was beginning to think he felt the same way."

The temptation to linger, even to suggest they have coffee together, was overwhelming, but Colby resisted. He was doing a lot of that where Valerie was concerned. Resisting. He only hoped his willpower held firm until she went back to Texas—and to Cassidy— where she belonged.

"Valerie," Steffie said, standing in the doorway outside Valerie's bedroom. "Have you got a moment?"

"Sure." Valerie was sitting up in bed reading, but her

mind wasn't on the latest computer technology she'd had every intention of studying. With infuriating frequency, her thoughts drifted away from high resolution monitors and narrowed in on Colby. She welcomed her sister's visit, not least as a distraction.

Steffie crossed the room and sat on the edge of Valerie's bed. "I made a complete fool of myself this morning," she said, her eyes downcast.

Valerie waited for her to explain, but further details didn't seem to be forthcoming. Her curiosity was aroused, but she didn't want to pry.

"With Charles," Steffie finally said, drawing her knees up and circling them with her arms. "It isn't the first time, either. He's the one person in the world I swore I'd never speak to again and then, the first few hours I'm home, I make an idiot of myself over him."

Valerie set aside her business journal and drew up her own knees. "He's been worried about you."

"You've talked to him? When? What did he say?" Steffie's head came up. Her long dark hair fell to the middle of her back, and her eyes probed Valerie's. Although Steff was almost twenty-seven, she looked closer to eighteen. Especially now, when she felt so embarrassed.

"Charles asked about you shortly after I got home, and later he was concerned because you didn't arrive when we expected you. Apparently he made some inquiries, trying to track you down. Both Norah and I were so caught up in what was happening with Dad that we weren't as worried about your late appearance as we should've been. Charles, however, seemed terribly anxious."

"He was just hoping I'd get home in time to make an idiot of myself, which I did."

Valerie thought that was unfair of Steffie. "Charles has been wonderful," she protested, still wondering exactly what Stephanie had done.

"To you and Norah. I'm the one he can't get along with." Steffie's shoulders rose as she gave a deep, heartfelt sigh. "How do you know when you're in love, really in love?" she asked plaintively.

Their mother should be the one answering that question. Not Valerie. She hadn't figured out her relationships with Colby *or* Rowdy. Bemused, she shook her head. She could outsmart the competition, put together some of the biggest deals in the industry, but she didn't know how to tell if she was in love.

"I wish I could answer that," Valerie said quietly. "I know next to nothing about love. I was sort of hoping *you'd* be able to enlighten *me*."

Steffie frowned. "Don't tell me we're going to have to talk to Norah about this."

"We can't," Valerie said, then started to laugh.

"What's so funny? Listen, Val, this isn't a time for humor, or even pride. If Norah knows more than we do, which she probably does, then we should forget she's the youngest and come right out and ask her."

"We can't ask Norah about love, because she isn't here," Valerie said. "She's on a date."

Steffie started to laugh, too, not because it was particularly funny, but because it was a rare moment of shared closeness.

"Reading between the lines of your letters, I assumed you'd fallen in love with your boss," she said next. "You never said as much, but the two of you seemed to be spending a lot of time together."

"I think I might've been half in love with him until I met Colby."

"Dad's heart doctor?"

Valerie nodded. "When I first got home, Dad was fully expecting to die. He actually seemed to be looking forward to it, which annoyed everyone. Although not being able to get home must have been a nightmare for you, it might be the one thing that kept him hanging on as long as he did."

"You're sidestepping the issue. Tell me about Colby."

"It started with Dad's matchmaking efforts, which I found rather amusing and Colby found utterly frustrating, but then as we got to know each other we realized there was a spark." More of a blowtorch than a spark, really, but she wasn't going to say that.

"If you're in love with Colby, then why do you look like you're going to cry?"

"Because we both know it wouldn't work. He's a small-town doctor, who also lectures at Portland University. Although he could practice anywhere, he wants to stay right here in Orchard Valley."

"And you don't?"

"I don't think I could be happy here," Valerie said miserably. "Not anymore. And there are other problems, too...."

"But if you truly loved each other, you'd be able to find a solution to your differences."

"That's just it. I don't know if this *is* love, and I don't think Colby does, either. Everything would be much easier if we did."

"Yes, but if he's the right person..."

"I don't know. I'm attracted to him. I think about him constantly, but is that enough for me to forsake all my ambitions? Give up my career? I don't know," she said again, "and it's got me tied up in knots. How do I decide? And if I *did* quit CHIPS and found some other job around here, how do I know I wouldn't resent him five years down the road? How do I know he wouldn't end up resenting *me* for not being a more traditional kind of woman—which is what he wants? Besides, even if I do love Colby, how can I be sure he feels the same way about me?"

"I wish Mom was here."

"So do I," Valerie said fervently. "Oh, Steffie, so do I."

Valerie didn't see Colby for several days. Four, to be exact. As her father's health improved, she spent less and less time at the hospital, therefore decreasing her chances of casually running into him. She was working out of the house, and that helped. Being in a familiar place, doing familiar tasks, allayed her fears and tempered her frustrations.

She knew she should think about returning to Texas. The crisis had passed, and by remaining in Orchard Valley she was creating one of a different sort. CHIPS, Inc., needed her. Rowdy Cassidy needed her. She'd already missed one important business trip, and although Rowdy had encouraged her to stay in Orchard Valley as long as necessary, he'd also let her know he was looking forward to her return.

Valerie had almost run out of excuses for staying in Oregon. Her father was going to be discharged in record time and Valerie, with her two sisters, planned a celebration dinner that included Colby.

She was surprised he'd accepted the invitation. Surprised and pleased. She was hungry for the sight of him. He was in her thoughts constantly, and she wondered if it was the same for him.

All afternoon, she'd been feeling like a schoolgirl. Excited and nearly giddy at the prospect of her father's homecoming—especially since Colby would be driving him back.

Norah had been in the kitchen most of the afternoon, with Stephanie as her assistant. Since Valerie's culinary skills were limited to salad preparation and napkin folding, she'd been assigned both jobs, along with setting the table.

"What time is it?" Steffie called from the kitchen.

Valerie, who was carefully arranging their best china on the dining-room table, shot a glance at the grandfather clock. "Five."

"They're due in less than thirty minutes."

"Do I detect a note of panic?" Valerie teased.

"Dinner isn't even close to being done," Steffie told her.

They'd chosen a menu that included none of their father's favorites. David Bloomfield was a meat-and-potatoes man, but that was all about to change. Colby had been very definite about that. From now on, David would be a low-cholesterol-and-high-fiber man.

"The table's set," Valerie informed the others. As far as she knew, it was the first time they'd brought out the good china since their mother's death. But their father's welcome-home dinner warranted using the very best.

Fifteen minutes later, Valerie glanced out the living-room window to see Colby's maroon car coming down the long driveway. "They're here!" she shouted, hurrying to the front porch, barely able to contain her excitement.

This moment seemed like a miracle to her. She'd come to accept that she was going to lose her father, and now he'd been given a second chance at life. This was so much more than she'd dared hope.

Steffie and Norah joined her on the porch. Colby climbed out of the car first and came around to assist David. It was all Valerie could do not to rush down the steps and help him herself. Although her father had made phenomenal progress in the eight days since his surgery, he remained terribly pale and thinner than she'd ever seen him. But his eyes glowed with obvious pride and satisfaction as he looked at his three daughters.

He turned to Colby and said something Valerie

couldn't hear. Whatever it was made Colby's eyes dart toward Valerie. She met his gaze, all too briefly, then they looked hurriedly away from each other, as though embarrassed to be caught staring.

"I'm afraid dinner's not quite ready," Norah said as Colby eased David into his recliner by the fireplace.

"I've been waiting two weeks for a decent meal," David grumbled. "Hospital food doesn't sit well with me. I hope you've outdone yourself."

"I have," Norah promised, smiling at Valerie. Their father wasn't expecting poached salmon and dill sauce with salad and rice, but he'd adjust to healthier eating habits soon enough.

"Can I get you anything, Dad?" Valerie asked, assuming he'd request the paper or a cup of coffee.

"Walk down and see if the Howard boy is still in the orchard, would you, Val?"

"Of course, but I don't think you should worry about the orchard now."

"I'm not worried. I just want to know what's been going on while I was laid up. I promise I'm not going to overdo it. Colby wouldn't let me. I tried to die three times, but he was right there making sure I didn't. You don't think I'd want to ruin all that work, do you?"

Valerie grinned. "All right, I'll check and see if the foreman's still around."

"Colby," David said, raising his index finger imperiously, "you go with her. I don't want her walking in the orchard alone."

The request was a shamefully blatant excuse to throw them together, but neither complained.

Colby followed her out the front door and down the porch steps. "You don't need to come," she said, looking up at him. "I've been walking through these orchards since I was a toddler. I won't get lost."

"I know that."

"Dad was just inventing a way for us to be alone."

"I know that, too. He told me while we were driving here that he intended to do this."

"But why?"

"Isn't it obvious?"

"Yes, but..." Her father had hinted more than once that he anticipated a prompt wedding between her and Rowdy Cassidy. He'd apparently dropped the idea of her marrying Colby—so did he want her to clarify that in person? He seemed downright delighted at the prospect of Rowdy as a son-in-law, talking about her marriage as if it were a foregone conclusion.

"How have you been?" Colby asked. They strolled in the late-afternoon sunshine toward the west side of the orchard, where the equipment was kept. There was a small office in the storage building, as well, and if Dale Howard was still in the orchard that was the most likely place to find him.

"I've been fine. And you?" Valerie could tell him the truth about her feelings or she could tell him a half-truth. She chose the truth. "I've missed you."

Colby clasped his hands behind his back, as she'd

seen him do before. It might have been wishful thinking on her part, but Valerie thought he did so in an effort to keep from touching her.

"I understand your boss is calling you every day," he said stiffly.

"I understand you took Sherry Waterman out to dinner this week," she retorted.

"It didn't help," he muttered. "The whole time we were together I kept thinking I'd rather be with you. Is that what you were hoping to hear?"

Valerie dropped her gaze to the dirt beneath her feet. "No, but I'll admit I'm glad."

"This isn't going to work."

How rigid his words sounded, as though he was holding himself in check, but finding it more and more difficult. "What isn't?"

"You…being here."

"Here? You didn't have to come with me! I've already explained that I'm perfectly capable of finding my way—"

"CHIPS stock went up two dollars a share last week."

Colby was leaping from one subject to the next. "That's great," she said cautiously. "I'm sure Rowdy's thrilled."

"You should be, too."

"As a stockholder myself I am, but what's that got to do with anything?"

"Houston is where you belong, with Rowdy Cassidy and all his millions."

Rowdy had been telling her the same thing. Not in

quite the same words, but he wanted her in Texas. With him. Not a day passed that he didn't let her know how much he missed her. Rowdy wasn't romantic; fancy words weren't his forte. He was as straightforward as Valerie herself. He missed her, he said, missed the time they spent together and the discussions they'd shared. He hadn't realized how much until she'd left.

"When are you going back?" Colby demanded.

Valerie understood that this was the whole purpose of their being alone together. This was the reason he'd fallen in with her father's schemes and had walked in the orchard with her. He wanted her out of Orchard Valley and out of his life.

"Soon," she promised, and her voice cracked with pain. The intensity of it took her by surprise; embarrassed, she increased her pace to a half trot, wanting to escape.

"Valerie." His voice came from behind her.

"No, please… You're right. I'll—" She wasn't allowed to finish her thought. Colby caught her by the upper arm and turned her to face him, bringing her into his warm embrace.

He took her wrists and placed them around his neck as though she were a rag doll, then circled her waist with his arms and brought her tight against him. Before she had a chance to catch her breath, his mouth was on hers.

Valerie felt as though she'd drown in the sheer ecstasy of being in his arms again. It wasn't supposed to be like this. It wasn't supposed to feel so right, so good. His mouth was eager and she opened to him as naturally as a flower to the sun.

She clung to him, and then he suddenly jerked his head away. Valerie pressed her face into his shoulder and shuddered. She might've been able to forget him, forget these feelings, if he hadn't kissed her again, if he hadn't taken her into his arms.

"Valerie, can't you see what's happening?"

She nodded. "I'm falling in love with you."

"We can't let this continue."

"But—"

"Are you willing to risk everything we've both worked all our lives to achieve? Are you going to change, or do you expect me to? The fact is, you know that *neither* of us wants to give anything up. So we've got to put an end to this. Because, Valerie, we have nothing in common."

Offhand, Valerie could think of several things they had in common, but she didn't mention them. There was no point. She understood what Colby was saying. If they went on as they were, it would lead to the inevitable, and they'd be so deeply in love that they'd forget what was keeping them apart. They'd choose to forget that Valerie had a brilliant career waiting for her back in Houston. They'd choose to forget that Colby wanted a woman who'd be a dedicated homemaker. They'd overlook even the most obvious differences. For a while, their love would be enough, but that wouldn't last, not for long.

"It's time to go back," Colby said, releasing her.

"Dad won't be worried."

"I'm not talking about your father. I'm talking about you, Valerie. Go back to Texas," he said, his dark eyes holding hers, "before it's too late." He turned and walked away. It was the second time he'd pleaded with her to leave, and this time hurt even more than the first.

# *Eight*

"Colby's taken Sherry Waterman out three nights in a row," Norah said casually over a cup of coffee Saturday morning. "They've gone out every night since Dad's been home." She nibbled her toast, but her gaze managed to avoid Valerie's, as though she felt guilty about relaying the information.

"I assume there's a reason you want me to know this."

"Yes," Norah murmured. "Sherry was at the hospital, and we had a chance to talk. She says she can't understand why Colby keeps asking her out. The spark just isn't there. They enjoy each other's company, but they're never going to be more than friends. It almost seems as if Colby wants to make it something it's not."

"Perhaps Sherry's reading more into the situation than is there." Valerie didn't actually believe that, but she felt compelled to suggest it. She knew exactly what Colby was doing—escaping her, fighting everything he felt for her.

"Sherry realizes Colby's in love with someone else, and she also knows he's fighting it." Norah's words were an eerie echo of her own thoughts. "It's you, isn't it, Val? Colby's in love with you."

"I can't speak for him," Valerie insisted, munching furiously on her toast.

"Do you love him?"

She gave a careless shrug and answered the question with one of her own, always a good business move. "What do I know about love?"

"You know enough," Norah argued. "Please, do everyone a favor and put the poor guy out of his misery."

"How would you suggest I do that?" Valerie asked, genuinely curious. She was miserable, too, but no one seemed to take *that* into consideration. In other circumstances, she would've talked to Steffie, but her middle sister was obviously having relationship problems of her own—not that she was forthcoming with the details.

"For the love of heaven," Norah cried, "just marry him. He's crazy about you. Any fool can see that, and you're in love with him, too."

"Sometimes love isn't enough."

"Yes, it is," Norah insisted.

Perhaps to Norah, who was young and idealistic. But there were too many complications Valerie couldn't afford to ignore in her relationship with Colby. Besides, he'd been pretty explicit about wanting her to leave.

"I think you should quit your job, move back home and marry Dr. Winston," Norah said decisively.

"And do what?" Valerie asked. "Take up politics? Learn to knit? If I was *really* lucky, I might find some job in town that's about a tenth as interesting as the job I have now. Listen, I've been an active business-woman for the past eight years. Do you honestly think I'd be happy sitting at home knitting sweaters for the rest of my life?"

"You would eventually. It'll take a little adjusting, that's all."

"Oh, Norah." Valerie sighed and gave her starry-eyed sister a pitying smile. "You make everything sound so simple. It just isn't. Colby isn't exactly pining away for me, not if he's spending all that time with Sherry. If he wants me to stay, he'll ask."

"What if he doesn't? Are you willing to throw away a chance at happiness because you've got too much pride? You should tell him you're willing to stay," Norah said heatedly. "Why does everything have to come from Colby?"

"It doesn't, believe me. But it's too late."

"What's too late?" their father asked from the kitchen doorway. He was dressed in his plaid housecoat, the belt cinched tightly at the waist. He ran a hand through his di-sheveled hair, looking as though he'd only just awakened.

Norah automatically stood and guided him to a chair.

"What are you two arguing about?" he asked. "I could hear you all the way in the back bedroom."

Their father was sleeping downstairs because Colby didn't want him climbing stairs yet. Although he hadn't complained, Valerie knew her father was anxious to return to his own room.

"We weren't arguing, Dad," Valerie said, paying no attention to Norah's angry look.

"I heard you," David countered, smiling up at Norah as she brought him a cup of coffee. "Seems to me I heard Norah suggest you should marry Colby. That's what I've been saying for weeks. So has everyone else who's got a nickel's worth of sense."

Valerie's throat seemed to close up on her. "He has to ask me first. And…and you acted as if you felt Rowdy and I—"

"Phooey. Rowdy Cassidy's a good man, but he's not for you. If it sounded like I thought you should marry Rowdy, that was just to get you—and that stubborn doctor—thinking. As for Colby not asking you, ask him yourself."

"Dad…" The list of objections was too long to enumerate. The best thing to do was ignore the suggestion.

"You've never been shy about going after what you want. I've always admired that about you. You love him, don't you? So ask him to marry you—or at least to give a relationship with you a chance. You might be pleasantly surprised by what he says," Norah told her.

"It wouldn't work," Valerie said sadly. "Colby's as traditional as they come. When he's found the woman he wants to marry, he'll propose himself."

Neither Norah nor her father offered a rebuttal, which suited Valerie. A few minutes later she left the kitchen and went up to her room to dress, but she didn't get far.

Sitting on the end of her bed, she closed her eyes and tried to think. Was she being unnecessarily stubborn? Was Norah right? Was she allowing pride to impede happiness? Questions came at her from all directions, and she felt at a loss to answer them.

There seemed to be only one way of learning what she needed to know and that was to confront Colby. For years she'd been finding solutions in all kinds of unlikely situations. It was her greatest strength in business; however, when it came to her own life, she drew a blank. There had to be an answer that suited them both, but she couldn't figure out what it was.

She was obviously the last person Colby expected to see when he answered his door. Valerie saw the astonishment in his eyes and felt encouraged. She'd hoped to catch him off guard and had succeeded.

"Hello, Colby," she said.

"Valerie…hello."

She'd dressed carefully, taking time to select the perfect outfit for her purposes. Something that would remind him that she was a woman—but not a pushover. She'd chosen a lovely pale pink sweater dress Steffie had brought with her from Italy.

"Would it be all right if I came in for a few minutes?" she asked when he didn't immediately invite her inside.

"Of course. I didn't mean to be rude. I was writing."

"Writing?" She followed him into his living room and when he gestured toward the sofa, she sat there, hoping she appeared cool and serene. As though her visit was nothing more than a social call, when in fact the direction of her whole life depended on it. She had too much experience in negotiating to permit her feelings to show, but she was more nervous about this meeting than any business deal she'd ever accomplished.

"I've been working on an article for the *American Journal of Medicine*," he elaborated. "The editor asked me six months ago if I'd be willing to contribute a piece and I'm only getting around to it now."

Valerie felt a surge of pride. Colby had an impressive future ahead of him. The world would be a better place because of his dedication and caring. Their eyes met, and Valerie wanted to tell him how much she respected him, how proud she was of him, but she couldn't. She didn't want anything she said now to sway his decision later.

"I have something to ask you," she said, standing abruptly. She glanced around, then sat down again.

"Yes?" His gaze fell to her hands and she realized she was rubbing her palms together. She stopped, embarrassed by this display of nervousness.

"The last time I saw you," she began in a voice that was more hesitant than she'd intended, "you asked me to leave Orchard Valley."

"Yes," he said harshly.

"Why?"

"You know the answer to that as well as I do. Your father's recovery has been a lot faster than we could've hoped. Eventually you're going back, so I can't see any reason to prolong this…interlude. Texas is where you belong."

"In other words, if a man's going to hold me and kiss me, it should be Rowdy Cassidy."

A brief flash of anger showed in his eyes, but was almost immediately quelled. "That's exactly what I mean," he returned smoothly.

"I can't help asking myself something," she said, her voice growing smaller despite her efforts. "Is my leaving what you *really* want?"

"What do you mean?"

"I could stay in Orchard Valley." Her gaze clung to his, hopefully, eagerly. "This is my home. It's where I was born and raised, where I attended school. Some of my friends still live here and I know just about everyone in town." The words were rushed, practically tumbling over one another.

Colby breathed in deeply and seemed to hold his breath. His hands tightened into fists. "Why would you do that?"

Valerie had wondered how he'd respond. She knew what she wanted him to say—that he needed her in his life. Instead, he'd responded with a cruelly flippant question.

"Why would I stay?" she repeated slowly, her eyes never wavering from his. "Because you're here."

Her words were met with a brief, tension-wrought silence as though her frankness had shocked him. He looked away.

"Are you saying you love me?" he demanded in a tone that suggested this wasn't what he wanted to hear.

"Yes." Her own voice was husky with something close to regret. "All morning I've been wishing I'd dated more in high school and college, because then I'd know what to say. I've always been too…direct. I can't help it. It's just part of my nature."

Colby didn't respond, which made her hurry to fill the silence.

"This is when you're supposed to admit you love me, too," she prompted anxiously. "That is, if you do… I may not have been a Homecoming Queen, but I'm woman enough to know you care for me, Colby. The least you can do is admit it and let me salvage what little pride I have left."

"Loving you has never been the problem."

"Thank you for that," she whispered.

"But love isn't enough."

"How do we know that?" she asked, although she'd said the same thing herself less than two hours earlier. "We haven't even tried. It seems to me no one would've gotten anywhere in this world if they'd decided to quit before even trying."

"You make it so tempting."

"I do? I really do?" His words thrilled her. They gave her the first sign of encouragement since her arrival. "I was thinking…there are companies in the Pacific Northwest I could work for…companies that would be glad to have me."

Colby stood and moved across the room. Not knowing what else to do, Valerie followed him.

"I think you should kiss me," she said hoarsely.

"Valerie." He turned as he said her name. He wasn't expecting her to be so close behind him, because he nearly collided with her. His hands reached for her shoulders to steady her.

It was exactly what Valerie had hoped would happen. She moved automatically into his embrace, wrapping her arms around his waist, hugging him close. She raised her mouth expectantly to his and wasn't disappointed.

With a groan, Colby claimed her lips. His hands were in her hair as he tilted her head back and kissed her with a hunger that left her breathless and weak.

"Valerie…no." Reluctantly he stepped away from her, bracing his hands against her shoulders.

"But why?" she pleaded.

Deftly Colby stepped farther back, putting as much distance as possible between them. "What's wrong with you?" he asked angrily.

"Wrong?" she repeated, still trapped in the excitement his kiss had aroused.

"Did you think coming here and seducing me would mean an offer of marriage? It's not very original, Valerie. I would have thought better of you."

"Seduce you?" Hot color sprang instantly to her cheeks. "I wasn't…I had no intention—"

"Well, that's the way it looked to me."

If he was trying to upset her, he was certainly doing an effective job. She forced herself to take several deep breaths. "I didn't come here to seduce you, Colby, nor am I going to let you annoy me into starting an argument. I came because I had to know. I had to find out for myself if there was a chance for us. If not, tell me so right now and I'll leave. I'll walk out that door and we'll both forget I was ever here." She paused. "Is that what you want?"

He frowned, his expression fierce, but he didn't answer.

"Say it," she demanded. "Tell me you don't want me. Tell me to get out of your life and I'll go, Colby. I won't even look back."

She remained on the far side of the room, frozen in misery.

Still Colby said nothing. Nothing.

"You don't need to worry about any unpleasant scenes. I'll pack up my belongings, drive myself to the airport, and you'll never hear from me again." Her voice remained steady despite the hoarseness of pain.

Silence.

"Just say it," she cried. "Tell me to go…if that's what you want. But if you had an ounce of sense, you'd ask me to stay right here and marry you. You don't have any sense, though. I know—because you're going to do what you think is the noble thing and send me away. Well, I won't make it easy for you, Colby. If you want me out of your life, you're going to have to say it."

"I might if I could get a word in edgewise."

Valerie choked on a sob and swallowed the laughter. "I love you! Doesn't that mean anything to you?"

His hands clenched into fists again, and his eyes, his beautiful eyes, didn't stray from her.

"Say it!" she shouted. "Tell me you don't want me. Better yet, tell me you're crazy in love with me and that you're willing to find a way to make everything right for us. Tell me that instead."

He closed his eyes.

"This is it, Colby. If I walk out that door, whatever was between us is over. I'll go about my business and you'll go about yours. I refuse to waste the rest of my life waiting for you." She dashed the tears from her cheeks with the back of one hand.

"You'll always be someone very special in my life." The words were so soft she barely heard them.

"That's not good enough," she sobbed. "Tell me to get out of your life. Make it really clear so I'll know you mean it, so I won't question it later. So *you* won't question it later."

"You don't belong here."

"That's better." She gulped. "But still not good enough. Haven't you ever heard of being cruel to be kind? Just make sure you mean what you say, because this is the only chance you'll have." Her voice broke. "You don't even have to promise to marry me. Just ask me to stay."

"No!" It was shouted at her, as though something had snapped inside him. "You want me to be cruel, is that what it takes? Does it have to come to this? You're an intelligent woman, or so I assumed, but this…this performance is ridiculous. I owe you nothing. You want me to tell you to go? Then go. You don't need my permission." He stormed to the other side of the room and held open the door for her. "Go back to Texas, Valerie. Marry your cowboy."

Stunned, she was afraid to move, afraid her legs would no longer support her. She nodded. She moved shakily past him.

"Goodbye," she whispered and then, unable to resist, brushed her fingertips down the side of his face. When she looked back at this moment, there would be no regrets. She'd offered him everything she had to give, and he was turning her away. There was nothing more she could do.

Colby glanced at his hands, the very hands he used to save lives, and saw they were trembling with the force of an emotion so strong it was all he could do not to smash them into a concrete wall.

When Valerie left, he'd been furious. He would have preferred it if she'd packed her bags and quietly disappeared. That was what he'd envisioned. Not this dreadful scene. Not dragging out their emotions, prolonging the pain.

It shouldn't have been so difficult for him. This wasn't a new decision, but one he'd made long before he'd ever kissed her, long before he'd held her in his arms and comforted her.

The phone rang and he seized it, grateful for the

reprieve from his thoughts. "Hello," he snapped, not meaning to sound so impatient.

"Colby, is this a bad time?"

"Sherry…of course not. I was just thinking…" He let the rest fade.

"I'm sorry, but I won't be able to make our dinner tonight, after all."

How sweet she sounded, Colby mused. Why couldn't he feel for her the things he felt for Valerie Bloomfield? Heaven knew he'd tried in the past few days. He'd done whatever he could think of to spark their interest in each other, but to no avail.

"My aunt Janice arrived and my parents asked me to take her over to my brother's place," Sherry explained. "I hope this isn't inconvenient for you."

"No problem." He heard something else in her voice, a hesitancy, a disappointment, but he chose not to question it.

"Colby."

"Yes?" The irritation was back, but it wasn't Sherry who'd angered him. It was his own lack of feeling for her. This past week, he'd spent four evenings with her. He'd held her and kissed her, and each time her kisses had left him cold and untouched.

"I don't mean to be tactless, but I don't think we should see each other anymore."

Her words shocked him. "Why not?" he asked, although he knew the reasons and didn't blame her.

"It's not me you're interested in, it's Norah's sister.

I like you, Colby, don't get me wrong, but this just isn't working. We've been seeing each other for over a year now, and if we were going to fall in love it would've happened before now."

"We haven't given it a real chance." Colby didn't understand why he was arguing with her when he was in full agreement. Sherry would make some man a wonderful wife. Some *other* man.

"You're using me, Colby."

He had nothing to say in his own defense. He hadn't realized until she'd said it, but Sherry was right. He *had* been using her. Not to make Valerie jealous, or in any devious, underhanded way, but in an effort to prove to himself that he could happily live without Valerie.

The experiment had backfired. And now he was alone, wondering how he could have let the only woman he'd ever loved walk out of his life.


"What's this I hear about you going to Texas?" David Bloomfield asked when Valerie joined him on the front porch following the evening meal. She sat on the top step, her back pressed against the white column while her father rocked in his old chair. She looked at the blooming apple orchard, breathed in the scent of pink and white blossoms perfuming the air. The setting sun cast a golden glow across the sky.

Valerie hadn't said anything at dinner about returning to Texas, and was surprised that her father was aware of her intentions. She'd sat quietly in her place at the table, pushing the food around her plate and hoping no one would notice she wasn't eating.

"It's time for me to go back, Daddy."

"It hurts, doesn't it?" he asked, his voice tender.

"A little." *A lot,* her heart cried, but it was a cry she'd been ignoring from the moment she left Colby's home. "Your health's improved so much," she said with forced cheerfulness. "You don't need me around here anymore."

"Ah, but I do," her father countered smoothly, continuing to rock. "Colby needs you, too."

His name went through her like the blade of a sharp sword, and her breath caught at the unexpected pain. Her father was the reason she'd come home, but Colby was the reason she was leaving.

"Love is funny, isn't it?" she mused, wrapping her arms around her knees the way she had as a young girl.

"You and I are so much alike," her father said. "Your mother saw it before I did, which I suppose is only natural. I'm proud of you, Valerie, proud of what you've managed to accomplish in so short a time, proud of your professionalism. Cassidy's lucky to have you on his team, and he knows it—otherwise he wouldn't have promoted you."

"I've got a terrific future with CHIPS." She said it to remind herself that her life did have purpose. There was somewhere to focus all her energy. Something that would help her forget, give her a reason to go on.

"Your mother's and my romance wasn't so easy, either, you know," her father said, rocking slowly. "She was this pretty young nurse, and I was head over heels in love with her. To my mind, she was lucky to have me. Problem was, she didn't seem to think so. I was a business success, a millionaire. But none of that impressed your mother." His smile was wryly nostalgic, his eyes gazing into a long-ago world. "Convincing Grace to marry me was by far the most difficult task I'd faced in years."

"She didn't love you?" That was impossible for Valerie to comprehend.

"She loved me, all right, she just didn't think she'd make me the right kind of wife. I was wealthy, socially prominent and, as you know, your mother was a preacher's daughter from Oregon. Before I contracted rheumatic fever I was one of the most sought-after bachelors in California, if I do say so myself. But I hadn't met the woman I wanted to marry until your mother became my nurse."

How achingly familiar this sounded to Valerie. She'd been content with her own life until she met Colby. Falling in love was the last thing she'd expected when she returned home.

"There were other problems, too," David went on. "Your mother seemed to think my work habits would kill me, and she wasn't willing to marry me only to watch me work myself to death."

"But you solved everything."

"Eventually." A wistful look stole over him. "I loved your mother from the first moment I opened my eyes and saw her standing beside my hospital bed. I remember thinking she was an angel, and in some ways she was." His face shone with the radiance of unending love. "I knew if she'd ever agree to marry me, I was going to have to give up everything I'd worked so hard to achieve. That meant selling my business and finding something new to occupy my time."

"You did it, though."

"Not without a lot of deliberation. I'd already made more money than I knew how to spend, but I realized I wasn't going to be happy retiring before the age of forty. I had to have something to do. It took a couple of years— and Grace's help—to figure out what that should be."

Valerie nodded. "I feel the same way. I'd never be happy just sitting at home— I'm too much like you." The extent of his sacrifice shook her. "How could you have given up everything you'd worked all those years to build?"

"Without your mother my life would've been empty. My work didn't matter anymore. Grace was important, and the life we were going to build together was important. I gave up one life but gained another, one I found far more fulfilling."

"But didn't you ever get bored or restless?"

"Some, but not nearly as much as I expected. When we'd been married a year or two, your mother saw I had too much time on my hands and we looked around for something to occupy me, some new interest. That was when we bought the orchard and moved here." He grinned. "My own Garden of Eden."

"I don't think I ever understood how much you'd changed your life to marry Mom."

"It was a sacrifice, and at the time it seemed like a huge one, but as the years passed, I realized she'd been right. I would've killed myself if I'd continued in business. Your mother brought balance into my life, the same way Colby will bring balance into yours."

She allowed a moment to pass before she spoke. "I'm not marrying Colby, Dad. I wish I could tell you I was, and that we were going to seek the same happiness you found with Mom, but it isn't going to happen."

It was as if she hadn't said a word. "You'll be so good for him, Valerie. He loves you now, and you love him, but what you feel for each other doesn't even begin to approach the love you'll experience over the years, especially after the children arrive."

"Dad, you're not listening to me." He seemed to be in a dream world that shut out reality. She had to make him stop, had to pull him out of the fantasy.

"He needs you, too, you know, even more than you need him. Colby's lived alone too many years. Only recently has he recognized how much he wants a woman in his life."

"He doesn't want *me*."

Her father closed his eyes and smiled. "You don't truly believe that, do you? He wants you so much it's eating him alive."

She lacked the strength to argue with her father, not after her confrontation with Colby earlier in the day. Nor did she have the energy to explain what had passed between them. In her mind, it was over. She'd told him she wouldn't look back and she meant it. She'd swallowed her pride and gone to him and he'd cast her out of his life.

She didn't hate him for being cruel; she'd asked for that. Nor had she made it easy for him to reject her. But he'd done it.

David sipped his coffee, and his smile grew even more serene. "You have such happiness awaiting you, Valerie. This problem with my heart is a perfect example of good coming out of bad. My attack was what brought you racing home. Heaven only knows how long it would've been before you met Colby if it weren't for this bum heart of mine."

Valerie reached for her own mug of coffee and took a sip. "You want anything else before I go inside?"

"So soon? It's not even dark."

"I have a lot to do."

"Are you going to think about what I said?"

She hated to disappoint him, hated to disillusion a romantic old man whose judgment was clouded by thirty years of loving one woman.

"I'll think about it," Valerie promised, but it was a lie. She intended to push every thought, every memory of Colby completely from her mind. That was the only way she'd be able to function. She got slowly to her feet.

"Good." He nodded, still smiling. "Stay with me, then. There's no need for you to hurry inside."

Valerie hesitated. This conversation was becoming decidedly uncomfortable. Despite her father's illusions, she had to face what had happened between her and Colby, accept it as truth and get on with her life. Pining away for him would solve nothing. And listening to her father only added to the pain.

"I need to do a few things before I leave." The excuse was weak, but it was all she could think of.

"There's plenty of time. Sit with me a spell. Relax."

"Dad…please."

"I want to tell you something important."

"What is it, Dad?" she asked with a sigh.

"I know for a fact that you're going to marry Colby," he said, smiling up at her, his eyes bright and clear. "Your mother promised me."

# Nine

"Dad," Valerie said, suppressing the urge to argue with him. "If it's about your dream, I don't think—"

"It was more than a dream! I was dead. I told you—ask Colby if you don't believe me. I crossed over into the valley of shadows. Your mother was waiting for me there and she wasn't pleased. No, sir. She was downright irritated with me. Said it wasn't my time yet, and I was coming home much too early."

"I'm sure this seemed very real to you—"

"It *was* real." His voice had grown louder. "Now you sit down and listen, because what I'm about to tell you happened as surely as I live and breathe."

Trapped, Valerie did as her father asked, lowering herself to the top porch step. "All right, Dad, I'll listen."

"Good." He smiled down at her, apparently appeased. "I've missed your mother, and I didn't want to continue living in this world without her. She told me my thinking was all wrong. She promised me the years I have left will be full and happy ones, with nothing like the loneliness I've endured since she's been gone."

"Of course they will." Valerie didn't put much stock in this near-death experience of her father's, but he believed it and that was the important thing.

"Problem was, I didn't much care about my life back here," he went on, almost as if he hadn't heard Valerie. "I was with Grace, and that was where I wanted to be. As far as I was concerned, I wasn't going back."

Valerie was familiar with her father's stubbornness; she'd inherited a streak of it herself.

"Your mother told me there was a reason for me to return. To tell you the truth, I'd already decided I wasn't going to let her talk me into it. She was darn good at that, you know. She'd drag me into the most outlandish things and make me think it was my idea."

Her father was grinning as he spoke, his eyes twinkling with a rare joy.

"That was when she told me about you girls. Your mother and I were standing by a small lake." He frowned, evidently trying to remember each detail of his experience. "She asked me to look into the water. I thought it was an unusual request, considering the discussion we were having."

"What did you see?" Valerie was picturing trout and maybe some bass, knowing how much her father enjoyed lazing away a summer afternoon fishing.

"I saw the future."

"The *future?*" This sounded like something out of a science fiction novel.

"You heard me," he said irritably. "The water was like a window and I could look into the years ahead. I saw you and your sisters, and you know what? It was the most beautiful scene I could ever have imagined. So much joy, so much laughter and love. I couldn't stop looking, couldn't stop smiling. There were my precious daughters, all so happy, all so blessed with love, the same way your mother and I had been."

"It sounds lovely, Dad." Her father had undergone traumatic surgery and just barely survived. If he believed in this dream, if he maintained he'd actually spoken to her mother, then Valerie couldn't bring herself to disillusion him. Nor did she want to argue. Especially not now, when her own emotions had taken such a beating.

"I remember every single moment of that meeting with your mother. I didn't see a single angel, though. I don't mind telling you, that was a bit of a disappointment. Nor did I hear anyone playing the harp."

Valerie hid a smile.

"You understand what I'm saying, don't you?"

"About angels?"

"No," he returned impatiently. "About you and Colby. He's the one I saw you with, Val. You had three beautiful children."

"Dad, why now?" At his quizzical gaze, she elaborated. "Why are you trying so hard to convince me to marry Colby? After the surgery, you seemed to have given up the idea. What happened to change your mind?"

"You did."

"Me?"

"You're both so darned stubborn. I hadn't counted on that."

"But you apologized for the matchmaking, remember?"

"Of course I remember. I gave it up on Grace's advice, but only because I felt you two wouldn't need any help from me. But I quickly found out you need my help more than ever. That's why I talked about Cassidy so much. To get you thinking about what you really wanted. And to make Colby a little jealous. Face it, Val. Eventually you're going to marry him."

"Dad, please, I know you want to believe this, but it just isn't going to happen." Without realizing what he was doing, her own father was making everything so much more painful.

"Don't you understand, child? Colby loves you, and you love him, and you're going to have a wonderful life together. Naturally there'll be ups and downs, but there are in any marriage."

"I'm not marrying Colby," she said from between gritted teeth. "For heaven's sake, I only met him a few weeks ago!"

"You think I'm an old man whose elevator doesn't go all the way to the top, but you're wrong." He gave her a lazy smile. "I know what I saw. All I'm asking is that you be patient with Colby and patient with yourself. Just don't do anything foolish."

"Like what?"

"Going back to Texas. You belong here in Orchard Valley now. It's where you're going to raise your children and where Colby's going to continue his practice."

"It's too late."

"For what?"

Valerie stood, her chest aching with the effort to breathe normally. She felt so empty, so alone. More than anything, she wanted to believe her father's dream, but she couldn't. She just couldn't.

"I've already booked my flight. My plane leaves in the afternoon." She didn't wait for her father to disagree with her, to tell her what a terrible mistake she was making. Instead she hurried into the house and up the stairs, not stopping until she was inside her room, with the door firmly closed.

She hauled her suitcase from the closet. There wasn't much to pack, and the entire process took her all of five minutes. She didn't weep. Her tears had already been spent.

When she returned to Texas, she'd be more mindful of love. It had touched her life once; perhaps it would again. In time. When her heart had healed. When she was ready.

With that thought in mind, she reached for the phone on the nightstand and held it in her lap, staring sightlessly at the keys. After an endless moment, she tapped out the long-distance number.

"Hello." The deep male voice sounded hurried and impatient.

"Hello, Rowdy," she said quietly.

"Valerie." He seemed delighted to be hearing from her. "I'm glad you phoned. I tried to reach you earlier in the day, but your sister told me you were out. Did she mention my call?"

"No. Was it something important?" Norah must have been the one who answered, since Steffie was out most of the day. Romantic Norah, who so badly wanted Valerie to marry Colby and live happily ever after.

"It wasn't urgent. I just wanted to see how soon CHIPS could have you back. There's been a big hole here since you left."

"I realize my being gone has been an inconvenience—"

"Don't be silly. I wasn't referring to the workload, I was talking about *you.* Like I told you before, I got used to having you around," he said gruffly, as though he was uncomfortable saying such things. "Doesn't seem right with you not here. You're an important part of my team. That's how come I'm giving you a ten percent raise—just so you'll know how much you're appreciated."

Valerie gasped. "That isn't necessary."

"Sure it is. Now, when are you flying home?"

*Home.* Home wasn't in Texas, it never really had been, but Rowdy wouldn't understand that.

"Valerie?"

"Oh, sorry. That was actually the reason for my call.

I've booked my flight for tomorrow. I'll arrive early in the evening and be at the office Monday morning." She forced some enthusiasm into her words.

"That's great news! It's just what I was hoping to hear. We'll celebrate. How about if I pick you up at the airport and take you to dinner?"

The invitation surprised her, although she supposed it shouldn't have. "Ah…" She didn't know what to say. She'd already promised herself she wasn't going to spend the rest of her life pining away for Colby Winston. Yet when the opportunity arose to put the past firmly behind her and begin a new life, she hesitated.

"I don't think so," she told him regretfully. "Not just yet. I'm going to need some time to readjust after being away for so long." It had been less than three weeks, but it felt like a whole lifetime.

"You've been gone *too* long," Rowdy said, his voice low and resonant. "I've missed you, Valerie. I haven't made a secret of it, either. When you get back, I'd like the two of us to sit down and talk."

Sudden dread attacked her stomach, her nerves. This wasn't what she wanted to hear. "I—I don't know if that'd be a good idea, Rowdy. I don't mean to be—"

"I know what you're thinking," Rowdy cut in. "And I have to admit, I share your concern. An office romance can lead to problems. That's why I want us to talk. Clear the air before we get involved."

It obviously hadn't occurred to Rowdy that she might

not be interested. But only a little while ago, the prospect of a relationship with him would have filled her with excitement.

Colby had hardly ever spent a more uncomfortable night. He hadn't been able to sleep and, finally giving up, had gone downstairs to read. Another hour ticked slowly by, and still his mind refused to relax. Feeling even more disgruntled, he set the novel aside.

It would have helped if Sherry had kept her dinner date, but she'd cancelled. Not only that, she'd let him know she didn't want to see him again. She was right to have done it, too—a fact that didn't improve his disposition.

When it came to his relationships with women, Colby just wasn't getting anywhere. Okay, so he was behind schedule. He'd underestimated the difficulty of finding the type of wife he wanted.

His requirements were very specific, which was why he'd intended to conduct his search in a methodical, orderly manner. It wasn't as though he'd discovered any shortage of "old-fashioned" girls, either. Unfortunately, most of them didn't appeal to him.

This only served to confuse him further. Obviously there was a flaw in his plan. Of one thing he was certain—Sherry was out of the picture. For that matter, so was Valerie.

*Valerie.*

Her name seemed to be engraved on his mind, but by

sheer force of will, he turned his thoughts in another direction. He got up and moved into his den to print out the article he'd been working on earlier that day. Although he'd shrugged off its importance when he spoke to Valerie, he was well aware that the invitation to submit it was a real honor. He'd done exhaustive research, and every word he'd written had been carefully considered.

But right then and there, Colby realized it meant nothing. Nothing. With an angry burst of energy, he crumpled the sheets and tossed them in his wastebasket.

Colby rarely acted in anger. Rarely did he allow himself to display any emotion. He'd schooled himself well; he'd needed to. He dealt with death so often, with fear, with grief. It became crucial, a matter of emotional survival, to keep his own feelings strictly private. Over the years, that had become second nature. For the first time in recent memory, he deplored his inexperience at expressing emotion.

He had no trouble recognizing that his inability to sleep, his lack of interest in a good novel, his discontent with the article he was writing, were all caused by what had happened between him and Valerie that morning.

He'd done what he had to do. It hadn't been easy— for either of them—but it was necessary. She'd made him angry with her demand that he be cruel. She wouldn't accept anything less. By the time she left, he'd been furious. She'd prodded and pushed and shoved until, backed into a corner, he'd had no choice.

Every harsh word he'd spoken had boomeranged back to hit him. She'd insisted repeatedly that he tell her to get out of his life. And he'd done it....

It was over, which was exactly what he wanted. Valerie would go back to Texas and he'd continue living here in Orchard Valley.

Her sad gray eyes would haunt him. And it had taken all afternoon to forget the feel of her fingertips as they grazed his face.

His intention had been to send her away, hurt her if he had to, so the break would be final. He hadn't grasped how much that would cost him.

Twenty hours later, he was still angry. Still in pain.

Walking back into his living room at 2:00 a.m., Colby sank into the recliner and reached for the television remote control. Surely there'd be some movie playing that would hold his attention for an hour or two.

He was wrong. All he could find—other than info-mercials and vapid talk shows—was a 1950s love story, filmed in nostalgic black and white. The last thing Colby was in the mood to watch was a sentimental romance with a happy ending. He turned off the television and stood up.

He hadn't been out to the Bloomfields' in three days. Although David was home and they'd scheduled an appointment at the office early in the week, it wouldn't be a bad idea to stop by and see how the older man was recovering. They were friends, and it was the least Colby could do—for the sake of a longstanding friendship.

That decision made, he found himself yawning loudly. Fatigue greeted him like an old comrade, and in that moment Colby knew he'd be able to sleep.

Valerie was dressed, her suitcase packed. She'd lingered in her room far longer than necessary. Her flight wasn't until 1:00 p.m.—not for another four hours—so she had plenty of time, yet she felt an intense need to be on her way. But there was another feeling that ran even deeper, even stronger: she dreaded leaving.

"Valerie?"

She turned to see Steffie standing in her bedroom doorway, frowning as she glanced at the suitcase. "Are you sure you're doing the right thing?"

Valerie gave her a wide and completely artificial smile. "I'm positive."

"How can you smile?"

"It's such a beautiful morning, how could I possibly *not* smile? Dad's home and thriving, you're here, and Norah's in seventh heaven because she's got someone to cook for."

Steffie grinned. "Yeah, I know. But I can't help feeling you shouldn't go."

"My life's in Texas now."

Steffie wandered into the room and sat on the edge of the bed. "If you're running away, it's a mistake. I made the same one myself three years ago. I embarrassed myself in front of Charles Tomaselli, and then because I was so mortified and because I couldn't bear to face him, I decided to study in Europe."

"You had a wonderful opportunity to travel. Do you honestly regret it?"

"Yes. Oh, not the travel and the experience. But leaving was wrong. I didn't realize it then, but I do now. I went into hiding. I know that sounds melodramatic, but it's the truth. At the time it seemed like the only thing to do, but I understand now that I should have swallowed my pride instead of walking away from everything I loved."

"Sometimes we don't have any choice."

"And sometimes we do," Steffie said. "Don't make the same mistake I did. Don't run away, because at some point down the road, you're going to regret it, just like I did."

Her sister's eyes were intent, silently pleading with Valerie to reconsider. If she hadn't gone to Colby the day before, Valerie might have hesitated, but there was no reason now for her to stay. There was no reason to hope Colby would change his mind.

"Someone's coming," Steffie said, walking over to look out Valerie's bedroom window.

Valerie moved aside the white curtains and peered outside. Steffie was right. A maroon car was making its way down the long driveway.

Colby.

A surge of excitement shot through her. He'd come to tell her he'd changed his mind, to ask her not to leave. Only seconds before, she'd been so sure there was no hope and now it flowed through her like current into an electrical wire. Try as she might, she couldn't squelch it.

"It—it's Colby," Valerie said, when she found her voice.

Steffie gave a cry of sheer joy. "I knew it! I knew he wouldn't be able to let you go. Everyone knows how he feels about you, how you feel about him. He'd be a fool if he let you go back to Texas."

"He didn't know I was leaving today," Valerie said calmly, although he must have figured it out for himself. He must've recognized that she wouldn't stay in Orchard Valley any longer than necessary.

"I'll find out what he wants," Steffie said, her voice high and excited. "Let's play this cool, okay? You stay up here and when he asks for you, I'll casually come and get you."

"Steffie…"

"Valerie, for heaven's sake, be romantic for *once* in your life."

"There could be plenty of other reasons Colby's here."

"Are you going to make him suffer, or are you going to forgive him right away? Personally, I think he should suffer…but only a little."

The doorbell chimed and Steffie hurried downstairs without another word.

Valerie couldn't keep her heart from racing, but she refused to play this silly game of wait-and-see. She reached for her suitcase and started resolutely down the stairs, the way she'd originally intended.

She was on the top step when she heard Colby ask to

see her father. *Her father—not her.* If it hadn't hurt so much, Valerie would have laughed at Steffie, who looked completely stunned. Her sister stared at Colby, her mouth open, hand frozen on the door, blocking his entrance.

"My father," Steffie repeated after a shocked moment. "You're here to see Dad?"

"He is my patient."

"I know, but…"

Some slight sound must have alerted Colby that Valerie was standing at the top of the stairs. His gaze rose and linked with hers before slowly lowering to the suitcase in her hand. Valerie detected a frown, as though he'd been caught by surprise.

"Valerie's leaving for the airport this morning," Steffie announced in a loud, urgent voice, implying that Colby had better do something fast.

What Steffie hadn't grasped was that Colby didn't want to do anything—other than bid her a relieved farewell.

"You should tell Dad that Dr. Winston's here," Valerie said mildly. "He's probably in the kitchen."

Steffie left, and Valerie gradually descended the stairs.

"Looks like you're packed up and ready to go," he said in a conversational tone.

She nodded. "My flight leaves at one."

"So soon?"

"Not soon enough, though, is it, Colby?"

He ignored the question, and Valerie regretted the pettiness that had prompted her to ask. He stood before her, his expression unreadable. She was grateful when her father appeared. Grateful because she wasn't nearly as expert at hiding her feelings as Colby. She was afraid he could read much more of her emotional turmoil than she wanted him to.

"Colby, my boy, good to see you. You've been making yourself scarce the last few days." David steered Colby into the kitchen, then glanced back at Valerie, scowling at the suitcase in her hand. "You've got plenty of time, Val. Come and have a cup of coffee before you leave."

For her father's sake, she resisted the temptation to argue. Shrugging, she set her luggage aside and dutifully followed Colby and David into the large family kitchen.

The two men sat at the table while Norah served them coffee. Valerie didn't sit with the others, but pulled out a stool in front of the counter and perched on that.

"I thought I'd check in and see how you were feeling," Colby was saying.

"Never felt better," her father said in response.

Valerie noticed how Colby avoided looking in her direction. He was uncomfortable with her; his back was stiff, his shoulders rigid with tension. Perhaps he'd expected her to have left by now.

Valerie sipped her coffee and briefly closed her eyes, wanting to savor these last few moments with her family. Norah, an apron tied around her waist, was busy pulling hot cinnamon rolls out of the oven. Homemade ones, from the recipe their mother had used through the years. The scent of yeast and spice filled the kitchen, and it was like stepping back in time. Their kitchen had always been where everyone gathered, a place of warmth and laughter and confidences shared.

Steffie couldn't seem to stand still. She paced to one side of the room, then crossed to the other, as though debating her next course of action.

Valerie found it endearing that her sister cared so much about what happened between her and Colby, especially when Steffie's own romance was so problematic. Valerie sensed that things weren't going well between her sister and Charles Tomaselli, but she wasn't in any position to be offering advice.

Steffie paused, her eyes pleading with Valerie. She seemed to be begging her to stay in Orchard Valley. To listen to her heart…

After a moment Valerie couldn't meet her sister's gaze and purposely looked away.

Conversation floated past her, but she wasn't aware of what was being said or who was saying it. The sudden need to leave was too powerful to ignore. If she didn't do it soon, she might never be able to. Slipping down from the stool, she deposited her mug, still half full of coffee, in the sink.

"The rolls will be ready to eat any minute," Norah said, looking at her anxiously. She, too, seemed to want Valerie to stay.

"Don't worry, I'll pick up something at the airport later."

"Are you going?" her father asked, as if this was news to him. "You've still got lots of time."

Valerie gave the first excuse that came to mind. "I've got to get the rental car back to the agency."

"You're *sure* you want to go?" Steffie asked forlornly, moving toward her sister.

"I'm sure," Valerie answered in a soft voice, throwing her arms around Steffie in an affectionate hug. "It isn't like I'll never be back, you know?"

"Don't let it take you three years, the way it did me," Steffie whispered into Valerie's ear. "I just can't help thinking you're making a mistake."

"What I'm doing is for the best," Valerie said.

Norah stood behind Steffie, waiting her turn to be hugged, her pretty blue eyes as sad as Steffie's. "I can't believe you're really going. I loved having you home."

"It's been good, hasn't it, Dad?" Valerie said, trying to lighten the atmosphere. "I'd like to suggest another family reunion, only next time let's plan things a bit differently. If I'm going to take three weeks away from CHIPS, I'd prefer to see more than a hospital waiting room."

David Bloomfield stood, his gaze holding Valerie's. He seemed to be asking her to remain a little longer, but she firmly shook her head. Every minute was torture.

She dared not look in Colby's direction. That made it easier to pretend he wasn't there.

"I have a great idea for a family reunion," Steffie said eagerly. "Why don't we all take a trip to Egypt? I've always wanted to ride a camel and see the pyramids."

"Egypt?" Norah echoed. "What's wrong with a camping trip? We used to do that years ago, and it was fun. I remember us sitting around the campfire singing and toasting marshmallows."

"Camping!" Steffie cried. "You can't be serious. I remember mosquitoes the size of Alabama."

"But we had fun," Norah reminded them.

"Maybe you did, but count me out," Valerie said, laughing quickly. "My idea of roughing it is going without room service." She glanced from one sister to the other, loving them both so much she thought she'd start to cry. Blinking rapidly, she stepped forward and flung her arms around her father's neck.

"Take care of yourself," she whispered.

"The dream," he returned, his eyes bright and intense. "I was so sure.…"

Valerie didn't need to be reminded of her father's dream. "Maybe someday it'll happen." But she didn't believe it, any more than she believed the dead could come back to life.

"You're going to say goodbye to Colby, aren't you?" her father urged.

She'd been hoping to avoid it. But she realized it would be impossible to leave without saying something to Colby, who was her father's doctor, her father's guest. David released her and she saw that Colby was on his feet and moving toward her. Her pride would've been salvaged, at least a little, if he'd revealed even a hint of sadness. But from all outward appearances she was nothing more to him than a passing acquaintance. It was as if he'd never held her in his arms, never kissed her.

"Goodbye, Colby," she said as cheerfully as she could. "Thank you for everything you did for Dad—for all of us. You were…wonderful." She extended her hand, which he took in his own. His fingers tightened on hers, his grip almost painful.

"Goodbye, Valerie," he said after a moment. As before, it was impossible to read his expression. "Have a safe trip."

She nodded and turned away, afraid that if she didn't leave soon, she'd do something utterly stupid, like burst into tears.

Everyone followed her to the front porch. Eager to get away now, Valerie hurried down the steps. Not bothering to open the trunk, she set her suitcase on the backseat.

"Phone once in a while, would you?" Steffie called.

Valerie nodded. "Take care of Dad, you two."

"Bye, Val." Norah pressed her fingers to her lips and blew her a kiss.

Rather than endure another round of farewells, Valerie slid into the driver's seat and closed the door. She didn't look at the porch for fear her eyes would meet Colby's.

Escaping was what mattered. Fleeing before she made a fool of herself a second time over a man who didn't want her.

She started the car, raised her hand in a brisk wave and pulled away. The tightness in her chest was so painful it was almost unbearable. For a moment she didn't know if she'd be able to continue. The thought that she needed a doctor was what dispersed the horrible pain. It broke free on a bubble of hysterical laughter.

She needed a doctor, all right, *a heart doctor.* With the sound of her amusement still echoing in her ears, Valerie looked back one last time, her gaze seeking Colby's.

Hard as it was, she managed a slow smile, a smile of gratitude for what they'd shared.

She drove away then and didn't glance back.

Not even once.

# *Ten*

For long minutes, no one said a word. Colby stood frozen on the Bloomfield porch, his eyes following Valerie's rental car as it sped down the driveway. His hands knotted into tight fists at his sides, and his chest throbbed with suppressed emotion.

The timing of this visit couldn't have been worse. He'd had no idea Valerie was leaving that morning, and like a fool he'd stumbled upon the scene. He cursed himself for not calling first.

He wasn't sure what he'd been thinking when he'd decided to come here. No, that wasn't true. Visiting David had been an excuse. He'd come to see Valerie. He'd hoped, perhaps, to find a private moment to talk to her. But for the life of him, he didn't know what he'd intended to say. He certainly hadn't changed his mind, hadn't planned to sweep everything under the proverbial rug and pretend that love would conquer all. He'd leave that kind of idealism to the world's romantics. He wasn't one of them; he was a physician and he dealt with reality. He had no intention of deluding himself into believing he and Valerie had a chance together, even if she did entertain thoughts like that herself.

"I can't believe this," Stephanie cried, glaring at Colby. Tears swam in her eyes. He'd always considered weeping females cause for alarm; he never knew what to say to them.

But there'd been that time with Valerie, the night of David's surgery, Colby reminded himself. She'd been sobbing out her grief and fear. With anyone else he would've sought another family member to offer the needed consolation. But he hadn't looked for Norah that night. Instead he'd gone to Valerie himself. He'd felt his own terrible loss. He couldn't hold out hope for her father's recovery, not when everything indicated that David probably wouldn't survive the night. And so he'd sat on the concrete bench beside her and placed his arm around her shoulders.

Valerie had turned to him, and buried her face against him. The surge of love he'd experienced in that moment was unlike anything he'd ever felt. Stroking her hair, he'd savored the feel of her in his arms.

"She'll be back," David said, interrupting Colby's memories.

"No," Stephanie argued in a trembling voice. "She won't. Not for a long time."

"Valerie's not like that," Norah said. "She'll visit again. Soon."

"Why should she, when everything she equates with home means pain? It's too easy to stay away, too easy to make excuses and be satisfied with a phone call now and then." Suspecting that David's second daughter was speaking from experience, Colby studied her.

She must have felt his scrutiny because she turned suddenly, undisguised anger blazing from her eyes.

"You might be a wonderful surgeon," she said, her gaze as hard as flint, "but you're one of the biggest idiots I've ever met."

Colby blinked in surprise, but before he could respond, Stephanie ran back inside the house. Shocked by the verbal attack, he looked at Norah. They'd worked together for a number of months and he'd always been fond of her.

"I couldn't agree with my sister more," Norah said with an uncharacteristic display of temper. "You are an idiot." Having said that, she stormed into the house as well.

David chuckled, and Colby relaxed. At least one member of this family could appreciate the wisdom of his sacrifice. Stephanie and Norah acted as if he should be arrested. Both seemed to think it'd been easy for him to let Valerie drive away, although nothing was further from the truth. Even now he needed to grab hold of the railing to keep from racing after her.

If only she hadn't turned at the last moment and looked straight at him. And smiled. The sweetest, most beautiful smile he'd ever seen. A smile that would haunt him to his grave.

"I love her," Colby whispered, his eyes never leaving the driveway, although Valerie's car was long out of sight. By now she was probably two miles down the road.

"I know," David assured him.

Something in the older man's tone made Colby glance at him. The inflection seemed to suggest that however much Colby might love Valerie, he didn't love her enough. But he did! He loved her so much that he'd sent her out of his life. It seemed that no one, not even David Bloomfield, could appreciate the depth of his sacrifice.

"Rowdy Cassidy will be a much better husband for her than I ever would," Colby said, steeling himself against the pain his own words produced.

"Maybe, but I doubt it," David responded, walking over to his wicker rocking chair and lowering himself into it. "I don't suppose you've noticed, but Valerie and I are a lot alike."

Colby grinned. The similarity hadn't exactly escaped him. Here were two people who each possessed a streak of stubbornness that was wider than the Mississippi. Both were intelligent, intuitive and ambitious. Hard-working. Single-minded.

"She'd never be happy living here in Orchard Valley," Colby said, his gaze returning to the driveway. He couldn't seem to make himself look away. It was as if that road was his only remaining connection to Valerie.

"You're right, of course. Valerie would never be content in a small town again. Not after living in Houston."

The reassurance should have eased the ache in his heart, but it didn't. He told himself there was no reason to linger. Carrying on a polite conversation was beyond him, yet he didn't seem to have the energy to leave.

"Did I ever tell you how I met Grace?"

"I believe you did." Valerie must be three or four miles down the road by now, Colby estimated.

"Our courtship was a bit unusual. It isn't every day a man woos a woman from a hospital bed."

Colby nodded. Before long, Valerie would be close to the interstate, and then it would be impossible to catch her. *Not* that he was going to chase after her.

"Grace wasn't keen on marrying me, for a number of reasons. All good ones, I might add. She loved me, that much I knew, but to her mind love wasn't enough."

David's words diverted Colby's attention from the road. He swiveled his gaze to the older man, who was rocking contentedly as though they were discussing something as mundane as the best bait for local trout.

"Grace was right. Sometimes love isn't enough," David added.

"In your case she was wrong," Colby mumbled, displeased. For the first time he understood where this discussion was leading. Valerie's father was going to force him to admit that he was as big an idiot as Stephanie and Norah had claimed. Though he might be a little more subtle about it.

"Not really. I knew I'd need to make some real changes before Grace would agree to marry me, but I was willing to make them because I knew something she didn't."

"What was that?"

A wistful look came over David, and his eyes grew hazy. "Deep in my soul, I knew I'd never love another woman the way I loved Grace. Deep in my soul, I recognized that she was the one chance I had in this life for real happiness. I could've done the noble thing and let her marry some nice young man. There were plenty who would've thanked me for the opportunity."

"I see."

"I have to tell you, though, it was the most difficult decision of my life. Marrying Grace was the biggest risk I ever took, but I never regretted it. Not once."

Colby nodded. David was telling him exactly what he wanted to hear. He, too, had made his decision; he'd set Valerie free to find what happiness she could. Rowdy Cassidy was waiting in the wings, eager to step into his place. Eager to help her forget.

Colby's mind flashed to Sherry Waterman. He liked her and enjoyed her company. He felt the same about Norah. But it was Valerie who set his heart on fire. Valerie who challenged him. Valerie whom he needed. Not anyone else, only Valerie.

"Don't you worry about her," David continued. "She'll be fine. In a while, she'll regroup and be a better person for having experienced love, even for such a short time. As for marrying Rowdy Cassidy, I don't think you need to concern yourself with that, either."

"Why not?"

"Because I know my daughter. I know exactly what I would've done had Grace decided against marrying me. I'd have gone back to my world, worked hard and made a decent life for myself. But I would never have fallen in love again. I wouldn't have allowed it to happen."

Colby didn't say anything. By now, Valerie was on the interstate. It was too late. Even if he did go after her, they wouldn't be able to stop. Not on the freeway with cars screaming past. It would be reckless and dangerous and beyond all stupidity to chase her now. Besides, what could he possibly have to say that hadn't already been said?

David stood. "You want another cup of coffee?"

"No, thanks. I should be on my way."

"I'll be in your office bright and early Tuesday morning, then."

Colby nodded. It was time to get back to his life, the life he'd had before he met Valerie Bloomfield.

Valerie refused to cry. She'd never been prone to tears and, except for a few occasions, had usually managed to fend them off. Even as a child, she'd hated crying, hated the way the salty tears had felt on her face.

What astonished her was how much it hurt to hold everything inside. It felt as though someone had crammed a fist down her throat and expected her to breathe normally.

In an effort to push aside the pain of leaving Colby, she focused her thoughts on all the good he'd brought into her life. Without him, she would have lost her father. Norah had told her as much that first evening. Colby was the one who'd convinced her father to go to the hospital. Colby was the one who'd performed the life-saving surgery.

If for nothing else, she owed him more for that than anyone could possibly repay.

But that wasn't all he'd given her. Dr. Colby Winston had taught her about herself, about love, about sacrifice.

She would always love him for that. Now she had to teach herself to release him, to let him go. Finding love and then freely relinquishing it might well prove to be a tricky business. She'd never given her heart to a man before. Loving Colby was the easy part. It felt as though she'd always known and loved him, as if he'd always been part of her life. It seemed impossible that they'd met only a few weeks ago.

Leaving him was the hardest thing she'd ever done.

The self-doubts, the what-ifs and might-have-beens rolled in like giant waves, swamping her with grief and dread.

Dragging in a deep breath, she fought the urge to turn the car around and head back. Back to Orchard Valley. Back home.

Back to Colby.

Instead, she exhaled, tried to relax, tried to tell herself that everything would feel much better once she got to

Texas. She'd be able to submerge the pain in her job. When she resumed her position with CHIPS, she could begin to forget Colby and at the same time treasure her memories of him.

Valerie didn't realize there were tears in her eyes until she noticed how blurry the road in front of her had become. Hoping to distract herself, she turned on the radio and started humming along with a country-western singer lamenting her lost love.

"Stop it," Valerie muttered to herself, weeping harder than ever. Irritably, she snapped off the radio, then swiped at the tears with the back of one hand, reminding herself she was too strong, too independent, for such weak emotional behavior.

Not until she was changing lanes on the freeway did she see the Buick behind her. A maroon sedan, traveling at high speed, passing cars, going well over the limit.

Colby? It couldn't be.

More than likely it was just a car that looked like his. It couldn't be him. He'd never come after her. That wasn't his style. No, if he ever had a change of heart, something she didn't count on, it wouldn't be for weeks, months. Colby wasn't impulsive.

The Buick slowed down and moved directly behind Valerie's car and followed her for a moment before putting on the turn signal. If it hadn't been for the tears in her eyes she would've been able to make out the driver's features.

The car honked. It *had* to be Colby. He didn't expect

her to stop on the freeway, did he? It wouldn't be safe. There was an exit ramp only a few miles down the road and she drove toward that, turned off when she could and parked. Luckily traffic was light, and the shoulders on both sides of the road were wide enough for her to park safely. When she did, Colby pulled in behind her.

She'd barely had time to unfasten her seat belt before he jerked open her door.

"What are you doing here?" she demanded.

"What does it look like? I'm chasing after you."

Legs trembling, she climbed out of her car and stood leaning against it, hands on her hips. "This better be good, Winston. I've got a plane to catch."

"You've been crying."

"There's something in my eye."

"Both eyes apparently."

"All right, both eyes." She didn't know what silly game he thought he was playing, but she didn't have the patience for it. "Why are you here? Surely there's a reason you came racing after me."

"There's a reason."

"Good." She crossed her arms and shifted her position. Whatever Colby wanted to say was obviously causing him trouble, because he started pacing in front of her, hands clenched.

"This is even harder than I expected," he finally admitted.

Not daring to hope, Valerie said nothing.

"I can't believe what a mess I've made of this.

Listen." He turned to face her, his expression as closed as always. "I want you to come back to Orchard Valley."

"Why?"

"Because I love you and because I'd like us to talk this through. You love me, too, Valerie. I don't think I realized how much until just now. It must've been so hard to come to me, to lay your heart out like that and then have me send you away. I—"

"You don't need to apologize," she broke in.

"I do."

Valerie had no idea, not the slightest, where all this was leading. She took a shaky breath. "All right, you've apologized."

"Will you come back?"

"If you want to talk, we can do it at the airport." That seemed like a fair suggestion.

"I want to do more than talk," he said. "I want you to show me how we're going to make this marriage work, because darned if I know. We haven't got one thing working in our favor. Not one."

"Then why even try?"

"Because if you leave now I'm going to regret it for the rest of my life. Sure as anything, I'm going to think back to this moment for the next fifty years and wish I'd never let you go. The problem is, I'm not sure what to do now—you've got me so tied up in knots I can't think straight."

"No wonder you don't look happy."

"You're right, I'm not happy. I'm furious."

Valerie grinned. "Love *is* rather frightening, isn't it?"

Colby grinned, too, for the first time. "But you know something? It's living without you, without your love, that frightens me."

"Oh, Colby…"

"Let's say we did get married," he said, the gravel under his feet crunching as he paced.

"All right, let's say we did."

"Are you going to want a job outside the home?"

"Yes, Colby, I will."

"What about children?"

"Oh, yes, at least two." She found it odd to be discussing something so personal while standing at the side of a road.

"How do you propose to be both a mother and an executive?"

"How do you intend to be both a father and a surgeon? Not to mention a husband? You have a career, too, Colby."

"You can't have it all, Valerie."

"Neither can you! Besides, it doesn't have to be either or. Half the women in America maintain a career *and* a family, but there have to be compromises. You're right, I won't be able to do everything. I couldn't even begin to try."

"I don't like the idea of farming our children out to strangers."

"Frankly, I don't, either, but there are ways of working around that. Ways of making the situation acceptable to both of us. For one thing, I could set up an office at home. It's pretty common these days with e-mail and teleconferencing and everything. Rowdy might be willing to start a branch of the company on the West Coast, and I think he might be persuaded to pick Oregon—especially if a hard-working executive chose to live there."

Colby nodded and thrust his hands into his pockets.

"I know I'm not what you want in a wife, Colby. You'd rather I was the kind of woman who'd be content to stay home and do needlepoint and put up preserves. But that isn't who I am, and I can't change. I'd give anything to be the woman you want, but if I'm not true to myself, the marriage would be doomed before we even said our vows."

"I don't think we should be concerning ourselves with some unrealistic image I've invented. What about the man *you* want?"

She smiled and looked away. "You're the only man I've ever wanted."

He reached for her then, wrapping his arms tightly around her, dropping a gentle kiss on the side of her neck. A deep shudder went through him as he exhaled.

"I'm never going to be able to stop loving you."

"Is that so terrible?" she asked in a whisper, her throat raw.

"No, it's the most wonderful blessing of my life." His eyes were warm and loving as he brought up his hands to clasp her shoulders. "I've been arrogant. Selfish. I nearly destroyed both our lives because I refused to accept the gift you offered me."

"Oh, Colby."

"There won't be any guarantees."

"If I wanted guarantees, I'd buy myself a new car. Everything in life is a risk, but I've never been more willing to take one than with you." She smiled. "I'm very sure of what I feel for you, even though it all developed so quickly."

"Like it sprang to life fully formed," he added.

"The most exciting thing is that we have a lifetime to get to know everything about each other."

"I'd say we're in for an adventure."

"Yes, but it'll be the grandest adventure of all." Valerie's arms went around his neck as he lowered his mouth to hers. One kiss wiped out the pain and the torment of these past few days. Colby must have felt it, too, because he kissed her again and again, their need insatiable, their joy boundless.

A car driving past honked noisily, disturbing them.

Valerie reluctantly broke off their kiss. "You might have chosen someplace a bit more private, Dr. Winston."

"Shall we try this again later, with champagne and a diamond ring?"

Valerie nodded because speaking when her heart was so full would have been impossible.

Her father was sitting on the porch when Valerie and Colby pulled up in front of the house late that afternoon.

"Did you tell Dad you were coming after me?"

"I didn't know it myself until I left here. Before I realized what I was doing, I was on the freeway, racing after you like a bat out of hell. I didn't have a clue what I was going to say when I found you."

Valerie tucked her hand in his and pressed her cheek to his shoulder. "You looked like you wanted to bite my head off."

"I looked like a man who was calling himself every kind of fool in existence."

"For coming after me?"

"No," he said quietly. "For letting you go."

Valerie rewarded him with an appreciative kiss on the corner of his mouth.

Colby groaned softly. "I'm not going to want a long engagement. The sooner we can arrange this wedding, the better."

"I couldn't agree more."

Colby kissed her lightly on the lips. "I have the sneaking suspicion your father hasn't moved since you took off for the airport."

They'd been gone for hours, returning the rental car to Portland, and then stopping for an elegant lunch in an equally elegant restaurant. Before leaving the city, they'd visited a well-known jewelry store where Valerie chose a beautiful solitaire diamond engagement ring. That very ring was on her finger now. It felt as if it had always been there.

"About time you two got back," her father said as

Colby helped her out of his car. "I was beginning to worry."

"How'd you know we were coming?" Colby asked.

"I knew before you left here that you'd be back with Valerie before the end of the day."

"Dad, you couldn't possibly have known." She waited for a protest, but none came. Her father sat back in his rocker and grinned happily.

"Oh, I know more than that about what's going to happen to you two."

"He's going to talk about that dream again," Valerie murmured, slipping her arm around Colby's waist and smiling up at him. He brought her close to his side.

"Love's shocked you both," David said, wagging a finger at them. "But there are a few more shocks in store for you. Just wait and see what happens when my twin grandsons are born."

"Twins?" Colby echoed incredulously.

"You're going to name them after their two grandfathers. The blond one will be David, and he'll be the spitting image of me."

"Twins," Colby said again.

"I don't know," Valerie said with a laugh. "I could get used to a few surprises now and then, especially if it means I can be with you."

Colby gazed down at her and Valerie realized her father was right. Love had caught them unawares, but it was the best surprise of their lives.

# STEPHANIE

For Heidi Pollard
A woman of letters

# *One*

Home.

Stephanie Bloomfield lugged her heavy suitcase up the porch steps of the large white-pillared house. She moved quietly, careful not to wake her two sisters, although it occurred to her that they might be at the hospital.

She herself had spent the best part—no, the *worst* part—of the past two days either on a plane or standing at the counter in a foreign airport. Or was that three days? She couldn't tell anymore.

Norah, her younger sister, had managed to call her in Italy nearly a week ago about their father's heart attack. The connection had been bad and she'd had difficulty hearing, but Norah's sense of urgency had come clearly over the wire. Their father was gravely ill, and Steffie needed to hurry home—something that turned out to be much easier said than done.

Steffie had been living just outside Rome, attending

classes at the university. She'd been participating in a special program, learning Italian and studying Renaissance history, culture and art. For three years she'd traveled effortlessly from one end of the country to the other. Now, when she desperately needed to fly home, the airports were closed by a transportation strike that paralyzed Italy. It didn't help that she'd been staying in a small, relatively isolated village hundreds of miles from Rome. She'd gone on a brief holiday, visiting a friend's family.

It had taken her several days and what felt like three lifetimes to arrange passage home. *Days,* when it should've been a matter of hours. This past week had been the most stressful of her life. She'd been in touch with her sisters as often as possible, and at last report Norah had said that their father was resting comfortably. Still, she'd heard the dread in Norah's voice. Her youngest sister had never been much good at hiding the truth. Although she'd tried to sound reassuring, Steffie was well aware that her father's condition had worsened. That was when she'd undertaken the most daring move of her life. She'd made contact with some men of questionable scruples, sold every possession of value and, at a hugely inflated price, obtained a means out of the country, by way of Japan, with layovers in places she'd never expected to visit. It was decidedly an indirect route to Oregon, but she was home now. Heaven only knew how much longer it would have taken if she hadn't resorted to such drastic measures.

After a whole day of waiting at the Tokyo airport,

fighting for space aboard any available flight to the States, and then the long flight itself, Steffie was frantic for news of her father. Frantic and fearful. In some ways, not knowing was almost better than knowing….

She opened the front door and stepped silently inside the sleeping house. She'd adjusted her watch to Pacific time, but her mind was caught somewhere between Italy and Tokyo. She was too exhausted to be tired. Too worried to be hungry, although she couldn't remember the last meal she'd eaten.

Setting down her impossibly heavy suitcase, she stood in the foyer and breathed in the scent of polished wood and welcome.

She was home.

Her father's den was to her right, and she immediately felt drawn there. Pausing in the doorway, she flipped on the light switch and stood gazing at the room that was so much her father's. A massive stone fireplace commanded one entire wall, while two other walls were lined with floor-to-ceiling bookcases.

She looked at his wingback chair, the soft leather creased from years of use. Closing her eyes, Steffie breathed in deeply, savoring the scent of old leather and books and the sweet pungency of pipe tobacco. This was her father's room, and she'd never missed him more than she did at that moment.

His presence seemed to fill the den. His robust laugh echoed silently against the walls. Steffie could visualize him sitting behind the cherrywood desk, the accounting ledgers spread open and his pipe propped in the ugly ceramic ashtray—the one she'd made for him the summer she turned eleven.

The photograph of her mother caught her eye. David Bloomfield could leave his daughters no finer legacy than the love he'd shared with their mother. He'd changed after Grace's death. Steffie had noticed it even before she left Orchard Valley. She'd guessed it from his letters in the years since. And she'd been especially aware of the changes when he came to visit her in Italy last spring. The spark was gone. The relentless passion for life that had always been so much a part of him was missing now. Each month his letters were more painful to read, more lifeless and subdued. Without his wife at his side, David Bloomfield was as empty as…as that chair there, his old reading chair, standing in front of the fireplace.

Steffie's gaze slipped to the newspaper spread across the ottoman. It felt as though, any minute, her father would walk through the door, settle back into his chair and resume reading.

*Only he wouldn't.*

He might never sit in this room again, Steffie realized, her heart constricting with pain. He might never reach for one of his favorite books and lovingly leaf through its pages until he found the passage he wanted. He might never sit by the fireplace, pipe in hand. He might never look up when she entered the room and smile when he saw it was Steffie—his "princess."

The pain in her chest grew more intense and the need

to release her emotions burned inside her, but Steffie ignored it, as she had a thousand times before. She wasn't a weeper. She'd guarded her emotions vigilantly for three long years. Ever since that night with Charles Tomaselli when he'd—

She brushed the memory aside with the efficiency of long practice. Charles was a painful figure from her past. One best forgotten, or at least ignored. She hadn't thought of him in months and refused to do so now. Sooner or later she'd be forced to exchange pleasantries with him, but when she did, she'd pretend she had trouble remembering who he was, as though he were merely a casual acquaintance and not the man who'd broken her heart. That seemed the best way to handle the situation—to pretend she'd completely forgotten their last humiliating encounter.

If he did insist on renewing their acquaintance, which was unlikely, she'd show him how mature she was, how sophisticated and cosmopolitan she'd become. Then he'd regret the careless, cruel way he'd treated her.

There was a sound in the hallway, and Steffie moved out of the den just as Norah reached the bottom of the stairs.

"Steffie? My goodness, you're home!" Norah exclaimed, rushing to embrace her.

And then, with a small cry of welcome, Valerie, the oldest of the three, bounded down the stairs, her long cotton gown dancing about her feet.

"Steff, I'm so glad you're home," Valerie cried,

wrapping her arms around both sisters. "When did you get in? Why didn't you let us know so we could meet you at the airport?"

"I flew standby most of the way, so I wasn't sure when I'd land. I caught the Air Porter and then a cab." She took a deep breath. "I'm just glad I'm here."

"I am, too," Valerie said with an uncharacteristic display of emotion, wiping the tears from her cheeks. Normally Valerie was a model of restraint. Seeing her this shaken revealed, more plainly than anything she could've said, how desperately ill their father was.

By tacit agreement, they moved into the kitchen. Valerie set about preparing a pot of tea. According to the digital clock on the microwave, it was a little past three. Steffie hadn't realized it was quite that late. She could hardly recall the last time she'd slept in a bed. Four days ago, perhaps.

"How's Dad?" It was the question she'd been yearning to ask from the moment she'd walked in the door. The question she was afraid to ask.

"He's doing just great," Norah said, her soft voice rising with delight. "We came really close to losing him, Steffie. Valerie and I were in a panic because things looked bad and Dr. Winston couldn't delay the surgery. And Dad pulled through! But…"

"But he…" Valerie began when Norah hesitated.

"He what?" Steffie prompted. Although she was thrilled with the news that her father had survived the crisis, she couldn't help wondering why both her sisters seemed reluctant to continue. "Tell me," she insisted. She didn't want to be protected from the truth.

"Apparently Dad had a near-death experience," Norah finally said.

"Isn't that fairly common? Especially during that kind of surgery? I've been reading for years about people who believe they traveled through a dark tunnel into the light."

"I wouldn't know how common it is to talk to someone in the spirit world, would you?" Valerie snapped.

"Dad claims he talked to Mom." Once again it was Norah who supplied the information.

"To Mom?" Steffie felt numb, unsure of how to react.

"Which we all know is impossible." Valerie hurried barefoot across the kitchen floor to pour boiling water into the teapot. She placed three mugs, three spoons and the sugar bowl on a tray; when the tea had steeped, she filled the cups, obviously preoccupied with her task. Carrying the tray to the table, she served her sisters, then leaped up to get a plate of Norah's home-baked cookies. "I think Dad needs to talk to a counselor," she said abruptly.

"Valerie." Norah sighed as though this was a well-worn argument. "You're overreacting."

"You would, too, if Dad was saying to you the things he says to me." Valerie stirred her tea without looking up.

Norah sighed again. "Dad honestly believes he spoke to Mom and if it makes him feel better, then I don't think we should try to discount his experience."

"What was Mom supposed to have said to him?"

Steffie asked, intrigued by the interplay between her two sisters. She helped herself to a couple of oatmeal cookies as she spoke.

"That's what worries me the most." Valerie raised her voice, clearly unsettled. "He's got some ridiculous notion that we're all going to marry."

"Now, that's profound." Steffie couldn't hide her amusement. The three of them were of marriageable age; it made sense that they'd eventually find husbands.

"But he claims to know *who* we're going to marry," Norah said, grinning sheepishly, as though she found the whole thing amusing.

"He's been wearing this silly smile for two days." Valerie groaned, dropping her forehead onto her arms. "He's been talking about a houseful of grandchildren, too. The ones *we're* supposed to present him with—and all in the next few years. If it wasn't so ludicrous, I'd cry."

"Has he said who I'm supposed to marry?" Steffie asked, curiosity getting the better of her.

Valerie lifted her head to glare at Stephanie, and Norah chuckled. "That's something else that irritates Valerie," she explained. "Dad hasn't told any of us, at least not directly. Not yet."

"He's acting like he knows this wonderful secret and he's keeping it all to himself, dropping hints every now and then. I swear it's driving me crazy."

"I don't mind it," Norah said. To someone else, she might have sounded self-righteous, but Steffie recognized her younger sister's compassion and knew that it edged out any hint of righteousness. "Dad's smiling again. He's excited about the future and even if he's becoming a bit…presumptuous about the three of us, I honestly can't say I mind. I'm just so glad to have him alive."

Valerie nodded, her argument apparently gone. "I guess I can put up with a few remarks, too."

"This is the first time one of us hasn't stayed all night at the hospital," Norah said, her mouth curving into a gentle smile. "Dr. Winston insisted there wasn't any need. Not anymore."

"Don't be fooled by that guy," Valerie muttered under her breath. "He may look like your average, laid-back country doctor, but he's got a backbone of steel."

He must have, if Valerie was reacting like this, Stephanie thought with sudden interest. It seemed that her sister had finally encountered a will as strong as her own. So, either Valerie had changed her ways or she had—could it be?—a soft spot for this Dr. Winston.

"In other words," Steffie said quickly, "I missed the worst of it. Dad's out of danger now and will eventually recover?"

"Yes," Norah said cheerfully. "Everything'll be back to normal."

"Not exactly." Valerie shook her head. "In a few weeks Dad will be the picture of health, but the three of us will be pulling out our hair after listening to all his talk about marriage, husbands and grandchildren!"

* * *

Bright sunlight poured through the open window of Steffie's bedroom when she woke. The house was quiet, but the sounds of the day drifted in from outside. Birds chirped merrily in the distance and a spring breeze set the chimes on the back porch tinkling and rustled the curtains lightly. She could hear work crews in the orchard—spraying the apple trees, Steffie guessed.

After those long days of struggling to get home, she exulted in the sensation of familiarity, wrapping the feel of it around her like a warm quilt. The crisis had passed. Her father would survive, and all the world seemed brighter, sweeter, happier.

Reluctantly she slid out of bed and dressed, pulling a pair of slacks and a light sweater from her suitcase.

She found a note on the kitchen table explaining that both Valerie and Norah were at the hospital. They were going to leave her arrival a surprise, so she could come anytime she was ready. No need to rush. Not anymore.

Selecting a banana from the fruit bowl on the kitchen counter, she ate that while reheating a cup of coffee in the microwave. As the timer was counting down the seconds, she walked into her father's den and reached for the newspaper, intending to take it with her to the hospital.

She would read it, Steffie decided, to catch up on the local news. But even as she formed this thought, she knew she was lying to herself.

There was only one reason she was taking the local newspaper with her. Only one reason she'd even picked it up. *Charles Tomaselli.* She turned to the front page. The *Orchard Valley Clarion.* She allowed her eyes to skim the headlines for a moment.

Emotion came at her in waves. First apprehension. She'd give anything to avoid seeing Charles again. Then anger. He'd humiliated her. Laughed at her. She'd never forgive him for that. Never. The agony of his humiliation smoldered even now, years later. Yet, much as she wanted to hate Charles, she couldn't. She didn't love him anymore. That was over, finished. He'd cured her of love in the most effective way possible. No, she reassured herself, she didn't love him—but she couldn't make herself hate him, either.

She could handle this. She had to. Besides, he was probably as eager to avoid any encounters between them as she was.

She gulped down half the steaming coffee. Then she tucked the paper under her arm and grabbed the car keys Norah had thoughtfully left on the kitchen table and headed out the door.

When she got to Orchard Valley General, Steffie paused, taken aback by a sudden rush of grief. The last time she'd gone through those doors had been the day her mother died. Steffie's heart stilled at the nearly overwhelming sadness she felt. She hadn't expected that. It took her a couple of minutes to compose herself. Then she continued toward the elevator.

When she arrived at the waiting room, she found Norah speaking to one of the nurses, while Valerie sat reading. It was so unusual to see her older sister doing anything sedentary that Stephanie nearly did a double take.

"Steffie!" Norah said, her face lighting when she saw her sister. "Did you get enough sleep?"

"I'm fine." That was true, although it would take more than one night's rest to recuperate from the past week.

"Did you fix yourself some breakfast?"

"Yes, little mother, I did. Can I see Dad now or is there anything else you'd like to ask me?" She slipped an arm around her sister's trim waist, feeling elated. It was wonderful to be home, wonderful to be with her family.

"You're here," Valerie said, joining them. "Dad asked me earlier when we'd last heard from you. I told him this morning."

"He's going to be moved out of the Surgical Intensive Care Unit tomorrow," Norah said happily. "Then we'll all be able to see him at once. As it is now, only one of us can visit at a time."

"Norah, would you like me to take your sister in to see your father?" Another nurse had bustled up to them.

"Please," Steffie answered eagerly before Norah could speak. The nurse led her through a hallway with glass-walled cubicles. Every imaginable sort of medical equipment seemed to be in use here, but Steffie barely noticed. She was far too excited about seeing her father. The nurse stopped at one of the cubicles and gestured Stephanie inside.

He was sitting up in bed. He smiled and held out his

arms to her. "Steffie," he said faintly, "come here, Princess." She saw that he was connected to several monitoring devices.

She walked into his hold, careful to stay clear of the wires and tubes, astonished at his weak embrace after the bone-crushing hugs she was accustomed to receiving. Her sisters had said the spark was back in his eyes. They'd talked about how well he looked.

Stephanie disagreed.

She was shocked by his paleness, by the gauntness of his appearance. If he was so much better *now,* she hated to think what he must have looked like a week ago.

"It's so good to see you," her father said, his voice cracking with emotion. "I've missed you, Princess."

"I've missed you, too," Steffie said, wiping a tear from the corner of her eye as she straightened.

"You're home to stay?"

Steffie wasn't sure how to answer. Home represented so much to her, much more than she'd realized, but she loved Italy, too. Still, just gazing out on the orchards this morning had reminded her how much she'd missed her life in Orchard Valley.

She'd left bruised and vulnerable; she'd returned strong and sure of herself. Being in Italy had helped her heal. But there was no longer any reason to stay away. She was ready to come home.

She'd been trying to decide what to do next when she'd received word of her father's heart attack. Her courses were completed, but remaining in Italy had a strong appeal. She could travel for a while, continue her studies, perhaps do some teaching herself. She could move to some place like Boston or New York. Or she could return to Orchard Valley. Steffie hadn't known what she wanted.

"I'm home for as long as you need me."

"You'll stay," her father insisted with unshakable confidence.

"What makes you so sure?"

He smiled mysteriously and his voice dropped to a whisper. "Your mother told me."

"Mom?" Steffie was beginning to appreciate Valerie's concerns.

"Yup. I suppose you're going to act like your sister and suggest I see some fancy doctor with a couch in his office. I did talk to your mother. She sends her love, by the way."

Steffie didn't know how to respond. Should she ask him to convey a message for her? "What did Mom...tell you?" she ventured instead.

"Quite a bit, but mainly she said I had quite a few years left in me. She promised they'd be good ones, too." He paused, chuckling softly. "Your mother always did know I had a soft spot for babies. And there's going to be a passel of them born in this family within the next few years."

"Babies?"

"An even dozen." The first sign of color crept into his cheeks. "Can you believe it? My little girls are going to make me a grandfather twelve times over."

"Uh…"

"I know it sounds like I've got a screw loose, but…"

"Daddy, you think whatever you like if it makes you happy."

"It's more than thinking, Princess. It's a fact, sure as I'm lying here. But never mind that now. Let me get a look at you. My goodness," he said, grinning proudly, "you're even lovelier than I remembered."

Steffie beamed with pleasure. She knew very well that she was no raving beauty, but her looks were nothing to be ashamed of, either. Her dark hair was straight as a clothespin, reaching to the middle of her back. She wore it pulled away from her face, using combs, a style that accentuated her prominent cheek-bones and the strong lines of her face. Her eyes were deep brown.

Steffie had just started to regale her father with the adventures of the past week when the same nurse who'd escorted her in to see him reappeared, ready to lead her back to the waiting area.

Steffie wanted to argue. They'd barely had five minutes together! But she forced back her objections; she wouldn't do anything that might upset her father. She kissed his leathery cheek and promised to return soon.

Valerie was waiting for her, but Norah was nowhere in sight.

"Well?" Valerie asked, glancing up from her magazine. "Did he say anything about talking to Mom?"

Steffie nodded, secretly a little amused. "He seems

downright excited about the prospect of grandchildren. I hate to see him disappointed, don't you?"

"Hmm?" Valerie muttered.

"Since you're the oldest, it makes sense you should be the first," she teased, enjoying her sister's blank look.

"For what?" Valerie asked.

"To produce a grandchild for Dad. The last time you wrote, I seem to remember you had quite a lot to say about Rowdy Cassidy. Might as well aim high—marry a multimillionaire—even if he is your boss."

"Rowdy," Valerie repeated as though she'd never heard the name before. "Oh…Rowdy. Of course there's always Rowdy. Why didn't I think of him?" With that, Valerie returned to her magazine.

Baffled, Steffie shook her head.

She wandered over to the coffeemaker, poured herself a fresh cup and sat down near her sister. She picked up the newspaper she'd brought with her and opened it to the front page, reading each article in turn. She was relieved to recognize several names; obviously not much had changed while she was away.

Folding back the second page of the weekly paper, she found that her eyes were automatically drawn to the small black-and-white photograph of Charles Tomaselli. For a wild second her heart seemed to stop.

He looked the same. Still as attractive as sin. No man had the right to be that good-looking. Dark hair, gleaming dark eyes. But what bothered her the most was the impact his picture had on her. It wasn't supposed to be like this.

She should be free of any emotional entanglement. She should be able to stare at that photograph and feel nothing. Instead she was swamped by so many confused, uncomfortable emotions that she could hardly breathe.

Determined to focus her attention elsewhere, she started on an article with Charles's byline. He'd written an investigative feature, clearly one of a series, about the unhealthy and often unsafe conditions under which many of the migrant workers lived and worked in the community's apple orchards.

Two paragraphs into the piece, Steffie had to stop reading. She'd come to her father's name, along with the name of their orchard. Obviously Charles hadn't done his research! Steffie knew how hard her parents had worked to ease the plight of the migrant workers. Her mother had set up a medical clinic. And unlike certain other orchard owners, her father had built them decent housing and seen to it that they were properly fed and fairly paid.

Steffie tried to continue reading, but the red haze of anger made it impossible. Her stomach twisted in painful knots as she rose to her feet, tucking the paper under her arm.

"Valerie," she demanded. "What was Dad doing when he suffered his heart attack?"

"I think Norah said he was sitting on the porch. What makes you ask?"

"He was reading the newspaper, wasn't he?"

"I wouldn't know for sure, but I don't think so."

"He must have been!" Steffie declared, walking

toward the elevator. She stabbed the button with her thumb, seething at the sense of betrayal she felt. All the evidence pointed to one thing. She'd found the paper spread open in his den. Her father had picked up the *Orchard Valley Clarion,* read the article and then in shock and dismay had wandered onto the porch.

"Steffie, what is it?"

"Have you *read* this?" she asked, thrusting the newspaper in front of her sister. "Did you see what Charles Tomaselli wrote about our father?"

"Well, I skimmed it, but—"

"Look at the date," she said, folding back the front page.

"Yes?" Valerie asked, still sounding confused.

"Isn't that the day of Dad's heart attack?"

"Yes, but—"

"You'd be upset, too, if you'd worked half your life improving the conditions of migrant workers only to have your efforts ridiculed before the entire community!"

"Steffie," Valerie said, gently pressing Steffie's arm. "Charles is Dad's friend. He's called several times to ask about him. Why, he was even here the night of Dad's surgery."

"He was probably feeling a large dose of guilt." It seemed perfectly obvious that Charles knew what he'd done. Her father's heart attack had happened the same day the article was published. So Charles *must* have known, must have figured it out himself. And that was why he'd come calling—she was sure of it.

But it was going to take a whole lot more than a few words of concern to smooth over what he'd done. Once Steffie had confronted Charles, she intended to stop at Joan Lind's office. Joan might be as old as a sand dune, but she was a damn good attorney and Steffie meant to sue Tomaselli for everything he ever hoped to have.

The elevator arrived and she stepped briskly inside.

"Where are you going?" Valerie asked as the doors started to close.

"To give Tomaselli a piece of my mind."

The doors blocked Valerie from view, but her sister's words came through loud and clear. "A piece of your mind? Are you sure you have any to spare?"

By the time Steffie reached Main Street and located a parking spot, the anger and hurt actually made her feel ill. Her cheeks were feverishly hot. Her stomach churned.

Charles disliked her, and he was taking it out on her father. Well, she couldn't let him do it.

She entered the newspaper office, then hesitated. There was a reception desk and a polished wooden railing; it separated the public area from the work space, with its computer terminals and ringing phones. Beyond it several desks occupied by reporters and other staff lined each side of the room, creating a wide center aisle that led directly to the editor's desk.

She noticed Charles immediately. As the *Clarion*'s editor, he had a work area that took up the entire end of the room. He was on the phone, but his eyes locked instantly with hers. There'd been a time when she would have swooned to have him look at her like this—with admiration, with surprise, with a hint of pleasure. But that time was long past.

Undaunted, she opened the low gate and walked purposefully down the center aisle until she got to his desk. She could hear the gate swinging back and forth behind her, keeping time with her steps. By now, Charles clearly understood that this wasn't a social call.

"Brent, let me get back to you." He abruptly replaced the receiver. "Well, well, if it isn't Stephanie Bloomfield. To what do I owe this visit?"

His casual insouciance infuriated her. Steffie slapped the newspaper down on his desk. "Did you really think you'd get away with this?" she asked, astonished by the calmness of her own voice.

Charles's eyes steadily held hers. "I don't know what you're talking about."

"You published this…piece, didn't you?"

"What piece do you mean? I publish lots of pieces."

His attitude didn't fool her. "The one about living conditions among migrant orchard workers. Now, I ask you, who owns the largest apple orchard in three counties? The first paragraph is filled with innuendo, but then you get right down to brass tacks, don't you—by naming my father!"

"Stephanie—"

"I'm not finished yet!" she shouted. In fact, she was

just warming up to her subject. "You didn't think any of us would notice, did you?"

"Notice what?" He crossed his arms over his chest as though he'd grown bored with her tirade.

"The date of the article," she said, gaining momentum. "It's the same day as my father's heart attack. The very same day—"

"Stephanie—"

"Don't call me that!" Tears rolled down her face. "Everyone calls me Steffie." Roughly, she wiped them away, hating this display of weakness, especially in front of Charles. "I—don't know how you can live with yourself."

"If you want the truth, I don't have much of a problem."

"I didn't think your sort would," she muttered contemptuously. "Well, you'll be hearing from Joan Lind."

"Joan Lind retired last year."

"Then I'll hire someone else," she said, turning on her heel. She marched through the office, slamming the low gate, which had only recently recovered from her entrance.

To her surprise, confronting Charles hadn't eased her pain.

When she pulled out of the parking space, the tires spun and squealed. She felt suddenly embarrassed. She hadn't meant to make such a dramatic exit. Nor was she pleased when she glanced in her rearview mirror to find that Charles had followed her outside.

# Two

With the hurt propelling her, Steffie raced home. In her present frame of mind, she didn't dare go back to the hospital. Now wasn't the time to make polite conversation with her sisters, or to meet her father's doctor. Not when she desperately needed to vent this terrible sense of frustration and betrayal.

Charles's treachery cut deep. They'd had their differences, but Steffie had never once believed he would purposely set out to hurt her or her family. She'd been wrong. Charles was both vindictive and unforgiving, and that was more painful than the things he'd said to her that last day they'd been together. That horrible day when he'd laughed at her.

She was shocked he still had the power to make her feel like this, but apparently his grip on her heart was as strong now as it had been three years earlier. The time she'd spent away from home, the time she'd given herself to heal, might never have existed. She was no less vulnerable to him now.

From the moment Steffie first met Charles, she'd been fascinated with him. Infatuated. In the beginning, she hoped he returned her feelings. She'd been attending the University of Portland, making the fifty-mile commute into the city every day. Her mother had died a few months earlier, so Steffie had decided against moving into a dorm, as she'd originally planned.

In her sorrow, she'd craved the comfort of familiar people and places. She was worried, too, about her father, who seemed to be walking around in a fog of grief.

Valerie was already living in Texas at that point, and although she'd come home often while their mother was ill, her work schedule had kept her from visiting much since.

Norah, who was in the university's nursing program, used to drive to Portland with her. But Steffie would have made the hour's drive twice a day by herself if she'd had to, simply so she could see Charles more often.

It mortified her now, looking back. Her excuses to see him had been embarrassingly transparent. She'd been so wide-eyed with adoration that she'd repeatedly made a fool of herself.

Her cheeks flamed as she recalled the times she'd followed him around like a lost puppy. The way she'd studied every word, every line, he'd written. The way she'd worshiped him from afar, until her love had burned fiercely within her, impossible to contain or control....

She didn't want to remember, and as she so often had in the past, she blocked the memories from her mind rather than relive the humiliation she'd suffered because of him.

Her anger had cooled by the time she'd finished the ten-mile drive out of Orchard Valley to the family home. Once she arrived, the thought of going inside held no appeal. She needed to do something physically demanding to work off her frustration.

The stables were located behind the house. Valerie and Norah had never really taken to riding, but Steffie, who was the family daredevil, had loved it. The sense of freedom and power had been addictive to a young girl struggling to discover her own identity. Some of the happiest memories of her childhood were the times she'd gone horseback riding with her father.

She knew from Norah's letters that he hadn't ridden much lately and had left exercising the horses to the hired help.

The stable held six stalls, four of them empty, and a tack room at the rear. Both Fury and Princess raised their sleek heads when she entered the barn. Princess was the gentle mare her father had purchased and named for her several years earlier; Fury was her father's gelding, large and black, notoriously temperamental. He pawed the ground vigorously as she approached.

"How're you doing, big boy?" she asked, rubbing his soft muzzle. "I'm not ignoring you, Princess," she told the mare across the aisle. "It's just that I'm in the mood for a really hard workout."

After allowing Fury to refamiliarize himself with her, Steffie collected saddle and bridle from the tack room. She slipped on Fury's bridle, then opened the stall gate and led him out. The gelding seemed to be as eager to run as she was to ride, and he shifted his weight impatiently as she tightened the girth and adjusted the stirrups.

Leading him out of the stable, she'd set her foot in the stirrup, ready to mount, when she noticed a small red sports car racing down the driveway. It didn't take her two seconds to recognize Charles.

Steffie had no intention of speaking to a man she considered a traitor. In fact, she didn't want to ever see him again. She planned to talk to her sisters, then seek legal counsel. Charles would pay for what he'd done to her father, and she'd make sure he paid dearly. Even if he retained bitter feelings about her, that was no reason to take vengeance on her family.

Reaching for the saddle horn, she hoisted herself onto Fury's back. She hadn't used a Western saddle since she'd left home and needed a moment to get used to it again. Fury scampered in a side trot as Steffie changed her position, leaning slightly forward.

"It's all right, boy," she assured him in a calm, quiet voice that belied her eagerness to escape—and leave Charles behind.

She ignored his honk and although it was childish, she derived a certain amount of pleasure from turning her back on him. She nudged Fury's sides and with her chin at a haughty angle, trotted away.

She'd only gone a short distance when she became aware that Charles was following her. Fury didn't need any encouragement to increase his steady trot to a full gallop. Although she was an experienced horsewoman, Steffie wasn't prepared for the sudden burst of speed. Fury raced as though fire was licking at his heels.

Holding on to the reins, Steffie adjusted as well as she could, bouncing and jolting uncomfortably, unable to adapt to Fury's rhythm. She'd ridden in Italy, but not nearly as often as she would've liked and always with an English-style saddle. Not only was she out of practice, she didn't have the strength to control a horse of Fury's size and power—especially one who hadn't been exercised lately. She should've thought of that, she groaned. Thank goodness he was familiar with the terrain. He galloped first along the dirt road, bordered on both sides by apple trees. He kicked up a cloud of dust in his wake, which made it impossible for Steffie to tell whether Charles had continued after her. She prayed he hadn't.

Only when Fury took a sharp turn to the left, through a rough patch of ground, did Steffie see that Charles was indeed behind her. She tried to pull in the reins, to slow Fury down to a more comfortable trot, but the gelding had a mind of his own. She tried to talk to him but her hair flew about her face, the long ends slapping her cheeks, blinding her. Between her bouncing in the saddle and the hair flapping in her face, she couldn't manage a single intelligible word.

By now she had a lot more than Charles to worry about. She was about to lose what little control she had of the horse. And on this rough ground, she feared for the animal's safety, not to mention her own.

Steffie remembered the land well enough to realize they were headed for a bluff that overlooked the valley. It was at the farthest reach of her family's property, and a place Steffie had often gone when she needed to be alone. She approved of Fury's choice, if not his means of getting there.

Her one consolation was that it would be virtually impossible for Charles to follow her any farther. His vehicle would never make it over the rock-strewn landscape. With no other option, he'd be forced to turn back. Or wait. And if he chose to wait by the side of the dirt road, he'd be out of luck—she'd simply take another route home, connecting with the road at a different point.

Once they reached their destination, Fury slowed to a canter. Steffie pulled back on the reins, slid out of the saddle and commanded her trembling legs to keep her upright. She wiped the sweat from the gelding's neck and rubbed him down with a handful of long dry grass, then led him to a nearby stream. She was loosely holding the reins, allowing him to drink the clear, cool water, when she saw a whirl of dust. Thinking at first that it might be a dust devil, she only glanced in that direction. Her heart sank all the way to her knees when she made out the form of a red sports car.

It wasn't possible. The terrain was far too uneven and

rocky. Charles must be insane to risk the undercarriage of his car by racing after her.

Squaring her shoulders, she turned to face him, refusing to give one quarter. Charles bounded out of the small car like a spring being released. She nearly flinched at the hard, angry set of his face.

"What do you think you're doing?" he demanded—as though he had a right to ask.

Steffie didn't acknowledge him but resumed her rubdown of the horse.

"You might have been killed, you idiot! And you might have killed that horse, too."

She was about to tell him she was no idiot, but she refused to become involved in a shouting match. And she *did* feel guilty about taking out a horse she couldn't control—her father's horse, yet. But Charles was a traitor, and worse. The next time she spoke to him, Steffie thought angrily, it would be through an attorney.

It looked for a moment as though he intended to grab her by the shoulders; in fact, what she heard him mutter sounded like a threat to "shake some sense" into her. He raised his hands, then briefly closed his eyes and spun away from her.

"You haven't changed a bit, have you?" he cried, jerking one hand through his hair as he stalked toward his car.

Still Steffie remained silent, although she had to bite her tongue in an effort not to lash back at him. He'd purposely hurt her family, hurt her. There was nothing left to be said.

He yanked his car door open, and Steffie blinked at the unexpectedness of his withdrawal. She wasn't sure what he'd planned to do, but this swift capitulation came as a surprise.

Not wanting him to assume she cared about his actions one way or the other, she tried to ignore him. She looped Fury's reins around a low branch and walked away. Her legs were trembling so badly that she decided to climb onto a boulder. Perched there, she gazed out at the sweeping view of the valley below, jewel-like in its green lushness.

Charles's footsteps behind her announced that he hadn't left, after all.

"Read it!" he shouted, slapping the very newspaper she'd given him against her thigh. "*This* time finish the article."

Steffie gasped, then pressed her lips together, tilting her head to avoid looking at him.

"Fine, be stubborn. That's nothing new. But if you won't read the article, I'll do it for you." He opened the paper.

Steffie wanted to blot out every word, but she wouldn't resort to anything quite as juvenile as plugging her ears. She cringed inwardly as his strong voice read the opening paragraph. On hearing it a second time, she felt the piece sounded even more hostile to her father than she'd believed earlier. It was as though Charles had taken the very heart of David Bloomfield's accomplishments and crushed it with falsehoods and accusations.

By the time he reached the spot where Steffie had stopped reading, where her father's name was mentioned, the anger inside her had rekindled. She closed her eyes to the wave of pain that threatened to overwhelm her.

He read on, and she waited with foreboding for the attack she knew was coming. But it didn't happen. As Charles continued, she suddenly realized how wrong she'd been. How *terribly* wrong. Her heart in her throat, she turned toward him. Charles went on, reading a direct quote from David Bloomfield in which he told of the changes he'd made over the years to aid migrant workers.

At first Steffie was convinced she'd misunderstood. Nor was she entirely sure she could believe Charles. He might be making it up as he went along, she thought wildly, instead of actually reading the article. She reached for the newspaper and snatched it away from him.

It only took her a moment to locate the paragraph he'd just read. He hadn't made it up! There, bold as could be, was the quote from her father, followed by two long paragraphs that reported the progressive measures Bloomfield Orchards had implemented over the years.

Her stomach plummeted, and she began to feel as though she were sitting in a deck chair on the *Titanic*. That feeling intensified as she finished reading the article. Because she soon discovered that not only was her father quoted—approvingly—several times, but their family orchard was used as a model for other local orchards to follow.

Steffie drew in a deep breath before she looked up at

Charles. Once again, she'd made a fool of herself in front of him. She cringed in acute embarrassment and self-contempt. What a jerk she'd been. What a total jerk.

She'd known that meeting Charles again was inevitable. She'd hoped that on her return he'd view her—from afar, of course—as mature. Sophisticated. She'd wanted him to see her as cosmopolitan and cultured, unlike the lovesick twenty-two-year-old who'd left Orchard Valley three years before.

She'd imagined their first meeting. She'd step forward, a serene smile on her face, and hold out her hand politely. She'd murmur ever so sweetly that it was lovely to see him again, but unfortunately she couldn't quite recall his name. Charles Something-or-other, wasn't it?

"It looks like I owe you an apology," she said instead, her voice quavering a bit despite her efforts to keep it even.

"Yeah, I'd say you owe me an apology!" he flung back. "I'd assumed you might have changed in three years. Instead you're an even bigger…nuisance."

His words felt like a slap across the face, and she flinched involuntarily. There wasn't a thing she could say in her own defense, nothing that would take away the shame of what she'd done. No words would erase the way she'd stomped into his office and created a scene in front of his entire staff.

"So it seems," she said as steadily as her crumbling poise would allow.

"You scared me, taking off like that," he raged. "You might have killed yourself."

Again, there was nothing she could say. Had she been in any other frame of mind, she would have recognized that with a horse like Fury, she was heading for trouble.

"You're a crazy woman!" he shouted, his anger fully ignited now. "How do you think I would've felt if you'd been hurt? What about your father? You accuse *me* of causing his heart attack! What do you think would've happened to him if you'd killed yourself?"

"I—I…" Hating the telltale action, she bit her lip to stop its trembling.

To Steffie's dismay, he reached down and pulled her to her feet. His hands clasped her shoulders and he drew her into his arms.

Before she had a chance to react, she was completely caught in his embrace, her hands trapped against his heaving chest.

One hand left her shoulder and slid into her long, tangled hair.

"Do you even have a clue what I was thinking?" he whispered. "Do you have any idea what was going through my mind?"

Her heart thundered. She should fight her way out of his embrace. She should demand that he release her, tell him he had no right to take her in his arms. But Steffie couldn't make herself move, couldn't make herself speak.

She didn't try to stop him even when it became obvious that he was going to kiss her. Mentally she braced herself, closing her eyes.

When his mouth found hers, it was a gentle brushing of lips. Her eyes opened in wonder and surprise.

Charles kissed her again, longer this time, his mouth gliding over hers. Before she realized what she was doing, she moved her arms upward and timidly locked them behind his neck. Her lips parted to his and he pressed her closer.

But only for a moment. "No, Steffie," he said in a raw whisper, clasping both wrists and breaking her hold. He stepped back. Their eyes met for several seconds before he turned and hurried away.

He left as abruptly as he'd arrived, his sports car spitting dirt and small stones as he roared off. She sighed and prepared to mount Fury for the long journey home.

Steffie took a nap that afternoon, waking sometime in the early evening. The sun was setting, dousing the orchards in a lovely shade of pink. Not knowing what time it was, she came downstairs to find Norah in the kitchen, emptying the dishwasher.

"Hi," Norah greeted her, smiling brightly when she saw Steffie. "I was beginning to wonder if you'd ever wake up. You must've been exhausted."

Steffie nodded.

"There's a plate for you in the oven. I bet you're famished."

The last thing she'd eaten had been that banana at breakfast. Murmuring her thanks, she walked across the room and removed the plate. Her sister had always been a good cook and Steffie gazed longingly at the broiled chicken breast, red new potatoes and fresh green beans.

"Where'd you go this morning?" Norah asked cheerfully, continuing to put the dishes away. "Valerie said you seemed upset about Charles Tomaselli."

Steffie pulled out a stool at the counter and sat down to eat. "I needed to ask him something."

"Did you get everything settled?"

Steffie lowered her gaze. "Everything's clear now."

"Good. He really has been wonderful through all this. Dad's pleased with how well the article on migrant workers was received. You read it, didn't you? The two of them spent weeks collecting facts, and Dad actually did a bit of undercover work. It was the first time since Mom died that he showed much interest in anything. I don't think even Charles knows how much Dad put into that piece. He must've gone over every detail a dozen times."

Steffie, who was just about to begin her meal, promptly lost her appetite. "I—I didn't realize that."

"I was planning to mail you the article, but then Dad had the heart attack and everything else fell by the wayside," Norah explained conversationally, leaning against the counter.

"Where's Val?"

"In the den. She's working. You know Val. She's got a mobile office set up there. Although I have to admit her mind hasn't been on the job lately."

"Oh?" Steffie made an effort to taste her meal. The chicken was tender and delicious. She took a second bite.

Norah wiggled her eyebrows playfully. "In case you hadn't noticed, there's a romance brewing between Val and Dr. Winston."

"There is?" Steffie asked, fork poised in midair. "What about Valerie's boss? Every time I got a letter from her it was Rowdy this and Rowdy that."

"I don't know about Rowdy, but I do know what I saw the night of Dad's surgery."

"Which was?" Steffie asked anxiously.

"Valerie fell apart after we were allowed to go in and see Dad. She didn't realize I knew how upset she was, but I figured she needed a few minutes alone. I hadn't seen Dad myself, and when I did, I could understand Valerie's concern. He was very close to death. I don't know how much anyone's told you about Dad's condition, but it's a miracle he survived the open-heart surgery. Anyway," she said with a sigh, "when I went in to see Dad I wondered if he'd last the night. I know Colby didn't think he would. Neither did any of the others on the surgical team. Naturally, they didn't say that, but I could tell what they were thinking. I've worked in surgery often enough myself to know who's likely to survive and who isn't. One look told me we'd be lucky if Dad lasted another few hours, although I was encouraged because he'd survived the surgery itself. There were plenty of complications, with the fluid in his lungs and all."

"Tell me about Valerie," Steffie urged.

"Oh, yeah, Valerie. Well, after she'd been with Dad

she went out onto the patio outside the surgical waiting room. She was crying, which we both know is rare for Val. I could tell she needed someone. When I got back from seeing Dad, I started to go out to her, thinking we'd be able to comfort each other, but I stopped when I saw that Colby was with her."

Steffie had heard wonderful things about Dr. Winston already, but his compassion for her sister confirmed everything she'd come to know of him. She said so to Norah, who nodded.

"They were sitting together and he was holding her in his arms. I don't know how to explain it, but he had this…look. As though he would've done anything within his power to take away her pain. I thought right then that he had the look of a man who's just discovered he's fallen in love."

"And Valerie?"

"I think she might have realized they were in love with each other before Colby did. You know how strong Valerie is, how she never wants to let anyone do anything for her. Well, for the first time since I can remember, she needed someone and Colby's the person she turned to."

"Valerie and Dr. Winston," Steffie said slowly. She'd often wondered what it would be like when her oldest sister fell in love. Valerie had always been so pragmatic, much too sensible to get involved in a relationship while she was in college. She was there to be educated, not to find a husband, she'd told Steffie.

"Then Dad began to improve," Norah went on, "and he started all this talk about the three of us marrying and having kids. I'm afraid Valerie's taking it much too seriously, worrying about it too much. But then, she's in love for the first time in her life and she's frightened half to death that Colby's the wrong man for her. Or more to the point, that *she's* the wrong woman for him."

"Love is love, and if they both feel so strongly, what's the problem?"

Norah's smile was sad and a bit hesitant. "Colby's as traditional as they come. I think he wants a woman straight out of the 1950s."

"Valerie knows this?"

"Of course she does. Colby's well aware of what Valerie's like, too. Her calling isn't the kitchen, it's the boardroom."

"I say more power to her." In Steffie's opinion, Colby Winston should appreciate her sister's God-given talents.

"Exactly!" Norah agreed. "But if Valerie marries Colby she'd probably have to quit her job. For one thing, CHIPS doesn't have an office in this part of the country. And she's worked too hard and too long to let go of her career."

"In other words, they'd both have to compromise— and they can't?"

"Exactly," Norah said again. She sighed. "No one ever told me love could be so complicated. I feel sorry for them both. They couldn't be more miserable."

Steffie finished off the last of the small red potatoes,

not wanting her sister to guess how curious she was about her father's "chat" with her mother. "What do you think of all this talk about Dad's...experience?"

Norah pulled up a stool and sat across from her. "I don't know. *He* believes he talked with Mom and that's what's important, don't you think?"

Steffie wasn't sure of anything anymore. She'd once been confident that she knew what she wanted in life. Then everything had fallen apart. But the time she'd spent in Italy had helped her regain a perspective on her own life...hadn't it?

It suddenly occurred to Steffie with a sense of horror that she'd spent three years studying and traveling in Italy, and her primary purpose had been *to impress Charles Tomaselli* when she returned.

She'd impressed him, all right, by making an even bigger fool of herself than before.

"Dad's been talking about his grandchildren all afternoon," Norah continued, breaking into Steffie's thoughts. Steffie was grateful for the intrusion.

"Grandchildren," she repeated softly. "From you, naturally?" She couldn't imagine Valerie as a mother, and she herself had no intention of marrying. When her father was well enough to come home, Steffie intended to find herself an apartment in Portland and to apply for a fellowship and begin her doctorate. She'd completed her master's in Italy after an intensive language program, and in her last year there, she'd also taken several advanced courses. It was hard to believe someone so well educated could be so dismally unaware of her own motives, she mused unhappily.

"Dad claims I'm going to present him with six grand-children," Norah said, barely restraining a smile. "Can you imagine me with *six* children?"

"Which means Valerie's going to be responsible for another six."

"No, three. According to Dad's ramblings, you're going to have three of the little darlings yourself."

Steffie grinned, in spite of her depression. The picture of her married and with a brood of children was some-what amusing. She'd only loved one man in her life and the experience had been so painful that she was deter-mined never to repeat the mistake.

"I guess we'll see," Steffie said, sliding off her stool to carry her now-empty plate to the sink.

"I guess we will," Norah concurred.

Although she'd slept for a good part of the after-noon, two hours later Steffie was yawning. Making her excuses, she returned to her bedroom, showered and got into bed, savoring the crisp, clean sheets.

Sitting up, her knees tucked under her chin, she pondered her conversation with Norah. In the years since she'd moved away, a number of her friends had married. She'd gotten wedding invitations, passed on by Norah, every few months. And several of her high school and college friends were already mothers, some two times over.

While she was in Italy, Steffie hadn't allowed herself

to think about anything more pressing than her studies, which had occupied most of her time. She'd traveled and studied and worked hard. But at odd moments, when she received a wedding invitation or a birth announcement, she'd occasionally taken a moment to wonder if her life was missing something. Or when she was with Mario, the adorable young son of her landlady in Rome, she'd imagined, more than once, how it would feel to have a family of her own.... She'd usually managed to suppress the yearning quickly.

And now she was experiencing it again, and more sharply than ever before. All this talk of weddings and children troubled her. She felt excluded, somehow. In the end, Valerie would probably marry her Dr. Winston, and there'd be a wonderful man for Norah, she was sure of it.

But for her? She found she couldn't believe in the same kind of happy ending.

# *Three*

Although she was exhausted, Steffie couldn't sleep. After tossing about restlessly and tangling her sheets, she sat on the edge of the bed and pushed the long hair away from her face.

She'd prefer to think the nap she'd taken that afternoon was responsible for this inability to sleep.

But she knew better.

She couldn't sleep because her thoughts wouldn't leave her alone. The memory of what a fool she'd made of herself with Charles hounded her until she wanted to scream.

With graphic clarity she recalled the first time she'd heard of Charles Tomaselli. She'd read his introductory column in the *Clarion* and had loved his wit. No matter what she thought of him now, she could never fault his talent as a writer. Charles had a way of turning a phrase that gave a reader pause. He chose his words carefully, writing in a clear, economical manner that managed to be both clever and precise. And he had a wide range of subjects, covering everything from social trends to the local political scene.

When she'd read his first few columns, she'd assumed he was much older, because the confidence of his observations and his style suggested a man of considerable experience. It wasn't until several weeks later that she actually met him. At the time she'd been so dumbstruck she could barely put two words together.

She'd tried to tell him how much she enjoyed his editor's column, but the words had twisted on the end of her tongue and came out sounding jerky and odd, like something a preschooler might say.

She'd been terribly embarrassed, but Charles had responded graciously, thanking her for the compliment.

It wasn't just the fact that he was in his late twenties—and not his fifties—that had taken Steffie by surprise. Nor was it the fact that he was strikingly handsome, although he was. What struck Steffie like a fist to the stomach was the instant and powerful attraction she felt for him.

Unlike Valerie, who'd gone out on only a handful of dates through high school and college, Steffie had had an active social calendar. She'd always been well liked by both sexes—popular enough to be voted Prom Queen her senior year of high school. But although she had lots of friends who happened to be boys, Steffie had never been in love. She'd thought, more than once, that she was, but she'd been wise enough to realize she was only infatuated, or in love with the idea of being in love.

Although she was twenty-one, going on twenty-two, she'd never been involved in a serious relationship. She hadn't considered herself ready for one—until she met the newly hired editor of the *Orchard Valley Clarion*.

When she met Charles, she knew immediately that she was going to love this man. How she could be so certain was unclear, even to her, but to the very depths of her young heart, she was absolutely convinced of it.

After that initial meeting, Steffie had driven home in a daze. She didn't tell anyone, including her sisters, what she felt. She didn't know how she could possibly explain her feelings without sounding silly. Love at first sight was something reserved for movies and romance novels.

She'd been filled with questions, wondering if Charles had felt it, too; she soon persuaded herself that he had.

He was older—twenty-seven, she discovered—amazingly mature and sophisticated, while she was an inexperienced third-year college student.

Steffie lived for the next edition of the *Clarion,* ripping open the newspaper until she found his column, and devoured each word Charles had written. Occasionally he wrote a feature article, and she read those just as avidly. She soon discovered that other people were equally taken with his work. He'd been in town for less than two months and had already become a source of pride and pleasure to the entire community.

Steffie straightened and reached over to turn on her

bedside lamp. Obviously she wouldn't be able to sleep, and sitting in her room, dredging up memories of Charles, wasn't helping.

The house was dark and silent, which meant Valerie and Norah were both asleep. Not wanting to wake either of her sisters, Steffie slipped quietly down the dimly lit stairs.

She thought about making herself a cup of tea, then decided against it. Instead, she tiptoed into her father's den. She turned on a soft light and reached for *Sonnets from the Portuguese*—an especially lovely edition her father had given her mother years ago, before they were married. Steffie cuddled up in his reading chair, already comforted.

The leather felt cool against her skin. An afghan her mother had knitted when the girls were still young lay neatly folded on the ottoman. Valerie must have brought it in with her, since it hadn't been there the night before.

Steffie reached for the rose-colored afghan and tucked it around her, then turned to one of her favorite poems.

She made it through two pages before her mind drifted back to Charles. Back to that first year…

He hadn't noticed her. Hadn't shared the instant attraction. In fact, he hadn't even remembered her name. Steffie was stunned. She'd dreamed of him every night since the day they met. Wonderful dreams of laughing and loving, of strolling hand in hand through the apple orchard, sharing secrets and planning the rest of their lives. Her heart was so full of love that it was all she could do not to tell him outright.

Getting a man to notice her was a new challenge for

Steffie. Until then, it had always been the other way around. The men—no, *boys*—had been the ones to seek her out. For the first time in her life, Steffie found herself at a disadvantage in a relationship. Clearly the only option open to her was to let Charles know as subtly as possible that she was interested. It shouldn't be such a difficult task for a former Prom Queen.

Except that it was...

The first thing Steffie did was to write him a letter commending his writing ability and his opinions. She'd agonized over every word, then waited nearly two weeks for a reply.

There hadn't been one.

Charles hadn't printed her letter and didn't respond, either. Steffie had been crushed. Never one to quit, though, she'd visited the newspaper office with suggestions for a wide variety of stories. As she recalled, she'd managed to come up with 150 such ideas. Admittedly some were better than others.

Charles had been polite, but had made it plain that although he appreciated her suggestions, he already had an enthusiastic staff whose job it was to come up with regional stories.

Her plan had been for Charles to be so awed by her concern about local issues and her invaluable ideas that he'd invite her to dinner to discuss her interest. Although, in retrospect, it sounded terribly naive, she'd actually believed this would happen.

Apparently, she spent more time than she realized

hanging around the newspaper office over the next few months because Charles unexpectedly asked her out for coffee one morning.

Steffie had been so excited that she could barely sit still. She was further encouraged when Charles chose a booth in the farthest, most private corner of the local coffee shop.

Even now, more than three years afterward, Steffie could recall how thrilled she'd been. She'd slid into the red vinyl seat across from him, sure he could read all the love and adoration in her eyes.

The encounter, however, proved to be a bitter disappointment for Steffie. Charles had been kind, but firm. He couldn't help noticing, he'd said, how much time she spent at the newspaper office, and was sure her studies must have been suffering. He'd also gotten her letter and the other notes she'd sent him, and although he was flattered by her attention, he was much too busy with the paper to become involved in a relationship.

When Steffie had pressed him for more of an explanation, he'd told her without a second's pause that he considered her too young for him. Furthermore, he felt she was…too innocent.

Steffie was aghast at his lack of foresight. She was a mature woman, and six years' difference in their ages was unimportant. If she didn't object, then he shouldn't, either.

As an active member of her high school debating team, Steffie had learned how to argue, and now she'd used every skill at her disposal.

It didn't work.

He'd finally told her she was a nice *kid* but he simply wasn't interested. That he was a busy man and didn't have the time or patience to be a babysitter. A babysitter! He wasn't exactly impolite, but it was clear he had no intention of asking her out. Ever.

Their coffee had just been served, and Charles hadn't taken more than a sip before he tossed some money on the table and left.

Steffie had remained there, too hurt to breathe, too numb to feel anything more than a painful disappointment. She couldn't remember how long she'd sat in the booth. Long after her coffee had cooled, she knew.

Obviously she'd sat there much *too* long because she'd decided that Charles Tomaselli was clearly lying.

"Steff."

The gentle voice was followed by a warm hand on her shoulder.

"What are you doing sleeping down here?"

Steffie raised her head and blinked. Valerie, dressed in a housecoat, stood beside her.

"What time is it?"

"Morning," Valerie said with a smile. "How long have you been here?"

Moving her legs, Steffie winced at the unexpected discomfort. Her legs were stiff and sore and the book still lay open on her lap.

"I was going to fix myself coffee and toast before heading to the hospital. Do you want some?"

"Please." She worked one shoulder and then the other and rotated her neck, hoping to ease the crick. Her thoughts had been so full of what had happened between her and Charles in those early days that she couldn't remember falling asleep. It surprised her that she had. She wondered if her musings had followed her into her dreams, then felt it would be better if they hadn't.

"I can't tell you how good Dad looks compared to a week ago," Valerie said when Steffie joined her in the kitchen.

"I'm sorry I wasn't there." She paused, shaking her head. "It was so crazy being stuck in Italy like that."

"You know—" Valerie paused, clutching a large earthenware mug "—in a way I'm grateful you couldn't get home for a while. It might be the one thing that kept Dad alive. He was determined to see you before he died."

Steffie wasn't sure she understood. "Do you mean to say Dad had a means of controlling the timing of his…demise?"

"Sort of. Death was what he wanted. If I've learned anything through all this, it's that the human will is incredibly powerful."

Steffie began making toast, taking the butter and Norah's homemade strawberry jam out of the refrigerator. "I'm not totally clear on what you mean about the human will."

"I don't know if I can explain it," Valerie said after a moment, her look distant and thoughtful. "All I know is that Dad was on the brink of death for days. When I first arrived, Colby told us Dad would require open-heart surgery. He wanted to perform the operation immediately but couldn't because of various complications Dad was experiencing. If you want the medical terms for all this you can ask Norah or Colby, but basically it boiled down to one thing. Dad had lost the will to fight for his life. He's been miserable without Mom. We both know that, but I don't think anyone fully appreciated exactly how *lonely* he's been."

"I shouldn't have left him." Despite Valerie's reassurances, Steffie partially blamed herself for her father's failing health. She'd known when he came to visit her in Italy last year that something was wrong. He'd taken the trip to Europe not out of any desire to travel but because Valerie and Norah had thought it would help revive his spirits. The fact that Steffie was living in Italy had been a convenient excuse.

Steffie had enjoyed the time with her father, and had been excited about showing him the country she'd come to love and introducing him to her new friends. She'd carefully avoided any conversation having to do with Orchard Valley or her mother. Her father had urged her to come home, but she'd already registered for new courses and paid her rent in advance and planned another trip. All excuses. Because it really came down to one thing: she'd been afraid to go home.

Steffie Bloomfield afraid! The family daredevil. Dauntless, reckless Steffie Bloomfield was afraid of a mere man. More precisely, she was terrified of having to speak to Charles again, of looking him in the eye and pretending it didn't hurt anymore. Pretending she didn't love him. Pretending she didn't feel humiliated.

She was incapable of shrugging off the past, especially when it was much simpler just to stay in Europe. She loved her art history courses, she enjoyed traveling throughout Italy, she was fond of her landlady's family, she had lots of friends and acquaintances. She'd discovered, too, that she had a real aptitude for languages; besides being proficient in Italian, she'd picked up some French and German and hoped to continue learning them. No, she'd decided, there were too many good reasons to remain in Europe. And so she'd stayed.

"Do you want to ride to the hospital with me?" Valerie asked, apparently deep in her own thoughts.

"Sure."

"I might need to do a few errands later, but you might be able to get a ride home with Norah if I'm not back."

"I'm not worried. I haven't been able to spend much time with Dad yet." Steffie felt guilty about rushing out of the hospital the day before without returning to see him.

As it turned out, Steffie couldn't have chosen a better morning to be with her father. It was the day he was being transferred out of the Surgical Intensive Care Unit and onto the surgical ward. His time in the SICU was only four days, his recovery nothing short of remarkable. Even Dr. Winston seemed to think so.

"I can't get over how beautiful you've become," her

father said when he woke from a brief nap. Steffie was sitting at his bedside, doing the *New York Times* crossword puzzle and feeling downright pleased with herself that she'd managed to fill in a good half of the answers.

"I'll tell you what I've become," Steffie said with a laugh, "and that's Italian. The first day after I left Rome I slipped from English to Italian and then back again without noticing. I think I spent twice as long clearing customs as anyone else, simply because the agent didn't know what to make of me."

"So can you cook me some real Italian spaghetti?" her father asked.

"I certainly can, and I promise it'll be so good you'll dream about it the rest of your life."

"With plenty of garlic?"

Steffie raised the tips of her fingers to her lips and made a loud smacking sound. "With enough garlic to ward off vampires for the next hundred years. Besides, I hear garlic's good for your heart."

"But lousy for your love life."

"I don't think either of us needs to worry about that," she teased.

"Ah." David Bloomfield shook his head. "That's where you're wrong, Princess. You, my darling Stephanie, are about to discover what it means to be in love."

Steffie didn't want to say she already knew all she cared to on that subject. *Thanks, Dad—but no thanks,* she told him silently. Falling in love wasn't an experience she wanted to repeat.

"You aren't going to argue with me like Valerie did, are you?"

"Would there be any point?"

"No," he said, smiling broadly.

"I didn't think so."

"You don't believe I really talked to your mother, do you?"

"Uh…" It wasn't that she disbelieved him exactly. *He* was convinced that something had happened, so her opinion was irrelevant. He claimed to have enjoyed a lengthy conversation with her mother while strolling around some celestial lake. Valerie had mentioned it soon after Steffie's arrival. Norah had talked about it, too. Steffie found their accounts fascinating. Did she believe it had happened? She didn't know. She was inclined to think he'd experienced some kind of revelation—but whether it was spiritual, as he thought, or a dream, or a fantasy of his own making, she had no idea. And it didn't matter.

"You won't be the only one who doesn't believe my talk with your mother was real."

"It isn't that, Dad."

"Don't you worry about it. Time will prove me right."

"Prove you right about what?" a distinctive male voice asked from behind her. Steffie froze and the dread washed over her.

Charles Tomaselli.

He was the last person she'd expected to meet here. The last person she wanted to see again.

"How're you feeling, David?" he asked.

"I've been better."

"I'll bet you have," Charles said wryly.

Steffie was on her feet immediately. "I'll leave you two to chat," she said with a cheery lilt, anxious to leave the room.

"There's no reason for you to go," her father countered, holding out his hand to her. "Your smile is the brightest sunshine I've seen in days. Isn't that so, Charles?"

Steffie cringed inwardly, and not giving Charles time to comment, quickly squeezed her father's hand. "I don't think it's a good idea for you to have too much company all at once."

"That's probably true," Charles agreed. "Besides, I've got some business to discuss with you. I thought you'd be interested in hearing what happened as a result of that article we did on the migrant-worker situation."

Steffie's breath caught in her throat until she realized Charles wasn't referring to the stunt she'd pulled in his office the day before. She went weak with relief when she heard him mention something about Commissioner O'Dell initiating an inspection program.

Steffie still hadn't looked at Charles, still hadn't turned to face him. She delayed it as long as possible, leaning forward to kiss her father's cheek. "I'll get a ride back to the house with Valerie or Norah, but I'll be in again this evening and we can finish our…discussion."

"I'll see you then, Princess."

Steffie nodded and mentally braced herself as she

turned away from her father's bed. She looked shyly at Charles. To her astonishment, their eyes met instantly. They seemed drawn to gaze at each other, as though neither could resist the pull of mutual attraction. Her own heart gave a small burst of joy and she wondered if, deep within, his did, too.

"Hello, Steffie."

"Charles." Her voice was low and wispy. "I'll see you later, Dad."

"Bye, Princess."

Her eyes skidded past Charles as she hurried from the room, eager now to make her escape. By the time she reached the end of the corridor, she heard a roaring in her ears and she was breathless—all because of a casual encounter with Charles. Obviously she'd need to prepare herself mentally for even such minor confrontations.

She hadn't been nearly as shy with him that summer evening three years earlier, she remembered with chagrin. It mortified her now to think of her brazen behavior....

If Charles considered her a *kid* when he'd invited her for coffee, then Steffie decided she owed it to herself to show him he was wrong. Without difficulty, she'd been able to discover where Charles lived. Crime had never been much of a problem in Orchard Valley, and Charles had been kind enough to leave his front door unlocked.

When he appeared several hours later, there were scented candles lit throughout the living room and a bottle of champagne chilling in the kitchen.

"Is that you, darling?" Steffie had called out from the bathroom. She'd been sitting in a bubble-filled tub for the better part of an hour, and her skin had started to shrivel. She was also worried about the candles dripping and the champagne getting warm, but she dared not leave, fearing she'd never be able to get the bubbles just right again. It was important that he think she was completely nude, though in reality she wore a skimpy bikini.

Charles didn't answer. He stalked into the room, stopping abruptly in the doorway as his shocked gaze fell on her.

"What the hell are you doing here?" he'd demanded.

"I thought you should know I'm not a child."

"Then what are you—a mermaid?"

She forced a soft laugh and said in what she hoped was a sultry, adult voice, "No, silly man, I'm a *woman* and if you'll come here, I'll prove it to you."

"Get out."

"Out? But…but I was hoping you'd join me."

"No way, sweetheart. Now either you remove yourself from my home or I'm calling the police."

She pushed her big toe under the water tap. "I think my toe might be stuck."

"Fine, I'll call the plumber."

"But, Charles, darling…"

"Charles, nothing," he snapped. Marching into the bathroom and gripping her by the upper arm, he lifted her halfway out of the tub. She screeched, stumbling to find her balance. As soon as she was upright, Charles tossed a towel at her and told her she had five minutes to leave before he called the police.

Steffie had fled, but she'd seen the gleam of male admiration in Charles's eyes, seen the way he'd looked at her for a second or two. And, fool that she was, she hadn't been the least bit discouraged. Instead, she'd devised yet another plan.

Steffie wandered into the waiting area searching for Valerie. One of the orderlies mentioned that her sister had gone to pick up office supplies. Steffie remembered hearing something about an errand, but she hadn't been paying enough attention to recall whether Valerie was returning to the hospital or going straight home.

Oh, well, there was always Norah.

Tracking down her youngest sister didn't take long. Within five minutes, Steffie found her in the emergency room—preparing to go on duty. The hospital was understaffed, and now that their father was beginning to recover, Norah had returned to work. Steffie didn't bother to ask for a ride.

Hoping Charles would be gone, she went back to the surgical ward. Her luck hadn't improved, and they met at the elevator.

"I thought you were headed home?"

"I'll have to wait for Valerie," she said, trying to edge past him. "Or get a cab."

His arm blocked her escape. "There's no need to do that. I'll drop you off at the house."

"No, thanks," she returned stiffly.

"I want to talk to you, anyway," he said, none too gently guiding her into the elevator. "And as they say, there's no time like the present."

"This really isn't necessary, Charles."

"Oh, but it is."

She noticed, when he led her out of the hospital to the parking lot, that he was driving the same red sports car she'd seen the day before. It eased her conscience a bit that it hadn't been damaged during his race across the countryside.

He opened the door for her, and Steffie climbed inside. She was adjusting the seat belt when Charles joined her. The space seemed to shrink like silk pressed against a hot iron. Their shoulders touched, their thighs, their arms. For a moment, Steffie held her breath.

"You said you wanted to talk to me?" she said after he'd pulled out of the hospital parking lot. She was leaning as close to the passenger door as she could.

"I thought we'd discuss it over a glass of iced tea. You *are* inviting me inside, aren't you?" He turned and grinned at her, that boyish, slightly skewed grin she'd always found so appealing.

She'd planned to tell him she had no intention of letting him in; instead she cleared her throat and said, "If you'd like."

"I would."

The ten-mile drive to the house generally took fifteen minutes. Steffie could have sworn Charles was purposely dragging out the time, driving well below the speed limit. They were so close in the small cramped car that she couldn't avoid brushing against him, even though she tried not to. She was trying to forget that he'd kissed her the day before, and this didn't make it any easier.

Steffie closed her eyes. It was all she could do not to shout at him to hurry. Why was he prolonging these moments alone? The least he could do was make polite conversation.

"My father seems cheerful, doesn't he?" If Charles wasn't going to say something, then she would. Anything to ease this terrible awareness.

"He certainly does."

"He's got a reason to live now, and that's made all the difference in the world. I'm not sure what to think about his dream, but—"

"What dream?"

"Uh…nothing… It's not important." Steffie couldn't believe what she'd done. In her nervousness, in her desperation to fill the silence, she'd blurted out what should never have been shared.

She relaxed when Charles finally turned off the road onto the mile-long family driveway. He parked in front of the house.

Steffie didn't wait for him, but threw open her door and jumped out, her keys already in hand. She had the front door open by the time he caught up with her, and tossing her purse onto the hall table, led him briskly into the kitchen.

Norah had made some iced tea that morning. Steffie silently thanked her sister for her thoughtfulness as she took out the cold pitcher. A minute later, she'd found two tall glasses, added ice and sliced a fresh lemon. Another minute, and the drinks were ready.

"What was it you wanted to say?" Steffie reluctantly asked. She hadn't realized how warm she was and held the glass between both hands, enjoying the coolness against her palms.

"It's about what happened yesterday," Charles said, walking away from her. He paused at the bay window that overlooked the backyard. Just beyond his view was the stable. "Or more appropriately, what *shouldn't* have happened."

# Four

"I'd rather not discuss it," Steffie said adamantly. She didn't want to hear any more about her irresponsible accusations and rash actions. Nor did she wish to hear how much Charles regretted kissing her.

"If anyone needs to apologize, it's me," she said quickly. "Why don't we just leave it at that? I was wrong."

Charles's back was to her as he stared outside toward the stables. "I don't think anyone's ever infuriated me this much," he said quietly. He turned, set his glass of iced tea aside and thrust his hands into his pockets. "I've never met a woman who manages to irritate me the way you do."

Steffie stiffened. "I've already apologized for leaping to conclusions. I admitted I was wrong." She shrugged elaborately. "My only excuse is that I spent a hellish week trying to get home and I haven't slept properly in days and I—"

"This isn't necessary," he said, interrupting her. "I'm not looking for an apology.... Actually I'm here to make my own. I want you to know I'm sorry about chasing after you. It was a dangerous thing to do. I might have spooked Fury into throwing you."

"Not to mention damaging your car."

"True enough."

"Let's put it behind us," Steffie suggested with a weak smile. "I was wrong to run away. It was...childish."

"You were angry, too."

"I've never met a *man* who manages to irritate me the way you do," she said, consciously echoing his words.

"We always seem to get on each other's nerves, don't we?" His grin was warm and gentle, just as his kiss had been. Strangely, Steffie found his smile no less devastating.

"We certainly have a history of annoying each other." It took her more courage than he'd ever know to refer to the past. But suddenly she hoped they could put that behind them, too.

"I'd never be able to forgive myself if anything had happened to you," he said.

"I wasn't really in any danger of Fury throwing me." Okay, so that was a slight exaggeration, but she *had* stayed in the saddle.

"It was, shall we say, a memorable way for us to meet again." Charles's voice was husky. He moved closer to her and she lowered her eyes, but not before she noticed how his attention seemed to center on her mouth.

"There's one thing I'm not sorry about." He took another step toward her and raised his hand to touch her cheek. His fingers brushed aside a stray lock of hair. Steffie couldn't move. She couldn't think coherently. She could barely breathe.

"I don't regret kissing you," Charles whispered.

Then she did move. Trembling, she stepped backward and bolted to the other side of the room.

"Stephanie?"

"Call—call me Steffie," she stuttered. Her hands were shaking so badly that she jerked them behind her.

"I prefer to call you Stephanie. You're not a little girl anymore."

She smiled brightly. Now was the perfect time to convince him how sophisticated she'd become after three years in Europe—sophisticated and *experienced.* She was sure that was the type of woman he expected, the type of woman he wanted.

"As kisses go, it was very nice," she agreed in an offhand manner. Was she overdoing it? she wondered. "Yours had a gentleness, and that was unusual. Most men aren't like that, you know? When they kiss a woman it's hot and sweaty. They leave a girl breathless."

"I see," Charles said, raising one eyebrow.

She placed her hands on her hips, fashion-model style, and tilted back her head, letting her long brown hair swing lightly. "I'm not the same person I was three years ago. You're right about that. I'm all grown-up now."

"So it seems."

"I appreciate the ride home," she said, walking out of the kitchen. She hoped Charles would follow her because she wasn't sure how much longer she could maintain this performance.

"Is there anything else these…hot, sweaty men taught you?" he asked in a dispassionate voice. He reached for his iced tea, apparently disinclined to leave quite so soon.

She turned around and smiled serenely. "You'd be surprised." Deciding to give him the answer he deserved, she rashly went on. "As you might imagine, I met men of all nationalities—students from all over Europe—and I sampled my fair share of kisses." Mostly chaste kisses of greeting or farewell, but he didn't have to know that. And then there were Mario's exuberant hugs…. Mario was only four years old, but Charles didn't have to know that, either.

Charles scowled, and set his glass down on the counter hard enough to slosh liquid over the edges. He stalked past her. "Goodbye, *Steffie*," he said coldly, throwing the words over his shoulder.

It wasn't until he'd slammed the front door that she understood his words had been meant as an insult. He was telling her he'd changed his mind, reconsidered. He'd seen through her little dramatization and decided he'd been wrong: she wasn't an adult. She remained a silly, immature girl.

Steffie wandered between two rows of budding apple trees, contemplating her latest disaster with Charles.

The setting sun cast a rosy splendor over the orchard. All her life, Steffie had come out here when she needed to think. This was where she found peace, and a tranquillity that eased her burdens. Since her last meeting with Charles, there'd been plenty of those. And regrets. She hadn't seen him in several days and that helped. But it also hurt. There were so many unanswered questions between them, so many unspoken words.

Hearing footsteps behind her, Steffie turned to see Norah walking toward her.

"You've got to do something!" Norah moaned.

"About what?" she asked when Norah moved three agitated paces ahead of her.

"You've got to help Valerie. You can give her advice. You've had more experience with men."

Steffie suppressed the urge to laugh at the irony of this statement, considering her ludicrous performance in front of Charles. She reached up to run her fingers along the smooth bark of a branch. "What's wrong with her?"

"She's making the biggest mistake of her life," Norah said dramatically. It wasn't often that her sister sounded so distraught. Unfortunately Steffie was hardly the ideal person to advise Valerie on romance.

"I told you before that Valerie and Dr. Winston are in love," Norah continued. "Everyone around them can see it. And whenever Valerie and Colby are together, they can't keep their eyes off each other."

"So what's the problem?"

"They aren't seeing each other anymore."

"What do you mean?"

"They're avoiding each other. I don't think they've talked in days."

Norah's words struck a chord in Steffie. She knew exactly what Valerie was doing, because she was guilty of the same thing herself. She hadn't seen Charles since the day he'd driven her home from the hospital. They were obviously taking pains to avoid each other—just like Valerie and Dr. Winston.

"I don't see what I can do," Steffie muttered.

"Talk to Val," Norah argued. "She might listen to you."

"What am I supposed to say?"

Norah hesitated, frowning. "I don't know, but you'll think of something. I've given it my best shot and I just wasn't getting through to her. Maybe you can."

"I'm glad you have so much faith in my abilities," Steffie said lightly.

"I do have faith in you," Norah said, her blue eyes serious. "You're different now than before you left."

"Three years in Italy will do that to a girl." As she had with Charles, Steffie strived to seem flippant and worldly.

"I don't mean that. You're more thoughtful. More— I don't know—mature, I guess. Before you left Orchard Valley you acted like you had to prove yourself to the world, but it isn't like that now. I can't see you doing some of the crazy things you used to do."

Just as well that Norah didn't know about some of her "mature" behavior these past few days. And thank heaven no one in the family had any idea of the embarrassing stunts she'd pulled trying to attract Charles's attention three years ago.

"I remember the time you stood on Princess bareback and rode around the yard. You were lucky you didn't break your neck."

Steffie remembered the incident well. It had been shortly before their mother died. She'd been grieving so terribly, and doing something utterly dangerous had helped vent some of her pain and grief. But Norah was completely right. She shouldn't have done it.

"Okay, I'll talk to Valerie," Steffie promised, "but I don't know how much good it'll do."

Steffie tried. But the conversation with her sister hadn't gone as planned. One look at Valerie told her how much her sister was suffering. Valerie tried to hide it, but Steffie knew the signs from her own limited experience with love.

They'd become involved in a lengthy discussion about love, then decided neither one of them was qualified to advise the other. They'd thought of bringing Norah in on the conversation but that suggestion had resulted in a bout of unexpected giggles. They couldn't ask Norah about falling in love because she was too busy dating.

One interesting detail that emerged from their talk was something Valerie mentioned almost casually. While Steffie was struggling to find a way home, Charles had seemed very concerned about her. He'd even pulled a few strings in an effort to help when she didn't arrive on schedule.

Although they'd never openly discussed her relationship with Charles, Valerie seemed to know how Steffie felt. It wasn't that Steffie had tried to conceal it; with one breath, she admitted she'd made a fool of herself over the newspaper article and with the next, she'd asked her sister about falling in love. Valerie was certainly astute enough to figure out Steffie's feelings for Charles.

David Bloomfield was now recuperating at home and doing well. Steffie still hadn't seen Charles. She'd thought maybe he'd be stopping by the house to visit her father, whose release from the hospital had been a festive event.

Steffie was pleased to see that Valerie and Colby were able to steal a few moments alone that afternoon, but she didn't think their time together had gone well. They'd gone for a walk in the orchard; Valerie had looked pale and sad when they returned, and Colby had remained silent throughout the celebration dinner that followed.

Knowing it was inevitable that she'd see Charles again, Steffie tried to mentally brace herself for their next meeting.

She couldn't have guessed it would be at the local gas station.

"Why, Steffie Bloomfield," Del of Del's Gas-and-Go greeted her when she went inside to pay for her fill-up and buy a bottle of soda. "I swear you're a sight for sore eyes."

She laughed. Del was pot-bellied and at least sixty, but he had to be the biggest flirt in town. "It's good to see you again, too. What do I owe you for the gas?"

"If I were a rich man, I'd say the gas was free. Looking at your pretty face is payment enough. Right, Charles?"

It always happened when she was least prepared, when seeing him was the last thing she expected.

"Yeah, right," Charles answered from behind her with a decided lack of enthusiasm.

"Hello, Charles," she said, turning around to greet him, trying to sound casual and slightly aloof. She pasted a smile on her face, determined not to let him fluster her as he had every single time they'd encountered each other.

"Stephanie."

"I don't know if you heard, but Dad's home now."

"I got word of that the other day." Charles took his wallet out of his hip pocket and paid for his gas.

Steffie twisted the top off her soda and took a deep swallow. It tasted cool and sweet, bringing welcome relief to her suddenly parched throat. "I was thinking you might stop by and visit." *Hoping* more aptly described her thoughts, but she couldn't admit that.

He didn't answer as he followed her outside. The service-station attendant was washing her windshield and Steffie lingered, wanting to say something, anything, to make a fresh start with Charles.

"As I recall, you wrote one of your first columns about Del's, didn't you?"

"You've got a good memory," Charles said, his words a bit less stiff.

The boy had finished with her windows and there was no further excuse to dawdle. Reluctantly she opened her car door. "It was good seeing you. Oh, by the way, Valerie told me you made several efforts to find me when I was trying to get home from Italy. I appreciate all the help you gave my family."

He shrugged. She set one foot inside the car, then paused and glanced back at Charles. She *had* to speak up—now. "Charles." He turned around again, a surprised expression on his face. "There's something you should know."

"What is it?"

"I'm very grateful for your friendship to my family— and to me." With that she ducked inside her car, heart racing, and drove off without looking back.

Unfortunately dinner that evening was a strained affair. Norah had come to Steffie an hour before with the news that Colby had dated another nurse, a friend of Norah's, three nights running. Norah didn't know whether to tell Valerie, and had asked Steffie's advice.

Steffie thought it best not to say anything to their sister until Norah had slept on the matter.

But Steffie suspected that Valerie was already aware of it, suspected that Valerie knew it in her heart. Although her sister hadn't said anything to the family, Steffie believed she'd quietly made arrangements to return to Texas and her job as vice president of CHIPS, a software company based in Houston.

Everyone could feel something was wrong, but no one said a word during dinner. Everyone was terribly polite—as though the others were strangers—which only heightened the tension.

Their father had made his excuses, claiming to be especially tired, and with Norah's help retired to his room almost immediately after dinner.

Apparently Valerie wasn't in the mood for company either, because she excused herself and retreated to her bedroom, leaving Steffie and Norah to their own devices.

After they'd finished clearing up after dinner, Norah left to attend a wedding shower for a friend.

Feeling at loose ends, Steffie inspected the kitchen. On impulse, she decided to make the spaghetti sauce she'd promised her father. She dragged out the largest pot she could find and began to assemble ingredients. Fresh tomatoes, onions, tomato paste, garlic. No fresh herbs, so dried would have to do. Oh, good, a bottle of nice California red…

Humming to herself, she put on a CD of Verdi's *Aida* and turned up the volume until the music echoed against the kitchen walls. The emotional intensity and dramatic characterizations of the Italian composer suited her mood.

She found an old white apron her father had used years before whenever he barbecued. Wrapping it around her waist, she drew the long strings around to the front and tied them.

Half an hour later, she was stirring the last of the tomato paste into the pot. She added a generous amount of red wine, all the while singing at the top of her lungs. The sound of someone pounding at the back door jolted her back to reality.

Running barefoot across the kitchen, she pulled open the door and saw Charles standing there, holding a pot of purple azaleas.

"Charles! What are you doing here?"

"No one answered the front door," he remarked dryly.

"Oh. Sorry." She walked to the counter to turn off her CD player. "Come in." The silence was nearly deafening.

"I thought you said your father was home from the hospital?" As though self-conscious about holding a flowerpot, he handed it to Steffie.

"He is," she said, setting the plant aside. "How thoughtful. I'm sure Dad will love this."

"It isn't for David."

"It isn't?"

"No, I was…we just got a full-page ad from How Green Is My Thumb Nursery and I felt it might be a gesture of good faith to buy something. I thought you'd appreciate an azalea more than your father would."

Steffie wasn't quite sure what to say other than a soft "Thank you."

He shrugged, apparently eager to leave. He stepped toward the door and she desperately tried to think of something to keep him there, with her.

"Have you eaten?" she asked quickly, even though the sauce was only just starting to simmer and wouldn't be properly ready until the following day.

"What makes you ask?"

"I was just putting together a pot of spaghetti sauce for tomorrow. Dad asked me to cook him an Italian meal and…well, if you wouldn't mind waiting a bit, I'll be happy to fix you a plate. It really needs to simmer longer, but I know from experience that it's perfectly edible after an hour." She sounded breathless by the time she'd finished.

"I've already had dinner, but thanks, anyway," Charles told her. "I could do with a cup of coffee, though." He nodded toward the half-full pot sitting beside the stove.

"Sure…great. Me, too. I'd get Dad but he's sleeping," she explained as she poured him a cup, then one for herself.

"Through that?" Charles motioned toward the CD player.

"Sure. He loves listening to the same music I do. Besides, he's way over on the other side of the house. I doubt he could even hear it." She didn't mention that a tragic love story might suit Valerie's mood, however. And since her sister's bedroom was directly above the kitchen she was the one most likely to have been serenaded.

Charles held the mug in both hands and walked over to examine her efforts. "So you learned to cook while you were away?"

"A little," she admitted.

"I wouldn't have guessed you were the domestic type." He stirred the sauce with a wooden spoon, lifted it out of the pot and tasted it, using one finger. His brows rose. "This is good."

"Don't sound so surprised."

"There must've been some Italian man you were hoping to impress."

The only man she'd ever wanted to impress was the one standing in the kitchen at that very moment.

"I was too busy with my studies to date much," she said, dumping the empty tomato-paste cans in the recycling bin.

"That isn't the impression you gave me the other day."

She hesitated, her back to him. "I know. I certainly seem to make a habit of playing the fool when I'm with you."

Charles's voice was rueful. "I've occasionally suffered from the same problem."

The unexpectedness of his admission caught her off balance, and she twisted around to face him. For a long, unguarded moment she soaked in the sight of him.

"There wasn't anyone I dated very often," she told him in a raw whisper.

"Surely there was someone?"

She shook her head. They gazed silently into each other's eyes, and Steffie seemed to lose all sense of time.

Charles was the one who broke the trance. "Uh, your pot seems to be boiling."

"Oh, darn, I forgot to turn down the burner." She

raced across the kitchen, flipped the knob on the stove and stirred the sauce briskly, praying it hadn't burned.

While she stood at the stove, Steffie basked in a glow of unfamiliar contentment. It felt so wonderful to be with Charles—not fighting or defensive, not acting like a love-struck adolescent. For the first time, she was truly comfortable with him.

"I'm sure the sauce will be fine," she murmured, picking up her coffee mug.

He pulled out a chair and sat.

As she was getting cream, sugar and teaspoons, she thought she heard some noise from upstairs. Glancing at the ceiling, she frowned.

"What's wrong?"

Steffie joined him at the table, adding only cream to her own coffee and pushing the sugar bowl toward Charles. "I'm worried about Valerie," she said frankly. "So is Norah. Everyone is, except Dad, which is for the best—I mean, he's got enough on his mind healing from the surgery. He shouldn't be worrying about any of us."

Charles added a level teaspoon of sugar to his coffee, then paused, the spoon held above his cup. "How'd you know I take sugar?"

Her gaze skirted away from his. "We had coffee together once before, remember?"

"No" came his automatic response.

Steffie preferred not to dredge up the unhappy memory again, especially since *he* didn't even seem to recall it. She stared down at the table. "It was the first time you asked me to—you know, leave you alone."

He scowled. "The first time," he repeated, then shook his head in apparent confusion. Just as well, Steffie thought to herself, astounded that he had absolutely no recollection of an incident she remembered in such complete and painful detail.

She decided to change the subject. "Norah baked cookies the other day, if you'd like some."

Charles declined. "Tell me what's going on with your sister." His eyes darted to the ceiling.

Steffie wondered how much of Valerie's dilemma she should confide in him, but then remembered Norah's telling her that Charles had been with them the night of her father's surgery. More than likely he knew how Colby and Valerie felt about each other.

"She's in love," she said after a moment.

"It's Doc Winston, isn't it?"

Steffie nodded. "They both seem to have fallen hard."

"So what's wrong?"

Steffie wasn't sure she could explain, when she didn't entirely understand it herself. So she shrugged and said, "I think Colby wants her to be something she can't. Valerie's an incredibly gifted businesswoman. But I gather he wants a woman who'd be happy to stay home and be a housewife—there's nothing wrong with that, of course, but it just isn't right for Valerie. It doesn't look like either one of them is going to compromise."

"If she loves him, maybe she should be willing to

compromise first," Charles said, then sipped his coffee. "Take the first step."

"What about Colby? Why does it always have to be the woman who compromises? Don't answer that, I already know. Women have been forced to adapt to men's fickle natures for so many generations that it comes to us naturally," she said with heavy sarcasm. "Right?"

Charles was silent. "I didn't come here to argue about your sister," he finally said.

"I know, it's just that I found your statement so—" She stopped in midsentence because she didn't want to fight with him, either. They'd done so much of that. And she didn't want this encounter to end the way all the others had.

"I'm sorry," she said. "I'm concerned about her, and I can't help feeling a bit defensive. I'm pretty sure she's making arrangements to return to Texas—and I wish she wouldn't."

"You haven't had much time with her, have you?"

Steffie tapped the mug with her spoon, staring into the dregs of her coffee. "That's not the whole reason I wish she'd stay." She was silent for a moment. "Leaving your problems behind simply doesn't work. Not unless you've exhausted every possibility of reaching a compromise. In fact, I think leaving can make everything much worse. The problem is, I can't tell Valerie that. It's one of those painful realities we each need to discover on our own, I guess. I'm going to talk to her, but I doubt it'll make any difference."

Charles's dark eyes were sympathetic. "I hope she listens."

Steffie thanked him with a smile. "I hope she does, too, but the three of us seem to share a wide streak of stubbornness."

Charles rubbed his eyes, and she realized he must be exhausted. "You won't get an argument out of me," he said with a tired grin.

"Are you still working as many hours?"

He nodded. "Fifty to sixty a week. We publish twice weekly now and eventually we're looking to go daily. Some days I feel like I'm married to that paper."

The word "married" seemed to hang in the air. At one time Steffie had been convinced beyond any doubt that *they'd* be married, she and Charles. It was this unshakable resolve that had created so many difficulties in her relationship with him. Naively, she'd assumed that all she had to do was *show* him they were meant to love each other and after a few short object lessons, he'd agree. Now she knew that life—and love—didn't work that way.

"Are you still a jack-of-all-trades at the paper?" she asked, remembering that his job meant he had a hand in every aspect of publishing the newspaper—from writing, editing and layout to distribution.

"Everything except the classifieds."

"Do you still have an intern?"

Charles relaxed against the back of his chair and nodded. "Wendy. She's a recent graduate from the University of Portland."

He smiled as he spoke, and a red light went on in front of Steffie's eyes. "What happened to Larry? I thought you were working with him?" The idea of Charles spending long hours with an attractive college student filled her with a sense of dread.

"No, he moved on to an Internet news service. So, Wendy's with me now."

*Wendy's with me now?* Then it came to her. She didn't need to worry about competing for Charles anymore.

She was out of the running.

# *Five*

"Is someone here?" Steffie heard her father even before he entered the kitchen. He was wearing his plaid house-coat, cinched at the waist, which emphasized the weight he'd recently lost. His white hair was rumpled from sleep.

"David, hello," Charles said, standing to shake hands with him. Her father slowly made his way to the table, declining Charles's gesture of assistance.

"I thought you were still asleep," Steffie said with a loving smile. She'd missed the worst of the crisis, but her sisters had repeatedly told her how close they'd come to losing their father. Now, every time she was with him, she felt a sense of renewed love and gratitude that his life had been spared.

"How do you expect a man to sleep with such deli-cious smells coming from the kitchen?" David grumbled good-naturedly. "I swear it's driving me to distraction."

"It's my Italian spaghetti sauce."

Her father squinted. "But we already ate dinner."

"I know. The sauce needs to simmer for several hours and it's even better if you let it sit overnight. I was hoping to surprise you tomorrow evening."

Her father nodded approvingly. "Sounds great, Princess." Then he grinned at Charles. "Good to see you, boy."

"You, too, old man."

She could tell that they'd often bantered like this. The atmosphere was relaxed, one of shared affection and camaraderie.

"You were in the neighborhood and decided to stop by?" David inquired. It wasn't likely Charles would come this way except to visit the Bloomfields, and they all knew it.

"I stopped in to check up on you," Charles said, but his gaze drifted involuntarily toward Steffie. Their eyes met briefly before she looked away.

"That's the *only* reason?" her father pressed.

"I, uh, brought that for Stephanie," he said and pointed in the direction of the potted azalea.

"You wouldn't by any chance happen to be sweet on my little girl, would you?"

"Dad," Steffie broke in urgently, "how about something to drink? Coffee, tea, a glass of water?"

"Nothing, thanks. I just came to see if I was dreaming about garlic and basil or if this was for real. I'll leave the two of you to yourselves now." He stood awkwardly, as though he wasn't quite steady on his feet. Steffie's instincts were to help him, but she knew it was important that he do as much as possible on his own. She stepped back, ready to assist him if necessary.

Charles must have been thinking the same thing because he stood beside her, a concerned look on his face.

"I'll see you to your room," she said. The effort of rising from his chair and walking a few paces seemed to deplete her father's strength.

"Nonsense," he objected. "You've got company. Charles isn't here to visit me. I heard him say so himself. That was just an excuse so he could bring you that pretty flower."

"Don't argue with me, Daddy."

Her father grumbled, but allowed her to wrap her arm around his waist to support him. She looked over her shoulder at Charles. "I'll be back in a minute."

"Take your time."

No sooner were they out of the kitchen than David came to a halt, wearing the most delighted grin Steffie had ever seen. "What's so amusing?" she asked.

"Nothing," he said. Then he started chuckling softly. "It's just that your mother was right about this, too. Surprises me, but it shouldn't."

"What? Right about what?"

"You and Charles."

"Daddy, there's nothing between us! We're hardly even friends."

"Perhaps, but all that's about to change. Soon, too. Very soon."

Her father continued to mutter under his breath, as pleased as ever. Steffie closed her ears to his remarks, knowing that he had to be referring to his dream—the time he'd supposedly spent tiptoeing around the afterlife, gathering information. It hadn't bothered her nearly as much when he was going on about Valerie and Colby, but now that it was her turn, she felt decidedly uneasy.

"Charles isn't here to see me," she insisted. "Bringing me the azalea didn't mean anything. He got a new advertising account, that's all. I'm sure he intended to give it to you, but you were sleeping."

"Whatever you say, Princess."

Arguing wouldn't get her anywhere, and besides, she didn't want to keep Charles waiting. She suspected he'd be leaving soon, anyway. Her father sat on the edge of his bed, his eyes curious as he smiled up at her. "I might have guessed. I wasn't sure what to think when your mother mentioned you and Charles. She told me you've been in love with him for quite some time. She's right, isn't she?"

Steffie kissed his brow and ignored his question. "Do you want me to tuck you in?"

"Good heavens, no! You hurry back to your young man. He's waiting for you. Has been for years."

"Good night, Dad," she said pointedly.

Her father's grin broadened. "By golly, your mother was right," she heard him mutter again. "I should've known. Forgive me, Grace, for doubting."

Outside the bedroom door, Steffie started to tremble.

Without directly saying so, her father was telling her what she'd most dreaded hearing, and at the same time what she desired above all.

Whether it was the result of fantasy, intuition or, as he believed, spiritual intervention, he'd become convinced that she'd be marrying Charles. The same way he was so certain about what would happen between Valerie and Colby Winston. And Steffie wasn't any more confident about her older sister's relationship than she was about her own with Charles.

"You look like you've seen a ghost," Charles told her when she rejoined him in the kitchen.

She raised her eyes to his, dismayed that he'd noticed. She needed to sit down. He was right, it *had* been a scare, listening to her father talk like that about the two of them, making marriage sound imminent.

"What is it? Is your father okay?"

She nodded. "Oh, he's fine, growing stronger every day…"

"It's good to see him smile again."

Steffie nodded and glanced at the simmering pot of sauce. Anything to keep her eyes away from Charles.

"What's really wrong?" he asked her. His concern was gentle and undemanding, and it touched her heart. This was the man she'd always known him to be. The man she'd fallen in love with—the man she'd never been able to forget.

Had it been anyone else, she would have laughed off her father's words. She would have joked with her "destined" husband-to-be about how her father was bent on playing matchmaker.

She couldn't do that with Charles, not when she'd so blatantly played the role herself. He'd assume, and not without justification, that she was up to her old tricks.

"It's nothing," she said, forcing herself to smile brightly. "I can't help thinking how lucky we are to have him with us again."

Charles studied her intently. "You're *sure* there's nothing wrong?"

"Of course." She looked at him in what she hoped was a reassuring manner.

"If there's anything I can do…"

"There isn't." She smiled, to take the sting from her words. "You've already done so much. We're all indebted to you…you've been wonderful."

"You make me sound like some saint. Trust me, Stephanie, no one's going to canonize me—especially with the things I'm thinking right now." He was behind her before she even realized he'd moved. His hands were on her shoulders and he drew her back and slipped his arms around her waist. He nuzzled her neck and breathed in deeply, as though to inhale her scent.

Deluged with warm sensation, Steffie closed her eyes and savored the moment. She'd never believed this could happen. She dared not believe it even now.

It would be so easy to turn into his arms, to bury herself in the comfort he offered. She'd dreamed of this for so long. But now that it was here, she was afraid.

Her hands folded over his, which were joined at her middle. "I—the flowers are…"

"A gesture of good faith."

His words confused her. He must have sensed her uncertainty because he spoke again in a low voice. "Let's start all over again, shall we? From the beginning."

"I— I'm not sure I know what you mean."

He softly kissed the side of her neck, then released her and turned her around so they were face to face. "Hello there, my name's Charles Tomaselli. I understand you're Stephanie Bloomfield. It's a real pleasure to meet you." He held out his hand to her, which she took. If his eyes hadn't been so serious, she would have burst into peals of laughter.

"Charles, you say? Anyone call you Charlie?"

"Hardly ever. Anyone call you Steffie?"

"Only when I was much younger," she teased. "A mere kid."

"I understand you're recently back in town. I don't suppose you've had time to notice, but there've been a few changes in Orchard Valley. How about if I drive you around, show you the place?"

She hesitated. "When?"

"No time like the present."

"But we've just met."

"I'm hoping that won't stand in your way. It shouldn't. I'm completely trustworthy."

"Then I'll accept your kind invitation."

"Do you want to bring a sweater?" he asked.

She shook her head.

He reached for her hand, his fingers entwined with hers as he led her toward the front door. It felt like the most natural thing in the world for them to be together.

They bounded down the steps, carefree and laughing. Charles opened the car door for her, helped her inside and without warning leaned forward to kiss her. Their lips met briefly, then lingered. When he broke away, Charles seemed surprised himself. Steffie glanced up at him, thinking she might read some sign of regret in his eyes, but there was none. Only a free-flowing happiness that reflected her own feelings exactly.

"Where were you last night?" Norah asked late the next morning. "I came home from Julie's wedding shower and you were nowhere to be found."

Steffie spread a thin layer of her sister's strawberry jam across her English muffin. "I went out for a while." She didn't add any details because her father was sitting at the table, lingering over his cup of coffee and the paper. He'd make all the wrong assumptions if he knew she'd been with Charles.

They'd spent nearly two hours driving around the area. Charles had taken her past several new businesses, including fast-food restaurants and some specialty boutiques. He'd shown her the recently constructed six-plex movie theater, a new housing complex and a brand-new mall on the outskirts of town. The drive had been highlighted by an ongoing commentary that included the latest gossip.

Steffie hadn't enjoyed herself so much in ages. Charles had been entertaining and fun, and he seemed to take pains never to refer to their past differences.

It was late when they'd gotten back to the house, but they sat in the car for another thirty minutes, talking, before Steffie went inside.

She'd fully expected to lie awake half the night savoring the time she'd spent with him, but to her astonishment, she'd fallen asleep immediately.

"Steffie was out with Charles," their father announced without looking up from his paper. "She didn't get home until late."

Steffie feverishly worked the knife back and forth across the muffin, spreading the already thin layer of jam even thinner.

"Charles Tomaselli?" Norah repeated as though she wasn't sure she'd heard correctly.

"Two girls and a boy," David returned cheerfully.

"I beg your pardon?" Steffie asked.

"You and Charles," he answered. "You're going to get married and within the next few years have your own family."

Rather than argue with her father or listen to more of this, Steffie glanced at her sister. "I need to do a few errands around town, but then I'm driving to Portland. Does anyone need anything?"

"Portland?" her father echoed. "Whatever for?"

"I thought it was time I applied for my doctorate and a part-time teaching position at the university. I *am* qualified, Dad, as you well know since you paid dearly for my education."

"But you can't worry about finding work now."

"I realize the country's in a recession, but—"

"I'm not talking about the economy," he said. "You're going to be married before the end of the summer, so don't go complicating everything with a job."

Steffie could feel the heat leap into her face. He seemed so certain of a marriage between her and Charles, and that exasperated her no end. "Dad, *please* listen—"

"It doesn't make sense for you to be starting a job or a course and then taking time off for a honeymoon."

Steffie wasn't sure if it was a good idea to humor him anymore. This had gone on long enough, but she didn't know what to say. She was aware that her father claimed everything would work out between Valerie and Colby, too. After seeing her older sister's pale, drawn features that morning, Steffie had no faith in her father's words. Not that she'd really ever believed him...

"I don't actually expect to make a lot of contacts, since most of the offices won't be open on a Saturday, but I'm hoping to look around, check out the library, get a few names. Obtaining a teaching position now might be difficult, anyway, especially for the fall session. But I'd like to get started on a thesis soon."

"In other words you're going to Portland, no matter what I say?"

"Exactly."

"Then go shopping when you're done," her father

suggested. "Try on a few wedding dresses. Both you and your sister are going to need 'em. Soon."

Norah was watching Steffie closely and spoke the moment their father had left the kitchen.

"What are we going to do?" Norah pleaded.

"I don't have a clue," Steffie said, fully agreeing with her sister's concern. "If Dad insists on believing—"

"Not Dad," Norah blurted out impatiently. "I'm talking about Valerie."

Steffie's exasperation with her father was quelled by her compassion for Valerie. "What *can* we do?"

Norah's face was pinched with worry. "That's the problem. I don't know, but we can't let her leave town like this. She came down early this morning…. I decided I had to tell her about Colby dating Sherry Waterman."

"How'd Valerie take it?"

"I don't know. She's so hard to read sometimes. It was as if she already knew, which is impossible." Norah frowned. "I wish you'd talk to her again. She's in her room now and, Steffie, I'm really worried about her. She's in love with Colby—she admitted it—but she seems resigned to losing him."

Steffie thought she understood her older sister's feelings.

"To complicate matters," Norah went on, "Valerie and I started talking and…arguing, and Dad heard us. He asked what we were fighting about."

"What did you say to him?"

"I didn't get a chance to say anything. Dad did all the

talking. At least he and I agree. Dad believes Valerie should go talk this out with Colby, too. But I don't think she will."

"Where's Valerie now?" Steffie asked.

Norah looked away. "She's upstairs."

"Doing what?" Her sister had been spending a lot of time alone in her room lately.

"I don't know, but I think you should go to her. Someone's got to. Valerie needs us, only she's so independent she doesn't know how to ask."

Steffie disagreed. Her sister was getting—and apparently ignoring—advice from just about everyone, when what she needed to do was listen to her own heart.

"What's all this about you and Charles?" Norah asked with open curiosity. "I didn't know you even liked him."

In light of their recent confrontation over the newspaper article, it was natural for her sister to assume that.

"We're just friends."

"Which is definitely an improvement," Norah muttered.

Eager to leave before Norah asked more questions, Steffie went upstairs to her room. She toyed with the idea of talking to her sister, of telling her that seeking a long-distance cure for a broken heart didn't work.

But Valerie was intelligent enough to make her own decisions, and Steffie didn't feel qualified to say or do any more than she already had.

She dressed in a bright blue suit for her trip to Portland, one Valerie would have approved of had she been home. Her sister had mysteriously disappeared without saying where she was headed.

Steffie was on her way out the door when her father stopped her. "Sit on the porch with me awhile, will you, Princess?"

"Of course." The wicker chair beside her father had belonged to her mother. Steffie sat next to him and gazed out over the sun-bright orchard she loved so much.

"Are you serious about this—getting a teaching position and all?"

"Yes. I can't stay home and do nothing. It'd be a waste of my education."

"Wait, Princess."

All his talk of marriage was beginning to annoy her. "But, Dad—"

"Just for a couple of weeks. You've been home such a short while— I don't want you to move away just yet. All I ask is that you delay a bit longer."

"I won't be moving out right away…" She hesitated. She couldn't deny her father anything, and he knew it. "Two weeks," she promised reluctantly. "We'll visit, catch up, make some plans. Then I'll start looking for an apartment."

"Is Charles coming for dinner tonight?"

"No." She'd invited him, but he had a late-afternoon meeting and doubted he'd be back in time.

"He's going to miss out on your Italian dinner."

"There'll be others."

"You should fix a plate and take it into town for him. A bachelor like Charles doesn't often get the opportunity to enjoy a home-cooked dinner."

"He seems to be doing just fine on his own," Steffie said, hiding a smile. Her father wasn't even trying to be subtle.

"He's a fine young man."

"Yes, I know. I think he's probably one of the most talented newsmen I've ever read. To be honest, I'm surprised he's still in Orchard Valley. I thought one of the big-city newspapers would've lured him away long before now."

"They've tried, but Charles likes living here. He's turned down several job offers."

"How do you know?" That he'd received other offers didn't surprise Steffie, but that her father was privy to the information did. Then she remembered he and Charles had worked together on the farm-worker article.

"I know Charles quite well," her father answered. "We've become good friends the past few years."

Steffie crossed her legs. "I'd forgotten the two of you wrote that article."

Her father shook his head. "Charles wrote nearly every word of that story. All I did was get a few of the details for him and add a comment now and then, but that was it."

"He credits you with doing a lot more."

Her father was silent for a few minutes, reflective. Steffie wondered if he was worrying about Valerie the way Norah had been. She was about to say something when her father spoke.

"Charles is going to make me a fine son-in-law."

Steffie closed her eyes, trying to control the burst of impatience his words produced.

"Daddy, don't, please," she murmured.

"Don't what?"

"Talk about Charles marrying me."

"Why ever not?" he asked, sounding almost offended. "Why, Princess, he's loved you for years, only I was too blind to notice. I guess I had my head in the clouds, because it's as clear as rainwater to me now. Soon after you left for Italy, he started coming around, asking about you. Only…he was so subtle about it I didn't realize what he was doing until I saw the two of you together last night."

"I know, but—"

"You don't have a clue, do you?" her father said, chuckling and shaking his head. "Can't say I blame you since I didn't guess it myself."

The way her father made it sound, Charles had spent the past three years pining away for her. Steffie knew that couldn't be true. He was the reason she'd left. He'd humiliated her, laughed at her.

"When your mother said you'd be marrying Charles—"

"Dad, *please*." Steffie felt close to tears. "I'm not marrying Charles."

He studied her, eyes narrowed in concern. "What's wrong, Princess? You love him, don't you?"

"I did…but that was a long time ago when I was young and very foolish." Her father had no way of knowing just *how* foolish she'd been.

Even after the incident in Charles's home, when she'd soaked in his tub until her skin resembled a raisin, she hadn't stopped. Some odd quirk of her nature refused to let her believe he didn't want her, not when she loved him so desperately.

Oh, no, she hadn't been willing to leave well enough alone. So she'd plotted and planned his downfall.

Literally.

Leaving a message at the newspaper office that her father needed to see him right away, Steffie had waited in the stable for Charles's arrival. She'd spread fresh hay in the first stall.

No one was home and she tacked a note on the front door directing Charles to the stable.

He'd arrived right on time. She had to say that for him; he was punctual to a fault. He hesitated when he saw she was there alone, then asked to talk to her father. He kept his distance—which might have had something to do with the pitchfork in her hand.

Steffie had planned this meeting right down to the minutest detail. She'd worn tight jeans and a checkered shirt, half unbuttoned and tied at her waist.

She remembered Charles repeating that he was anxious to talk to her father. Among other things, he'd told her, he wanted to clear the air about what was happening between him and Steffie.

At the time she'd nearly laughed out loud. *Nothing* was happening, despite her best efforts.

Steffie remembered again how perfect her timing

had been. As she was chatting with him, explaining that she wasn't sure where her father had gone, she set aside the pitchfork and started up the ladder that led to the loft. At precisely the right moment, she lost her balance, just as she'd planned. After teetering for a second, she dropped into Charles's arms.

He broke her fall, but the impact of her weight slamming against him had taken them both to the floor, and into the fresh hay. For a moment, neither said a word.

"Are you all right?" He spoke first, his voice low and angry.

Steffie had never been more "all right" in her life. For the first time she was in Charles's arms and he held on to her as though he never intended to let her go, as though this was exactly where he'd always wanted her to be.

Steffie had gazed down on him and slowly shaken her head. His gaze had gone to her parted lips and then his hands were in her hair and with a groan he'd guided her mouth to his. The kiss was wild, crazily intense. No man had ever kissed her with such hunger or need. Steffie didn't understand what she was feeling; all she knew was that she wanted Charles more than she'd ever wanted anything. So she'd done what came instinctively. She'd kissed him back with the same searing hunger, until it seemed neither of them would be able to endure the intensity any longer.

Steffie would never forget how he'd rolled away from her, bounding effortlessly to his feet, breathing hard.

At first he'd said nothing. Steffie knew she'd have to

speak first. So she'd looked up at him and said what had been on her heart from the moment they'd met. She'd told him simply, honestly, how much she loved him.

Steffie would forever remember what happened next.

Charles had stared down at her in silence for several heart-stopping seconds, and then he'd begun to laugh. Deep belly laughs, as though she'd said the funniest thing he'd ever heard.

She was exactly what he needed, he'd said with a twinge of sarcasm—a lovesick girl running after him. How many times did he have to tell her he wasn't interested? When he was ready for a woman in his life, he wanted exactly that, a *woman,* not a child. Especially not one as immature as she was.

He'd said more, but by then Steffie was running toward the house, tears streaking her face. The sound of his laughter had followed her, taunting her, ridiculing her.

"Charles has loved you all these years," her father said now. He spoke confidently, crashing into her memories and dragging her back to the present. The past was so painful that Steffie was content to leave it behind.

"He's never loved me," she whispered through a haze of remembered pain.

"Ah, my sweet Princess," her father countered. "That's where you're wrong."

# *Six*

"Dad, listen to me." Steffie stood, turning her head for fear her father would see the tears glistening in her eyes. "Whatever you do, please don't say anything to Charles about—you know?"

"Being in love with you?"

"That, too," she pleaded, "but I'm particularly concerned about this marriage thing."

"That worries you?"

"Yes, Dad, it worries me a great deal."

"You don't understand, do you?" he asked softly.

"Oh, Dad, you're the one who doesn't understand."

"Steffie, my Princess, don't limit yourself to the things you understand," her father said in the gentlest voice imaginable, "otherwise you'll miss half of what life has to offer."

She had to leave, had to escape before she dissolved into an emotional storm of tears. Not until she was in the car, heading she didn't know where, did she realize her father hadn't promised one way or the other. He might well blurt everything to Charles.

By the time Steffie had reached Orchard Valley, she'd composed herself. She'd do her errands—pick up dry cleaning, visit the small local library, mail a birthday card to little Mario in Italy—before she drove to Portland. Because it was Saturday, Main Street was busy and she was fortunate to find a parking spot. Not so fortunate as she would have liked, however, since the only available space was directly in front of the newspaper office.

For at least ten minutes, Steffie sat in the family station wagon, considering whether to talk to Charles herself. *Should* she warn him about her father's crazy dream, his matchmaking hopes?

She was still debating the issue when she saw him, talking to the girl at the front desk. Her heart gladdened at the mere sight of him. He'd removed his suit jacket and the sleeves of his white shirt were rolled halfway up his arms. He was so attractive, so compelling. For several minutes she watched him, mesmerized.

At first glance, Steffie thought Charles might have been talking to Norah, but that was impossible. The resemblance was there, though. This young woman was blonde and exceptionally pretty. Even from inside her car, Steffie could see how she gazed up at Charles with wide, adoring eyes.

The dread that went through her was immediate and

unstoppable. She was jealous, and she hated it. The blonde was probably Wendy, the apprentice Charles had mentioned, and Steffie didn't doubt for an instant that she was in love with him. Not that Steffie blamed her; she'd once played the role of doting female herself. Was playing it even now, despite her most strenuous efforts.

Charles was still talking to his intern, his hand resting against the back of her chair. He leaned forward as the two of them reviewed something, their heads close together. The blonde laughed at some remark of his and smiled up at him, her heart in her eyes.

Steffie couldn't watch any more. It was like looking back several years and seeing what a fool she'd made of herself. Hurriedly she got out of the car and swung her purse over her shoulder. Forcing her eyes away from the newspaper office, she locked the car door. She was about to walk down the street when Charles stepped onto the sidewalk.

"Stephanie, hello." He sounded surprised to see her. More than that, he sounded pleased.

"Hi," she returned awkwardly, feeling guilty, although she wasn't sure why. It wasn't as if she'd actually been spying on him.

"Where are you headed?" he asked, giving her business suit an appreciative glance.

"I—I was thinking about driving into Portland and visiting the university after I do some errands here. I plan eventually to rent an apartment in the city, but Dad…" She hesitated.

Charles grinned knowingly. "But your father wasn't delighted with the idea."

"Exactly. I promised him I'd wait another couple of weeks."

"Why two weeks?"

"Uh…" For a few seconds, she panicked, wondering if Charles had guessed, wondering if her father had mentioned his dream, praying he hadn't. "It seemed like a reasonable compromise."

"Have you got a moment? I'd like you to meet Wendy. She's the intern I was telling you about. Bart's here, as well. You remember Bart, don't you?"

Steffie bit her lip, feeling reluctant. The last time she'd been to the newspaper office she'd come bent on vengeance, with threats of a lawsuit burning in her eyes.

"Tell you what, I'll throw in lunch. I've got an appointment at one, but it's barely twelve now."

She was still caught in the throes of indecision, when Charles took her firmly by the elbow and escorted her inside. She felt a wave of relief; after all, the opportunity to spend time with him, even a few minutes squeezed in between appointments, was too precious to decline.

It might have been Steffie's imagination, but the people in the newspaper office seemed delighted to see her. She wondered what Charles could possibly have said to salvage her reputation.

A couple of the reporters, one of whom she remembered from high school, welcomed her back to Orchard Valley. Bart, the pressman, inquired about her father's health. Even Wendy seemed inclined to like her, which raised Steffie's guilt by several uncomfortable notches.

"I'll be back at one," Charles said as he guided Steffie out the front door.

"But—" Bart stopped abruptly when Charles cut him off with a glare.

"I'll be here in plenty of time," he promised. "What's your pleasure?" he asked, smiling down at her.

"Whatever's most convenient for you."

"The Half Moon's serving sandwiches now. How does that sound?"

"Great." When Steffie left for Italy, the Half Moon, just down the street from the *Clarion,* had been a small coffee shop.

Now she saw that it had been expanded and modernized. While Charles placed their order, Steffie found them a table. Several customers, old acquaintances, greeted her and asked about her father, and before she realized it, she was completely at ease, laughing and joking with the people around her.

When Charles returned with their turkey-and-tomato sandwiches and coffee, she smiled at him happily, content to shed the troubled thoughts she'd carried into town with her. At least for the moment...

"How's your father this morning?" Charles asked, holding his sandwich with both hands to keep bits of tomato and lettuce from escaping.

"Cantankerous as ever." Opinionated, too, and occasionally illogical, but she didn't say any of that. Even if she decided to warn Charles, now didn't seem to be the time. Not when they were sitting across from each other, relaxed and lighthearted, and all the world felt right.

The hour passed quickly. This kind of pure, simple happiness never lasted, she told herself. But, oh, how she wished it could. Charles seemed equally reluctant for their visit to end.

Steffie walked back to work with him. "Thanks for lunch," she said, standing on the sidewalk in front of the office.

"I'll call you," Charles promised as Bart came out, looking anxiously at his watch. "I'll be right there," Charles told him, a bit impatiently. He turned back to Steffie. "Sometime tomorrow?"

"Sure." She nodded eagerly.

*Sometime tomorrow.* A few short hours and yet it felt like a lifetime away.

Valerie was leaving.

Steffie did try talking to her. She'd tried to explain that running away from love wouldn't help; it would just follow her wherever she went. Her sister had listened, then quietly packed her bags.

Sunday morning, when Valerie was about to go, Colby showed up unexpectedly. Steffie was thrilled; it was as if everything she'd read about the power of love, everything she'd always secretly believed, was true. Colby would prove it. He'd come to declare his love and sweep Valerie off her feet.

It soon became clear, however, that Colby wasn't there because of Valerie. He hadn't known she was catching a flight that afternoon, and when he heard, he seemed to accept it as inevitable. Furthermore, he had no intention of stopping her. No intention of asking her to stay. If anything, he seemed almost relieved at her imminent departure.

When the moment came for Valerie to go, Steffie thought she might burst into tears herself. She'd so desperately wanted to believe in the power of love, in its ability to knock down barriers and leap over obstacles.

Valerie hugged them all farewell, and with shoulders held stiff and straight, walked from the porch to her rental car. Then, just before she left, she turned and looked at Colby.

Steffie would always remember the tenderness she saw in her sister's eyes. It was as though she'd reached back, one last time, to say goodbye…and to thank him. At least, that was how it seemed to Steffie. She'd never been so affected by a mere glance. That look of Valerie's was full of love, but it also expressed dignity and a gracious acceptance.

Steffie was trying to sort out her mingled emotions of anger and pain as Valerie drove away. She turned to Colby, who still stared after her sister's car. It took every ounce of self-control she had not to scream at him. Only the anguish in his eyes prevented her from lashing out, and when she recognized the intensity of his pain, her own anger was replaced by a bleak hopelessness.

"She's gone," he whispered.

"She'll be back," her father said with the same un-questioning confidence that had driven Steffie nearly mad with frustration.

"No," she insisted, her voice quavering. "She won't. Not for a very long time."

Then, unable to face either Colby or her father, she dashed back into the house. Norah followed soon afterward, and Steffie realized that her younger sister was crying.

"She's going to marry Rowdy Cassidy," Norah wailed. "What's so terrible is that she doesn't even *love* him."

"Then what makes you think Valerie would do anything so foolish?" Steffie asked calmly. Valerie might be unhappy about losing Colby Winston, but she was too sensible to enter into a loveless marriage.

"You don't understand," Norah said as she continued to sob. "*He's* in love with her. He's called nearly every day and sent flowers and…and Valerie's so vulnerable right now. I just know she's going to make a terrible mistake."

"Val's not going to do anything stupid," Steffie reassured her sister. Valerie wouldn't marry her boss on the rebound—Steffie was confident of that. Deep down, she knew exactly what her sister would be doing for the next three years—if not longer. She knew because she'd done it herself. Valerie would try to escape into her work, to the exclusion of everything else. Because then she wouldn't have time to hurt, time to deal with regrets and might-have-beens. She wouldn't have time to look back or relive the memories.

An hour later, Steffie took a glass of iced tea out to her father, who stubbornly refused to leave the porch. He sat in his rocking chair, anxiously studying the road. "They'll both be back," he said again.

Steffie didn't try to disillusion him. By nightfall he'd be forced to accept the truth without her prompting.

Within ten minutes of Valerie's departure, Colby had left, too. He hadn't raced down the driveway in hot pursuit or given the slightest indication that he was going anywhere but back to town.

"Mark my words," her father said confidently. "Valerie and Colby will be married before the end of June."

"Dad…"

"And you and Charles will follow a few weeks later. All three of my daughters are going to be married this summer. I know it in my heart, as surely as I know my own name."

Although she nearly choked, Steffie swallowed her words of argument.

Needing some physical activity to vent her frustrations, she saddled Princess. She knew better than to try her luck with Fury again. But the mare, who was generally docile, seemed to sense Steffie's mood and galloped down the long pasture road and across the rocky field until they reached the bluff. The same place Fury had taken her.

Holding the reins, Steffie slid off the mare's back and sat on the very rock she had before. She lost track of time as she sat looking out on the valley, thinking about Valerie. And Colby. Remembering her own disastrous relationship with Charles, and how her willful behavior had destroyed any chance they'd had three years ago. Now there seemed to be a fresh beginning for her and Charles, however fragile it might be. Not for Valerie, though… Life wasn't fair, she thought, and love didn't make everything perfect.

She rode slowly back and had just finished rubbing down Princess and leading her into her stall when Charles appeared. "I thought I heard someone here." He stood by the stable door, hands on his hips, smiling.

"Charles." She shouldn't have been so surprised to see him. After all, he'd made a point of telling her he'd be in touch.

"Your dad figured you'd gone out riding, but he seemed to think you'd be home soon."

"Have you been waiting long?"

"Not really. Your father's kept me entertained."

"Is he still on the front porch?"

"He hasn't moved since I got here."

Dispirited, Steffie looked away. "That's what I was afraid of. Valerie's gone, and he seems to believe she'll come back if he sits there long enough."

Charles frowned heavily. "Is something going on? A problem?"

"No," she answered quickly, perhaps too quickly because Charles's eyes narrowed suspiciously. "I mean, nothing you need to worry about. Dad desperately wants to believe Colby and Val will kiss and make up—that's the reason he's being so stubborn. By dinnertime he'll have to recognize that it simply isn't going to happen."

It might've been because she was nervous and flustered, or maybe she just wasn't watching where she was going, but Steffie tripped over a bale of hay.

Although she threw out her arms in an effort to right herself, it was too late. She fell forward, but before she completely lost her balance, Charles caught her around the waist. He twisted his body so that when they went down, he took the brunt of the fall.

It was as though the years had evaporated. They'd been in virtually the same position on that previous occasion, with Steffie sprawled over him, her heart pounding. Only this time she hadn't manipulated the circumstances. This time she wasn't in control.

They were both breathing hard. A tumult of confused emotions raged within her, and she braced her arms against him, ready to get up and move away. Instead, his arms, which were around her waist, held her firmly in place.

"It seems we've been here before," he said, his eyes gazing into hers.

"I—" She stopped abruptly and nodded.

"Do you remember what happened that day?"

Incapable of speaking, she nodded again.

"Do you remember the way we kissed?"

She couldn't look at him, couldn't allow him to read the answer in her eyes.

He held her fast for another long moment before he gradually eased his hold. "Let's talk about that time."

"No!" she cried. The instant she was free, she rushed to her feet, not realizing she must have sprained her ankle. But when she placed her weight on her left foot she experienced a sharp stabbing pain. She couldn't suppress a whimper as she leaned against the stall door for support.

"You're hurt," Charles said, immediately getting to his feet. He slipped his arm around her waist.

"I'm sure it's nothing. I've just twisted my ankle— it hardly hurts at all," she lied.

Without another word, Charles effortlessly scooped her into his arms.

"Charles, please," she said, growing angry. "I'm perfectly fine. It's a minor sprain, nothing more. There's no need for this."

He didn't reply but began to carry her out of the stable.

"Where are you taking me?" she demanded.

"The kitchen. You should put ice on it right away."

"I want you to know I don't appreciate these caveman tactics."

"That's too bad." He was short of breath by the time he reached the back door, which infuriated Steffie even more. "Put me down this instant," she snapped.

"In a minute." He managed, after some difficulty, to open the door, then deposited her unceremoniously in a chair—like a sack of flour, she thought with irritation. He was pulling open the freezer section of the refrigerator and removing the ice-cube tray.

She rested her sore foot on her opposite knee and was about to remove her shoe when he stopped her. "I'll do that."

"Charles, you're being ridiculous."

He didn't answer, but carefully drew off her shoe and sock. His fingers were tender as he examined her ankle, and it felt strangely intimate to have him touch her like this.

"I told you already—it doesn't hurt anymore," she argued. "I might have gotten up too fast or put my foot down wrong. I don't feel a thing now."

"Try standing up."

Cautiously she did. His arm circled her waist as she gingerly placed her weight on the foot. "See," she said, feeling both triumphant and foolish. "There doesn't seem to be any damage."

"I wouldn't be so sure. Try walking."

The floor felt cool against her bare foot as she took a guarded first step. There was barely a twinge. She tried again. Same result. "See?" she said. "I'm fine." And she proceeded to prove it by marching around the kitchen.

"Good." Charles replaced the ice-cube tray in the freezer, but he was frowning.

"Don't look so disappointed," she teased as she pulled on her sock and shoe.

He glanced at her, then smiled slowly, sensually. "I've heard of some inventive ways to avoid kissing a man, but…" He let the rest fade as he sat down beside her, then pulled her chair toward him until they sat face to face, so close their knees touched.

Steffie shut her eyes as his hands came to rest on her shoulders. His breathing grew ragged and he whispered her name. "Stephanie," he said, leaning forward to touch her lips with his own.

Steffie was afraid—of his kiss and of her own response. But she felt a thrill of excitement, too. He must have sensed that, because the quality of his kiss changed from gentle caress to fierce desire.

Charles groaned, and she slid her hands up his chest, delighting in the feel of hard, smooth muscles as she gave herself fully to his kiss.

Suddenly he broke away, his shoulders heaving. Steffie let her eyes flutter open and for a long silent moment they stared at each other.

His hand reached out to touch her hair, a small, intimate gesture that moved her unbearably.

Then he stretched out his arms, clasping her by the waist and lifting her from the chair to set her securely in his lap. She wasn't given the opportunity to protest before his mouth claimed hers once more.

This time his kiss was slow and gentle, as tender as the earlier kiss had been hungry and demanding. She felt herself melting in his arms, surrendering the last of her resistance.

"I want to talk about what happened," he whispered.

She knew what he meant, and she wanted none of it. That scene in the stable—the fall she'd faked—was much too embarrassing to examine even now. "That was in the past."

"It has to be settled between us."

"No," she said, trying to change his mind with a deep, hungry kiss.

His voice was rough when she finished. "Steff, we have to clear the past before we can talk about the future."

"We only just met, remember?" He was the one who'd suggested they start over. He couldn't bury the past and then ask that they exhume it.

"Just listen to me…"

"Not yet," she pleaded. Maybe never, her heart whispered, balking at the idea of reliving a time that had been so painful for her.

"Soon." He tangled his fingers in her hair and spread kisses across her face.

"Maybe," she agreed reluctantly.

The sound of laughter broke into the haze of her pleasure. At least Steffie assumed it was laughter. It took her a wild moment to realize the sound was coming from the porch, and that it must be her father. Not knowing what to think, she slowly broke away from Charles.

"Is that David laughing?" he asked.

Steffie shrugged. "I'd better find out if something's wrong."

He nodded, and they walked hand in hand to the porch.

"Dad?" she asked softly when she saw her father, rocking contentedly. His smile broadened when he noticed her and Charles. His gaze fell to their hands, which were still clasped tightly together, and his eyes fairly twinkled. "Check the freezer, will you? By heaven, I wish I'd thought of this sooner."

"The freezer?" she repeated, glancing at Charles, wondering if her father had lost his wits. "Why do you want me to check it?"

"We need something special to fix for dinner tonight. We're going to have a celebration!"

Steffie frowned in puzzlement. "What kind of celebration?"

"There's going to be a wedding in the family."

Steffie groaned inwardly. "Dad…"

"Don't argue with me, Princess, there isn't time."

"But, Dad…"

"See there?" he said, pointing toward the long stretch of driveway. "What did I tell you?"

Steffie looked, but she couldn't see anything except a small puff of dust, barely discernible against the skyline.

"I was about to give up on those two," he said with a wry chuckle. "They're both too stubborn for their own good. I have to admit they gave me pause, but your mother was right. Guess I shouldn't have doubted her."

"Dad, what are you talking about?"

"Your sister and Colby. They're on their way back to the house now."

Steffie glanced up again, and this time the make and color of the car was unmistakable. Colby was returning to the house. And although she couldn't clearly tell who the passenger was, she knew it had to be her sister.

# *Seven*

"Even now I can't believe it," Valerie said wistfully, sitting cross-legged on her bed. Steffie and Norah lounged on the opposite end, listening.

"Colby actually chased you down on the freeway?" Norah wanted to know.

Valerie's smile lit up her whole face as she nodded. "It really was romantic to have him race after me. He told me he didn't realize he was planning to do it until he was on the interstate."

"You've got everything worked out?" Steffie asked. From what Norah had told her, and from remarks Valerie herself had made, she knew there were a lot of obstacles standing in the way of this marriage.

"We've talked things out the best we can. It's been a struggle to come up with the right compromises. I've got a call in to Rowdy Cassidy at CHIPS. I think I can talk him into letting me open a branch of the company in

Oregon. He's already done a feasibility study for the Pacific Northwest. He was just waiting until he could find the right person to head it up. He didn't originally have me in mind, but I don't think he'll have a problem giving it to me. Then again—" she paused thoughtfully "—it may be better to discuss this in person."

"Colby doesn't mind if you continue working?" Norah's voice was tinged with disbelief.

"No. Because it's what I need. Naturally he'd rather I was there to pamper him when he gets home from the hospital every night, but this way we'll learn to pamper each other."

"I'm so happy for you." Steffie leaned forward to hug her sister. Valerie's eyes reflected an inner joy that Steffie had never seen in her before. This was what love—real love—did for a person. When two people cared this deeply for each other, it couldn't help but show.

"Now that we've decided to go ahead with the wedding, Colby wants to do it as soon as possible," Valerie went on to say. "I hope everyone's willing to work fast and hard because we've got a wedding to plan for next month."

"Next month!" Norah's blue eyes widened incredulously.

"I was lucky to get him to wait *that* long. Colby would rather we flew to Vegas tonight and—"

"No way!" was Norah and Steffie's automatic response.

"I never thought I'd be the sentimental sort," Valerie admitted sheepishly, "but I actually want a large fancy wedding. Colby loves me enough to agree, as long as I organize it quickly. Once that man makes a decision, there's no holding him back."

Steffie smiled to herself. Dr. Colby Winston was in for a real surprise. Valerie was talented enough in the organizational department to manage the United Nations. If he gave her a month to arrange their wedding, she'd do a beautiful job of it with time to spare.

A wedding so soon meant the family was about to be caught up in a whirlwind of activity, but that suited Steffie. It was time for them to celebrate. The grieving, the anxiety, were over.

"You've been seeing a lot of Charles lately, haven't you?" Norah asked, looking expectantly at Steffie. "Do you think we could make this a double wedding?"

Valerie smiled broadly at Steffie, as though she'd be in favor of the idea, too.

"I haven't been seeing *that* much of Charles," Steffie answered, thrusting out her chin. She realized she sounded defensive. "Well, I—I suppose we have been together quite a bit lately, but there's certainly never been any talk of marriage."

"I've always liked Charles," Norah said, studying Steffie closely. "I mean, I could go for this guy, given the least bit of encouragement. First Valerie falls in love and now you. You know, it's a little unfair. I'm the one who lives at home and you two fly in and within a few weeks nab the two most eligible men in town."

"Me?" Steffie argued. "You make it sound like a done deal. Trust me, it isn't."

"You're in love with him," Valerie said quietly. "Aren't you?"

Steffie didn't reply. She was unwilling to openly admit her feelings for Charles. It would be so easy to fool herself into believing he held the same tenderness for her. But he'd never said so, and other than a few shared kisses he hadn't given her any indication he cared.

*But he had,* something inside her said.

Steffie refused to listen. She couldn't, wouldn't, forget that she'd made a fool of herself over him, not once but three times. Because she'd cared, and he hadn't.

"I don't know how Charles feels about me," Steffie said in a soft steady voice.

"You're joking!" Norah exclaimed.

And Valerie added, "Steffie, it's obvious how he feels."

Steffie discounted their assurances with a shrug. "For all I know, he could be hanging around me in order to get close to Norah."

"Charles? No way." Both Valerie and Norah burst into loud peals of laughter.

"Are you saying you wouldn't mind me dating him?" Norah teased, winking at Valerie.

"Feel free." In fact, Steffie would throttle Norah if she went within ten feet of Charles, though she could hardly say so.

"I hope you're joking," Norah said, shaking her head. "I should've seen what was going on a long time ago. I don't know how I could've been so dense. Charles and Dad became friends shortly after you left—good friends."

"That doesn't mean a thing," Steffie insisted. She didn't need anyone else building up her hopes, and although her sisters meant well, their encouragement would only make her disappointment harder to bear.

"It wouldn't mean much if Charles hadn't made a point of asking about you every time he stopped by," Norah was saying. "I have to hand it to the guy, though—he was always subtle about his questions."

"Now that you mention it, whenever I talked to Charles, Steffie's name cropped up in the conversation," Valerie reported thoughtfully. "I should have guessed myself."

"You were too involved with Colby to see anything else," Norah teased and then sighed. She crossed her arms and rested them atop her bent knees. "Don't get me wrong, I'm happy for you two, but I wish I'd fall in love. Don't you think it's my turn?"

"Aren't you leaping to conclusions here?" Steffie asked. She wasn't exactly sporting an engagement ring the way Valerie was. She and Charles hadn't arrived at that stage of commitment—and probably never would. Besides, her past mistakes with him had been the result of leaping to certain incorrect conclusions about his feelings, and she wasn't ready for a repeat performance.

Steffie didn't see Charles again until Tuesday afternoon. She wasn't surprised not to hear from him, knowing how involved he was with the production of the paper during the first part of every week.

Valerie and Steffie had driven into town to visit The

Petal Pusher, the local flower shop. Valerie had decided on a spring color theme for her wedding and had already chosen material for Steffie's and Norah's gowns in a pale shade of green and a delicate rose.

Valerie angled the car into the slot closest to the flower shop. Since the newspaper office was almost directly across the street, it was natural for her to glance curiously in that direction.

"You haven't talked to Charles in a couple of days, have you?"

"He's busy with the paper."

"There's time to stop in now and say hello if you want. I'll be talking to the florist, so you might as well."

Steffie was tempted, but felt uncomfortable about interrupting Charles at work. "Some other time," she said with a feigned lack of interest, though in actuality she was starving for the sight of him. Helping Valerie plan her wedding had forced some long-buried emotions to the surface. Steffie hadn't admitted until these past few weeks how deeply she longed for marriage herself. A family of her own. A husband to love and live with her whole life.

A husband.

Her mind stumbled over the word. There'd only ever been one man she could imagine as her husband, and that was Charles. Even though Steffie knew it was unwise, she'd started dreaming again. She found herself fantasizing what her life would be like if she was married...to Charles. She wanted to blame her sisters for putting such thoughts in her head, but she couldn't. Those dreams and fantasies had been there for years. The problem was that she couldn't suppress them anymore.

An hour later, at the same moment as Steffie and Valerie were leaving the flower shop, Charles happened to step out of the *Clarion* office.

Steffie instinctively looked across the street, where he was walking with Wendy, deep in conversation. Something must have told him she was there because he glanced in her direction. He grinned warmly.

Steffie relaxed and waved. He returned the gesture, then spoke to Wendy before jogging across the street to join Steffie and her sister.

"Hello," he said, but his eyes lingered on Steffie. He barely seemed to notice Valerie's presence.

"Hi." It was ridiculous to feel so shy with him. "I'd have stopped in to say hello, but I knew you'd be busy."

"I'm never too busy for you." His eyes were affectionate and welcoming.

"See," Valerie hissed close to Steffie's ear. Then, more loudly, "I've got a couple of errands to run, if you two would like a chance to talk."

Charles checked his watch. "Come back to the office with me?"

"Sure." If he'd suggested they stand on their heads in the middle of Main Street, Steffie would have willingly agreed.

Valerie cast a quick glance at the clock tower. "How about if I meet you back at the car in—"

"Half an hour," Charles supplied, reaching for

Steffie's hand. "There's something I'd like to show you," he told her.

"Fine, I'll see you then, Steff," Valerie said cheerfully. She set off at a brisk walk, without looking back.

Their fingers entwined, Charles led Steffie across the street to the newspaper office. "I was going to save this for later, but now's as good a time as any." He ushered her in and guided her down the center aisle, past the obviously busy staff, to his desk.

Steffie wasn't sure what to expect, but a mock-up of the *Clarion*'s second page wasn't it. As far as she could see, it was the same as any other inside page she'd read over the years.

"Clearly I'm missing something," she said after a moment. "Is the type different?"

"Nope, we've used the same fonts as always." He crossed his arms and leaned against the desk, looking exceptionally pleased with himself.

"How about a hint?" she asked, a bit puzzled.

"I might suggest you read the masthead," he said next, his dark eyes gleaming.

"The masthead," she repeated as she scanned the listings of the newspaper's personnel and the duties they performed.

"All right, I will. Charles Tomaselli, editor and publisher. Roger Simons—"

"Stop right there," he said, holding up his hand.

"Publisher," she said again. "That's new. What exactly does it mean?"

His smile could have lit up a Christmas tree. "It means, my beautiful Stephanie, that I now own the *Orchard Valley Clarion*."

"Charles, that's wonderful!" She resisted the urge to throw her arms around him, but it was difficult.

"My dream's got a mortgage attached," he told her wryly. "A lot of folks think I'm an idiot to risk so much of my future on a medium that's said to be dying. Newspapers are folding all over the country."

"The *Clarion* won't."

"Not if I can help it."

Her heart seemed to spill over with joy. She knew how much Charles loved his work, how committed he was to the community. "I'm so excited about this."

"Me, too," he said, his smile boyishly proud. "I'd say this calls for a celebration, wouldn't you?"

"Most definitely."

"Dinner?"

She nodded eagerly and they set the date for Thursday evening, deciding on a restaurant that overlooked the Columbia River Gorge, about an hour's drive north.

Steffie felt as if her feet didn't touch the pavement as she hurried across the street thirty minutes later to meet her sister. Never, in all the time she'd known Charles, had she seen him happier. And she was happy with him, and *for* him. That was what loving someone meant. It was a truth she hadn't really understood before, not until today. This intense new feeling had taught her that real love wasn't prideful or selfish. Real love meant sharing the happiness—and the sorrows—of the person you loved. Yes, she understood that now. She realized that her past obsession with Charles had focused more on her own desires than on his. Her love had matured.

Charles had wakened within her emotions she hadn't known it was possible to experience. Emotions—and sensations. When she was with him, especially when he kissed her, she felt vibrant and alive.

"You look like you're about to cry, you're so happy," Valerie said when Steffie joined her in the car. "I don't suppose Charles popped the question."

"No," she said with a sigh. "But he asked me to dinner to help him celebrate. Guess what? Charles is the new owner of the *Clarion*."

Valerie didn't seem nearly as excited as Steffie. "He's going to be working a lot of extra hours then, isn't he?"

"He didn't say." If he spent as much time at the newspaper as he had three years earlier, there wouldn't be any extra hours left.

"I suppose his eating habits are atrocious."

Steffie suspected they were, but she shrugged. "I wouldn't know."

"I bet he'd enjoy a home-cooked meal every now and then, don't you?"

Steffie eyed her sister suspiciously. "Is there a point to this conversation?"

"Of course," she answered with a sly grin. "I think you should heat up some of that fabulous spaghetti sauce and take it to him later. You know what they say about the way to a man's heart, don't you?"

"Funny, that sounds exactly like a suggestion of Dad's. What's your interest in this?"

"Well," Valerie said coyly, "that way I wouldn't feel guilty about asking you if I could take some to Colby's. If he tasted your spaghetti sauce and happened to assume, through no error of mine, that I'd cooked this fabulous dinner—" she paused to inhale deeply "—he'd be so overcome by the idea of marrying such a fabulous cook that he'd go over the wedding list with me and not put it off for the third time."

"There's method in your madness, Valerie Bloomfield."

"Naturally. Colby doesn't know that I can't tell one side of a cookie sheet from the other. I don't want to disillusion him quite so soon. He suggested I make dinner tonight and, well, you get the picture."

"I do indeed. I'll be happy to share the spaghetti sauce with you."

"I'll hang around the kitchen to be sure some of the aroma sticks to me."

"I'll give you the recipe if you want."

"I want, but if I have trouble cooking with a microwave, heaven only knows what I'll do once I'm around a stove. One with burners and a real oven."

Steffie chuckled. She certainly had no objection to helping her sister prepare dinner for Colby, but she wasn't sure taking a plate over to Charles's house was such a good plan.

Valerie and Norah convinced her otherwise.

"Charles never did get to sample your cooking," Norah reminded her. "He stopped by and you offered him dinner, but he'd already eaten. Remember?"

"How'd you know that?"

Norah looked mildly surprised, as though everyone must be aware of what went on between Steffie and Charles. "Dad told me."

Her dear, matchmaking father. Steffie should have known.

"It isn't going to hurt anything," Valerie reminded her. "If you want, you can ride into town with me. I'll go over to Charles's house with you and we can drop off the meal, then I'll drive you home."

Steffie still wasn't sure, but Norah and Valerie believed it was a romantic thing to do. They both seemed to think Charles was serious about their relationship.

As for Steffie, she didn't know what to think anymore. In fact, she preferred not to think about their relationship at all. And yet...

She remained hesitant about this project of delivering him a surprise dinner but Valerie and Norah were so certain it would be a success that she went ahead with it.

They were apparently right.

She'd found his door open—that hadn't changed, she thought with a twinge of embarrassment—and had left a container of the sauce, some noodles with instructions and a couple of last-minute extras on his kitchen table.

Steffie was propped up in her bed reading a new

mystery novel at ten-thirty that night. Her bedroom window was open and a breeze whispered through the orchard. The house was quiet; her father had gone to bed an hour earlier, and her sisters were both out for the evening.

When the phone chimed, she answered on the first ring, not wanting it to wake her father.

"How'd you do it?" Charles asked, sounding thoroughly delighted. "I came home exhausted and hungry, thinking I was going to have to throw something in the microwave for dinner. The minute I walked into the house, I smelled this heavenly scent of basil and garlic. I followed my nose to the table and found your note."

"You should thank Valerie and Norah. The whole thing was their idea." Had he been furious, Steffie would gladly have shifted the blame, so she figured it was only right to share the credit.

"I haven't tasted spaghetti that good since my grandmother died. I'd forgotten how delicious homemade sauce can be."

Steffie was warmed by the compliment. "I'm glad you enjoyed it."

"Enjoyed it! You have no idea. It was like stepping back into my childhood to spend the evening with my grandmother. She was a fabulous cook, and so are you."

Steffie leaned against the heap of pillows and closed her eyes, savoring these precious moments.

"The bottle of red wine and the small loaf of French bread were a nice touch," he told her.

"I'm glad," she said again. A dozen unnamed emotions whirled inside her.

"I wish you didn't live so far out of town," Charles said next. "Otherwise I'd come over right now—to thank you."

"I wish I didn't live so far out, too."

"Since we're both making wishes, there are a few other things I'd like, as well," he added in tones as smooth as velvet.

"You're limited to three." How raspy her own voice sounded.

Charles chuckled. "Only three? What happens if I want four?"

"I'm not sure, but I seem to remember reading about a handsome young newsman who was turned into a frog because he got greedy about wishes."

"How many have I got left?"

"Two."

"All right, I'll choose carefully. I wish we were together in your father's stable right now."

"You're wasting one of your wishes on the stable?"

"That's what I said. It seems as though every time I'm there, you end up in my arms. In fact, I'm looking forward to visiting your father's horses again soon."

"That can be arranged. Fury and Princess will be thrilled."

"I'm glad to hear it," he murmured. Steffie could picture him sprawled comfortably on his sofa, talking to her, a glass of wine in his hand.

"Be warned, you have only one wish left."

"Give me a moment—I want to make this good. I've had two glasses of wine and in case you haven't noticed, I'm feeling kind of mellow."

"I noticed." She smiled to herself.

"Know what I'd like?"

"You tell me," she teased.

"With my last wish, I'd like to wipe out the past."

"That one's easy," she said, and even though he couldn't see her, she made a sweeping motion with her hand. "There. It's gone, forgotten, never to be discussed again."

"Uh-oh. I think I made a mistake."

"Why's that?"

"We can't sweep it away."

"Why not?" she asked, striving for a flippant air. "It was one of your wishes, and it's in my power to grant it, so I have."

"But I don't want it wiped out *completely*. Let's talk about it now, Stephanie, get this over with once and for all."

Steffie's heart jolted. "Sorry, it's gone, vanished. I haven't a clue what you're talking about." Willfully she lowered her voice, half pleading with him, not wanting anything to ruin these moments.

The silence stretched between them. "You're right, this isn't something we can discuss over the phone. Certainly not when I'm half drunk and you're so far away."

"You're tired."

"It's funny," Charles told her, and she could hear the satisfaction in his voice. "I'm so exhausted I'm dead on my feet, and at the same time I feel so elated I want to take you in my arms and whirl you around the room."

"You never once mentioned buying the paper." She didn't mean it as a criticism. But he'd managed to keep it a secret not only from her, but from just about everyone in town. When Steffie had mentioned Charles's news to her father, he'd been as pleasantly surprised as she.

"I couldn't, but believe me, I was dying to tell you. Negotiations can be tricky. I was prohibited from saying anything until I'd reached an agreement with Dalton Publishing and the financing had been arranged."

Steffie snuggled down against her pillows. "So much is happening in our lives. First there was Dad's heart attack, and now Valerie's wedding. Oh, Charles, I wish you were here to see Valerie. I didn't know anything in the world could fluster my sister, but I was wrong. Being in love flusters her.

"I was with her Monday when she tried on wedding dresses. My practical, levelheaded older sister would stand in front of a mirror with huge tears running down her cheeks."

"She was crying?"

Steffie smiled at the memory. "Yes, but these were tears of joy. She never allowed herself to believe that Colby loved her enough to work through the things that stood between them. The two of them are so different, and that's been the problem all along. But neither of them seems to understand, even now, that it was those very differences that attracted them to each other."

"*We're* different."

His words gave Steffie pause. "I know but—"

"And I'm attracted to you, Stephanie. Very attracted."

It was ironic that she'd told him how love had completely unsettled her sister, only to be sitting on her own bed a few minutes later with the phone pressed against her ear and the tears sliding down her cheeks.

"Aren't you going to say anything?"

"Yes," she whispered in a trembling voice.

"Stephanie? What's wrong? You sound like you're crying."

"That's the silliest thing I ever heard," she rallied, rubbing her eyes with one hand.

"I wish I was there."

"Sorry," she said, laughing and crying at once, "you're flat out of wishes."

# *Eight*

"More wine?" Charles asked, reaching for the bottle of Chablis in its silver bucket.

"No, thanks," Steffie said, smiling her appreciation. Their dinner had been delectable. It was one meal she wouldn't soon forget, although it was Charles's company that would linger in her mind more than the excellent halibut topped with bay shrimp.

"How about dessert?"

Steffie pressed her hands to her stomach and slowly shook her head. "I couldn't."

"Me neither." He leaned against the back of his chair and gazed out the window to the Columbia River below. The gorge was in one of the most scenic parts of Oregon. Steffie had always loved this view of the mighty river coursing through a rock-bound corridor.

"I've looked forward to this evening for a long time," Charles said, turning back to her.

"I have, too." Until tonight, Steffie had only dreamed of being with Charles like this. As his equal, an adult...a woman in love.

"I don't think I've ever seen you look more beautiful, Stephanie."

His words brought a flush of color to her cheeks. Steffie had dressed carefully, choosing an elegant Italian knit dress in a subdued shade of turquoise. Valerie had lent Steffie her pearl necklace and earrings, and Norah had contributed a splash of her most expensive perfume.

Her sisters and her father, too, had put a good deal of stock in this evening's date. Steffie wasn't sure what her family was expecting. No doubt some miracle. For herself, she was content just to spend the evening with Charles.

"You look wonderful yourself." She wasn't echoing his compliment, but was stating a fact. He'd worn a dark suit with a silk tie of swirling colors against a pale blue shirt.

"Then we must make an attractive couple tonight," Charles commented, rotating the wine goblet between his fingers.

"We must," Steffie agreed.

Charles finished off the last of his wine and set the glass aside. "You were generous enough to grant me three wishes the other night, remember?"

Steffie wasn't likely to forget. She felt warm and shivery inside whenever she thought about their late-night telephone conversation.

"Being the honorable gentleman I am, not to mention talented and handsome, as you so aptly pointed out, it seems only fair that I return the favor. You, my lady, are hereby granted three wishes."

"Anything I want?" Steffie cocked her head.

"Within reason. I'd be willing to drive you to Multnomah Falls to watch the water by moonlight, but I might have a bit of trouble if you decide you want world peace."

"The Falls by moonlight?"

"I was hoping you'd ask for that one."

She blinked at the way he'd turned her question into a pre-approved wish. "Charles," she said, "you're a romantic."

"Don't sound so shocked."

"But I am. I'd never have guessed it."

She was teasing him, and enjoying it and was surprised when he frowned briefly. "That's because we've never discussed what happened—"

"Not tonight," she said, holding a finger to his lips. "It's one of my wishes. We'll discuss nothing unpleasant."

His frown deepened. "I think we should. There's a lot we—"

"You're the one who granted me three wishes," she reminded him solemnly.

He nodded, his expression somewhat disgruntled. "You're right, I did, and if you want to squander one of your wishes, then far be it from me to stop you."

"It's too lovely a night to dredge up the past, especially when it's so embarrassing. Let's just look forward—"

"Fine," Charles agreed quickly and turned to thank their waiter when he brought two cups of steaming coffee to the table. "We'll just look ahead. Now, remember you have one remaining wish."

Steffie hesitated. "Do I have to claim it now?"

"No, but the wishes expire at midnight."

Steffie laughed softly. "You make me feel like Cinderella."

"Perhaps that's because I'd like to be your prince."

His gaze was dark and unguarded. Steffie lowered her eyes, for fear he'd read all the love that was stored in her heart.

"Do I frighten you?" he asked after a moment.

Steffie's eyes flew back to his. "No. I thought I frightened you!"

He laughed outright at that. "Not likely."

They drank their coffee in silence, as though afraid words would destroy the mood. After Charles had paid the bill, he drove toward Multnomah Falls, managing the twisting narrow highway with ease. Steffie had visited the Falls many times, but had always been a bit scared of the drive. However, Charles took the sharp turns in slow, controlled moves, and she relaxed, enjoying the trip.

The rock walls along the road were built of local basalt more than seventy years earlier, during the Depression.

"I love this place," Charles said as they reached the parking area across the roadway from the waterfall. Because it was a weeknight, there were only a few cars in the lot.

Dusk was settling, and the tall, stately firs bordering the falls were silhouetted against the backdrop of a cloud-dappled sky. The forested slopes were already dark as Steffie and Charles began the gradual, winding ascent to the visitors' viewpoint.

A chill raced down her arms and Steffie was grateful she'd brought a thin coat with her. Multnomah Falls was Oregon's highest waterfall, plummeting more than six hundred feet into a swirling pool, then slipping downward in a second, shorter descent. The force of the falling water misted the night.

With his hand at her elbow, Charles guided them to the walkway that wove up the trail. When they got to the footbridge that spanned the falls, Steffie stopped to gaze at the magnificence around her. The sound of falling water roared in her ears.

"If we wait a few minutes, the moon will hit the water," Charles told her. He stood behind her, shielding her from the wind that whipped across the water's churning surface.

Steffie closed her eyes. Not to the beauty of the scene before her, but to the sensation she experienced in Charles's protective embrace.

"I've dreamed of holding you like this," he whispered. "Of wrapping my arms around you and feeling you next to me. I love the way your hair smells. It reminds me of wildflowers and sunshine."

Steffie couldn't speak. She couldn't get even one word past the knot in her throat. She swallowed and slowed her breathing, hoping that might help, because there was so much she longed to say, so many things she yearned to tell him.

"I don't ever want to be separated from you again," Charles told her, his voice raw.

She didn't understand. Charles had all but sent her away. He'd all but cast her out of his life. She turned in his arms until they faced each other and raised her hands to his face.

Charles smiled then and gently gripped her wrists. He moved his head until his mouth met the sensitive skin of her palm, and he kissed her there.

"You know, three years ago there was so much I couldn't tell you," he began.

"I have one wish left," she reminded him. "I want you to kiss me. Now."

"With pleasure." She could hear the smile in his voice.

They'd kissed before, but they'd never shared what they did in those moments. Charles's lips found hers in the sweetest, most loving exchange she'd ever experienced, and Steffie's emotions exploded to life.

Steffie wanted this, wanted it more than anything she'd ever known, yet at the same time she felt overwhelmed by confusion. Charles had ordered her out of his life, laughed at her declaration of love, humiliated her until she couldn't bear to live in the same town. Now, he seemed to be suggesting that he *hadn't* wanted her to go, and that he never wanted her to leave again.

Steffie wasn't sure what to believe. With all her heart

she longed to lose herself in Charles's kiss, to savor all the sensations that flooded her. And yet the uncertainty remained. Did he merely desire her, or did he, too, feel a forever kind of love?

But his kiss wiped out all thought as the joy rushed through her, replacing fear and doubt.

"Someone's coming," Charles whispered suddenly. He broke away, still holding her shoulders, and brushed his mouth against her forehead. Then he released her.

Steffie's father was sitting by the fireplace in his den when she let herself into the house later that night. She saw the lamplight spilling into the entryway and decided to check on him.

"Dad?" David was sitting in the wingback leather chair beside the fireplace, her mother's afghan tucked around his legs. His head drooped and his lips were slightly parted.

Steffie had spoken before she realized he was asleep. But just as she turned to tiptoe from the room, he stirred.

"Steffie?"

"I didn't mean to wake you," she told him quietly.

"Good thing you did. I was waiting up for you." He ran one hand through his hair and sat up straighter. "How was your dinner with Charles?"

Steffie sank onto the ottoman, angling her legs to one side. She knew her eyes had a dreamy look, but she didn't care. "Wonderful."

"Did Charles ask you anything?"

"Ask me anything?" she repeated, feigning ignorance. "What could he possibly have to ask me?"

David Bloomfield frowned. "Plenty. I thought—I hoped he was going to mention…an upcoming event."

"Oh, that!" she said with a light disinterested laugh. If the evening hadn't been so wonderful, she would've felt irritated with his pressure tactics. But she found it impossible to complain when she was this happy.

"He did, you mean? And what did you tell him? Don't keep me in suspense, Princess."

Steffie splayed her fingers and studied the smoothly polished nails before sighing. "I told him we'll see about it on Sunday."

"Sunday? You're going to keep that boy in agony until Sunday?"

She nodded, affecting a complete lack of concern. "He wanted to know if we could go horseback riding, and I said we could probably do it on Sunday. That's the question you're referring to, isn't it?"

"No," came his disappointed reply. "And well you know it. I expected that boy to ask you to marry him."

"Well, he didn't and even if he had—"

"Even if he had, what?" The frown slid back into place. "I tell you, Stephanie, you're as stubborn as your mother when it comes to this sort of thing. You can't fool me—you've been in love with Charles for years. If he asks you to marry him—"

"But he hasn't and from what I could see, he doesn't have any intention of doing so."

"I don't agree."

"You're free to think what you want, Dad, but keep in mind that this is *my* life and I won't take kindly to your interfering in it. And remember that Charles values his privacy, too."

"He didn't ask you to marry him," her father muttered under his breath. "You don't think he intends to, either?" he demanded, louder now.

"Not to my knowledge."

A look of righteous indignation came over him. "Then I'd better have a talk with that boy. I won't allow him to trifle with your affections."

"Dad!" Steffie had trouble not laughing over the old-fashioned terms he used. She was sure Charles would find it humorous, too, if she suggested he was "trifling" with her heart.

"I mean it, Steffie. I refuse to let that young man hurt you again."

"He only has that power if I give it to him—which I won't. You're looking at a woman of the twenty-first century, Dad, and we're too smart to let a man *trifle* with us."

"Nevertheless, I'm having a talk with him."

Her expression might have been outwardly serene, but Steffie's insides were dancing a wild jig. "You'll do no such thing," she insisted.

"Apparently Charles Tomaselli doesn't know what's good for him."

"Dad! We talked about this before, remember?"

Her good mood was quickly evaporating. "Now I want you to promise you're not going to interfere with Charles and me."

Her father refused to answer.

"I'll be mortified if you even bring up the subject of marriage to him."

"But—"

"I'm trusting you, Dad. Now good night." She stood and kissed his forehead before hurrying up the stairs to her own bedroom.

"I appreciate the ride to the airport," Valerie said as they drove out of town early Saturday afternoon. Her sister's flight was scheduled to leave at six, which gave them plenty of time for a leisurely trip into Portland. Valerie was going to meet with Rowdy Cassidy to tell him about her engagement and request a job transfer.

"I'm glad to do it," Steffie assured her older sister. Now that Valerie had set the preparations for her wedding in motion, she was free to return to Texas. There were several tasks, besides the discussion with Cassidy, that she needed to take care of. She had to pack her personal things, deal with her furniture and put her condo on the market.

"Colby wanted to come with me, but his schedule's full," she explained wistfully. "That's something we'll both have to adjust to."

"Heavy schedules?"

Valerie nodded. "I'll talk to Rowdy about that while I'm in Houston."

"Do you think he'll agree to let you head up the West Coast branch of CHIPS?"

"It's hard to say…. I don't think he's going to be pleased about my wanting to leave Houston, but he hasn't got a choice." Steffie noticed a hesitancy in her sister that she hadn't seen earlier. "Rowdy can be hard to predict," Valerie added. "He might be absolutely delighted for me and Colby. But there's also a chance that he'll be angry I took an extended leave of absence to plan my wedding." She sighed. "I didn't tell him the whole truth about why I didn't return the day I said I would."

"Why not?" Steffie prodded, briefly taking her eyes from the road when Valerie didn't immediately offer the information.

"I know I should have, but it just didn't seem right to do it over the phone. Besides, I'm afraid Rowdy might be…have been interested in me himself. At one point, I even thought I was interested in him! Good heavens, I didn't know a thing about love until I met Colby. I don't mean to hurt Rowdy's feelings but I can't give him any hope."

"Do you want me to fly back with you?"

"Oh, no. Rowdy's really a gentleman beneath that cowboy exterior."

Steffie's suspicions were raised. "Does the good doctor know how Rowdy feels about you?"

"I think he might. Then again, we've never really discussed Rowdy, and why should we? If you want the truth, I think Colby would rather forget about him."

"Maybe he should take his head out of the sand."

"Don't you go saying anything to him," Valerie said vehemently. "I mean it, Steff. What happens between Rowdy and me is between Rowdy and me."

"Is Colby the jealous type?" Steffie remembered how she'd felt the day she saw Charles standing next to Wendy, the intern at the *Clarion*. Until that moment, she'd never thought of herself as jealous. Even now the blood simmered in her veins when she recalled how the little blonde had gazed up at Charles, her blue eyes wide with open admiration.

"I don't know if Colby is or not. I only know how I'd feel if the situation was reversed." Valerie seemed to consider her next words. "Before Colby and I became engaged he was dating a nurse named Sherry Waterman, a friend of Norah's. Apparently he'd been going out with her for quite a while. Everyone was expecting them to announce their engagement. Norah seemed to feel otherwise, but that's another story."

"I swear Norah's got a sixth sense about these things."

Valerie nodded. "I think she does, too. At any rate, Colby and I decided that although we were attracted to each other, a long-term relationship was out of the question. Colby…asked me to hurry up and leave because my staying made everything so much more painful for us both."

"He didn't!" Steffie was outraged. "It's a good thing he didn't say that around me."

Valerie laughed. "He didn't really mean it. Oh,

maybe he did at the time, but I didn't make falling in love easy for either of us."

Valerie's stubbornness was a trait the three Bloomfield sisters shared, Steffie thought with a small, rueful grin.

"After we talked, Colby started dating Sherry again. I think they went out four or five nights in a row. I didn't know about it, but in a way, I guess I did. I certainly wasn't surprised when I heard.

"Poor Norah felt she had to let me know what was happening. I think it was harder on her than on me."

"Were you jealous?"

"That's the funny part," Valerie said pensively. "At first I was so jealous I wanted to scratch Sherry's eyes out. I fantasized about hunting down Colby Winston and making him suffer."

"You should've asked me to help you. I'd gladly have volunteered."

Valerie smiled and patted Steffie's forearm. "Spoken like a true sister, but as I said that was my *first* reaction. What I found interesting was that it didn't last.

"I sat down and thought about it and realized how selfish and unfair I was being to Colby. If I truly loved him, I should want him to have whatever made him happy. If that meant marriage to Sherry Waterman, then so be it."

"In other words you were willing to let him go."

"Yes. And that was a turning point for me. Don't misunderstand me, it hurt more than anything I've ever done. Remember the day I was supposed to fly back to Houston?"

Steffie wasn't likely to forget it. "Of course."

"When I got ready to leave, I really had to work at controlling myself. I wasn't sure I could make it down the front steps without bursting into tears."

"I knew you were upset,...."

"Naturally, Colby would have to choose right then to stop in for a visit. That man's sense of timing is going to be a problem." Valerie shook her head in mock exasperation.

Steffie laughed. Give Valerie a week and she'd have Colby's life completely reorganized.

"Somehow I managed to pull it off," Valerie continued. "I remember sitting in the car and—this is odd—I felt a sense of peace. I don't know if I can explain it. I felt this incredible...nobility. Don't you dare laugh, Steffie, I'm serious. I didn't stop loving Colby—if anything, I loved him more. Here I was, willingly walking away from the first man I'd ever loved."

"I wanted to throttle Colby about then."

Valerie grinned. "I remember learning about the tragic hero in my college literature courses. In some ways, I felt like I qualified for the tragic heroine."

"You weren't sorry you'd fallen in love with him, were you?"

"No, I was grateful. I was leaving him and at the same time I was giving him permission to find his own joy. And like I said, that somehow...ennobled me."

Steffie recalled the farewell scene on her front porch when she'd been so angry with Colby. "I...don't know if I could be that noble about Charles."

"What's happening with the two of you?"

"I'm not sure." Steffie was being entirely honest. "We had a wonderful dinner on Thursday, then we drove to Multnomah Falls and watched the moonlight on the water."

"That sounds so romantic."

"It was. We walked up to the footbridge and...talked."

"I'll bet!" Valerie laughed.

"We did—only we did more kissing than talking." Steffie knew that Charles had wanted to talk, wanted to discuss the past with her. She hated the thought of reliving all that pain. But more than anything she dreaded examining her utterly ridiculous behavior. Every time she recalled the scene in his bathroom, with her playing the role of waterlogged enchantress, she burned with humiliation. Someday they'd talk about it, but not now. It was too soon.

"Dad seems to think you two will get married."

This discussion was a repeat of the one she'd had with her father every day for the past two weeks. "You know Dad when he's got a bee in his bonnet. I've had to make him promise not to say a word about marriage to Charles."

"Do you really believe he listened to you?" Valerie asked.

"I hope so," she muttered.

Valerie frowned as she turned to stare out the car window. Steffie's hands tightened on the steering wheel and she glanced around her. Wild rhododendrons blossomed along the side of the road, their bright pink flowers a colorful contrast to the lush green foliage.

"I'm worried about Dad."

Valerie's words surprised Steffie. "Why? He's getting stronger every day. His recovery is nothing short of miraculous. I've heard you say so yourself, at least a dozen times."

"All right, I'll rephrase that. I'm worried for you."

"Me? Whatever for?" As far as Steffie was concerned, her life had rarely been better. She'd applied for late admission to the Ph.D. program and planned to begin researching thesis topics soon. As for Charles... well, things were wonderful. Yes, she still had a lot of murky ground to cover with him, but there'd be time for that later.

"Dad's riding high on success," Valerie reminded her. "He seems to think that because everything fell into place with Colby and me, it should for you and Charles, as well. Remember he's supposed to have dreamed all this."

"I know. We've had our go-arounds on that issue. He's told me at least twice a day for the past two weeks that I'm going to marry Charles by the end of the summer. Now I just smile and nod and let him think what he wants."

"It doesn't bother you?"

"It drives me nuts." Possibly because she wanted to believe it so badly...

"Aren't you nervous that Dad's going to get impatient and say something to Charles?"

"No," Steffie answered automatically. "Dad and I've been over this. He knows better than to say anything to Charles."

Valerie nodded. "I wish I shared your confidence."

Steffie put on a good front for the remainder of the drive, but she was growing more and more concerned. She knew one thing; she didn't have the personality to take on the role of tragic heroine. She'd leave that to her older, wiser sister.

As soon as Valerie had checked in for her flight to Texas, Steffie headed back to Orchard Valley. As the minutes ticked away, she became increasingly anxious to get home.

It was just like Valerie to plant the seeds of doubt and then fly off, leaving Steffie to deal with the result—a garden full of weeds!

When she pulled into the driveway, Steffie experienced an immediate sense of relief. Her world was in order; her fears shrank to nothing. All was well. Her father was rocking on the front porch, the way he did every evening. He smiled and waved when he saw her.

"Hello, good-lookin'," she said as she climbed out of the car. "How was your day?"

"I had a great afternoon. Every day's wonderful now that I've got all these reasons to live. Oh, before I forget, Charles stopped by to see you. Guess he must've been in the neighborhood again." A smile twinkled from her father's eyes. "You might want to call him. I suspect he's waiting to hear from you."

Steffie froze. Doubt sprang to new life. "You didn't say anything to him about…what we discussed, did you?"

"Princess, I didn't say a word you wouldn't want me to."

"You're sure?"

"As positive as I'm sitting here."

Steffie went inside the house, reassured by her father's words. Norah was busy in the kitchen, kneading bread dough on a lightly floured countertop.

"Did you happen to see Charles?" Steffie asked in passing. She opened the refrigerator and removed a cold soda.

"He stopped by earlier and sat on the porch with Dad. I think he was here for about fifteen minutes."

Steffie swallowed a long cool drink. "I'll give him a call."

"Good idea."

She waited until she was in her room, then sat on her bed and reached for the phone. Although it had been several years since she'd called Charles, she still remembered his number. The same way she remembered everything else about him.

He must have been sitting by the phone, because he answered even before the first ring was finished.

"Charles, hello," she said happily. "Dad said you came by."

"Yes, I did."

His voice was cool, and Steffie paused as the dread took hold inside her. "Is something wrong?"

"Not wrong, exactly. I guess you could say I'm disappointed. I thought you'd changed, Steffie. I thought you'd grown up and stopped your naive tricks. But I was wrong, wasn't I?"

# *Nine*

"**D**ad!" Steffie struggled to keep the anger and distress from her voice. She hurried to the porch, her fists clenched against her sides. "You told me…you promised…" She hesitated. "What *exactly* did you say to Charles?"

Her father glanced upward momentarily, clearly puzzled. "Nothing drastic, I assure you. Is it important?"

"Yes, it's important! I need to know." She had to call on every ounce of self-control not to shout at him and demand an explanation. She longed to chastise him for doing the very thing she'd begged him not to.

"You look upset, Princess."

"I am upset and I'm sure you know why… Just tell me what you said to Charles."

"Sit down a bit and we'll talk."

Steffie did as her father requested, sitting on the top

porch step near his chair and leaning back against the white pillar. "Charles stopped in this afternoon, right?"

"Yes, and we had a nice chat. He tried to make me think he was here to visit me, but I saw through that." Her father's smile told Steffie all she needed to know. For one angry second, she thought he resembled a spider, waiting patiently for someone to step into his web.

"Obviously I was the subject under discussion, wasn't I?" She forced herself not to yell, not to rant and rave at a man so recently released from the hospital.

Her father rocked back and forth a few times, then nodded. "We talked about you."

Steffie closed her eyes, her frustration mounting. "I see. And what did the two of you come up with?"

"Let me tell you what Charles said first."

She balled her hands into fists again, praying for patience. *"What did he say?"*

"Well, Charles stopped by, as I said, pretending it was me he was here to visit, when we both knew he was coming to see you. I went along with it for a while, then asked him flat out what his intentions were toward you. I fully expected you to be wearing an engagement ring by now, and I let him know it."

"Dad!" Without meaning to, Steffie sprang to her feet. "You breached a trust! I trusted you to keep your word, not to talk to Charles about this. And now you pass it off as…as nothing. Don't you realize what you've done?"

For the first time he looked chagrined. "I did it because I love you, Princess."

"Oh, Dad…you've made everything so much more difficult."

"Aren't you interested in what he had to say?" His smile was bright and cocky again. "Well, aren't you? Now sit back down and I'll tell you."

"Oh, all right." She sighed, lowering herself onto the porch step, her legs barely able to support her. She was shaking with trepidation.

"Charles seemed more concerned with the fact that I'd asked than with answering the question. To be perfectly honest, Princess, he wasn't overly pleased with me."

"I can't believe he even answered you."

"Of course he did. He said if the subject of marriage did come up, then it was between the two of you, and not the three of us. It was a good response."

"You never should've said *anything* about us marrying."

"Well, Princess, the way I figured it, he was going to pop the question, anyway. Besides, I don't want Charles leading you on, or hurting you again."

"Dad, you've made it nearly impossible for me now and—"

"Let me finish, because there's more to tell you." But after silencing her, he went strangely quiet himself.

"Go on," she urged, clenching her jaw.

"I'm just trying to think of a way to tell you this without annoying you even more. I told Charles something you didn't want me to tell him."

"The dream?" The question came out a whisper. "But

you said you hadn't told Charles anything I wouldn't want you to. And before—you *promised* you wouldn't mention marriage!"

"No, Princess, I never did promise. I took it under consideration, but not once did I actually say I wouldn't discuss this with Charles. Now don't look so worried. I didn't tell him a thing about talking to your mother or about the three precious children the two of you are going to have someday."

"What did Charles say? No," she amended quickly, "tell me *exactly* what you said first."

"Well, like I already told you, we were chatting—"

"Get to the part where you brought up marriage."

"All right, all right. But I want you to know I didn't say anything about the dream. Not because you didn't want me to, but because when it came right down to it, I didn't think he'd believe me. You three girls are having trouble enough, so I can hardly expect someone outside the family to listen."

"You told Colby about it."

"Of course I did. He's my doctor. He had a right to know."

"Great. In other words you blurted out that you expected Charles to marry me—because you didn't want him trifling with my heart?" Spoken aloud, it sounded so ludicrous. Not to mention insulting. No wonder Charles was cool toward her.

"Not exactly. I asked his intentions. He said that was between the two of you. As I already explained."

"Good." Steffie relaxed a little. "And that was the end of it?" she murmured hopefully.

"Not entirely."

"What else is there?"

"I told him you were anticipating a proposal of marriage, and for that matter so was I."

Steffie ground her teeth to keep from screaming. It was worse than she'd feared. Sagging against the pillar, she covered her face with both hands. It would've been far better had he told Charles about the dream. That way, Charles might have understood that she'd had nothing to do with this. Instead, her father had made everything ten times worse by *not* mentioning it.

Charles was angry with her; that was obvious from their telephone conversation. He'd refused to discuss it in any detail, just repeating that he was "disappointed." He seemed to believe she'd manipulated her father into approaching him with this marriage business. He wasn't likely to change his mind unless she could convince him of the truth.

"Where are you going?" her father asked when she left him and returned a moment later with her purse and a sweater.

"To talk to Charles—to explain things, if I can."

"Good." David's grin was full. "All that boy needs is a bit of prompting. You'll see. Once you get back, you'll thank me for taking matters into my own hands. There's something about making a commitment to the right woman that fixes everything."

Steffie was drained from the emotion. She found she couldn't remain angry with her father. He'd talked to Charles with the best of motives. And he didn't know what had gone on between her and Charles in the past—the tricks she'd played. So he couldn't possibly understand why Charles would react with such anger to being pressed on the issue of marriage.

"I'll wait up for you and when you get home we'll celebrate together," he suggested.

Steffie grinned weakly and nodded, but she doubted there'd be anything to celebrate.

She took her time driving into town, using those minutes to organize her thoughts. She hoped Charles would be open-minded enough to accept her explanation. Mostly, she wanted to reassure him that she hadn't talked her father into interrogating him about marriage. They'd come so far in the past few weeks, she and Charles, and Steffie didn't want anything to spoil that.

Charles was waiting for her, or he seemed to be. She'd barely rung his doorbell when he answered.

"Hello." His immediate appearance took her by surprise. "I—I thought it might be a good idea if the two of us sat down and talked."

"Fine." He didn't smile, didn't show any sign of pleasure at seeing her.

"Dad told me he talked to you about…the two of us marrying." The words felt awkward on her tongue.

"He did mention something along those lines," Charles returned stiffly.

He hadn't asked her to make herself comfortable or invited her to sit down. It didn't matter, though, since she couldn't stand still, anyway. She paced from one side of his living room to the other. She felt strangely chilled, despite the warm spring weather.

"You think I put Dad up to it, don't you?"

"Yes," he said frankly.

He stood rooted to the same spot while she drifted, apparently aimlessly, around the room. His look, everything about him, wasn't encouraging. Perhaps she should have delayed this, let them both sleep on it, instead of forcing the issue. Perhaps she should've dropped the whole thing, and let this misunderstanding sort itself out. Perhaps she should go home now before the situation got even worse.

"I didn't ask Dad to say anything to you," she told him simply.

"I wish I could believe that."

"Why can't you? This is ridiculous! If you intend to drag the past into every disagreement, punish me for something that happened three years ago, then—"

"I'm not talking about three years ago. I'm talking about here and now."

"What do you mean?"

"I'll say this for you, Steffie, you've gotten a lot more subtle."

"How…do you mean?"

"First, you park in front of the newspaper office just as I happen to—"

"When?"

"Last week. I was talking to Wendy, and when I looked up, I saw you sitting in your car, staring at us. Just how long had you been there?"

"I...don't know."

"Now that I think about it, I realize what a fool I've been. You've been spying on me for weeks, haven't you?"

The idea was so outlandish that Steffie found herself laughing incredulously. Nothing she said would make any difference, not if he believed what he was saying. Because if he did, there was nothing of their relationship left to salvage.

"There's no fooling you, is there?" she threw out sarcastically. "You're much too smart for me, Charles. I've been hiding around town for days, following you with binoculars, charting your activities. It's amazing you didn't catch on sooner."

He ignored her scornful remarks. "Very convenient the way you twisted your ankle the other day, too, wasn't it? Somehow you managed to fall directly into my arms."

"The timing was perfect, wasn't it?" she said with a short, humorless laugh. "You're right, I couldn't have planned that any better."

He frowned. "Then there was the dinner waiting for me at the house the other night. Italian, too, just the way my grandmother used to make it."

"Interesting how I knew that, huh?"

"All of this adds up to one thing."

"And what might that be?" she asked scathingly, folding her arms. She'd assumed far too much in this relationship. She'd lowered her guard and actually believed Charles loved her, because she loved him so deeply. Now she understood how wrong she'd been.

"It adds up to the fact that you're playing games again."

"Don't forget the moonlight the evening we were at Multnomah Falls. I arranged that, too. I have to admit it took some doing."

"There's no need to be sarcastic."

"I don't agree," she returned defiantly.

Charles frowned and muttered something she couldn't hear.

"I must say I'm surprised you caught on so quickly, what with me being so subtle and all."

"Let's clear the air once and—"

"But the air *is* clear," she said, waving her arms wildly. She knew she was going too far with this, but the momentum was building and she couldn't seem to stop. "I've been found out, and now it's all over."

"Over?"

"Of course. There's no need to pretend anymore."

"What are you talking about?"

"Revenge. It's supposed to be sweet, and it would've been if you hadn't caught on when you did."

"Just what did you intend to do?" he demanded.

"You mean you don't have that figured out, as well?"

"Tell me, Stephanie." His voice was hard as ice and just as cold.

"Fine, if you must know. Once I got you to the point of proposing—" she paused dramatically "—I was going to laugh and reject you. It seems only fair after the way you humiliated me. You laughed at me, Charles, and it was going to be my turn to laugh at you. Only you found me out first…."

His frown deepened into a scowl. "Your father—"

"Oh, don't worry, he didn't know anything about that part. Getting him to shame you into a marriage proposal was tricky, but I managed it by telling him I was afraid you were…trifling with my affections." She gave a deep exaggerated sigh, astonished that he seemed to believe all this.

"I see."

"Oh, you're too clever for me, Charles. What can I possibly say?"

"Perhaps it would be best if you left now."

"I think you're right. Well, at least you know what it feels like to have someone laugh at you."

Charles walked to his front door and held it open for her. With a jaunty step, Steffie walked out of his house. "Well, I'll see you around, but you don't need to worry—I won't be spying on you anymore."

His jaw was clamped tightly shut, and Steffie realized she'd succeeded beyond all her expectations. Charles was disgusted with her. And furious. So furious that he couldn't get her out of his home fast enough.

"You can't blame a girl for trying," she said with a shrug once she'd slipped past him.

In response, Charles slammed his door.

By the time Steffie was inside the car, she was shaking so badly that she could hardly insert the key into the ignition. Her breath seemed to be trapped in her chest, creating a painful need to exhale.

Like Charles, she was angry, angrier than she'd ever been in her life. In one rational corner of her mind, she knew—had known all along—that it was a mistake to goad him with all those ridiculous lies.

But the shocking thing, the sad thing, was that he'd believed them. To his way of thinking, apparently, it all fit. And as far as Steffie was concerned, there was nothing more to say.

In time, she'd regret her outburst, but she didn't then. At that moment, she was far too infuriated to care. In time, she'd regret the lies, the squandered hopes—but it wouldn't be soon.

"Well?" her father asked, his expression pleased and expectant as she let herself into the house an hour later. "Are you two going to look for an engagement ring in the next few days?"

"Not exactly," Steffie said, moving into his den. As he'd promised earlier, her father was waiting up for her, reading in his favorite chair.

His face fell with disappointment. "But you did talk about getting married, didn't you?"

"Not really. We, uh, got sidetracked."

"You didn't argue, did you?"

"Not really." Steffie was unsure how much to tell him. She worried that if he knew the extent of the rift between her and Charles, he'd feel obliged to do something to patch things up.

David set aside his reading glasses and gazed up at her. "You'll be seeing him again soon, won't you?"

Living in Orchard Valley made that very likely. It was the reason she'd chosen to study in Europe three years earlier. "Naturally I'll be seeing him."

David nodded, appeased. "Good."

"I think I'll go up to my room and read. Good night, Dad."

"Night, Princess."

On her way up, Steffie met Norah at the top of the stairs. Her younger sister glanced in her direction and did an automatic double take. "What's wrong?"

"What makes you think anything's wrong?"

"You mean other than the fact that you look like you're waiting to get to your room before you cry?"

Her sister knew her too well. Steffie felt terrible—discouraged, disheartened, depressed. But in her present mood, she didn't have the patience to explain what had happened between her and Charles.

"What could possibly be wrong?" Steffie asked instead, feigning a lightness she didn't feel.

"Funny you should say that," Norah said, tucking her arm through Steffie's and leading the way to her bedroom. "Valerie asked me nearly the same thing not long ago. What could possibly be wrong? Well, I'd have to say it's probably trouble with a man."

"Very astute of you."

"Obviously it's Charles." Norah didn't react to Steffie's mild sarcasm.

"Obviously." She was tired, weary right down to her bones and desperately craving a long, hot soak in the tub. Some of her best thinking was accomplished while lazing in a bathtub filled with scented water. She'd avoided bubble baths since the time she'd spent hours in one waiting for Charles.

"Did you two have a spat?"

"Listen, Norah, I appreciate your concern—really, I do... I don't mean to sound ungrateful, but I'm tired and I want to go to bed."

"Bed? Good grief, it's only seven."

"It's been a long day."

Norah eyed her suspiciously. "It must have been."

"Besides, I have a lot to do on Monday."

Norah's interest was piqued. "What's happening then?"

"I'm going to Portland to see about my application at the university and to find an apartment."

For a moment Norah said nothing. Her mouth fell open and she wore a stunned look. "But I thought you told Dad you were going to wait on that."

"I was..."

"But now you aren't? Even after you promised Dad?"

Steffie glanced away, not wanting her sister to see

how deeply hurt she was. How betrayed she felt that Charles would believe she was deceitful enough to trick him into marriage. It seemed that whenever Charles Tomaselli was involved, she invariably ended up in pain.

"I feel better than I have in years." David greeted Steffie cheerfully early the next morning. He was sitting at the kitchen table, drinking a cup of coffee and studying the Portland Sunday paper. He welcomed her with a warm smile, apparently not noticing his daughter's lackluster mood. "Beautiful morning," David added.

"Beautiful," Steffie mumbled as she poured herself a cup of coffee and staggered to the table. Her eyes burned from lack of sleep, and she felt as though she was walking around in a nightmare.

She'd spent the entire night arguing with herself about the lies she'd told Charles. In the end, she'd managed to convince herself that she'd done the right thing. Charles *wanted* to believe every word. He'd seized every one of her sarcastic remarks, all too ready to consider them truth.

"What time will Charles be by?" her father asked conversationally.

"Charles?" She repeated his name as though she'd never heard it before.

"I thought the two of you were going horseback riding this afternoon."

"Uh…I'm not sure Charles will be able to come, after all." The date had probably slipped his mind, the way it had hers. Even if he did remember, Steffie sincerely doubted he'd show up. As far as she was concerned, whatever had been between them was now over. In fact, the more she reviewed their last discussion, the angrier she became. If he honestly believed the things she'd suggested—and he certainly seemed to—then there was no hope for them. None.

"I'll get dressed for church," Steffie said bleakly.

"You've got plenty of time yet."

"Norah has to get there early." Her sister sang in the choir. Generally Norah left the house before the others, but Steffie thought she'd ride with Norah this morning, if for no other reason than to escape her father's questions. From the looks David was giving her, he was about to subject her to a full-scale inquisition.

Attending church was an uplifting experience for Steffie. During that hour, she was able to forget her troubles and absorb the atmosphere of peace and serenity. Whatever solace she found, however, vanished the minute she and Norah drove into the yard shortly after noon.

Charles's car was parked out front.

Steffie tensed and released a long, slow sigh.

"Problems?" Norah asked.

"I don't know."

"Do you want to talk to him?"

"No, I don't." But at the same time, she wasn't about to back down, either. She wouldn't allow Charles to chase her from her own home. He was on her turf now, and she didn't run easily.

Steffie parked behind Charles's sports car and willed herself to remain calm and collected. Her father must have heard them because he stepped outside the house, his welcoming smile in place. He still moved slowly but with increasing confidence. It was sometimes hard to remember that he was recovering from major surgery.

"Steffie, Charles is here."

"So I see," she said with a distinct lack of enthusiasm.

"He's in the stable, waiting for you."

She nodded and, with her heart racing, walked up the steps and past her father.

"Aren't you going to talk to him?"

"I need to change my clothes first."

"To talk? But…" He hesitated, then reluctantly nodded.

By the time Steffie was in her bedroom, she was trembling. Her emotions were so confused that she wasn't sure if she was shaking with anger or with nervousness. But she did know she wasn't ready to face him, wasn't ready to deal with his accusations or his reproach. For several minutes she sat on her bed, trying to decide what to do.

"Steffie." Norah stood in the doorway, watching her. "Are you okay?"

"Of course, I—no, I'm not," she said. "I'm not ready to talk to Charles yet."

"Nothing says you have to talk to him if you don't want to. I'll make up some excuse and send him packing."

"No." For pride's sake, she didn't want him to know how badly she'd been hurt by their latest confrontation.

"You look like you're about to burst into tears."

Steffie squared her shoulders and met her sister's worried eyes. "I'm not going to give him the satisfaction."

"Attagirl," Norah said approvingly.

Changing into jeans and a sweatshirt, Steffie went down the back stairs into the kitchen. She didn't expect to find Charles sitting at the table chatting with her father. What unsettled her most was that he gave no outward sign of their quarrel. Steffie slowed her pace as she entered the room.

Charles stopped talking and his eyes narrowed briefly. "Hello, Stephanie."

"I'll leave you two alone," her father said before Steffie could answer Charles's greeting. He rose, a bit stiffly, and made his way to the door. "I guess you've got plenty to discuss."

Steffie wanted to argue, but knew there wasn't any point. She merely shrugged and remained where she was, standing a few steps from the back stairs. She didn't look at Charles. The silence between them lengthened, until she couldn't endure it any longer.

"I didn't expect you to come," she said in a harsh voice. "It certainly wasn't necessary."

"I'm aware of that."

"I'm not in the mood to go riding and I don't imagine you are, either." In other words, she wasn't in the mood to go riding with *him*.

"I'm not here to ride."

"Then why are you here?"

Apparently Charles didn't have the answer because he got to his feet and walked over to the window. Whatever he saw must have fascinated him because he stood there for several minutes without speaking.

"Why are you here?" she asked a second time, on the verge of requesting him to leave.

He finally turned around to face her. "I don't know about you, but I couldn't sleep last night."

Steffie refused to admit that she'd fared no better, so she made no response.

"I kept going over the things your father said and the things you told me," Charles went on.

"Did you come to any conclusions?" Pride demanded that she not look at him, or reveal how much his answer meant to her.

"One."

Steffie tensed. "What's that?" She had to look at him now.

His eyes finally met hers. Although nearly the entire kitchen separated them, Steffie felt as though he was close enough to touch.

"It seems to me," he began, "that since your father's so anxious to marry you off, and you seem to be just as eager, then fine."

"Fine?" she repeated, wondering if this was some joke and she'd missed the punch line.

"In other words," Charles returned shortly, "I'm willing to take you off his hands."

# Ten

"What? Take me off Dad's hands?" Steffie echoed. Surely he wasn't serious. No woman in her right mind would accept such an insulting proposal.

"You heard me."

"Tell me you're kidding."

Charles shook his head. "I've never been more serious in my life. You want to marry me, then so be it. I'm willing to go along with this, provided we understand each other...."

"In that case I withdraw the offer—not that I ever *made* an offer."

"You can't do that," Charles argued, looking surprised. "Your father thinks we should get married and, after giving it some thought, I agree with him."

"That's too bad, since I'm not interested."

Charles laughed softly. "We both know that's not true. You've been crazy about me for years."

Steffie whirled around and crossed her arms, as though to fend off his words. "I can't marry you, Charles."

"Why not? I know you love me. You said so yourself before you left for Italy, and I know that hasn't changed."

"Don't be so sure."

"Ah, but I am. And recently you showed me again."

"When?" she demanded, trying to recall the conversations they'd had since her return to Orchard Valley.

"The afternoon we met at Del's."

Steffie cast her mind back to that day. They'd met by accident as they'd gone in to pay for their gas. Steffie remembered how glad she'd been to see him, how eager to set things straight. But she couldn't remember saying one thing that would lead Charles to believe she still loved him.

"I didn't say anything."

"Not in so many words, true, but with everything you did. The same holds true for the night I dropped off the azalea and you asked me to dinner. Remember?"

"Yes, but what's that got to do with anything?"

"A whole lot, as a matter of fact. You were continually making excuses for us to be together."

Steffie's face flooded with color. "What's that got to do with anything?" she asked again.

He ignored her question. "We had fun that night, touring Orchard Valley. Didn't we?"

Steffie nodded. She wasn't likely to forget that evening. For the first time in her relationship with Charles, she'd felt a stirring of real promise. Not the kind of hope she'd fabricated earlier, but one based on genuine companionship. Charles had enjoyed her company and they'd laughed and talked as though they'd been friends for years.

"You told me that when you lived in Italy you were too busy with your studies to date much," Charles reminded her.

"So?"

"So that led me to conclude that you hadn't fallen in love with anyone else while you were away."

"I hadn't."

"Your father came right out and told me on several occasions that he was concerned about you because you didn't seem to be dating anyone seriously."

Steffie glared at him, feeling trapped. "I still don't understand what this has to do with anything."

"Plenty. You loved me then, and you love me now."

"You've got some nerve, Charles Tomaselli." She glowered fiercely, hoping he'd back off. "What makes you so sure I'm in love with you now?"

"I know you better than you realize."

"What nonsense!" She managed a light laugh. "You don't know me at all, otherwise you—" She stopped abruptly.

"Otherwise what?"

"Nothing." *Otherwise he wouldn't have believed the things she'd told him.*

"Don't you think it's time we stopped playing games with each other?" he suggested.

"What games?" she snapped. "I gave those up years ago."

Charles frowned as though he wasn't sure he should believe her.

Hurt and angry, Steffie raised her hand and pointed at him. "*That's* the reason I refuse to marry you," she cried. Restraining the emotion was next to impossible and her voice quavered with the force of it. "I suppose I should be flattered that you're *willing* to take me off Dad's hands," she said sarcastically. "Every woman dreams of hearing such romantic words. But I want far more in a husband, Charles Tomaselli, than you'd ever be capable of giving me!"

"What do you mean by that?" Before she had a chance to reply he muttered, "Oh, I get it. You're afraid I'm going to be financially strapped with the newspaper, aren't you? You think I won't be able to afford you."

Steffie was stunned by his remark. Stunned and insulted. "You know me so well, don't you?" she asked him, her voice heavy with scorn. "There's just no pulling the wool over your eyes, is there?" She drew in a deep breath. "I think it would be best if you left." She walked across the kitchen and held open the back door. "Right now."

Charles shook his head. "Sorry," he said. "I don't want to leave." He pulled out a chair and threw himself down. "We're going to talk this out, once and for all," he told her.

"You're too stubborn."

"So are you."

"We'd make a terrible couple."

"We make a good team."

Steffie didn't know why she was fighting him so hard—especially when he was saying all the things she'd always dreamed of hearing.

"I realize I've made some mistakes with this," he said slowly. "It might have sounded callous, offering to marry you the way I did."

"I'll admit that *taking me off Dad's hands* does lack a certain romantic flair," she agreed wryly. She crossed over to the counter for a coffee mug, filling it from the pot next to the stove. If they were going to talk seriously, without hurling accusations at each other, she was going to need it.

"I was angry."

"Then why'd you come here?" she asked, claiming the chair across from him.

"Because," he answered in a tight, angry voice, "I was afraid I'd lose you again."

"Lose me?" That made no sense to Steffie.

"You heard me," he growled. "I was afraid you'd return to Italy or take off on a safari, or go someplace equally inaccessible."

"Portland. I'm moving to Portland, but it isn't because of what happened with you. I intended to do that from the moment I got home." She folded her hands around the hot mug. "Why should you care where I go?"

"Because I didn't want you leaving again."

"Why do you want me to stay, especially if you believe the things I told you yesterday?"

His eyes held hers. "I don't believe them."

"You gave a good impression of it earlier," she reminded him. A fresh wave of pain assaulted her and she looked away.

"That's because I was furious."

"That hasn't changed."

"No, it hasn't," he agreed, "but the simple fact is I don't want you to leave again."

"Unfortunately you don't have any say in what I do."

Charles frowned. "Now *you're* angry."

"You're right about that! Did you really think I was so desperate for a husband I'd accept your insulting offer? Is that what you think of me, Charles?"

"No!" he shouted. "I'm in love with you, dammit! I have been for years. I had to do something to keep you here. I don't want to wait another three years for you to come to your senses."

His words were followed by silence. Steffie stared down into her coffee, and to her chagrin felt tears well up in her eyes. "I'm afraid I don't believe you."

Charles stood abruptly and walked to the window again. Hands clasped behind his back, he gazed outside. "It's true."

"It couldn't be." She wiped the tears from her face. "You were so…so…"

"Cruel," he supplied. "You'll never understand how

hard it was not to make love to you that first time in the stable. I've never been more tempted by any woman."

"I...tempted you?" Her voice was low and incredulous.

He turned around and smiled, but it was a sad smile, one full of doubts and regrets. "I remember when you started hanging around the newspaper office. I was flattered by the attention. Soon I found myself looking forward to the times you came by. You were witty and generous and you always had an intelligent comment about something in the paper. I quickly discovered you were much more than a pretty face."

"I never worked harder in my life to impress anyone," she murmured with self-deprecating humor.

But it didn't take Steffie long to get back to the point. "If that was how you felt, then why did you ask me not to come around anymore?"

"I had to say something before I gave in and threw caution to the wind. You'd recently lost your mother and you were young, naive and terribly vulnerable. I struggled with my conscience for weeks, trying to decide what I should do about you. In case you haven't noticed, I'm six years older than you. That made a big difference."

"The gap in our ages hasn't narrowed."

"True enough, but you're not a girl anymore."

"I was twenty-two," she argued. "At least by the time I left."

"Perhaps, but you'd been pretty sheltered. And you

were still dealing with your grief. Your entire life had been jolted, and I couldn't be sure if what you felt for me was love or adolescent infatuation."

Steffie closed her eyes and let the warmth of his words revive her. "It was love," she told him. A love that had matured, grown more intense, in the years that separated them.

"It probably doesn't mean much to you now, but I want you to know how hard it was for me the night I came home and found you in my bathtub."

"But you were so angry."

"It was either that or take you into my room and make love to you."

Steffie still felt confused. "You laughed at me when I told you how I felt that day in the stable…."

"I know," he said simply. Steffie heard the pain and remorse in his voice. "I've never had to do anything that's cost me more. But I never dreamed you'd leave Orchard Valley."

"What did you expect me to do? I couldn't stay—that would've been impossible. So I did the only thing I could. I left."

Charles's hand reached for hers, twining their fingers together. "I'll never forget the day I learned you'd gone to Europe. I felt as if I'd been hit by a bulldozer."

"I had to go," she repeated unnecessarily. "It was too painful to stay."

His fingers tightened around hers. "I know." Slowly he raised her hand to his lips. "I've waited three long years to tell you how sorry I was to hurt you. Three years to tell you I was in love with you, too."

Steffie attempted with little success to blink back the tears.

"If it had been at any other time in your life, if I could've been sure you weren't just trying to replace your mother's love with mine—then everything would've been different. But you were so young, so innocent. I couldn't trust myself around you, feeling the way I did."

"And you couldn't trust me."

He nodded his agreement. "I'm sorry, Stephanie, for rejecting you. But it was as painful for me as it was for you. Perhaps more so, because I knew the whole truth."

"You never wrote—not once in all that time. Not so much as a postcard. Not even an e-mail."

"I couldn't. I wanted to, but I didn't dare give in to the impulse."

"So you waited."

"Not patiently. I expected you to come home at least once in three years, you know."

"I dreaded seeing you again. I was thousands of miles away from you and yet I still loved you, I still dreamed about you. It didn't seem to get any better. Even after three years."

"A few weeks ago, you'd finished your classes and you were in the process of deciding if you were going to stay on in Italy."

"How'd you know that?"

"Your father. He was the only way I had of getting information about you, and I used him shamelessly."

"He told me you started coming by for visits shortly after I left."

"I'm surprised he didn't figure out how I felt about you. I don't think I could have been any more obvious if I'd tried."

"Dad didn't have a clue until recently and then only because of the—" She stopped when she realized what she was about to tell him.

"Of what?" Charles prodded.

"I…it would be best if you let Dad explain that part."

"All right, I will." He looked away from her momentarily. "Although you never seriously dated anyone, there *was* someone in Italy, wasn't there? A man you cared about?"

"Who?" Steffie frowned in bewilderment.

"A man named Mario?"

"Mario…a man?" He was four now, and the delight of her heart while she'd lived in Italy.

"He caused me several sleepless nights. Your father only mentioned him once. Said you 'adored' him. I went through agonies trying to be subtle about getting information on this guy, but your father never brought him up again."

"Mario," Steffie repeated, smiling broadly. "Yes, I did adore him."

Charles scowled. "What happened?"

Still smiling, Steffie said, "There was a slight discrepancy in our ages. I'm more than twenty years older."

"He's a kid."

"But what a kid. My landlady's son. I was crazy about him." Spending time with a loving, open child like Mario had helped her through a difficult period in her life.

"I see." A slow, easy smile slipped into place. "So you like children."

"Oh, yes, I always have."

"I hope that young man appreciates everything he put me through."

"I'm sure he doesn't, but I certainly do. I know what it's like to love someone and have that someone not love you."

Charles considered her words for a moment. "I've always loved you, Stephanie, but I didn't dare let you know. I couldn't trust what we felt for each other then—but I can now."

She avoided his gaze. She had to ask, although she was afraid to. "If that's true, why were you so angry when Dad suggested we get married?"

Charles sighed. "Frustration, I guess. I'd intended to propose the night we went for dinner. I had everything planned, down to the last detail."

"But why didn't you?"

"I couldn't, not when the past still came between us. You made it clear you didn't want to discuss our misunderstandings. So my hands were tied. I hate to admit it, but I was nervous—even if you didn't seem to notice."

"I made it one of my wishes—I didn't want to talk about the past," she recalled, experiencing an instant twinge of regret.

"And I had to go along with it," he said.

"That still doesn't explain why you were so offended when Dad suggested we marry." His reaction was a mystery in light of the things he was telling her now.

"A man prefers to propose himself," Charles offered as a simple explanation. "I don't think I could've made my intentions any plainer if I'd hired a skywriter. Then to have first your father and then you—"

"Me?"

"Yesterday I suddenly felt so afraid that you *weren't* lying about why you'd stopped by the house. To deliver the finishing blow, to get me to admit I loved you and then laugh at me…"

"I—I made that part up! I was so mad—"

"*You* were mad?"

"I know, I know. It's just that I had to say something. I didn't think you'd believe all those ridiculous lies, and then you seemed to and that made everything a thousand times worse. I was just beginning to hope we might have a future together."

"I was, too. That's why it hit me so hard."

"I could never intentionally hurt you, Charles. Not without hurting myself."

His eyes held hers, and everything around Steffie faded into insignificance. She was on the verge of disclosing her love when there was a knock at the kitchen door, followed by her father poking his head inside. "Is it safe yet? You two looked like time bombs about to explode twenty minutes ago."

"It's safe," Charles answered, smiling at Steffie.

"I hope you've got everything worked out because I'm tired of waiting, The way I figure it, you should be married by the end of the summer. Your oldest—"

"Dad," Steffie cut in. "I don't think Charles is interested in discussing it right now. Why don't you leave all of that to us?"

"Our oldest?" Charles asked, frowning.

"Child, of course. A girl, then a son and then another daughter. Sweethearts, all three of them. The boy will be the spitting image of you, Charles—same dark brown eyes, same facial features."

Charles glanced at Steffie as though he was questioning her father's sanity.

"I think you'd better tell Charles about the dream, Dad."

"You mean you haven't?" He sounded surprised.

"No, I didn't want to frighten him out of marrying into the family."

"What's going on here?" Charles's eyes roved from Steffie to her father and back.

"You may have trouble accepting this," David said, pulling out a chair and settling himself. He grinned, happy as Steffie could ever remember seeing him. "But I got a glimpse of the future. It was a gift from Grace. She wanted to be sure I had a reason to live and so she—"

"But isn't Grace—"

"She's in heaven, but then so was I, briefly. It was what they call a near-death experience. You can ask Colby if you want."

"Colby?" Charles repeated.

"I'm not convinced he believes me one hundred percent, but time will prove me right. Look at what's happened with Valerie and Colby, just like I said it would. And with you two. You're going to marry this little girl of mine, aren't you?"

"In a heartbeat," Charles confirmed.

Her father's grin practically split his face. "That's what I was counting on. You love him, don't you, Princess?"

Steffie nodded. "More than I thought possible," she said in a hushed voice.

David smiled knowingly and stood up from his chair. "In that case, I'll leave you two to discuss the details of your wedding. I'd like to suggest midsummer, but as I said, I'll leave that up to you." He sauntered out of the room.

"Midsummer?" Steffie shrugged.

"Sounds good to me. Does that give you enough time?"

She laughed. "Sure, and I'll be able to register for my courses, according to plan—if that's okay with you?" At his enthusiastic agreement, she added, "Uh…what do you think about Dad's dream?"

"A boy and two girls, he says."

Steffie nodded shyly.

"How do *you* feel about that?" he asked.

"Good, very good."

Charles reached for her then, taking her in his arms

with the strength of a man who'd been too long without love. He buried his face in the curve of her neck and breathed deeply. "I nearly lost you for the second time."

"You'd never have lost me, Charles. I've loved you for so long, I don't know how not to love you."

"I love you, too, Stephanie. Give me a chance to prove it."

In her eyes, he'd proved it when he hadn't laughed at her father's dream. She knew what he was thinking, perhaps because she was thinking the same thing herself. They were in love and had already decided to marry, so it didn't matter what her father had predicted after his supposed sojourn in the afterlife. It was the course they'd willingly set for themselves.

He kissed her then, and her heart seemed to overflow with love, just as her eyes overflowed with tears.

"Stephanie," Charles whispered, his lips against hers. "We have a lot of time to make up for."

"It'll take at least fifty years, won't it?"

"At the very least," he murmured, kissing her again with a need that left her breathless.


David Bloomfield relaxed in his rocker on the front porch, his smile one of utter contentment. It was all coming to pass, just as he'd known it would. Just as Grace had told him. First Valerie, and now Steffie. His grin widened.

*My goodness,* he thought. *Norah's in for one heck of a surprise.*

\* \* \* \* \*

# REQUEST YOUR FREE BOOKS!

## 2 FREE NOVELS
## FROM THE ROMANCE COLLECTION
## PLUS 2 FREE GIFTS!

**YES!** Please send me 2 FREE novels from the Romance Collection and my 2 FREE gifts (gifts are worth about $10). After receiving them, if I don't wish to receive any more books, I can return the shipping statement marked "cancel." If I don't cancel, I will receive 4 brand-new novels every month and be billed just $5.74 per book in the U.S. or $6.24 per book in Canada. That's a saving of at least 28% off the cover price. It's quite a bargain! Shipping and handling is just 50¢ per book.* I understand that accepting the 2 free books and gifts places me under no obligation to buy anything. I can always return a shipment and cancel at any time. Even if I never buy another book, the two free books and gifts are mine to keep forever.

194/394 MDN E7NZ

| | | |
|---|---|---|
| Name | (PLEASE PRINT) | |
| Address | | Apt. # |
| City | State/Prov. | Zip/Postal Code |

Signature (if under 18, a parent or guardian must sign)

### Mail to **The Reader Service:**
**IN U.S.A.:** P.O. Box 1867, Buffalo, NY 14240-1867
**IN CANADA:** P.O. Box 609, Fort Erie, Ontario L2A 5X3

Not valid for current subscribers to the Romance Collection
or the Romance/Suspense Collection

**Want to try two free books from another line?**
**Call 1-800-873-8635 or visit www.morefreebooks.com.**

* Terms and prices subject to change without notice. Prices do not include applicable taxes. N.Y. residents add applicable sales tax. Canadian residents will be charged applicable provincial taxes and GST. Offer not valid in Quebec. This offer is limited to one order per household. All orders subject to approval. Credit or debit balances in a customer's account(s) may be offset by any other outstanding balance owed by or to the customer. Please allow 4 to 6 weeks for delivery. Offer available while quantities last.

**Your Privacy:** Harlequin Books is committed to protecting your privacy. Our Privacy Policy is available online at www.eHarlequin.com or upon request from the Reader Service. From time to time we make our lists of customers available to reputable third parties who may have a product or service of interest to you. If you would prefer we not share your name and address, please check here. ☐

**Help us get it right**—We strive for accurate, respectful and relevant communications. To clarify or modify your communication preferences, visit us at www.ReaderService.com/consumerchoice.

MROM10R

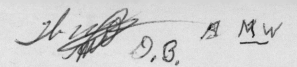

Dear Friends,

I'm excited that Norah, Valerie and Stephanie, three sisters I first introduced to readers in the early 1990s, are returning to print. Their stories were the precursors to the Cedar Cove series and the Blossom Street books. These three novels stand out for me for another reason, too. This was the first time I wrote such closely connected stories, and the lessons I learned in the process have stayed with me all this time.

Lesson number one: I will never again write books that take place simultaneously. I can't even begin to tell you how many headaches this brilliant idea of mine gave my editor, Paula Eykelhof, and me.

Speaking of my editor, I've had the rare privilege of working with Paula for nearly twenty-four years. As she often reminds people, that's longer than some marriages, and she's right. (She generally is!) We make a good team and have from the start. Paula worked on these books when I originally wrote them and she's helped me refresh them all these years later.

As often happens, the idea for this plot came from my own life. My father nearly died following his second heart surgery, and the thought of losing him shook our entire family. Thankfully (unlike the dad in these stories) my father didn't wake up convinced he could see the future. Although the stories' underlying premise is based on something serious, I believe you'll find plenty of reasons to smile as you read about the adventures—and misadventures—of the Bloomfield sisters and their friend Sherry Waterman.

Oh, that's lesson number two: I didn't want to stop. Once I got to know these sisters and I'd written their stories, there was another one begging to be told, so I wrote it, too. You'll learn more about Sherry in August (when *Orchard Valley Brides* comes out—it also includes *Norah*).

Now you understand why, when I write about Cedar Cove and Blossom Street, the stories just keep coming—and I just keep writing.

Enjoy!

*Debbie Macomber*

P.S. I love hearing from readers. You can reach me through my Web site, www.debbiemacomber.com, or by writing me at P.O. Box 1458, Port Orchard, WA 98366.

# Praise for the novels of Debbie Macomber

# Also by Debbie Macomber

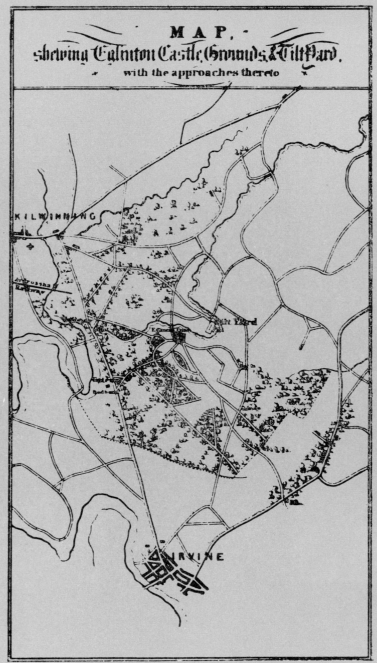

MAP,

shewing Eglinton Castle, Grounds, & Tilt Yard,

with the approaches thereto

Maclure & Macdonald lith. 57 Buchanan St. Glasgow

# THE KNIGHT AND THE UMBRELLA

1. The King's Champion casting his glove at the Coronation
of George IV in Westminster Hall

# THE KNIGHT
## and the
# UMBRELLA

An Account of
THE EGLINTON
TOURNAMENT
1839
by
IAN ANSTRUTHER

GEOFFREY BLES · LONDON

© IAN ANSTRUTHER, 1963

*Printed in Great Britain*
*by Willmer Brothers & Haram Ltd, Birkenhead*
*and published by*

GEOFFREY BLES LTD

52 DOUGHTY STREET, LONDON, W.C.I.
33 YORK STREET, SYDNEY
531 LITTLE COLLINS STREET, MELBOURNE
47–53 CASTLEMAINE STREET, BRISBANE
CML BUILDING, KING WILLIAM STREET, ADELAIDE
WYNDHAM STREET, AUCKLAND
10 DYAS ROAD, DON MILLS, ONTARIO
P.O. BOX 8879, PALLSTATE HOUSE
51 COMMISSIONER STREET, JOHANNESBURG

*First published 1963*

*For*
*J. C.*

# Contents

# Illustrations

## Plans

## Endpapers

(x)

# *Preface*

'The good old times—all times when old are good—'
                                        Byron *The Age of Bronze*

The urge to think of times gone by as somehow better than the present day is one of the deepest instincts in human nature. We read in the sixth chapter of Genesis: 'There were giants in the earth in those days; and also after that, when the sons of God came in unto the daughters of men, and they bare children to them, the same became mighty men which were of old men of renown.' This was the world before the Flood and, according to the presumed testament of Noah whose own grandfather was the famous Methuselah, the latter descended from Adam and therefore from God.

The above is merely a handy example, easily matched in other mythologies, of the way in which from the earliest times men have seen their ancestors larger than life. For the same reason, naturally, too—a primitive urge to honour the dead—they have always taken a magnified view of all the things they did.

Throughout Europe in the 19th century but first especially in the British Isles, people began to turn their thoughts to the Middle Ages. The basic reason for this was a feeling of change. New methods of working the land and new processes of manufacture with power supplied by enormous steam engines and quantity achieved by mass

(xi)

production had completely altered the pattern of social life. The Romantic Movement, at the same time, backed by men like Hume and Gibbon who supplied a mass of historical facts, and others like Scott and Bishop Percy who published the ballads of the Middle Ages, revealed to the literate and cultivated world not only the beauties of savage nature but, at least as it appeared to some, the grand simplicity of English medieval life. In a shifting world of factories and steamships, people thought of the past with pride and nostalgia; a mechanical era might lie ahead but nothing, surely, could beat the good old days.

In this atmosphere of change and progress in the year 1838, a young nobleman, the Earl of Eglinton, who longed for the ordered, feudal life and the thrilling combats of his fighting ancestors, decided to revive a tournament. His proposal, now, seems quite ridiculous but at the time it was taken seriously, just as today, in the 20th century, the current fashion for the arts of the Regency, and especially the passion for Georgian architecture with modern villas in the classical style being built by speculators throughout the country, will certainly, in a hundred years, appear to be idiotic. What happened when the tournament took place forms the principal theme behind this book.

The other theme, in a way subsidiary, and yet, in a way, the more important is why he instead of someone else—anyone at all amongst his friends—was the one who actually gave it. There were many people who were just as rich, many who lived in Gothic castles, many who admired the Middle Ages, and many who, better than himself, could have staged such a tournament easily; but the fact remained that it fell to him; and all students of human nature who love the play of chance and character will enjoy watching how these worked and seeing what, in the end, occurred to his scheme.

From the point of view of social history and the general development of the Gothic Revival, the Eglinton Tournament came at a critical moment. The last genuinely 'Gothik' folly of the type invented in the 18th century, it was, too, like the Houses of Parliament—of which the cornerstone had just been laid—the first accurately medieval spectacle of the new Victorian epoch. It forms thus a distinctive landmark between the old and the new, and divides the fashion for the 'picturesque' from the mawkish mania for knights and tournaments and all the trappings of the Middle Ages which first inspired and finally destroyed the country's popular taste.

It was not the first to be held in Europe or, indeed, in the United States (some 18th and 19th century Tournaments are listed in Appendix I), for the Gothic Revival and the Romantic Movement affected people all over the world, but it was the first as well as the last to be held in the United Kingdom; because, in the British Isles at least, the right conditions never appeared again. Not only are such revivals expensive, but also all the feeling in the world for the days gone by and the deeds of chivalry were never enough in later decades to animate even the richest enthusiasts to follow Lord Eglinton's example.

For, in holding such a tournament, he was caught unaware in a net of circumstances; and thus he lost an ancient fortune, not for honour, nor for glory, nor even for the love of a beautiful woman, but simply because he was drowned in the sea of his time.

2. The medieval games at Firle Place, 1827 (artist unknown)

3. Eglinton Castle, from *Survey of Ayrshire*, W. Aiton, 1811

# *Acknowledgements*

Much research is needed to write a book like this especially if, as proved the case, there is no central source of documents; and as a result, over a period, a large number of people have helped me complete it. To record their names would require a page and, for this reason, I do not propose to do so; but to them first, once again, I should like to offer my thanks.

I must, however, mention a few: Mr A. B. Thompson of the Meteorological Office in Edinburgh for providing figures of rainfall in Ayrshire; Dr James Corson, the authority on Scott, for sending me data on the sales of *Ivanhoe*; Mr Kenneth MacKelvie, Chartered Accountant, for helping me to study the Eglinton accounts; Colonel Evelyn Arthur for lending me books; The Marquess of Waterford for bringing me miniatures; The Duke of Atholl for offering me photographs; Sir James Hunter Blair for loaning me letters; Commander Hamilton for giving me papers; Mr and Mrs William Mure for technical advice; Mr Robert Oattes for presenting me with a bowl; Mr James Campbell for the use of a valuable scrapbook.

This last belonged to Joseph Train, the devoted admirer of Sir Walter Scott who wrote that he wished

'to convert into a more permanent form the various accounts of the Tournament contained in the floating periodical literature of the day with the aim of affording

(xv)

at some future period the accurate and interesting details of an exhibition which, although likely to be only incidentally alluded to in the histories of the time, certainly in its object as well as in its execution stood out in bold and prominent relief amid the events of the day.'

The antiquary's foresight has now been justified, and to him also, although long dead, I would like to acknowledge my debt.

It became necessary in the course of the work to put on a suit of armour, and this was arranged by the late Sir James Mann to whom I render particular thanks as I do, also, to William Reid, the expert esquire who armed me.

Next, I should like to thank Mrs Bonnaire for typing the MS a thousand times; Sir James Fergusson, Keeper of the Records of Scotland, for making available the Eglinton muniments; the skilled staff of the London Library and also that of the Library at the War Office for saving me many hours of research; Jocelyn Gibb, my friend and publisher, for spurring me on with genial encouragement; and my wife, Honor, for patience and help.

Finally I come to the two families, those descended from the Lambs of Beauport and the present heir of the 'Tournament Earl'—Miss Harbord of Mousehold, Norwich and William, 17th Earl of Eglinton—on whose private papers this book is based. For rendering me access to their personal archives, giving me their time and hospitality, allowing me to borrow precious volumes, patiently answering innumerable letters, appealing to the press for missing material and, during the many months when it seemed that nothing would ever be written, giving me advice, support and encouragement, I cannot, as every biographer will guess, ever properly express a fraction of my thanks.

(xvi)

# THE EGLINTON TOURNAMENT

'Some people despise and abuse it, and rejoyce that it has cost Lord Eglinton . . . a great sum of money. Others laud it as an original and noble idea, far beyond hunting or shooting or racing, and hold that his Lordship deserves immortality. . . .'

HENRY THOMAS COCKBURN
*Memorials of his Time*
entry dated 15th October, 1839.

## PART ONE

## The Background

### THE CORONATION OF WILLIAM IV 1831
### 'THE HALFCROWNATION'

'As the economy of the age did not allow His Majesty to give his Peers the usual coronation dinner in Westminster Hall, he privately entertained a large party at St. James's.'

*Ann. Reg.*, 1831, p. 155


### QUEEN VICTORIA'S CORONATION 1838
### 'THE PENNY CROWNING'

'The Coronation of Queen Victoria was conducted in most respects after the abridged model of that of her immediate predecessor; the walking procession of all the estates of the realm, and the banquet in Westminster Hall, with all the feudal services attendant thereon, being wholly dispensed with; not, however, without many complaints and various public struggles, as well on the part of the antiquaries, as on that of the tradesmen of the metropolis.'

*Ann. Reg.*, 1838, p. 96, *Chron.*

# Chapter One

THE CORONATION of Queen Victoria, which was held on 28th June, 1838, came at a time of extraordinary progress and change.

The railway age, which for many years had remained a mere dream, had at last become a reality for, during the reign of her uncle and predecessor, William IV, from 1830 to 1837, the power of steam which had been developing steadily for half a century suddenly reached a point of dramatic expansion and, just as suddenly, the homely plod of hoof and sail and the ancient limits of a day's journey started to crumble and vanish.

In 1829 George and Robert Stephenson had successfully demonstrated their famous steam engine 'Rocket', and a year later the first passenger railway in the world had been opened from Manchester to Liverpool. This was followed by the line from Liverpool to Birmingham in 1837, and in 1838, the year of the coronation, by the final, triumphant link from Birmingham to London.

The first official journey over this last route of 112 miles, which had taken ten years to plan and construct and had cost the enormous sum of five million pounds, was performed in four hours and fourteen minutes at an average rate of twenty-six miles per hour. This was twice the speed of the 'Tally-ho', the swiftest stage coach running between the same cities, and from this moment it was clear to everybody that the coaching era was finished.

In the very same summer an identical milestone was reached in the development of steamships. For a number

3

of years small paddle steamers had plied about the coast and across the Channel and once in a while one of them had crossed the Atlantic, but in 1838, the year of the coronation, three gigantic wooden liners, the *Royal William*, the *Sirius* and the *Great Western*, were all launched within a few weeks of each other and began to steam back and forward to the United States regularly.

The most famous of these was the *Great Western*, which was designed by Isambard Kingdom Brunel. She was 212 feet in length, 35 feet in breadth between the paddles, 23 feet in depth, of 2,300 tons displacement, of 750 horses power, as it was described in those days, and of $8\frac{1}{2}$ knots in speed.

She was both the greatest ship in the world and the first in the world to make the crossing by steam alone, which she did steadily in fifteen days and sometimes in twelve and a half. This was four times as fast, at least, as the average time by sail, and from this moment it was clear, too, that the days of sail were over.

These two developments alone, apart from a number of others which were just as important but less spectacular— like the first adoption of Nasmyth's steam hammer, the first commercial use of the electric telegraph, the first employment of the railways for carrying the mails, the first bicycle, even the first expresso steam coffee-pot—convinced everyone, like it or not, that the country stood on the brink of a different epoch.

For this reason, because of the great change in the times, because of the happy contrast between George IV, the last monarch to be crowned with traditional ceremony, and Queen Victoria; because, too, of a useful precedent in the coronation of William IV which had been curtailed because of the riotous state of the country, it was decided to make a change in the coronation.

4

The antiquated and now pointless ceremonies which had been held previously in Westminster Hall after the service in the Abbey, the public state banquet for the Peers, and the knight in armour, the hereditary King's Champion who challenged all comers to deny the sovereign's right to succession, were abolished. A gay, simple procession from Buckingham Palace, up Constitution Hill, along Piccadilly, down St James's Street, via Pall Mall to Charing Cross, and thence by Parliament Street to the Abbey was arranged to take their place.

This change, however, which was announced in the *London Gazette* on the 10th of April by Lord Melbourne, the Whig Prime Minister, and which was clearly in keeping with the times did not, to a large number of conservative citizens, seem to be necessary in the least.

'I am a plain country gentleman of the old school . . . but my blood is up . . . and I must take leave to ask a few unsophisticated questions,' one of them wrote to the editor of *The Times* three days afterwards.

Was it not typical of the present, penny-wise government of Whigs to pretend they could not afford a few thousand pounds for a coronation when every year they wasted millions on popular reform? And was it not the case that the cancellation of the banquet and the King's Champion was merely a political trick to catch the support of the working classes and snub the old Tory aristocracy?

These were the views of a large number of Englishmen and especially, naturally enough, of the many peers who had taken part in the banquet for George IV and had found it a noble symbol of ancient homage and chivalry. It was a great event, one of the oldest institutions in the monarchy, and the last relic of the days when kings dined in state before their subjects. Furthermore, apart from the ceremony of the Royal Champion, it was the scene of

5

many other feudal customs of equal charm and antiquity.

The Earl Marshal, the Lord High Steward and the Lord High Constable had to ride into Westminster Hall with the first course to escort the dish to the royal table and, once it was served, they had to retire backwards, still mounted on their horses. The Archbishop of Canterbury, as Lord of the Manor of Bardolf, had to present the King with a mess of dilligrout. This was a watery porridge with plums in it, much favoured by William the Conqueror and ordained by him as the manorial fee in perpetuity. The Duke of Atholl, as Lord of the Isle of Man, had to provide the King with two falcons. Thomas Rider, Esq., Lord of the Manor of Nether Bilsington, had to produce three maple cups which were then given to the Mayor of Oxford in exchange for a bowl of wine.

In spite of the interest of these and many other traditional activities—like the washing of hands and the strewing of herbs to prevent pestilence—nothing compared to the ceremony of the King's Champion which had been performed by the same Lincolnshire family of Dymoke for nearly six centuries.

Immediately after the first course the Champion had to appear in full armour on a caparisoned charger, just as he would for a tournament, preceded by two trumpeters, two esquires holding his shield and lance, and escorted by the Lord High Constable and the Earl Marshal. The Knight Marshal, the Earl Marshal's deputy, had to clear the way and, after a flourish of trumpets, the Lancaster Herald called on all persons of any degree whatsoever to declare themselves and fight if they disputed the claim of the new sovereign to ascend the throne.

The Champion then threw down his gauntlet, which was picked up and returned to him by the Herald after a pause of a few moments.

This was performed three times—at the entrance to the hall, at the centre and at the top end before the King's table. After the last challenge the King drank to the Champion from a gold cup which he handed to the Champion and from which the latter drank to the King in return. When he had drained the cup he was allowed to keep it as his fee. After this he shouted 'Long life to his Majesty the King', and then, bowing to the Monarch, backed his horse away from the royal table. He had to continue backing all the way down the hall to the entrance. This was an extremely difficult feat, especially in full armour.

As invariably happens in public life when a large body of people are discontented, one man at last came forward and became their official spokesman. In this case it was Charles William Stewart, 3rd Marquess of Londonderry, the half-brother of the famous Lord Castlereagh, himself a distinguished soldier and diplomatist and friend and staff officer of Wellington during the Peninsular War.

On the day following the Prime Minister's cancellation of the banquet in Westminster Hall he spoke in the House of Lords. He deplored, he said, the abrogation of so many ancient ceremonies. The great changes in the present time ought to inspire the Government to keep the old traditions instead of putting an end to them.

These remarks had no result and a month later he presented a petition to the same effect from five hundred merchants of the City of London, for the City, too, like the Lords of Manors, enjoyed many ancient privileges at coronation banquets of which, now, they were being deprived.

Finally, on the 28th of May, when none of these moves had any effect whatever, he asked the Prime Minister not to crown the Queen at all. What was the point of doing so, he asked furiously, glaring across the floor of the House of

Lords at the Government's spokesman, Lord Fitzwilliam. Let the noble Earl present a motion to abolish the coronation altogether and then—ha ha, bitterly!—let him present another to abolish himself.

But Lord Londonderry was well known as a root and branch reactionary, to such a degree, in fact, that a mob of enraged reformers had once torn him off his horse in Hyde Park; so the Government took no notice of him. There were the strongest possible reasons for not having an old fashioned coronation and Lord Melbourne and other members of the administration made them clear to the public convincingly.

The banquet for George IV, seventeen years earlier, had cost the enormous sum of twenty-five thousand pounds. Now, the exchequer was short of funds and the last budget, just declared, had shown a deficit of one and a half millions. Therefore, all departments had to economise, and certainly nothing at all could be spared for what, in fact, with George IV, had only developed into an orgy.

Added to this was the great changeover to mass production in industry. Thousands of people were out of work and at this moment fifty-thousand weavers were literally starving. It was clearly impossible, under these circumstances, to hold a public state banquet for the peers, let alone for the Queen to partake of it with them.

As to the appearance of the King's Champion—at the coronation of George IV, a clanking youth, who had challenged no one except the antiquaries because he had carried the wrong shield—there was every chance that the whole ceremony would simply become a pantomime. For this had happened during the past on three different and calamitous occasions.

At the coronation of William and Mary in 1689 the Champion had lost his Champion's glove. An old crone had picked it up, laughed mysteriously, and disappeared with it. A romantic stranger, whom all the Jacobites knew to be Bonnie Prince Charlie, had done the same thing at the coronation of George III in 1761. He had seized the Champion's glove from the floor, thrown another, and immediately vanished.

In 1685, at the coronation of James II, the Champion had suffered a truly immortal humiliation. He had flung his glove to the ground so furiously that he had flung himself to the floor in pursuit of it. He had lain on his back like a winded beetle. In the first moment of frightful silence the Queen had snorted and the King had actually laughed.

Lord Melbourne recalled these incidents pointedly. No Government could risk this sort of catastrophe, he said. He was quite sure that on reflexion every sensible person would agree with him.

Thus it came about that Queen Victoria was crowned with only simple pageantry. The state banquet in Westminster Hall, the romantic challenge by the Royal Champion and all the other picturesque ceremonies were done away with. Like the feudal homage they represented, they became themselves things of the past.

In spite, however, of the Prime Minister's reasonable hope that everyone who thought about his arguments would agree with him, many people refused to do so, especially the old Tory aristocracy, and particularly one of them—a dashing, wealthy nobleman of twenty-six, head of an ancient Scottish family; Archibald William Montgomerie, the 13th Earl of Eglinton.

He was perfectly mortified at being deprived of the coronation banquet and all its feudal solemnities. For apart from being a true product of his times, born at the high tide of the romantic movement, steeped in the myths and lore of chivalry and thoroughly addicted to medieval ceremonies, it so happened that his step-father, Sir Charles Lamb—who had brought him up like a son—was the Earl Marshal's deputy, the Knight Marshal of the Royal Household, and ought to have marshalled the Champion for Queen Victoria.

So as well as feeling annoyed at being done out of the banquet, to which he had looked forward all his life and to which his rank entitled him, he was highly irritated at being denied the fun of watching his step-father, clad in a scarlet dress slashed with blue and a scarlet cloak and blue stockings, clear the floor of Westminster Hall for the Champion. He was also perfectly incensed at missing the spectacle of the Champion himself, a veritable knight in armour, in flesh and blood, casting his steel gauntlet as though at a tournament.

Therefore, after the coronation in the summer of 1838, he returned home to his Ayrshire seat, a vast, modern, Gothic castle, thoroughly exasperated at missing these famous ceremonies. For the worst of it was that Queen Victoria was very young and very unlikely to die before him; and so he had almost certainly lost the only chance of his life.

During the first week of August a guest* or neighbour whose name is forgotten but which ought to be written in black, funereal Gothic type in the family records and cursed for ever, made a suggestion which slightly cheered him up.

At his next private race meeting at Eglinton Park, annually held in the spring at Bogside, he might add to the

---

* This was possibly Henry Gage, the Knight of the Ram at the Tournament, a friend and exact contemporary of Lord Eglinton's and a neighbour of the latter's step-father in Sussex. Gage's father, Viscount Gage, had held a party of this nature at his home, Firle Place, in 1827.

amusements by instituting medieval games. One of his friends could appear in armour and perform the ceremony of the challenge, while others could run at rings and tilt at quintains.

This idea, at which Lord Eglinton laughed and to which he agreed, started an extraordinary rumour: that in the spring he planned a medieval tournament; and because of the great number of people like himself who were sorry about the Champion; because, too, of the spell of the Gothic Revival which made them interested in medieval life; and because, finally, of a frivolous hoax in the *Court Journal* the year before which had announced a tournament at Windsor Castle for the Queen's accession, practically everybody believed it.

They wrote in hundreds to congratulate him and ask for details, while the *Court Journal* and other popular society newspapers ironically welcomed the return to the age of chivalry.

At first, Lord Eglinton simply laughed at all this. But after a day or two he began to think about it.

For unluckily for him, his step-father, Sir Charles Lamb, who was still smarting, too, at being done out of the ancient ceremonies, thought the idea was captivating. Because, as Knight Marshal of the Royal Household, he could then appear in correct regalia, holding his baton and leading his marshalmen, and perform his authentic medieval role as a principal umpire of a tournament.

It happened, also, that Sir Charles's son, Lord Eglinton's half-brother, a dreamy artistic boy who naturally knew Lord Eglinton intimately, shared his father's enthusiasm—although for entirely different reasons. For oddly enough, by a strange and unhappy twist of fate, he had nursed a passion for tournaments all his life—in fact was positively obsessed by them—and even as a man, at the age of twenty-three, lived entirely in a private world of shining knights and chivalry.

So, pushed along by his step-father and half-brother, who looked for the fun and none of the expense, Lord Eglinton announced that the rumour was correct.

What was more, he said, he would follow it up with a medieval banquet. There would be roast peacocks, boars' heads, barons of beef and bowls of dilligrout, with every other antiquated delicacy, and afterwards a dance to the strains of lutes and harpsichords. By doing this he might even discredit the Government. For such an act of private hospitality would mock their parsimony at the coronation and would surely make Lord Melbourne blush with shame.

In taking this decision, Lord Eglinton embarked on the greatest folly of the century. He soon discovered that however cheap and commonplace it might have been to arrange a tournament in the age of chivalry, however simple for the heralds to announce it and however easy for a knight to take part in it, in the age of steam it was hardly a possibility.

The organisation of all the participants—all of whom had to be enlisted—and of armour, lances, costumes and tents—all of which had to be made—required a staff of hundreds, while the cost of mounting and equipping even one single combatant proved to be astronomical.

Being a spoilt, impulsive young man, immensely rich and used to having his smallest wish even at the slightest pretext, he simply waved his hand when all this became evident and said he would do it anyway.

And he carried it through to the end, even though he had to postpone it, had to pledge a large part of his ancestral estate to pay for it, had to suffer the ridicule of the press throughout the world and, finally, to endure an ultimate affliction of Providence.

Any ordinary person would have been crushed by all this, but Lord Eglinton almost thrived on it. Beneath a delectable manner he was a man of fine courage, too, with plenty of pride, common sense and capability. For the first time in his life he was really put to a test and, although the trial was absurd and the defeat agonising, he displayed such extraordinary cheerfulness and sportsmanship that in the end the jeers were drowned by a murmur of congratulations.

He became as a result, and by general acclamation, the most popular nobleman in Scotland, and this position he held for the rest of his life. He was loaded with honours in the world of sport, and, later on, when Lord Melbourne's government was out and the Tories in office, with coveted political distinctions.

Twenty years afterwards and not long before his comparatively early death—by then twice Lord Lieutenant of Ireland, patron of the Turf, Derby winner and for many years 'the excellent and justly popular nobleman' of his epitaph in Burke's *Peerage*—he wrote an account of his life.

He composed it privately, just for his family, in neat, close handwriting, in a small locked leather diary, and only recorded those details of his career which he thought had been interesting. Of the year 1839 and its great *débâcle*—the one event for which he is now remembered and for which at the shallow edge of social history he is certain of immortality—he wrote merely, 'I gave a tournament at Eglinton.' That, except for a few irrelevant remarks, was the only mention he made of it.

He said nothing at all of the difficulties, humiliations, notoriety and disappointments, nor did he mention the cost. Throughout his life he spent his money in a golden shower so he probably never assessed it. And although, in fact, the expense was gigantic, compared to his losses afterwards on bets, wagers, carriages and racehorses, it was certainly only a drop in the bucket.

But there was, too, possibly another reason for hardly mentioning the tournament. For him, at least, it had broken the spell of the Gothic Revival, the magic enchantment of the Age of Chivalry, the charmed aura of his vanished youth; and he himself, in a way like Orpheus, by looking back, had caused the death of the thing he loved the most.

In wearing armour, couching a lance, paying *devoirs* to a Queen of Beauty and trying to evoke the days of tournaments, he had learnt nothing of medieval habits and only discovered a prosaic truth:

That the past can never be brought to life, and that ancient pastimes and decorative arts should never be imitated in a different age.

Lord Melbourne had been proved to be right. The olden days were not so good and to revive chivalry in the Age of Steam was only to invite an absurd catastrophe.

# Chapter Two

THE FAMILY of the Earls of Eglinton, the Montgomeries of Eagleshame and, through the female line, the Setons of Seton, had one of the oldest Norman pedigrees in Scotland, which stretched back to a French knight called Mundegumbri who settled in what is now Ayrshire in the twelfth century.

It was always supposed that the Mundegumbris came from France with William the Conqueror, and were in descent from the ancient French family of Montgommerie, but the only certain fact was that this particular Mundegumbri acquired the lands of Eagleshame from the High Steward of Scotland at some time after 1157. He was called Robert, and he married the High Steward's daughter, Marjory, so perhaps the lands were her dowry. He died about 1178.

For the next two hundred years his successors lived the life of small but important landlords, fighting in local feuds, attending the Scottish court, supporting the King at war and all the while, by purchase and marriage, slowly increasing the family property and influence.

In 1388 the 9th descendant, Sir John Montgomerie, fought in the famous battle of Otterburn and captured Harry Hotspur, the renowned son of the Earl of Northumberland. For this exploit he was immortalised in Scottish ballad and forced his captive, by way of ransom, to build a castle at Polnoon on the Eagleshame estate. He did well in domestic matters, too, for he married the only daughter of a neighbouring landlord, Sir Hugh Eglinton, and

15

c

through her gained the Eglinton and Ardrossan estates.

One more generation passed and then the family became enobled. Sir Alexander Montgomerie, 11th of Eagleshame, who was a Privy Councillor, a Lord of Parliament, and three times the King's representative at treaties of peace with England, was created the 1st Lord Montgomerie by James II in 1445.

This gave the family a position of much greater authority and it was not long before they took advantage of it. Lord Montgomerie's eldest son died before him and never succeeded, but his grandson and great grandson both inherited his ability and strength of character, and the latter, by supporting the future James IV in the struggle against his father, gained a position of Royal favour which finally earned him the Earldom in 1506. He, too, like his great grandfather, was a Lord of Parliament, a Privy Councillor and a constant holder of many high and important appointments throughout his life; and during sixty years of influence he greatly increased the family estates. In him, Hugh Montgomerie, 1st Earl of Eglinton and 13th holder of the lands of Eagleshame, the direct descendants of Robert Mundegumbri reached their peak after a steady climb of seventeen generations.

Then there was a change. In 1612, the 5th Earl, the great grandson of the 1st Earl, died childless. Perhaps this was the result of too much family ambition, for his uncle who was the heir-apparent but without sons, broke the rules of blood relationship and married the Earl to his eldest daughter.

Whatever the cause, the 5th Earl left no descendants and thus, after more than four hundred and fifty years, the male line of the Mundegumbris became extinct.

In those days, however, there were more ways than one of keeping a great family intact and before he died the Earl obtained a Crown Charter to name an heir in the female line.

His maternal aunt, Lady Margaret Montgomerie, had three sons by her husband, the 1st Earl of Winton, and he chose the last of these, Sir Alexander Seton.

In this way the family preserved their identity. For although in lineal terms they became Setons, they kept their own name of Montgomerie and all their old estates and privileges.

In the end they came out better than before. One hundred and fifty years later the Setons themselves became extinct, with their own ancient baronies of Seton and Tranent and their earldom of Winton.

Then the Montgomeries claimed these honours because of the fact that in birth they were really Setons. They still kept the name of Montgomerie, however; for the Crown Charter gave them the right and just because of a little blood they saw no reason to insult their ancestors and substitute the name of Seton for their own noble Norman patronymic.

The chapter of family history which opened now with the new heir, Sir Alexander Seton, continued without a break to the 13th Earl of Eglinton who gave the Tournament. Sir Alexander did not inherit entirely without opposition, for in spite of the Crown Charter, his right to the Earldom was challenged by James VI and he had to struggle hard to establish it. He was obliged, too, to make a large payment to a neighbouring peer, Lord Balfour of Burleigh, who had laid claim to part of his estate of Kilwinning. Also, in compensation to the last Earl's wife, as Dowager Countess and eldest child of the former heir-presumptive, he was forced to raise a substantial sum in hard cash, equivalent to thirty-two thousand pounds today (1960).

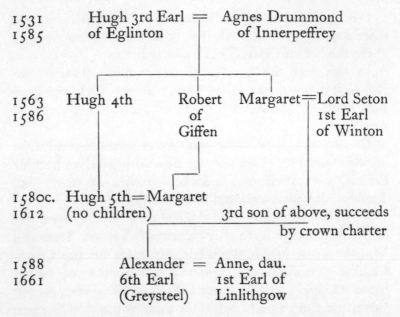

1531    Hugh 3rd Earl  =  Agnes Drummond
1585    of Eglinton         of Innerpeffrey

1563   Hugh 4th      Robert    Margaret=Lord Seton
1586                 of                  1st Earl
                     Giffen              of Winton

1580c.  Hugh 5th=Margaret
1612    (no children)        3rd son of above, succeeds
                                        by crown charter

1588    Alexander  =  Anne, dau.
1661    6th Earl      1st Earl of
        (Greysteel)   Linlithgow

But 'Greysteel', as he came to be called because of his quiet but dangerous temperament, brushed aside the financial difficulties and, showing a princely disregard for the inconvenience of debt, which appeared again in many succeeding generations, pledged his entire property to obtain the funds.

'God send us some money, for they are little thought of that want it,' he is said to have prayed many years afterwards.

Although this transaction placed him in great financial straits for the rest of his life, he lived to see his titles and estates firmly established with every hope of passing them on to his children.

This ambition was doubly fulfilled. Through him, two hundred years later, the male line of the family was saved

*Diagram showing the descent of Lord Eglinton
from 'Greysteel'*

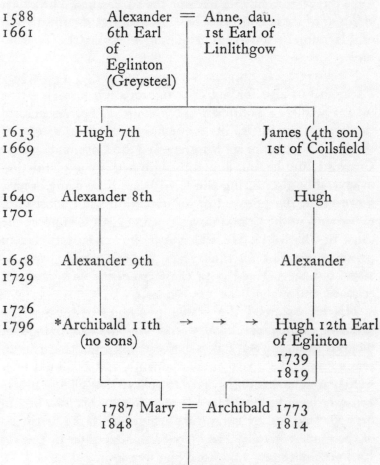

| | | |
|---|---|---|
| 1588<br>1661 | Alexander<br>6th Earl<br>of<br>Eglinton<br>(Greysteel) | = Anne, dau.<br>1st Earl of<br>Linlithgow |
| 1613<br>1669 | Hugh 7th | James (4th son)<br>1st of Coilsfield |
| 1640<br>1701 | Alexander 8th | Hugh |
| 1658<br>1729 | Alexander 9th | Alexander |
| 1726<br>1796 | *Archibald 11th<br>(no sons)  → → → | Hugh 12th Earl<br>of Eglinton<br>1739<br>1819 |

1787 Mary = Archibald 1773
1848            1814

ARCHIBALD WILLIAM 13th Earl
who gave the
Tournament

* Succeeded his brother, 10th Earl, not shown.

from extinction a second time. His eldest son's direct descendant, the 11th Earl, had no sons and his fourth son's direct descendants became the successors. The eldest children of these two branches married and the fourth son of this union became Lord Eglinton who gave the Tournament.

'Greysteel' was famous not only for saving the family Earldom but also for living a vigorous life himself. As a man, a soldier, a politician and a courtier, he was held in the highest regard by his contemporaries. He was one of the many Scottish peers who renewed the Covenant against Charles I, and he fought against him with great distinction in several battles during the Civil War. Like many others, however, he disapproved of his execution and he lost faith in the aims of the Commonwealth and began to support the cause of Charles II. He was captured in 1651 and kept in prison at Berwick for nine years, forfeiting all his possessions, but he survived until the Restoration and was then released and given back his estates.

His life spanned the whole era which witnessed the ultimate decline of chivalry and saw the beginnings of modern thought. As a boy he certainly must have worn armour and taken part in tournaments, and as an old man he may well have found it hard to believe that such pastimes had ever been fashionable. He was thus, in his own life, in his own time and by hereditary achievement, the first head of the modern family. He married the daughter of the 1st Earl of Linlithgow who bore him five sons and he died in 1661 at the age of seventy-three.

From now on, for the next six generations, right up to the time of Lord Eglinton who gave the Tournament, two interwoven themes formed the pattern of family development. The first of these was consolidation and increase of all that 'Greysteel' had left them, and the second, always dragging close behind, was the need to find enough money to achieve it.

There are many papers about debts from this time onwards in the family archives. Some of these are classified 'good', others 'doubtful' and some 'desperate'. Seven years after 'Greysteel's' death his son had to sell £29,000 worth of property to meet some urgent creditors, and three generations and eighty years had to pass before every one of them was satisfied.

'Greysteel's' great-grandson, the 9th Earl, brought the family to solvency. But he no sooner did this than he borrowed huge sums himself and passed the burden on to his successors.

From this moment, in the early years of the reign of George I, the family debt was perpetual. Long minorities, faithful trustees and Acts of Parliament made no difference to it. It was like the sea which washed away the Eglinton Harbour at Ardrossan. It rose and fell and imperceptibly sucked the soil from the roots of the family tree.

The most interesting feature of the family history from the time of 'Greysteel's' death to the succession of Lord Eglinton's paternal grandfather at the end of the 18th century was the fact that for one hundred and twenty years the estates were managed by only three members of the family. This came about because 'Greysteel's' grandson was not interested in estate management and handed over the whole property to his son on his eighteenth birthday. This son who became the 9th Earl controlled the estates for fifty-three years, first with such economy that all the debts were extinguished and then with such enthusiasm that every one of them was resuscitated.

In a way, he was quite justified in acting in this manner, for all the projects for which he borrowed money— enclosure, drainage, building and especially planting trees—greatly increased the potential value of the estate. All that his children had to do was to live the way he had done himself—at first plainly for forty years, paying off the debts, and then on a moderate scale with their unencumbered income.

His sons, however, found this philosophy tiresome and each succeeding generation only accepted the convenient parts of it, taking loans as fast as they could and admonishing their children to pay them back.

The 9th Earl was responsible, too, for a special Will which in later years brought an irreparable family disaster. He entailed the lands which he had bought himself—Dundonald, Kilmaurs, Glassford and Southennan, on his children generally, male or female. The great danger in this arrangement lay in the chance that one of his heirs might have only daughters. For if an Earl died with daughters but no sons, the old Eglinton estates and titles would pass to the nearest male relatives but the new lands of the 9th Earl would remain in line to his own female children. So the new heir would only inherit half the total estate.

This precise event happened in 1796 with Lord Eglinton's father and mother, for his mother became heiress to the 9th Earl's new estates and his father, a cousin, the heir-apparent to the old family lands and Earldom; since the two married, the whole inheritance was kept intact.

In the 19th century, however, it happened a second time and the old titles and estates and the new lands again became separated. The estate was split and ever since the two valuable parts have remained in different possession.

After the death of the 9th Earl in 1729, only two earls remained before the succession changed to 'Greysteel's' younger line, the Montgomeries of Coilsfield.

These two were brothers, Alexander the 10th and Archibald the 11th, and they both showed particular ability combined with all the best traits of their ancestors. They were manly, generous, amusing and hospitable; intelligent farmers, distinguished courtiers and efficient holders of many important administrative posts. The 10th Earl, especially, made real contributions to Scottish agriculture by adopting the latest methods on his estates and breaking down many old-fashioned prejudices by the success of his experiments.

Some people thought him a crank because he tried to discard his peerage, finding the House of Lords frustrating and believing that he could be more useful in the House of Commons.

He was not really a peer, he said, because he had lost his patent, and therefore he ought to be treated as a commoner.

The Dean of the Faculty of Advocates in Edinburgh, however, ruled that the loss of patent was no proof of loss of nobility and doubtless the Earl's heir, his brother Archibald, was extremely glad to hear it; but for some time he renounced his title and called himself Mr Montgomerie.

'Don't forget horse howing if you love Scotland,' he wrote to his brother when the latter was on the eve of a duel, his passion for agriculture making him forgetful of the possibility of his brother's death.

But the 10th Earl himself was the one to lose his life. He was shot by a poacher on his own estate in 1769 and died, unmarried, at the age of forty-six.

With the succession of Archibald Montgomerie, 11th Earl, Lord Eglinton's maternal grandfather, the senior male line of the Setons came to an end. Almost two hundred years had passed since 'Greysteel' had staked his career to uphold the Montgomerie titles and estates and not one of his children, grandchildren, great-grandchildren, great-great-grandchildren had shown themselves unworthy of it. They had lived honourably and usefully, serving their country and increasing their estates, and if they had also borrowed money, there were few landowners who had behaved differently, and at least they had never done so for themselves but always in the best interest of the family.

When the 11th Earl died, only four years before the beginning of the 19th century, the family had reached their highest level of magnificence. They were rich, grand, influential and popular and could look back on 700 years of ancestry with frank and open pride.

The one thing they lacked was an up-to-date castle. The ancient house at Eglinton—'strong but rude', according to a contemporary—was small and old fashioned and altogether unfitted for modern life.

Luckily the new Earl who now succeeded happened to have a penchant for architecture and had just built a delightful small house on his own estate at Coilsfield.

The moment his cousin died he sent for an architect.

It was no good, late in life and rather unexpectedly becoming Earl of Eglinton, Lord Montgomerie and twenty-fourth holder of the lands of Eagleshame if he had to live in a ruin.

He realised he would have to find some money; but if twenty-four generations had managed to do so, he felt convinced that he could find some, too.

In Hugh Montgomerie, 12th Earl, and Lord Eglinton's paternal grandfather, all the family characteristics burst forth uncontrollably. He had spent many years in the Army, seeing active service in America, and had then retired to his family home of Coilsfield and become a Member of Parliament. Since he was only a third cousin of his two predecessors, he might have expected to receive only a third part of their ancestral temptations, but instead he inherited three times the force of every one of them. The excitement of being the Earl unhinged him and, having passed fifty-seven years of his life in comparative simplicity, he now determined to live as he really liked.

As well as delighting in architecture, he particularly enjoyed surveying and civil engineering, having, in the latter part of his career, been Government Inspector of military highways in Scotland and having, with great pleasure and regardless of cost, surveyed and constructed dozens of roads and bridges.

He now, therefore, surveyed and inspected the Eglinton Estates and at once he observed the need for several improvements.

First, he demolished Eglinton Castle to the ground and rebuilt it, ignoring the architect, in a style, as his factor put it, 'uncommonly elegant and peculiarly his own.'

Next, he rejuvenated his accounts by taking control of the richer half of the family estate which had just passed by tail general to his cousin, the late Earl's eldest daughter. He arranged her marriage to his eldest son and appointed himself trustee of her settlement.

Then he embarked on a major work of hydraulic engineering. He commenced a gigantic harbour on his estate at Ardrossan on the Firth of Clyde designed to hold a hundred ships of all sizes, and began a canal at Glasgow at the same time by which to connect his harbour direct to the city. The idea behind this was that ships could then avoid the longer tidal route of the river and be towed conveniently straight to the centre of the metropolis.

Two things went wrong with these arrangements. Every winter the sea destroyed the work he had done in the summer and every year the hazards of navigating the river by sail were diminished by the increased efficiency of steamships.

The whole magnificent project became a failure. The canal was never finished; the harbour was hardly advanced beyond a breakwater, and the only thing that was ever completed was a charming small house at Ardrossan called The Pavilion—a kind of luxury surveyor's office from which he issued his instructions.

In spite of all these disasters, however, the scheme was sound in its day and the very best experts were used to survey it. The chief of these was Thomas Telford, the famous designer of many other canals and dockyards whom the Earl had known personally for many years.

> This canal (wrote Telford afterwards), is a striking instance of the risk which exists in an active nation of undertaking any new work which requires much time in completion; for although it may be very hopeful when projected, yet so rapid has of late years been the progress of invention that some novelty is frequently introduced which totally alters the case, and interferes with former establishments; for instance, no person in 1805 suspected that steam boats would not only monopolise the trade of the Clyde, but penetrate into every creek where there is water to float them in the British Isles . . .*

This was certainly true; but long after the general scheme was abandoned, enormous sums had to be poured into the enterprise. The sea kept silting up the harbour and washing it away, and more and more money had to be spent on simply preserving the foundations.

The old Earl was annoyed by set backs, but not in the least dispirited. Steam ships or sail, he remained convinced that in the end it would pay the family to finish the harbour, if nothing else. He borrowed money again and again and, like so many of his ancestors, justified himself by saying

* Life of Thomas Telford by himself, 1838, p. 69.

that the only thing his successors would have to do would be to live simply for the next forty years and then enjoy the fruits of his investment; for he himself had lived like this as a young man and he knew the value of economy.

Happily, too, in this case he was in a position to insist on it. His son was dead and his grandson, the future Lord Eglinton who gave the Tournament, was only a baby, so he tied him up with knots of trustees and forced him to live beside him at Eglinton Castle.

The old man loved the child tyranically, beating him and giving him candy. In after years Lord Eglinton described him: he was 'little, ugly, hardheaded and irritable,' his nose stuffed with quids of tobacco, and still wearing his hair in the old-fashioned military pigtail. He spent his days racing and hunting and his evenings entertaining his friends; when he was alone he wrote poetry*, played the violin or read about his forbears in the peerage.

Lord Eglinton was happy with him for, although his mother had married again and was living in England, her place was filled by a loving spinster aunt. Like most other boys of his generation, he was brought up on tales of knights and chivalry and he passed his childhood contentedly in the castle, dreaming of days gone by and filling the bright new rooms with the ghosts of his medieval ancestors.

And although Eglinton Castle was only twenty years old, it was just the place in which to imagine past generations of the Montgomeries. It was built in the latest romantic style like a medieval fortress, with turrets, battlements, castellations and a moat.

---

* He is said to have written the Canadian Boat Song:
  'From the lone shieling of the Misty Island
  Mountains divide us, and a waste of seas,
  Yet still the blood is strong, the heart is Highland,
  And we in dreams behold the Hebrides.'

The old Earl was immensely proud of it, far prouder than if he had finished twenty harbours and canals from Glasgow. For it stood for the things he valued most—the respectable wealth, noble status and genuine medieval origin of the family.

It is not easy to maintain a dynasty successfully, and more than male heirs or money, luck or even a Crown Charter are necessary. A sense of history is needed, too, to appreciate the inherited honours and to play the part of tenant-for-life constructively. Without this historical instinct—the enjoyment of family possessions, the pride in past achievements and perhaps, too, ambition to add to them—no succession is likely to last for many generations.

But the heirs of the Montgomeries had all possessed this instinct and none more strongly than the 12th Earl who built the castle.

When he died at the age of eighty in 1819, there were only forty-two earls in Scotland and his creation was older than all but six of them. Twenty-four generations lay behind him, and also three flourishing cadet branches, all with their own estates.

Eglinton Castle was indeed a fine home for the head of such a dynasty—a massive symbol of all their characteristics, their antiquity, importance, generous hospitality and perhaps, as well, their disregard of economy.

Its antique elevations, beautiful round hall and spacious, comfortable rooms gave just the right impression. They gave a feeling of graceful nobility and of all those honours and achievements which their founder Robert de Mundegumbri must have wished for his descendants six hundred and sixty-two years earlier when he married the High Steward's daughter and acquired the nearby lands of Eagleshame.

The medieval lines of Eglinton Castle gave one other

impression, too, which became extremely important to Lord Eglinton.

At this time, in the last years of the Regency, the Gothic idiom was overwhelming the 18th century taste for

*Table of Debts left by the Earls of Eglinton*
1665–1819

| Ref: | Earl | Date of debt | Merks Scots | £ Stg | £ Stg 1952 |
|------|------|------|------|------|------|
| | Greysteel 6th, died 1661. No record | | | | |
| Slip 1079 | 7th | 1665 | M.328,484 | £20,000 | £140,000 |
| | 8th | No record | | | |
| | 9th | c1700 | | NIL | NIL |
| Slip 7571 | 9th | 1729 | | £18,000 | £126,000 |
| Slip 7571 | 10th | 1769 | | £60,000 | £360,000 |
| Slip 7571 | 11th | 1796 | | £40,000 | £160,000 |
| Trust A/C | 12th | 1819 | | £269,000 | £720,000 |

1. Scots pound = one twelfth of pound Sterling = 1/8d.
2. Merk = two thirds of a Scots pound = 1/3d.
   (Both these statements come from the O.E.D. under 'pound' and 'mark', and the equation of Scots to Sterling pounds is taken at the date of the union of the crowns, 1603).
3. Conversion to the 1952 equivalent. The tables used for this conversion are those in *Economica*, November, 1956, 'Seven centuries of the prices of consumables'.
4. The Slip numbers refer to documents in the Scottish Record Office.

Classical simplicity, and the more romantic and picturesque a building looked, the better it pleased the fashionable imagination.

Already the 19th century craze for the Middle Ages was almost universal. Medieval history absorbed the writers of the western world and architecture stood on the brink of the Gothic Revival.

Thus the antique design of Eglinton Castle was a massive symbol of social taste as well, of the taste of the times and the mood of the family, their contemporary outlook and modern ways, which set them up in the front of fashion, themselves a symbol of Gothic enthusiasm.

In this form Lord Eglinton was to immortalise them. For the Gothic mood was expressed in many other ways besides historical novels, poetry and architecture.

It appeared in politics, machinery, dress, conversation and in every other field of the national existence. A strange medieval fever swept over the European continent. The days of chivalry obsessed the minds of everybody and knights in armour stirred a thousand dreams.

4. Lady Jane Montgomerie and the infant 13th Earl of Eglinton
(by Raeburn, c. 1816)

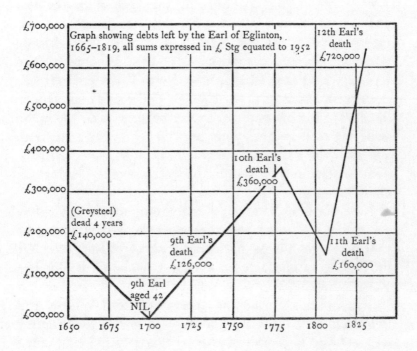

Graph showing debts left by the Earl of Eglinton, 1665–1819, all sums expressed in £ Stg equated to 1952

£700,000

£600,000

£500,000

£400,000

£300,000

£200,000

£100,000

£000,000

12th Earl's death £720,000

10th Earl's death £360,000

(Greysteel) dead 4 years £140,000

9th Earl's death £126,000

11th Earl's death £160,000

9th Earl aged 42 NIL

1650   1675   1700   1725   1750   1775   1800   1825

# Chapter Three

LORD EGLINTON was born on the 29th of September, 1812, at the Casa Mistretta, Palermo, the fourth and last legitimate child of the 12th Earl's heir, Lord Montgomerie. He was christened Archibald William by the Rev. Eyre Obins, Chaplain to Lord William Bentinck, the British Minister to the Sicilian Court and Commander in Chief in the Mediterranean. In the same week and in the same house a daughter was born to his father's mistress, and this child was called Elizabeth. Lord William Bentinck with General and Mrs Campbell of Inverneil became the children's godparents.

Lord Eglinton's father, Lord Montgomerie, the eldest son of the 12th Earl, was then aged thirty-nine, a man of charm and good looks but of no great personality who left little mark on his contemporaries. A Major General in the Royal Glasgow Regiment, he was placed in charge of the British Mission during the absence of Lord William the following year, but 'The poor man,' according to the latter, was 'reduced to death's door by the anxiety and annoyance he has experienced from these people.'* His health failed and, forced to sail for home, he died of consumption at Alicante on the 4th of January, 1814, at the age of 41, and was buried at Gibraltar.

The rest of the family who had travelled, too, reached Scotland safely, including the future Lord Eglinton; being

* The Bentinck Papers, Nottingham University, Bentinck to Admiral Hallowell, 23rd Oct. 1813.

then still an infant and having an elder brother, Hugh, who became the heir, no one took any notice of him.

The next year his mother married again. From the point of view of the Tournament, this proved an event of the utmost importance, for his mother's choice, Charles Lamb, as well as being heir to a baronetcy, together with several estates including the one in which he lived called Beauport, near Battle in Sussex, and a comfortable income of £12,000 per year, was due to become the Knight Marshal of the Royal Household.

This appointment carried a salary of £2,000 per year and—at least according to Sir Charles—conferred precedence over all other baronets in the Kingdom. In medieval times, as deputy to the Earl Marshal, it had been a valuable position, giving access to many of the Earl Marshal's prerogatives, including the arrangement of court functions and the judgment of combats and disputes of chivalry. It was now only a sinecure but it came to life at the time of a coronation. Then the Knight Marshal had to ride in the royal procession and manage the ceremony of the Champion in Westminster Hall.

But Lord Eglinton's grandfather who knew the Lambs, and did not like them, was not impressed by Sussex baronets or indeed by anything else. Having always approved of Lord Eglinton's mother because, as the family's richest heiress, she had sensibly married his eldest son and properly given him several grandsons, he was now thoroughly displeased with her. If she married an Englishman like Lamb, the whole income from her enormous fortune would be lost to the Eglinton Trust for the rest of her life.

This would not do when every penny of it was needed to support his harbour, the biggest single investment the family had and from which her eldest son would eventually benefit.

He explained the matter as patiently as he could, reminding her of his position as head of the Montgomeries and trustee of her marriage settlement. If she wanted to marry again she must choose another cousin and keep her fortune within his control. If she persisted in espousing Lamb she would only commit an act of selfishness for which she alone must take the consequences.

He did not bother to explain this threat but the moment she married Charles she discovered his intentions. Under a medieval Scottish law, known as Tutory Dative, she was forced to place her sons under the guardianship of their next male agnate over the age of twenty-five—in this case Lord Eglinton's grandfather—and leave them behind at Eglinton Castle. They were to be looked after by their Aunt Jane, her late husband's sister. Their mother could see them whenever she wished but, since her home was now 450 miles away in Sussex, this privilege was virtually meaningless. It only served as a cruel reminder that in reality she would hardly see them at all.

Thus her marriage to Charles Lamb had two results for Lord Eglinton. It caused him to lose his mother at an early age and in effect become an orphan; and it gained him a step-father in later years who, because of his inherited position, was one of the few people in the world who was personally interested in reviving a tournament.

Two years after this, his elder brother died of croup and left him the Eglinton family title of Lord Montgomerie and made him heir to the earldom and both his mother's and grandfather's estates. Although he was only four years old at the time, he never forgot the terrible effect which this tragedy had on his grandfather.

' I remember to this hour the storm of grief by which the old man was struck down,' he wrote in his diary forty-four years later.

The old earl erected a monument to the dead child and inscribed it with the characteristic elegance of his own vanished 18th century.

TO THE MEMORY OF HIS BELOVED GRANDSON,
HUGH
WHO DIED THE 13TH JULY 1817,
AT THE AGE OF SIX YEARS AND A FEW MONTHS:
A CHILD OF PROMISE.
ON THIS SPOT, ONCE HIS LITTLE GARDEN,
THIS STONE IS ERECTED
BY HIS AFFLICTED AND DISCONSOLATE GRANDFATHER,
HUGH EARL OF EGLINTON.

He made no mention of the child's mother and it is unlikely that he even thought about her. Life for him, at the age of seventy-seven, was too short to bother with sentimentality. There was only time for matters of real importance. He raised a further £150,000 by sales and mortgages and, with one last exasperated turn of energy, flung it all into the harbour at Ardrossan.

The effect on Lord Eglinton's character of this bereavement was no more than anyone might have expected. Suddenly becoming the direct heir of a 750 year old dynasty, he soon became unmanageable. His aunt Jane who looked after him was 'affectionate, warm hearted, pious, excellent in every relation of life . . . a bright example of every precept she inculcated,' but she was no good as a disciplinarian. She dressed him up like a courtier in sky blue suits with gold frogs, and adored him, petted him and allowed him to do whatever he liked.

Each birthday she composed him an ode, and this year's, which ran to eighteen stanzas, contained the following:

*I*

'All hail, dear boy! whose merits claim
This tribute from a Bard ethereal:—
(I own my calling; but my name
Is like my nature—*immaterial*!)

*II*

'Of all the Sylphs who dwell in air
(Not AYR, for female Sylphs so noted)
Few tend the objects of their care
So well as I—your own devoted!

*III*

'Your playful JOLIE\*, but for me
Would grow so fierce, you could not trust her,
And worthless would your DIAMOND† be
Did not my care preserve his lustre.'

*XVI*

'I mark your Mother's happy smile,
I see your fond Aunt's flush of pleasure,
And watch your Grandsire's eyes, the while
He gazes on his cherished treasure!'

*XVIII*

'Farewell, dear boy! my song must end,
Your fond and faithful Sylph remember
Thro' life; for *every* month your *friend*,
And *Poet Laureate* for *September*!'

From this it seems that he did at least see his mother
occasionally. It was no wonder that, growing up in the
beams of so much doting attention, he remembered this
time of his childhood with happiness.

The year after this, in 1819, his grandfather died and
he came into his inheritance at the age of seven as the
13th Earl of Eglinton. His mother certainly must have
hoped that now she would get possession of him; but it

---

\* A favourite dog.    † His pony.

turned out otherwise. Under his grandfather's will he was left to his Aunt Jane and five tutors to live at Eglinton for the next seven years until he reached the age of fourteen. After that he could live with whom he liked although the tutors would still be responsible for him. This, too, was to have an important influence on his character. He was not used to having five apparently aged men telling him what to do with himself. Whenever he had the chance he tried to annoy them. He was backed up in this by his mother. She maintained a polite and sufficient relationship with them but swore she would have a revenge.

It was only now, when the old Earl was dead, that the family found out the terrifying state of his finances. Under his will which he had drawn up when Lord Eglinton had become his heir in 1817, he had left £1,000 a year to Aunt Jane and £4,000 a year to his harbour. After dealing with a few other small annuities to servants and specifying other annual expenses as might be necessary—such as the upkeep of Eglinton Castle for which he allocated £700— he instructed his trustees to pay the balance of income each year against his debts. Only when they had settled everything could the Trust be liquidated and the management of the estate be handed over to Lord Eglinton.

The very first glance at the balance sheet showed this to be impossible. It was simply a repetition of the old family philosophy of expecting the heir to live on a bean for forty years until, towards the end of his life, he became solvent and could start to spend freely. At the present rate of nett income, it would have taken at least thirty years to discharge the debt without any allowances for emergencies. The gross income for the first year, 1820, was £27,435; the minimum expenditure was £17,881; the outstanding debt was more than a quarter of a million.

The trustees—or tutors, as they were known in Scotland—originally appointed under the will were as follows:

Sir David Hunter Blair, aged 52, a neighbour and friend of Lord Eglinton's grandfather; Lt. General James Montgomerie, aged 65, Lord Eglinton's great uncle; Richard Alexander Oswald of Auchincruive, aged 49, Lord Eglinton's uncle by marriage; Alexander West Hamilton of Pinmore, aged 55, Lord Eglinton's first cousin once removed by birth and also by marriage; George Russell, Writer to the Signet (Solicitor), aged about 42, of the firm of Tod & Hill in Edinburgh. Alexander West Hamilton acted as agent to the trustees and held the title of Commissioner.

Their first decision, taken at once, was to disregard the testator's instructions and cease all except the most vitally essential payments to the harbour. At this moment it was a pure white elephant. No ships of any size could berth in it. The canal from Glasgow had never been finished so that nothing could reach it from the land.

This necessary and sensible economy was the best of many which the tutors were forced to take during the next twelve years and no group of five men, faced with many vexatious problems, ever sacrificed their time more freely or sensibly, or ever received less appreciation from those to whom they gave it.

The greatest difficulty which confronted them was the calamitous depression in agriculture which followed the end of the Napoleonic war. Nearly all the Eglinton fortune came from farm rents and in 1817, when the will had been drawn, all land and farm produce had been more valuable than at any time in living memory, due to the usual shortages produced by war. During this year, many farm leases had fallen in and these had naturally been renewed at the currently augmented level. All plans set out in the will had been based on this inflated income.

But when the war came to an end food was once more easily imported and farm prices began to drop.

The annual rental value of one of the Eglinton farms called Caprington, for example, fell from £390 in 1819 to £285 in 1827 and this latter figure was fixed, according to a note in the Trustee's Minute Book, after the farm had been 'much improved by the tenant.'

Each year between 1820 and 1827 the Trustees were forced to allow abatements of rent, often as much as 20 per cent, and only by the most extraordinary care and economy were they able to end these years with any surplus. West Hamilton, the Commissioner, generously declined all his fees although he was entitled to £300 per year, and this selflessness was typical of all of them.

Each year they managed to balance the books and to put aside seven or eight thousand pounds towards the mortgages. The worst year of all, and one of national crisis, was 1826. After this things got easier, so far as the management of the estate was concerned; but then they had to deal with Lord Eglinton. On the 12th of September he reached the age of fourteen and was, according to Scottish law, partially able to manage his own affairs. He could make decisions so long as the Trustees approved of them. This meant, in other words, that he could legally make a nuisance of himself. That he meant to do so was fairly quickly seen.

Apart from Aunt Jane's birthday eulogies there are few papers about his childhood before this point. He was taught lessons first of all by a small Irish tutor called John Kerr who was left £100 in the 12th Earl's will and who also wrote him long birthday paeons. They were no good and Aunt Jane must have laughed at them. Kerr was followed by a tall Englishman who was succeeded by a petulant Welshman. Then there was school. Lord Eglinton remembered nothing about his tutors in later years except their relative size, but the fact that he got through three of them in three summers shows that he was difficult. The Trustees thought so, certainly, and when he was nine, in 1821, they recorded in the Minute Book that it was time he went to school. He was too young to go to Eton and they sent him to one at Mitcham, probably Richard Roberts', one of the two small boarding academies there which prepared the sons of gentlemen for public school, though its name is not recorded. Here, for the first time, 'Young Hopefull' as he described himself sardonically, discovered what life from home could be like.

Even at this distance of time I shudder at the very thought of it (he wrote in his diary forty years later) and I cannot understand how I could have been kept there so long, but I suppose my just complaints were not credited. A more selfish, ill tempered, niggardly brute than the Master (there was but one for 18 boys) never existed, and any interference of his wife was always to our detriment. We were abused and cudgelled, we had no amusements, we were half starved and washing was unknown. For breakfast three small pieces of dry bread and a mug of milk was the allowance, for supper one piece with a smaller quantity of milk, and for dinner one plate of meat and a helping of pudding. On Friday evenings two foot-pans, without any change of water, did service for the whole eighteen boys, and on Saturday our necks and arms were washed, but all other portions of our bodies were left to the chance of what might happen in the holidays.

At the end of four years he left and spent the summer at Richmond with his Aunt Jane before going to Eton. He began to develop his lifelong interest in the turf and appeared for the first time in the Racing Calendar, winning a match against Sir James Boswell of Auchinleck for 100 gns over half a mile with a grey mare called Violet, ridden by a famous jockey called Tommy Lye. He began, too, to show signs of the family carelessness about finance, and Sir David Hunter Blair, the principal Trustee, had to remind him about economy. But this was the final summer before his fourteenth birthday and he paid no attention to him.

His mother, with whom he stayed, too, during these holidays, encouraged him in this attitude and made mischief between him and the Trustees deliberately. She did not blame Sir David for having kept her child because, after all, he was only doing his duty, but she did blame him for nagging the boy about money before he had actually got into debt. Being extremely rich herself, she had never bothered about this sort of thing. She thought it was ridiculous and only likely to make a person grow up extravagant. Quite unexpectedly, at this moment she was given a chance to cozen the Trustees out of a useful slice of capital, and both she and her husband, Charles, laughed so much about it that they nearly gave themselves apoplexy. Having worked out the necessary tactics, she made the Trustees a proposition. With all the innocence of their own honesty they discussed it at a meeting and, finding it apparently to the benefit of the family, wrote that they agreed.

When her first husband, Lord Montgomerie, had died in 1814, she had been given a life interest in a house called Coilsfield, the family seat of Lord Eglinton's grandfather, in which she and her husband had lived after they were married. It was a pleasant modern house in the classical style, small by the standards of those days, with 140 acres of park. She had filled it with her own inherited furniture and pictures and, after her husband's death, had let it furnished to the Earl of Glasgow for £1,000 per year; for when she had married Lamb she had moved to the south and never had any use for it.

She now wrote to the Trustees that, as she was never going to live there again, she would like to give it up. If they would buy all its contents she would, in return, surrender her life interest.

Since the furnishings were entirely hers and, if any disaster had happened to Lord Eglinton, they would all have gone to her children by Lamb, and since they were all of family interest, the Trustees agreed unanimously. They offered her £4,000 for the lot and thanked her for taking the trouble to think of it. They recorded in the Minute Book that they thought this was a 'most advantageous transaction'. For they also considered the annual rent of £1,000 from Lord Glasgow. After saving it for four years to replace the capital, they could use every penny as surplus income towards the payment of the debt.

The moment the money was paid and everything was settled, Lord Eglinton's mother sprang the trap. She had quite forgotten, she said, to mention the fact that Lord Glasgow was giving up his lease. She was most sorry to have been so stupid. She hoped they would find another tenant soon.

The Trustees were fearfully angry at this development and even their calm report in elegant script in the Minute Book shows their frenzy. They could not sell Coilsfield because it was part of the entailed estate and in this year, when bad weather had caused an almost total failure of crops and the whole country was gripped by economic depression, nobody was renting furnished houses in the country. The hopes of finding another tenant were nil. They were forced to manage Coilsfield themselves and when they did so they found it extremely expensive.

Quite certainly because of this transaction, they took an obstructive line shortly afterwards when they met to decide Lord Eglinton's allowance for Eton. He had asked for enough money to take some horses with him. With an instantaneous, firm and quite unanimous voice, they refused it. He was not going to Eton to spend his time and the family money galloping back and forward to Ascot. If he wanted exercise, he could play games and if he needed a horse he could be like everybody else and manage with Shanks' pony.

This rebuttal caused a storm of which there is still an original account and it gives an interesting picture of at least one side of Lord Eglinton's character at this age.

Lord Eglinton was furious and wrote Sir David Hunter Blair a rude letter. Sir David became furious, too, and rode over to Eglinton Castle one Sunday morning from his home nearby, marched him into a dressing room and gave him the sharpest lecture that any earl at the age of 14 had ever endured in his life. Lord Eglinton sat in a chair and glared at Sir David and said nothing. Sir David then went home to Blairquhan but Lord Eglinton continued to sit in the same chair and refused to eat or speak or move for the rest of the day until he went to bed in a rage at nine o'clock. Every half hour Aunt Jane popped in to console him with love and sweetmeats, but he sulked on and would not be comforted.

The next morning Jane wrote to Lord Alloway, now one of the Trustees, a poignant letter on mauve paper. She knew that the Trustees must do what was right, but she begged them to allow Archy just one little horse. He was truly contrite, thoroughly understood the principles of economy and would never spend an extra penny again.

She made Lord Eglinton write him a letter, too, in the same vein which contained the statement that he only wished to be on good terms with his guardians and had no wish to change them. This was a reference to the fact that he was now in a position to do so, having passed his fourteenth birthday. It was a plain lie and he admitted it afterwards. Possibly at that moment he may have meant it, held as he probably was in the consoling arms of Aunt Jane whom he loved genuinely; but as soon as he went south to Sussex and talked to his mother he quickly changed his mind.

At last, now, his mother had reached the moment for which she had waited for more than eleven years. She had no doubt prepared the ground for a long time and no doubt, also, she found it easy enough to persuade a spoilt boy of 14, who only wanted to please the person nearest him, that he ought to make up his mind and live beside her. No doubt, reasonably enough, too, he was more than ready to do so from natural affection.

Yet it was also a decision for which he felt ashamed for the rest of his life, for perhaps no mother in the world can love a boy so much as a spinster aunt, and certainly no aunt ever gave a nephew more love and devotion than Aunt Jane who for twelve years had truly dedicated her life to him.

But having resolved to make a change, he did so at once and whatever pangs he may have suffered when he thought of the pain it would cause his aunt, he certainly must have grinned at the thought of the shock on Sir David Hunter Blair to whom, on the 6th of November, 1826, he addressed the following letter:

My dear Sir David.

As I am now determined to live in future with Mamma, I think it right to inform you of it, and I beg you will make this known to the other guardians, and I hope that none of you will object to it.
Eglinton.

What Sir David wrote in reply is not recorded but the Minutes relate that it pained the guardians considerably. Its abrupt tone was quite unnecessary, and it followed by only four weeks the note which had said exactly the opposite. Since the request was reasonable enough, however, and because they only wished Lord Eglinton well, they decided not to make any difficulty.

Lord Eglinton interpreted this differently and recorded in his diary that they received his letter with consternation and astonishment. The only reason that they ever gave in to it was because they had not the power to do the reverse.

There was nothing more for the Trustees to do now except to arrange his annual maintenance, and his mother wrote that if they would give her 'undisputed care of his person' she would undertake to pay all his school expenses, clothes and servants' wages for the next four years for a round sum of five hundred pounds a year. The Trustees thought this was reasonable and agreed to it. She thanked them and, being always ready to release a parting shot, added that she had not, of course, meant this to include the cost of his journeys to Scotland. If any of them wanted to see him, they must find the money for this journey themselves.

This was a dig at Aunt Jane who had generously offered to stay in the Castle and keep it aired until he should want it. Only a year later, however, she became engaged to a neighbour—John Hamilton, a brother of Alexander West's, the Commissioner—and moved to a pleasant small mansion called Rozelle, somewhat like Coilsfield, which was also part of the family estate. Lord Eglinton offered it to her for life, rent free. This, in turn, was a dig at Alexander West who was then living there. He resigned his lease but also resigned his appointment as Commissioner. He must have felt that to receive notice was really the last straw after all he had done, including foregoing his salary. In fact, there was more to come for he could not even, without the greatest difficulty, get an expense of £862 which was then owing to him. Lord Eglinton travelled up to the Castle and, when he had settled down, sent Sir David Hunter Blair an enormous account for the cost of moving in there. His mother came with him and so did her husband, Sir Charles Montolieu Lamb.

It was only natural from now on that Sir Charles Lamb, by mere proximity if not because of his position as step-father, should help to form Lord Eglinton's character; and this he certainly did. He had succeeded his father in 1824 as 2nd baronet and Knight Marshal and at this time, as he approached forty, had become a fading Regency Buck and a rich, worldly court functionary. His own family had mixed feelings about him. They all agreed that at home in Sussex he was a kind, hospitable and amusing host, but they also agreed that, although he was wealthy and often extremely generous to servants, it never seemed to enter his head to give presents to anybody else, particularly to themselves, his penurious relations.

He liked living with people who agreed with him and, except for an odd fancy for music, for which he had no ability at all, he had no time for the arts or intellect or any of the people who had anything to do with them and in this respect he was even conspicuous amongst his friends who shared the same opinions. He spent much of his time abroad, having villas in France, Italy and Switzerland, and he travelled between them in two huge, four-wheeled mustard coloured carriages, known as Berlins—one for himself and one for his wife—followed by an enormous retinue of servants. He caused Nice to become a popular wintering place, as Lord Brougham had done similarly to Cannes, and he earned the title of '*Le Milord Paysan*' by

5. Sir Charles Lamb at Geneva, from an engraving (artist unknown)

riding about the countryside in Byronic *déshabille*, scattering coins in the streets of the villages.

In 1831 he was painted at Geneva by an unknown artist, possibly Danby, by all accounts very characteristically.

Years later Lord Eglinton wrote that 'He was, without exception, the most selfish, arrogant and immoral man I ever met with';* and certainly, seen in this portrait with a wicked, melancholy smile on his lips, the only features which seem to be missing are a pair of satyr's horns on his brow and cloven hoofs splitting the toes of his pumps.

He seduced women wherever he went and encouraged Lord Eglinton to do the same, often passing his mistresses on to him. For a boy of fifteen this was a fresh experience and Lord Eglinton rather enjoyed it. Sir Charles assured him it was quite normal although, of course, better concealed from his mother.

Lord Eglinton's career at Eton, where he now went, was not marked by any kind of distinction either in work or sport. He lived with a tutor of his own—as many students did in those days—and shared lodgings with a boy called James Bruce, son of the Earl of Elgin. These rooms were over a confectioner's in the High Street and, primed in the technique as he was by Sir Charles Lamb, he soon won the confidence of his landlord's daughter, spending the afternoons in her arms, consuming bottles of gin and bowls of quinces. His first tutor was a friend of the family's, to whom he was much attached and who left after a year to marry a cousin, an unidentified Miss Montgomerie. During this time he learnt a certain amount and was kept in control. But his next tutor, although also officially living with him in the same lodgings, actually stayed in Windsor and from then on Lord Eglinton did as he liked.

The headmaster of Eton at that epoch was the famous

* Diary.

47

and terrifying Dr Keate who once publicly flogged eighty boys with a birch in one day, but in spite of Lord Eglinton's easy habits and inattention to work he was only beaten once, having been caught in one of the fields up the river shooting partridges.

Many boys were there with him who took part in the Tournament 12 years later and six of them played a major part in it and became knights—Lords Waterford, Alford and Cranston, Sir F. Johnstone and Sir F. Hopkins, and his half-brother Charlie Lamb, while many others became their Esquires. His future brother-in-law was there, too, Thomas William Newcomen, son of the 2nd and last Viscount of the same name who ought, therefore, to have been an 'Honourable' but in fact was not because he was illegitimate. Lord Eglinton preferred rowing to cricket and won an oar in Britannia in the 4th of June regatta. He was much annoyed from time to time at being called Lord Eddystone Lighthouse. But this feeble joke was also inappropriate, for he was not particularly tall or strong at that time and only achieved his fine slender figure and exceptional ability at games several years later after he left.

He did this at the age of 16 when he went to live with his mother and Sir Charles Lamb in charge of another tutor. This man was no better than the last and his main accomplishment was billiards at which, in consequence, Lord Eglinton acquired an exceptional ability. From now on for the next five years, until he became of age, he simply enjoyed himself, travelling about Europe, falling in love, becoming well known as a crack steeplechaser and learning to drink the extravagant amounts of claret that young men of his set had to be able to consume without becoming incapacitated. Little record of his life during this period exists except his own.

The quantity of claret I imbibed during that winter was fabulous (he wrote of 1832, the year before his majority), the bets and matches of all sorts I made were innumerable, the scenes at night were far from creditable, and the headaches in the mornings were dreadful to think of.

So great a gap exists between his age and ours today that such a life may seem disreputable, especially for a young man who was born to wealth in spite of debts and to great social position and consequent responsibility.

1832 was the year of the Reform Bill, a year of poverty, hunger, cholera and tumult—one of the most critical in England's history when civil war seemed inevitable. But Lord Eglinton never mentioned these things in his diary once. He took a long time to grow up and mature and become the serious and responsible member of the aristocracy for which his family remember him with pride. In his late teens and early twenties he just moved in his own exclusive set of hunting dandies, dressed as they did in the young-exquisite style of amazingly tight buckskin breeches, Hessian boots and sublimely coloured tail coats, and lived, loved and laughed throughout the year from early morning until late at night.

His mother was rich and gave him plenty of money; even so, he was constantly running short of it. The Trustees' Minute Book records this. In the autumn of 1829, after leaving Eton, he asked that the £500 previously allowed to his mother should be given to himself and also be doubled. This was agreed. In 1831 he asked if the sum could be doubled again as £1,000 had proved 'quite inadequate.'

The reason for this appears in the Racing Calendar. He had opened a stud and begun racing seriously with three horses, Paul Pry, Lucifer and a beautiful grey mare called Queen Bathsheba which brought him his first success by winning the Ayr Plate. The Trustees received this request more unwillingly. Eventually they acceded to it but they wrote in their minutes that they thought it was too much. Under all the economic circumstances that still prevailed, and considering all their efforts, they felt that £1,500 ought to have been enough.

In regard to this they were certainly quite correct, having themselves set a fine example of economy. During the last thirteen years, in spite of the steady fall in the value of money and the fall, too, in estate income because of the unavoidable abatements in rents, they had managed every year to put aside seven or eight thousand pounds towards the payment of mortgages. Now, in the last month of their management, when they came to draw a consolidated statement of their activities, they saw they had saved £89,000, of which £20,000 had been put to the redemption of shares in the railway to the harbour and the balance in paying off the debt. They had maintained the Castle and park and gardens, paid all the annuities regularly, reduced the expenses on the harbour to a minimum and had permitted Lord Eglinton a fair allowance. They themselves had taken nothing, even although they were entitled to their expenses, and quite certainly they were more than justified in telling Lord Eglinton not to be extravagant.

Advice and restrictions of this nature were not to Lord Eglinton's taste for under the will of the 12th Earl he acquired an annual allowance of £5,000 when he came of age but he did not gain control of his estates until the Trustees had extinguished the debt. This was going to take them another thirty years at the present rate—so far as he was concerned, more than a lifetime—and they did, in fact, only wipe it out just before his death twenty-four years later. Furthermore, £5,000 a year for a man in his position was no more than pin money. This was not merely by the standards of a spendthrift. As things were by then, it was hardly more than half the amount in real money that it had been fifteen years earlier when settled under his grandfather's will; and even if it had been doubled, it would hardly have maintained him more than adequately. His mother's income alone, for example, was £18,000 per year, so that £5,000 for her son who was head of an ancient and noble family with huge estates and equivalent responsibilities was obviously totally inadequate.

Luckily enough, however, the Trustees agreed about this, too, and a memorandum still exists in the hand of Sir David Hunter Blair proposing to change the will by Act of Parliament. This must have been the first suggestion he had made in twelve years with which each of his colleagues and Sir Charles Lamb, Lady Montgomerie and even Lord Eglinton all concurred instantly.

# Chapter Four

THE ACT of Parliament which changed the will of the 12th Earl received the Royal Assent on the 27th of June, 1834. It was called an 'Act to enable the Trustees of Hugh Montgomerie of Skelmorlie, Earl of Eglinton . . . to sell part of the Trust Estates . . .'* and it was backdated by eight months to take effect from Lord Eglinton's birthday. It made him achieve at one stroke the very dream of every man who has ever felt that he ought to be rich but found himself chained to five trustees who were only bent on saving his money.

He acquired complete, free and absolute control of all his estates and escaped from the grip of Sir David Hunter Blair for ever. At the same time he left the responsibility and payment of all the mortgages to the Trustees. By way of a pinch of salt to flavour the arrangement, he added the cost of the Act of Parliament, itself £4,805 8s. 10d.

To enable them to meet these obligations, he arranged for Coilsfield house and park—which was well known to be a liability—to be sold as quickly as possible and also, without sentiment for the past, the whole estate at Eagleshame, the original family property which his remote ancestor, Robert de Mundegumbri, had worked so hard to obtain from Walter the Steward seven hundred years earlier.

He himself accepted responsibility for the payment of all his grandfather's annuities—£300 per year to both his great-aunt Maria and to Aunt Jane;† £20 per year to his

* 4 & 5 Gulielmi IV. Cap. 21.

† Aunt Jane had married by this time and only received £300 per annum, instead of £1,000 in the will.

retired nurse called Jane Wilson; and a few other small amounts to similar faithful retainers. These added up to the fair sum of £820 but, with the exception of Aunt Jane's, they were not likely to need paying for long; for all the other recipients were old and would soon be dead.

From Lord Eglinton's point of view all this was exceptionally satisfactory but it was, too, naturally enough, because of the probity and good sense of Sir David Hunter Blair and the other Trustees, much the best of the many alternatives which might have been adopted. Lord Eglinton probably laughed and thought he had got the better of Sir David but he ought, in fact, to have thanked him sincerely for having forgiven past ingratitudes and for still only truly thinking in terms of the family's benefit. It was certainly an unhappy decision to sell the estate of Eagleshame which had belonged to the Montgomeries since 1157 but the property was much the furthest from Eglinton Castle and therefore the least pleasure to Lord Eglinton personally, and also it was valued at—and in fact fetched—£220,000, almost exactly the amount of the outstanding debt.

As to the settlement of the debt itself, this, too, had become a problem of real urgency. The country was in a state of great turmoil and at any moment a sudden crisis might have caused foreclosure of all the outstanding mortgages. A financial earthquake of this kind would almost certainly have ruined everybody. To get rid of the debt by a sale—and as soon as possible—was therefore by far the wisest course. It was hoped, too, that other parts of the estate which were soon due to be connected to a railway and which already contained profitable coal mines and also —if it were ever finished—Ardrossan harbour, would all in time and with careful management increase in value and make up for the sale of the estate of Eagleshame.

All this would have come into effect if it had not been for Lord Eglinton's extravagance. But at twenty-one, with no debts and the captivating prospect of great income actually available in ready cash—and also having inherited both his grandfather's liberality and his mother's carelessness, to say nothing of having been educated by Sir Charles Lamb, a well known libidinous spendthrift—there was no possible hope of his being either frugal or practical.

The pity was that Sir David Hunter Blair did not have the wisdom or perhaps the means to anticipate this and prevent Lord Eglinton from getting his hands on everything. If he had allowed him, for example, one estate and some of the securities—enough, say, to provide an income of £10,000 per year—and kept the remainder within the Trust, the whole financial history of the family might have been different. For although Lord Eglinton might have been short for a while, he would in the end have inherited his mother's income of £20,000 free of trust, and until that time he might have been reasonably careful.

In the event he did gain control of everything, skilfully countering every argument and refusing every compromise. For the influence of old families like the Montgomeries was still, at that time, enormous, and any desire by a young peer to manage his own estates invariably commanded support in Parliament and general public sympathy.

So, in spite of the loss of £9,000 per year from the sale of Eagleshame, Lord Eglinton still inherited £20,000 per year with the prospect of the same sum again on the death of his mother who was then aged 46—a combined income which would have made him very rich indeed.

Unless a man of his standing and upbringing was born prudent and naturally interested in developing his estates he could not possibly have resisted the temptation to live extravagantly, at least for many years of his early life; and Lord Eglinton was not a man like this.

Shortly after the Act of Parliament had been passed, he discovered a trick he could play on Sir David Hunter Blair which made his mother and Sir Charles Lamb laugh so much that this time they nearly choked for a week. Once again it concerned the furniture at Coilsfield.

By some oversight, this furniture was not included in the agreement which placed the house in the hands of the Trustees for sale and Lord Eglinton tumbled to the fact that everything still belonged to him. He therefore told the Trustees that he wanted it. He well knew, however, that this was impossible, for the house had only recently been let with great difficulty, fully furnished, long after Lord Glasgow had left it in 1826, and the Trustees would be quite unable to break the tenancy and give him the furniture. So they found themselves forced to buy it again for £4,000, the very price they had already given his mother for it seven years previously. This practically finished all their dealings with him. It was, of course, the very line that Lord Eglinton hoped they would follow.

As his 21st birthday approached he travelled up to Scotland with his mother, step-father and half-brother, Charlie Lamb, and spent the last few weeks before the 29th of September supervising the plans for a grand parade and banquet for all the tenants at Eglinton Castle. This month the weather was beautiful and all the riots of the past year connected with the Reform Bill were forgiven and nearly forgotten. All his hundreds of thousands of valuable acres were bathed in peace and warmed in the bright, sunny, soft September air.

A printed list of instructions, with a plan of the procession, surmounted by a coronet, still survives amongst

Aunt Jane's papers at Rozelle and it gives an interesting picture of how such events were arranged at that time and also, so far as the procession was concerned, carries a significant foretaste of the same thing for the Tournament six years later, for which indeed it may have formed a precedent.

At half past nine on the day after his birthday, Monday morning the 30th of September, the whole of Ayrshire was rocked by congratulatory salutes of cannon at Ardrossan harbour and all the tenants assembled at Towerlands, a mansion two miles west of the Castle, and moved off, two by two, in the direction of Eglinton Mains, one of the principal entrances.

They were grouped according to the various estates on which they worked and were led by a Marshal, a band of music, a man on horseback carrying a banner and a Captain Orr, the tenant of Towerlands, who, with a Committee which walked after him, had dealt with the practical arrangements.

After the committee marched the groups of tenants, each preceded by its own band, drums or piper and each symbolised by a man dressed in rustick character such as a sower, or else by a horseman carrying an emblem like a tile, a cheese or a plough, according to the nature and produce of its district.

When they arrived in front of the Castle they were deployed round a prepared space which was roped off. Selected tenants danced a fling, while all the others were told to stand still and not to emulate them. After a reasonable time had been spent in this, as the instructions put it, 'healthful and enlivening exercise', a bugle was blown and the whole party marched off for sports and races at Bogside, Lord Eglinton's private racecourse within the park where he kept his stud.

Finally they returned to Eglinton Castle for the banquet. A number of official toasts and speeches were given, recitations were declaimed, a band struck up and everybody joined in songs and choruses. Some of these were traditional and well known but others were written especially for the occasion and handed round to be sung by those who could read them.

One was composed by a local physician, Dr Gibs, who described Lord Eglinton as a 'gem of the first water.' This lapidary tribute went down so well that it was still remembered six years afterwards and brought him a bit of luck. When the time came to apply for tickets to the Tournament, Dr Gibs wrote to Lord Eglinton, reminding him of this sparkling moment and, as a result, he received a ticket for the grandstand.

Lord Eglinton enjoyed the evening enormously and so did everyone else. No doubt, on this occasion, the Trustees paid for it since the Act did not come into effect until the following morning. But it must have been the last entertainment for which they agreed to provide.

From the next day, the 1st of October, 1833, legally, financially and traditionally, Lord Eglinton pushed off into the world on his own.

As a parting gift the Trustees gave him a bonus of £5,000—a single payment of what would otherwise have been his total annual allowance under his grandfather's will.

But also, in a last brutal measure of financial integrity, they gave away to his creditors all the rest of the money they had in the bank in cash at that moment. It was practically a whole year's gross income, fifteen thousand pounds.

Lord Eglinton's career from now on until he gave the Tournament, and indeed for the next quarter of a century until he turned his attention to politics, can be summed up in a single word of five letters—sport.

He never bothered with social life and, during the next five years, he was only mentioned four times in the national newspapers like *The Times* or the *Court Journal* for doing anything of general interest to Society.

On the 31st of July, 1833, he betted an officer in the Ayrshire Yeomanry that he could race him fifty yards round a post and back again if he were on foot and the officer on horseback. The officer took the bet and Lord Eglinton won it easily.

On the 1st of May, 1834, he took his seat in the House of Lords as Lord Ardrossan, the family's barony of the United Kingdom which had been granted to his grandfather in 1806. He supported the Tories and did so, without wavering, for the rest of his life.

Then, on the 30th of November, 1835, he fell badly while hunting in Leicestershire and broke his collar bone.

He received, on the 16th of July, 1836, an honorary appointment held by both his maternal and paternal grandfathers before him: the Colonelcy of the Ayrshire Militia.

He can be seen as he must have appeared at the age of 21 when he raced the officer in a life-sized portrait by the Edinburgh artist, Blackburn, no doubt commissioned by Aunt Jane, for it still hangs above the stair at Rozelle. His expression appears to be rather peevish but perhaps he was bored by having to be painted, compelled to sit against his will, unable to curb his aunt's adoring insistence.

So far as his own account of his life in these years is concerned there was, according to his own words in his diary, nothing of public interest worth noticing and nothing of private concern that could be decently recorded. He kept women as he kept horses—amongst them possibly Elizabeth Howard who became famous as the Comtesse Beauregard, mistress of Napoleon III. She came to the Tournament rehearsals in St John's Wood, to which Lord Eglinton may have invited her, although at that time she was kept by another. But no woman is identified, even by an initial, except one who cannot be traced, a 'beautiful Fanny B.'

Apart from the outline of these activities which, in spite of the encouragement they received from Sir Charles Lamb, were quite normal for a young man of wealth at that time, there is no mention in his diary of any incident during these years except vague references to playing cricket in Switzerland and hunting stags with the Duke of Orleans in the forests of Compèigne. In other words, even when he was abroad, he spent his time in sport.

Naturally enough, when he was passing through London on his way to or from Sussex or Ayrshire, he went to Court, attended balls, lounged at Crockfords, and left his card on various hostesses of the day, in his case principally Lady Blessington, whose salon happened to contain the group of people he found most interesting.

Benjamin Disraeli was among them, having just then, in 1837 at the age of 33, been elected to Parliament for the first time, and Prince Louis Napoleon, afterwards Emperor of the French, who began his first exile in England in 1838 and attended the Tournament as the principal Visiting Knight.

Lord John Manners was often there, too, with his cousin, Baillie-Cochrane, afterwards Lord Lamington, a neighbour and close friend of Lord Eglinton's in Scotland, and also George Smythe, later Lord Strangford, who became Cochrane's cousin by marriage. These three were as deeply, unconsciously steeped in the current romantic vogue for the Middle Ages as Lord Eglinton himself. They were all elected to Parliament shortly afterwards and, under the nominal and sympathetic leadership of Disraeli, they formed what was known as the Young England Party and preached a return to a more feudal way of life as the only cure for the evils of the industrial revolution.

This proved to be unrealistic but not because they lacked sense or ability. They failed to understand their times economically, although socially they epitomised them. In their admiration of the Middle Ages, in their pride of the part that their ancestors played in its history, in their appreciation of the remains of its splendid architecture and in their devotion to what they believed was its simple, feudal, chivalrous life, they were living symbols of the Gothic spirit, the inescapable, hypnotic essence that dominated their time.

These contacts were rare and casual for beyond his own county of Ayrshire Lord Eglinton did not bother with social life at all and, generally speaking, until he proclaimed the Tournament and became a figure of national interest, he was unknown except in the world of sport.

This exception, however, formed his whole life. During these early years of his twenties every season he became better known and more popular and his colours of blue and green tartan, embroidered with golden thistles and with yellow sleeves and cap, became more widely recognised and acclaimed at every racecourse from his own local one at Ayr to the great courses such as Doncaster and Newmarket.

In 1831, two years before his majority, he had started his stable with three horses and, riding himself at 12 st. 7 lb., had achieved local celebrity by winning three steeplechases in one day. Then, in 1833, he increased his string to five and was noted in the Racing Calendar for winning 100 sovereigns at Edinburgh with a bay gelding, Paul Pry, over two miles in a match against a friend who came to the Tournament as an Unknown Knight, Walter Little Gilmour. In 1834 he added three more horses, bringing his string to eight, and the next year he added a ninth and raced at Newmarket for the first time with a colt called Black Diamond, a name inspired, no doubt, by that of his boyhood pony so fondly immortalised in his 8th birthday ode by Aunt Jane. Finally, in 1838, he doubled the strength of his whole establishment and, with eighteen horses, let himself go on a racing career which became itself part of the great and exciting history of the English turf. His superb victories in the Derby, the St Leger, the Ascot Cup, the Goodwood Cup and the 'immortal' match with The Flying Dutchman against Lord Zetland's Voltigeur did not take place until after the Tournament and were thus still many years ahead of him. But in 1838 he won both the Northumberland Plate and the Liverpool Cup with a brown colt called St Bennett and eleven races out of nineteen with a bay gelding called The Potentate. He was, too, in this year, elected to the Jockey Club which even then with its membership limited, as it still is, to 75, was the most exclusive and coveted club in the country.

From the point of view of finance, however, all this was not done for nothing. Such incomplete personal accounts as still exist show that he lived at once to the full extent of his income and that very soon he began raising extra money by selling various estates which was, so far as the family were concerned, really worse than if he had done so by borrowing.

In 1834 he received as income from his factor and solicitor £13,200 and probably much the same sum in the years following, for which there are no accounts. In 1838, the next period for which there is any record, he received only £11,445, but he supplemented this sum by selling a small estate called Carcluie for £10,000.

This was the first of a series of sales which the whole County of Ayrshire began to enjoy as an annual event and on one particular occasion, 1847, the year before the death of his mother, they raised his income by £57,000.

The year previous to this he had sold the family harbour at Ardrossan to the Glasgow, Kilmarnock and Ardrossan Railway Co. for £74,000, possibly one tenth of the amount his grandfather had spent on it. And in the year before that, 1845, if not many years earlier, he had begun borrowing. A memo for that year shows a loan from the National Bank of Scotland in Edinburgh for £15,000. For he had sold most of his estates by that time although he had not, in every case, received the money, and he clearly began to look round for other sources of revenue.

Under the Act of Parliament he had received £50,000 in cash and securities as well as his estates and as time went on he seems to have spent this also. At all events, by the end of his life, all these sums of money—and doubtless many more that were not accounted for—had vanished without a trace.

But in 1838, the year before the Tournament, and for that matter for many years afterwards, he was still enormously rich and the cost of racing never really worried him. He never failed to win money with his horses and in 1849, when he won the Derby with Flying Dutchman, he netted £19,500 which at that time was a record, while for more than a quarter of a century his average winnings were more than £4,000 per year. He was lucky, too, with his wagers. He collected £30,000 in one day in 1842 when he won the St Leger with Blue Bonnet, and during his racing career, taking all his wins and losses against each other, he

gained about £80,000. Of course, in terms of the cost of
the whole, this was a trifle but it did at least prove a
certain success.

In this year, 1838, with his election to the Jockey Club,
and with his colours carried at all the great race meetings
in the kingdom, life really began for him.

The great sporting journalist, Henry Hall Dixon, who
was known as 'The Druid', wrote in the *Doncaster Gazette*
that 'From 1838-40 the Eglinton Stud became a great
fact.

For all the rest of the world in England in this year, the
social world, the business world and, indeed, the entire
community, literate or otherwise, who had ever inhaled the
ubiquitous breath of romantic medievalism, ever heard
of King Arthur's knights, ever turned a page of *Ivanhoe*,
ever admired Gothic architecture or ever watched the sun
setting against a crumbling battlement and felt the strange
charm of history, the 'great fact' about Lord Eglinton was
something entirely different.

It was first a rumour, then confirmed by a small entry
on page 538 of the *Court Journal* for the 4th of August,
that he planned to give a tournament.

At this moment, romantic interest in the Middle Ages
which had appeared first a century earlier in the books and
architecture of a few antiquaries was rapidly becoming a
national mania.

The Oxford Movement had just developed in order to
revive the medieval status, discipline and ritual of the
Church, an ambition in its own field that was close to that
of the Young England Party in politics. The Gothic
Revival in architecture had just received public national
approval by the choice of Barry's Gothic plan for the new
Houses of Parliament. Tennyson's *Morte d'Arthur*, *Lady
Clara Vere de Vere* and many other immortal medieval

63

poems had just been written, were circulating privately and were about to be published to form the first landmark in this popular field of Victorian literature. The Gothic wave was about to break.

Thus, because at this moment Lord Eglinton happened to announce his Tournament, he was acclaimed in a way that at all other times would have been impossible.

He was destined to become known throughout Europe for prowess in the lists as one of his kinsmen had been known before him, Count Montgomerie who killed the King of France in a tournament in 1559. He was due, too, to become the most widely known and popular nobleman in the country.

He was doomed, finally, to make his name a symbol of extravagance, to burden the family with a great debt and to provide history, in the Tournament itself, with the last example of a Gothic folly of the type common in the 18th century—the romantic product of a genuine enthusiasm which a more factual Victorian society was soon to ridicule and sweep away.

# Chapter Five

'WHEN THE Eglinton Tournament was first suggested,'
wrote Grantley F. Berkeley, 2nd son of the 5th Earl of
Berkeley, in his memoirs thirty years afterwards,

> I know of nothing that ever seized on the minds of
> the young men of fashion with such force as it did, or
> held out apparently so many romantic attractions. I can
> safely say that, as far as I was concerned, I was seized
> with an extraordinary desire to be one of those who
> would enter the lists, without at first considering the
> consequences which must inevitably attend on such a
> proceeding. Perhaps, assisted by the narratives of the
> *Wizard of the North*, and other illustrators of the olden
> times, all that I thought of for the moment was a
> Queen of Beauty, brave deeds, splendid arms, and
> magnificent horses.

This reaction of Berkeley's was characteristic of almost
all the young men and women of his class. Every one of
them had been steeped in the history of the Middle Ages
since their first efforts to absorb anything. Every girl at
some time or another had dreamed of being acclaimed a
Queen of Beauty by a knight in shining armour, and every
boy had day-dreamed similarly of thundering down the
lists in terrific jousts to deserve the love of a chaste paramour who would then crown him Lord of the Tournament.
To a generation christened Tristram, Launcelot, Isolde
or Guinevere and taught to read from the tales of King
Arthur's Knights, the thought of actually doing any of

65

these things was intoxicating. From the very first chance of its possibility, the Eglinton Tournament was news.

There is no way of understanding the extraordinary force and hypnotic power with which the image of the Middle Ages obsessed the minds of men and women at this time without studying the history of the movement from its beginning. It is often felt of those days which had no fast, multiple means of communication that no form of mass enthusiasm, no kind of universal craze, could ever have moved entire continents in the way that fashions move them today.

This is not true at all. Long before the reign of Queen Victoria, the romantic charm of the Middle Ages was felt in almost every corner of the globe, and the world sales and influence of a book like *Ivanhoe*, for example, with its famous description of the tournament at Ashby de la Zouch, were just as great, taken over a decade, as those of any successful book today.

The only difference was that ideas took longer to circulate. But when a fashion developed, it went deeper and stayed longer and often lasted for a generation. It sometimes influenced a complete era. And this was the case with the vogue for the Middle Ages. It took nearly a century to arrive, but when it came it dominated an epoch.

The last jousts to be held on English soil, the last friendly tilts between armed knights in the genuine un-broken tradition of the 12th century, took place in the reign of Charles I. They were held at Court for the cele-brations at Easter and Whitsun, under the direction of Sir Henry Herberte, Knight, assignee to Sir John Ashley, Knight, Master of the Revelles, and are mentioned in his accounts for 1626.* There may have been others later, for the Easter Revels went on until 1638, but no mention is made of 'tyltinge'. It is quite certain that in this year,

* The Public Record Office, E351/2805, 1623–26.

when civil war broke out in the North, all sports like jousting came to an end.

During the next hundred years, public interest in medieval life declined with each generation until it virtually ceased to exist. This was true of Gothic architecture particularly and also of heraldry, the only aspect of chivalry which still had any practical function. Coats of arms remained fashionable during the Restoration but the heralds themselves became pedantic and expensive, their visitations increasingly unpopular, and after the Revolution of 1688 they were forced to give them up. Once they ceased to record and control coats of arms by calling on families personally, all knowledge and enthusiasm for the subject vanished. Applications for confirmation and grants of arms grew fewer and fewer. According to figures published by the Harleian Society* there were two hundred of these in the first decade of the 18th century, but in the fourth there were only forty. This was only four per year and meant that only one person approached the Herald's College for a coat of arms every three months. It seemed clear that quite soon nobody would bother to apply to them.

In 1732, in a last effort to save themselves from oblivion, the heralds convened the ancient Court of Chivalry, the supreme arbiter of heraldic disputes on the field of the tournament. Many gross breaches of their medieval privileges had been committed in the last fifty years and they felt it was time to assert their authority and put a stop to them. A particularly outrageous case had been that of a Mrs Radburne, a merchant's widow of Mark Lane, London, who, in 1728, had given her husband a heraldic funeral when her local herald, Clarenceaux King of Arms, had told her not to do so. She had designed the hatchment

* Vols lxvi, lxvii, lxviii.

and all the trophies of honour herself instead of having them done by the College of Arms, itself a fearful breach of heraldry, and then, naturally enough, because of ignorance, had mounted them all on the coffin backwards.

Although the Court sat lugubriously for several years, it found there was no means of making Mrs Radburne or anyone else pay any attention to it. The public simply laughed at the heralds and said they were fools with long memories. They were forced to adjourn without achieving anything and their successors did not convene again for two and a quarter centuries, until 1954 when asked to settle a case for the Corporation of Manchester.

After this there was nothing left of all the past magnificence of Chivalry except the presence on a few state occasions of a handful of havering heralds in tarnished tabards who appeared solemnly with rattling parchments and proclaimed announcements which nobody could hear.

'The boast of heraldry, the pomp of pow'r,
And all that beauty, all that wealth e'er gave,
Awaits alike th' inevitable hour,
The paths of glory lead but to the grave.'

Thus wrote the poet, Thomas Gray, in his famous *Elegy* which he began in 1742. He spoke from his own experience for, having lived in London close to the College of Arms where the heralds convened the Court of Chivalry, he himself had witnessed heraldry's extinction.

The mere fact that he wrote about it like this, however, with a certain nostalgia, showed, too, that he sensed the spell that was soon to revive it. He was charmed by its crumbling antiquity and for this reason, as well as lamenting its inevitable death, he preserved its spirit, used it in his work, and thus earned his place as the first major contributor to the medieval revival in literature. For he was, like

68

all creative artists, ahead of the taste of his time; and, in finding emotional expression in the Middle Ages, he perfected an idiom which was not to be widely appreciated for another generation.

In the 1740's, therefore, interest in medieval life reached its lowest point and also started to revive. For in these years a small group of amateur antiquaries like Gray himself—Sanderson Miller, the architect, and Horace Walpole—began to study and appreciate many aspects of medieval life that were then unpopular. In this decade, Sanderson Miller built the first sham castles and ornamental Gothic summer houses. In 1739 Gray, on the Grand Tour with Horace Walpole, first recorded his interest in Gothic architecture. This was exactly a century before the Tournament. In this year, too, Lord Eglinton's grandfather was born.

In nearly every case and in nearly every stage, individually and collectively, the revival of interest in medieval life began with an interest in its architecture. The reason for this was simple. Suits of armour, manuscripts and most other material relics of the time were scarce, but Gothic buildings, decayed or otherwise, were still in use and could easily be studied anywhere.

The best known example of this sequence of development is that of Horace Walpole. First of all, in 1748, he bought his famous villa, Strawberry Hill at Twickenham, and after a few years turned it into a 'little Gothic Castle.' This is generally considered the first landmark in the history of the Gothic Revival in architecture, for although several other people were doing the same thing with their houses at the same time, his position in society, his great circle of acquaintances and his long life gave him a position of leadership.

He held the lead not only in architecture. As everyone

else discovered who took to living in a Gothic house during the next one hundred and fifty years, a new Gothic house needed Gothic furniture to give it authenticity; tapestries and suits of armour to increase its atmosphere; and coats of arms emblazoned here and there to suggest the medieval connections of the family who lived in it. As time went on, Walpole collected all these things, and set an example which many people imitated.

And, like a great number of other people who came after him, amateur as well as professional, many of whom had less ability, he wrote stories about the Middle Ages, too. In 1764, he published a novel called *The Castle of Otranto* which, like the purchase of Strawberry Hill in the field of architecture, is generally considered to mark the beginning of the medieval revival in literature.

It was a tale of the 12th century, filled with knights, castles, ghosts and combats. Walpole wrote it, so he recorded in the preface, after he dreamed of a gigantic hand in armour crashing on to the stair at Strawberry Hill.

As in everything else, he carried away the prize, too, in the field of Gothic dreams.

At this point in the history of the revival—at about the time of the accession of George III in 1760—it becomes necessary to specialise. Every aspect of life began to be affected by it. Not only the great obvious items like literature and architecture, but also the shape of the furniture, the binding of books, the layout of gardens and even the construction of domestic hardware.

A typical example of this was the stove designed by the architect John Soane for Lord Abercorn for the hall at Bentley Priory. It was six feet six inches high and cast in the form of a suit of armour.

Another was a mechanical hermit built for Lord Hill for his garden at Hawkstone in Shropshire. It lived in a

Gothic grotto and whenever anyone opened the door of its cell, it nodded its head.

Other people had real hermits installed in their grottos; but these living beadsmen were not so good, for they developed rheumatism, lost their tempers and failed to nod when visited.

Because all these things developed more or less at the same time, however, it is not so hard to form a complete picture of the movement as it might be otherwise. The history of one aspect was very like the history of all the others, and this is particularly true of the revival of heraldry. It developed hand in hand with architecture and literature. More people in more castles became more enchanted by Gothic literature, built more pediments for coats of arms, took more interest in their own antiquity and had more ambition for heraldic funerals. Thus, side by side with everything else, the interest in heraldry revived.

The first landmark in this particular revival was made in 1764 by a man called Norborne Berkeley, a distant relative of the earls of that family. First of all he followed Walpole's example and converted his house, a Tudor manor called Stoke Gifford in Gloucestershire, into a castellated mansion. It was 'helmèd with a gothic roof'* according to Henry Jones, a local bard, and its great front portico was graced with a huge coat of arms, while its battlements were fretted into the letters of Berkeley's motto: MIHI VOBISQVE.

Next, as soon as the building was finished, he applied to the College of Arms for a pedigree; for during the course of a study of his family's coats of arms and quarterings in the Middle Ages he had found out that he might be heir to a peerage. This was the ancient barony of

* *Clifton* a poem dedicated to Norborne Berkeley in 1768.

Botetourt: it had been created in 1305 but for three hundred and fifty-eight years nobody had heard of it because it had lain in abeyance.

A title falls into abeyance if it is claimed equally by more than one heiress, the direct male line having failed. Such an event evolves through the following anomalies: there is no law of primogeniture amongst women to direct it to the eldest; it can not be shared; it can not be deemed extinct so long as there are heirs to it. This happens only to medieval titles known as baronies by writ, and naturally only to those which pass in the female line. It occurs automatically if one of these titles descends to several heiresses.

Once this has taken place, the title rests in abeyance indefinitely. It can only be claimed, unless awarded by the Sovereign personally, by an heiress or one of her descendants who can prove that all the co-heirs and all their descendants are dead.

In the matter of the barony of Botetourt, however, Norborne Berkeley decided that this was the case. He therefore submitted his claim to the House of Lords.

After a number of hearings which caused a good deal of public interest and of which Horace Walpole wrote that 'the town thinks much, and I not at all',* the Committee of Privileges found that Berkeley's claim was substantiated.

The principal evidence had been his new pedigree and for this reason the heralds received a great deal of excellent publicity. For, having composed it from records made at the time of their medieval visitations, they demonstrated that after all—even three hundred and fifty years afterwards—they and their work were not entirely useless.

From their point of view, as well as Norborne Berkeley's, they scored another success which was almost better than

* Walpole to Lord Hertford, 27th Mar. 1764.

the peerage itself and which set them up and established the value of heraldry in the eyes of the public for ever.

In the records of Parliament and on all occasions of ceremony and protocol, Berkeley was given the precedence he would have had if his family had held the title continuously since 1406. And because there was only a handful of barons whose families had actually held their titles longer than this, Berkeley's rank and seniority amongst his peers turned out to be nearly the highest in the House.

The results of this piece of heraldic lifemanship were instantaneous. Every peer who had to walk behind Berkeley was furious. Every commoner of old family who had always known he was heir to a peerage began to study heraldry to see if he could prove it.

Norborne Berkeley died only six years afterwards at the age of fifty-three, a 'cringing, bowing, fawning, sword-bearing'* courtier, according to the bitter pen of 'Junius', and 'totally ruined but quite charmed'†, according to Horace Walpole. He went bankrupt because of the cost of his case, gambling, extravagance and investment in a company which tried to convert copper into brass, and he earned the hatred of 'Junius' for having acquired the post of Governor of Virginia through Court influence.

He was an inconspicuous man and, except for his claim to the barony of Botetourt, nobody would ever have heard of him. But in the revival of heraldry, his success formed an important landmark as well as a critical precedent in peerage law. And during the next seventy years it inspired enthusiasm for heraldry enormously.

One of the direct and earliest consequences of Berkeley's case was a great increase in the number of books about the peerage.

* Wade's edition of *Junius;* V.2. p. 212.
† Walpole to H. S. Conway. Aug. 9th, 1768.

Before the accession of George III in 1760, there were few works on this subject available to the ordinary reader—Dugdale's *Baronage* of 1676 and Collins' *Peerage* of 1709 or its later editions being the only two to be found in most private libraries. But it was not long before others began to appear and before the end of the Georgian era at least twenty different peerages could be bought on any bookstall.

Some of these were plagiarised miniatures of existing publications and contained nothing original, while others were works of real scholarship and were so huge that two footmen with stepladders were needed to get them down from a shelf and carry them out of a library. Most of them never appeared again but a few were reprinted with new editions for more than a century and two of them—Debrett's and Burke's, which were first published in 1802 and 1822 respectively—are still standard works in print today.

The proprietors of some of the earlier peerages continued to republish, too, and in 1806 Collins' decided on a new 6th and enlarged edition. They looked round for a suitable person to supervise it and they finally settled on a man who had already published some gothic verses, two novels after the style of *The Castle of Otranto* called *Mary de Clifford* and *Arthur Fitzalbini* and who had, too, established a reputation as a meticulous and fervent heraldic genealogist.

He was called Samuel Egerton Brydges and his mania for pedigree was a byword. It became afterwards, as the years passed, a genuine case of gothic delirium.

Samuel Egerton Bridges—Bruges, Burges or Brydges, as the name had been spelled at different times—was born in 1762, two years before Norborne Berkeley's claim to the barony of Botetourt, the eighth child and second surviving son of a comfortable Kentish family. He lived to believe that his line was of great nobility and antiquity but one of the heralds proved during his lifetime that it sprang from inferior yeoman stock. From the age of eight, he developed a mania for heraldry and genealogy, and he used to pray for tempestuous weather to make all hunting, cricket and other forms of exercise impossible and to allow him to stay indoors by the fire in the library with a good, fat, complicated peerage. He was educated locally and at Cambridge and in 1783 he came to London, took chambers in the Temple and read for the Bar.

By the time he was called, in 1787 at the age of twenty-five, he had already pursued his own pedigree for many years and had pushed it back to the Earl of Comyn who came to England with William the Conqueror. He had shown, too, that more recently it came from the third son of the first Lord Chandos, a peerage created in 1554, and he had reached the conclusion that when the present holder of this barony died his elder brother who was called Tymwell would become the heir to it. Up to this moment he had spelt his name 'Bridges' but, to show his newly discovered kinship with the Baron's family who spelt it 'Brydges', he changed the 'i' to 'y'. He also, naturally, made his brother who was thirteen years older than himself, and in his view 'had no judgment at all', do the same thing. When the Barony became vacant two years later because of the death of its owner the Duke of Chandos, he forced his brother to make a claim for it.

The proceedings which followed were perhaps the most tedious and most farcical that have ever wasted the time of the House of Lords. When the claim was turned down for lack of proof, Brydges produced some more, and when this, too, was pronounced inadequate he began to forge it. As the years went by he conjured up every piece of mysterious evidence that was ever devised by a medieval necromancer.

He found a little black box in an attic which was full of documents, but they vanished when anyone lifted the lid. He quoted entries in parish registers, but these were spirited away when anybody wanted to see them, or else the pages—obviously tampered with—were unexpectedly turned into dust. He actually produced one crinkled parchment but, since there seemed to be nothing on it except a coat of arms and some hyroglyphics, a Mr Robert Lemon, an antiquary from the Tower of London, was called to apply a magic liquid which was said to revive invisible ink. This was done but if any ink had ever been applied it still could not be seen.

At last, in 1803, after thirteen and a half years in which the Committee of Privileges had sat twenty-seven times, they presented their opinion to the House of Lords that Tymwell Brydges 'had not made out his claim to the said Barony.'

If such a verdict were not enough, Egerton and Tymwell —by then on the brink of hysteria—proceeded to urge every peer by circular letter to attend the House to vote against it. This was considered a gross breach of privilege and finally wrecked their case. One of the very few peers who voted in favour of it was the infamous Duke of Cumberland. He did not care for the Barony or Egerton or Tymwell, but his current mistress happened to be Tymwell's wife.

Tymwell died four years later; but for Samuel Egerton this agonising and humiliating public defeat which, as he wrote in his autobiography, 'was received by our enemies with grins of extreme delight', was only a beginning.

During the next six years in which he was compiling the new edition of Collins' *Peerage*, a gigantic work which still serves as the standard reference of its kind for the Georgian era and for which his name will always be remembered, his own supposed rank and family antiquity obsessed his thoughts with the blind force of madness.

Every other consideration of health, sense or duty to his wife and children went down before it. From the date of his brother's death and his own supposed succession, he used the title as if he actually owned it and signed his letters '(*Per legem terrae*) Baron Chandos of Sudely'. When he came to describe the family of Chandos in his peerage, he explained his own claim for thirty-six pages, and once the whole work was finished he threw every other interest aside and wasted the rest of his life and his entire fortune in struggling to prove that his claim was valid.

In one year, 1823, he wrote thirty-three letters to the Prime Minister, almost none of which were answered. He then published at his own expense a thick book called *Lex Terrae* in which he pointed out to the members of the House of Lords that their powers were limited, and explained that in common law he was not bound to pay any attention to them. Finally, he compiled an enormous tome called *Stemmata Illustria* in which with a great shield showing three hundred and sixty quarterings he proved over three hundred pages his descent from the Merovingian kings in the 5th century and showed in more than two hundred and fifty different pedigrees that more blood of Charlemagne flowed in his veins than it did in those of the Royal Family.

In doing all this, he spent more than one hundred thousand pounds and all that he earned was a baronetcy for his work on Collins' *Peerage* and the doubtful honour of being parodied in Disraeli's novel, *Sybil* as a luminous genealogist called Baptist Hatton.

The time described in this novel is exactly that of the Eglinton Tournament and, being a satire of contemporary events, it gives an authentic picture of the extent to which the mania for claiming old peerages had spread. For by that time hundreds of people were chasing them.

'You would like to be a peer, Sir?' Baptist Hatton asks an old baronet, Sir Vavasour Firebrace. 'Well, you are really Lord Vavasour, but there is a difficulty in establishing your undoubted right from a single writ of summons . . . Your claim on the barony of Lovel is good: I could recommend your pursuing it, did not another more inviting still present itself. In a word, if you wish to be Lord Bardolf, I will undertake to make you so . . . It will give you precedence over every other peer on the roll, except three, and I made those.'

'It is wonderful,' exclaimed Sir Vavasour. 'And what do you think our expenses will be in this claim?'

'Bagatelle!' answered Mr Hatton. 'It will not cost you a paltry twenty or thirty thousand pounds.'

In 1837 when Sir Samuel Egerton Brydges died at the age of seventy-five—the last of a line that did not exist—his passion for pedigree and his obsession for composing great heraldic shields of coats of arms and quarterings had already become an accepted part of medieval revivalism. Many people of all literate classes did the same thing, while many others had, in spite of its absurd failure, become impressed by his furious pursuit of his medieval barony.

For slowly but steadily, over the long period since Norborne Berkeley had first successfully claimed his own, the ever widening spread of the medieval revival had made such claims more and more popular.

It was worked out by one enthusiast that since the year 1265 at least one hundred-and-one baronies by writ had fallen into abeyance. There was, for example, the barony of Sampson whose heirs had vanished in 1306 and which

6. Lord Eglinton, aged 24, on Black Diamond
(a painting by Ferneley, 1836)

might, therefore, be claimed by anybody. All that was needed was a nice foolproof pedigree to show that the claimant was a missing heir and a few copies of medieval documents to prove that all the other possible claimants were dead. These were not so hard to find as they might be. All the certificates could be supplied easily by any peerage lawyer or professor of heraldic genealogy.

For these experts were now in good supply. The heralds themselves, many solicitors and a whole group of fraudulent amateurs had appeared conveniently to fill the demand for them. In actual practice, it was almost impossible to prove a unique claim but, for all that, as this particular medieval virus reached the stage of an epidemic, more and more wealthy people determined to have a go at it.

Amongst those who failed were Henry Dymoke, the King's Champion, who claimed the barony of Marmion; Sir Robert Burdett who did not wish to waste his money and claimed five at the same time, Tyes, De Badlesmere, Latymer, Berkeley and Berkeley; Charles Kemys Kemys Tynte whose claim for the barony of Wharton was found to be in abeyance still between himself and four others. One of these was the friend and Ayrshire neighbour of Lord Eglinton's, a keen member of the Young England Party, whose name was long enough as it was: Alexander Dundas Ross Cochrane Wishart Baillie, afterwards Lord Lamington.

Many others succeeded, especially those of old family whose pedigrees were well authenticated already. The peak was reached in the years just before and after the Tournament when five baronies were claimed successfully which had such immense periods of abeyance that even the claimants themselves could hardly remember their origins.

These were Vaux in 1838, Camoys in 1839, Braye in 1839, Beaumont in 1840 and Hastings in 1841. The sum of the lengths of their abeyances came to one thousand seven hundred and fifty-three years.

The longest was Hastings which had lain dormant since 1290 and was claimed by Sir Jacob Astley as the junior co-heir of the junior co-heiress.

Technically, the best was Camoys. This had been held for only forty-three years after its creation in 1383 and had then been forgotten completely. It gave its new owner, the 3rd baron, precedence over the 17th baron Stourton whose family had held his title continuously in male descent for three hundred and eighty-four years.

Lord Stourton was absolutely exasperated by this, and so were many of his colleagues. They decided that it was high time that this particular heraldic dragon was knocked on the head; and since that day, with rare exceptions, only claimants with outstanding pedigrees have been considered for baronies by writ which have lain in abeyance for many centuries.

Although this decision spoilt the game of claiming abeyant peerages, it only encouraged the adoption of other methods of displaying family antiquity and medieval enthusiasm.

A group of baronets under a man called Sir Richard Broun, whom Disraeli caricatured in *Sybil* as Sir Vavasour Firebrace, tried to prove that the medieval status of the baronetcy as a whole had been that of another estate of the realm and, therefore, that all baronets ought to have seats in Parliament. Sir Richard claimed, too, that they ought to be styled 'Honourable' and before he succeeded to his father's baronetcy he demanded for himself the privilege of knighthood which, he said, had been promised by James I in 1616 to all baronets' heirs apparent. When the Lord Chancellor refused to present him to the Queen for this purpose, he assumed the prefix of 'Sir' anyway and signed himself 'Sir Richard Broun, *Eques auratus*'. Finally, in exactly the same manner as Sir Egerton Brydges, he compiled a book, *Broun's Baronetage*, in which he filled the preface with twenty pages of his own arguments and gave his own family three times as much space as anybody else's. He described himself as a 'feudal Baron' and 'chief of his race in North Britain'; for by that time his father had died and at least his rank as a baronet was indisputable.

Another and less elevated section of the community decided not to bother with the House of Lords at all and, taking a different tip from Sir Egerton Bridges or Brydges, took the matter into their own hands and simply changed their names from Smith or Green to what they supposed they had been in the Middle Ages, sometimes adding the particle 'de' in front of them.

De Burghs, De Veres, De Greys and De Beauchamps, all multiplied uncontrollably. A family called Mullins changed their name to De Moleyns. Another in Wales called Wilkins received a royal licence in the same year as the Tournament to assume the surname of De Winton. A few years afterwards, Thackeray's famous character, James Plush, the footman who made a fortune in railway stock, appeared in *Punch* as Jeames de la Pluche, and announced that his direct ancestor, Hugo, had landed in Sussex with William the Conqueror.

It has since been shown by historical research that, except in a few cases like those of Howard de Walden and Willoughby de Broke, the particle 'de' was never used in the Middle Ages except to denote where a person lived, and was never taken in a surname or written in a document except by accident. So that now practically all names of this nature are seen to be concoctions and, instead of proving their medieval origins, reveal themselves as Victorian gothicisms.

But at that time nobody knew or cared about this and several writers besides Thackeray made fun of those who adopted the Gothic particle.

'What can delay De Vaux and De Saye . . .
   And De Nokes and De Styles and Lord Marmaduke
      Grey,
   And De Roe? And De Doe?
Poynings and Vavasour?'

wrote Richard Barham in his *Ingoldsby Legends*, a popular collection of satires on this and other medieval affectations, published in 1839.* For the same reason, too, Tennyson wrote the lines:

> 'A simple maiden in her flower
> Is worth a hundred coats of arms'

and also:

> 'From yon blue heavens above us bent
> The Gardener Adam and his wife
> Smile at the claims of long descent.
> Howe'er it be, it seems to me,
> 'Tis only noble to be good.
> Kind hearts are more than coronets,
> And simple faith than Norman blood.'

both in the same poem, pointedly entitled *Lady Clara Vere de Vere*. His uncle who had inherited his father's birthright and whom he disliked had just taken the additional surname and arms of d'Eyncourt; and this had inspired him to write so contemptuously.

However trite Tennyson's remarks might have been, the mania for heraldry was so great by that time that few families amongst the upper classes or aristocracy wholeheartedly believed them. They felt that a maiden with sixteen quarterings had twice as much charm as one with only eight, unless the one with eight—perhaps the

* *The Lay of St Cuthbert.*

daughter of one of the new, rich manufacturers—had sixteen times as much money.

Even those families who had many titles and quarterings already, like the Montgomeries, were bitten frequently by this form of medievalism and spent fortunes trying to substantiate their rights as heirs to others. Many a dripping interminable Scottish night was spent by Lord Eglinton's grandfather working out his claim to the Earldom of Mount Alexander, an old family honour which had gone to an Irish branch in the Middle Ages and which the Lyon King of Arms in Edinburgh told him was extinct but which he himself believed to be only dormant. He failed to prove it and all his time and effort were brought to nothing.

Lord Eglinton himself was luckier. In 1840 he was served heir male general to the Earls of Winton. This title, granted to the father of 'Greysteel' in 1600, had been attainted after the rebellion of 1715 and had thus automatically fallen dormant. In normal circumstances such an attainder would have caused a bar to any succession, but Lord Eglinton determined to get round it. With careful presentation, plenty of money, good solicitors and expert heraldic advice, he managed to prove his case by 'Speciality'.

Finally, for all those antiquaries, humble or great, professional or amateur, who had no ambition to change their names, to claim peerages or perhaps no money with which to do so, there was always the study of heraldry and genealogy for itself.

They could use heraldic terms as a form of wit in ordinary conversation like the boring herald, Memblazon, in *Kenilworth* who spoke of 'sejeant' instead of 'sitting' and 'reguardant' instead of 'looking', or else they could pass their time alone in their Gothic villas or mansions or chambers, reading peerages and composing enormous shields of coats of arms and pedigrees.

For at this moment in the 19th century when the aristocracy still took a romantic view of medieval life, and the middle classes had not yet spoilt the fun by treating it seriously, there was one thing that everyone wanted—rich, or poor, hoary earl or modern industrialist:—a big bright coat of arms with dozens and dozens and dozens and dozens of quarterings.

This pattern of development of the medieval revival in the field of heraldry—its last use on the field of the tournament in the reign of Charles I; its ultimate decline and apparent extinction in the 1730's; its sole preservation in the hands of a few antiquaries during the following decades; its reappearance and steady return to fashion amongst the upper classes from about the accession of George III in 1760; its final restoration to a state of universal national popularity in the reign of William IV and the early years of Queen Victoria—this cycle over the period of two centuries was the same for all other branches of the Gothic movement and thus for the movement as a whole.

Naturally enough there were variations in time and subject and in this decade or that certain aspects, like jewellery or archery, might be more revived than others, like music or the theatre, but taking the whole movement over the entire period, this was the general graph of its death and renascence.

The history of heraldry illustrates it well for several reasons. The facts are clear, simple and well authenticated by many contemporary documents; the life span and life's work of one man—Sir Egerton Brydges, 1762-1837— precisely covers the whole revival of it and stands as a symbol of all its values—its historical worth, artistic merit and pointless worship of often imaginary ancestors; and heralds and heraldry, being living relics of the days of chivalry in which they developed, were thus, naturally, of particular interest to all those who took part in the Eglinton Tournament.

Moreover, the influence and example of Sir Egerton Brydges' life impinged on the Tournament, too, in another way for, apart from every connection he had or thought he had with everyone else, he did have a genuine link with the family of Lamb of Beauport. It so happened that in 1821, because of inheritance, they had adopted the name of Lamb, but before that they had been called Bruges, Burges, Bridges or Brydges, and they also, like Sir Egerton, claimed kinship with the barons and dukes of Chandos. Furthermore, they were well acquainted with him, for although he lived in Geneva in voluntary exile, Sir Charles Lamb had many maternal relatives and a house in Geneva,* too, and for this reason he and the rest of his family often met him there.

Although most of them laughed at Sir Egerton and his claims and quarterings and ravings about pedigree, yet one of them took him seriously, loved and admired him, to some extent became his pupil and, from his early youth, like Sir Egerton himself, spent his days buried in books on the peerage and passed his sleep dreaming about knights and chivalry.

He gave his toys Gothic names as soon as he was old enough to call them anything; he drew his first heraldic shield with eight quarterings correctly blazoned in gay tinctures for a pet guinea-pig before he reached the age of ten; he began to write his first medieval manuscript on parchment and illuminate it with heraldic signs and knights in combat before he passed the age of puberty;

* The Chateau Banquet.

and he bought his first suit of armour and rescued his first damsel in distress even before he took part in the Tournament.

He was brought up in the same house and at the same schools side by side with a contemporary and half-brother with whom he shared all these dreams and possessions.

This half-brother was Lord Eglinton. The boy himself was the heir to the baronetcy of Lamb of Beauport and to the enchanting, authentic, medieval post of Knight Marshal of the Royal Household—the eldest son of Sir Charles Lamb and Lady Montgomerie: Charles James Saville Montgomerie Lamb.

# Chapter Six

CHARLES LAMB, who was known as Charlie in the family to distinguish him from his father, was born at Beauport on the 7th of October, 1816, four years and one week after Lord Eglinton, and was baptised on the 3rd day of the next month by the Rev. H. Rule Sarel, the local curate of Hollington in whose parish Beauport Park was situated.*

The Lamb family was an old one—Burges, as it was still called at the time of Charlie's birth—and it traced itself back with authenticity to a Giles Burges who was M.P. for Reading at the end of the fifteenth century, while it claimed descent in family legend from a Flemish merchant who came to England in 1230, calling himself Burges or Bruges after the city of his birth.

Whatever its precise origins, the family was one of age and reputable connections and its members had marked the pages of history from time to time in a small but honourable way. Colonel Roger Burges, a direct ancestor of the 17th century, had acquired fame in the Civil War by defying Cromwell successfully and holding the town of Faringdon in Berkshire. A century later, George Burges, another soldier, had taken part in the battle of Culloden and captured the standard of Prince Charles' body-guard, born by the Duke of Atholl.

This man's son, James Burges, the first baronet and Charlie's grandfather, had spent most of his life as an active Member of Parliament and had held the post of

* Hollington Parish Register.

Under Secretary of State for Foreign Affairs. He had resigned from politics in 1795 and had then achieved his baronetcy.

At the same time he had received the appointment of Knight Marshal of the Royal Household. He had asked for this because he wanted a position at Court and also because he had fallen under the prevailing spell of the Middle Ages and wished to assume the mantle of a medieval functionary.

Once he had retired from public life, he took to literature and, in 1818, the year before Sir Walter Scott published *Ivanhoe* and brought literary medievalism to a climax, he produced an epic in twelve cantos entitled *The Dragon Knight*.

A mere chance brought him the Lamb estate. This inheritance—which was worth about six thousand pounds per year and included properties in Hertfordshire, Suffolk and Leicestershire as well as a row of houses in Palace Yard, Westminster and a mansion in Golden Square—belonged to a Mr John Lamb, a friend and contemporary of his father's who had made money as an army agent and who, having no relations and being a bachelor, had bequeathed it to him in his father's memory. When Lamb died in 1798, however, he directed it first to another friend called Henry Cock for life and by all normal expectations Cock ought to have outlived Burges by several years. But Cock expired suddenly of a heart attack in 1821. So Burges came into it, and in that year he and his family changed their name by Royal Licence to Lamb.

The house and estate of Beauport where the family had lived for a number of years before they acquired the additional estates of John Lamb had been bought by James Burges in 1794 and was in East Sussex on top of the Downs, facing south towards Hastings, with superb views in all directions. In 1767 it had belonged to General James Murray, one of Wolfe's commanders in Canada, who had rebuilt it in the classical style and changed its name from Beacon Hill to commemorate the Manor House of Beauport near Quebec which had been Montcalm's headquarters before the battle of the Heights of Abraham in which he had taken part. Before him it had been owned by a local family of hop growers and brewers called Rivers. In all probability this was the family who built it.

As a place to live in it was well designed and comfortable and, apart from having an almost perfect situation, it was near the sea, had splendid woods close to it and also, beyond them, the great bare sweep of the open Downs.

It was a plain and pleasant rectangular mansion with sash windows and vaguely symmetrical proportions and was considered, naturally, by all the Gothic enthusiasts of the 19th century as a typical specimen of boring classical architecture.

In compensation, its local village was Battle whose single, straight, ancient street was dominated by the towers and castellated battlements of the great gateway of Battle Abbey. They marked the spot where William the Conqueror had defeated Harold in 1066, and thus they stood as a romantic reminder of the very advent of English chivalry.

Whether or not the existence of such a hoary and picturesque Gothic edifice so close to Beauport inspired the infant mind of Charlie Lamb with medieval ambitions as he walked or rode past it in his early years cannot be calculated.

Certainly it was a fact that almost as soon as he could read and write he began to do so about the Middle Ages and, even before that, to populate the woods and fields around Beauport in his imagination with as many knights and dragons as other children at other times might have filled them with goblins and fairies.

His childhood letters and manuscripts which, strangely enough, have managed to survive although the male line of the family has been extinguished, all the possessions sold or discarded and the house burnt and turned into an hotel, reveal his interests with charming enthusiasm.

In the earliest of the letters, written to his mother on the 16th of October, 1823, one week after his seventh birthday, he announced in the first sentence—without wasting time on preliminary civilities about the weather or anybody's health—that he was going to write the history of his life and adventures, another about the life of Miss Johnson, his governess, and a third concerning Minnikin, Pin and Toby, his guinea pigs.

After stating this, he reverted to everyday matters and said that he had been down to the sea to collect shells, an occupation which, like the study of the Middle Ages, absorbed him constantly throughout his life and which, on this Thursday, made him late for tea.

Then, after tea, Miss Johnson had read to him. She must have done so for several hours, for she got through the whole history of the Wars of the Roses and the reign of Edward IV. Charlie was perfectly entranced by it and told his mother that Edward was 'marvellously handsome but horridly cruel.'

So far as is known he did not, at that time, compile an account of his own life and adventures or of Miss Johnson's, but he did begin and actually finish during his childhood a complete history of the lives of many of his guinea pigs.

These animals, which were favourite pets of the 19th century and which, like shells, were one of the passions of his life, lived in the grounds of Beauport in what became a miniature guinea pig city. It was named Winnipeg and a great castellated hutch called Guinea Pig Castle stood in the middle of it, specially built by the estate carpenter for the King and Queen who were known as Geeny and Cavia.

The manuscript of this chronicle—16,000 words in length, half as long, for example, as the story of Alice in Wonderland—is entitled *The History of Winnipeg from the foundation to the Present time. BY ROYAL COMMAND.* and is written in eight tiny fat volumes which are bound in red and green leather. The style is a comic mixture of biblical phraseology and cockney slang and the narrative is drawn from his imagination, experience and also, according to the first paragraph of the eighth chapter of the third volume, 'from an ancient illumined parchment entitled register of Zeleyor which hath lately been discovered.'

It is illustrated with portraits in water colours of the guinea pigs, drawn from life, with their coats of arms correctly blazoned and tinctured and sometimes described as, for example, those of a warrior called Keelrat, 'a noble Winnipeg who bore for his arms—Arg$^t$ three rats keeled prop$^r$—'.

For, naturally enough, all the guinea pigs were of old Saxon, Norman or even Roman and Greek descent and anxious to prove it, either by displaying their coats of arms or else by assuming the Gothic particle. For 'every lord wished to be a Duke—every Squire a lord.'

The third chapter of the fourth volume which is a good example of the whole work begins as follows:

*The Reign of Albineus*
*the Yellow*
*Earl of Newton*

On the death of Polydorus, the unanimous voice of the people chose Albineus Earl of Ayton and Newton to be Lord Protector of the Kingdom of Winnipeg, with full and regal power. At the time of his accession he was

Warden of the marches, Hyparch of Winnipeg and Viceroy of the Kingdom—mighty offices such as were never before combined in one individual. And he had acquired vast renown in the border wars. Much was expected of him, and much indeed was required. For at this time the state of the Kingdom was seedy indeed. From a commission of enquiry instituted in May year 11 Farai was ruinous, and nearly deserted and the whole country of the border was desolated with war and abandoned by its people. A Census of the whole population including the people of Ermineus shews an amount of three decads and a half. But the spirit of energy, peace being restored, was soon infused into the people. Ino FitsRedais, surnamed the just was appointed bailiff of Peektown, and warden of the gate, bearing the same powers as Hyparch of Winnipeg, he was vigourous but gentle. Altogether perhaps the most perfect character in Winnipeg history. The numbers of the people under the firm rule of these Nobles augmented considerably. It was in August year eleven, that the Earl of Newton, the now a lover lover of peace, yet unwilling that chivalry should languish, inspired, likewise, with the love of Rosabel, Countess of Zelia, instituted the farfamed knightly order of the White Rose, with its well known device *'Sur tous les fleurs la Rose est Belle.'* This high honor was first conferred upon Sir Ino Fitsreds, Knight, Sir Heliodorous, Prince of Rarribun, Sir Alexander Lilli, Kt and Turkwine de Newton, Captain of the guard.

These noble and medieval guinea pigs and their lives and adventures absorbed Charlie for many years, at least until he was past the age of eleven, for he wrote to his mother from Eton on the 6th of February, 1828, and commanded her, as his Agent, to supervise the erection of a tombstone to Cavy, the first chatelaine of Guinea Pig Castle. Cavy seems to have died in the Christmas holidays and, since guinea pigs live for about six or seven years, her birth can be guessed at the early 1820's; and these years must roughly date the beginning of the Beauport dynasty.

As a piece of literature and an example of nursery Georgian gothicism, his work must be unique and, unlike most childish compositions which are soon forgotten, it lay in his mind and inspired him years later to go to the Tournament as a representative of its noblest Order of Chivalry.

In this way, in the best tradition of all fairy stories, the guinea pigs slept in their tiny graves for twenty years and then awoke as shining knights.

For although it was thought to be Charlie who galloped down the lists inside the armour of the Knight of the White Rose, in fact it was nothing of the sort, but the incarnation of one of the four original members of this Order who took it in turns to embody him. The Prince of Rarribun, Sir Ino FitsRedais, Sir Alexander Lilli or Turkwine de Newton, the finest flowers of the Chivalry of the city of Winnipeg.

There are two portraits of Charlie during his childhood, one painted by Kinson in Paris in 1821 and the other by Ferneley at Melton Mowbray in 1822. Kinson's was burnt at Beauport a century later and a poor copy of it, done by an old gentleman called Brooke which hung at Eglinton Castle was sold when the place was demolished in 1925 to an unidentified Mr Fraser for six guineas and has since completely vanished. A faded photograph of it exists, however, and also a lithograph. Ferneley's portrait, with all the charm and excellence for which that artist remains admired today, escaped the fire at Beauport because it was small enough to be snatched up and rescued, which

Kinson's was not, and it still belongs to one of Charlie's descendants.

Of the two, Kinson's is easily the worse, but it has more value from the biographer's point of view because it includes the only known portrait of Charlie's mother. It shows Charlie in life size, standing beside her in a smock against the marbled entrance of an Italianate room, looking past the head of a gigantic St Bernard which is lounging near her feet and staring up at her moodily. The family always considered that Kinson had made a good likeness of Charlie but had drawn Lady Montgomerie two inches too short, and the apparent magnitude of the dog which looks enormous seems to justify this criticism.

Ferneley's portrait shows Charlie in a grey top hat and pink riding costume, trotting across a field on a black horse with a collie running ahead of him, a hoary oak in the right foreground and the great classical portico of an unidentified mansion in the far distance beyond a lake. In this work all the subjects retain their expected sizes.

As might be expected from Charlie's manuscripts and letters, he appears in both pictures—and also the lithograph which has slight differences from the original—as a dreamy boy with a look of intelligence and sensitivity. His face is small, delicate and pointed and his head covered with jet black curls like those of his father. His hair and brows and eyes are so black and his skin so dark that he might indeed have inherited Moorish blood, as was often said of both of them. But no trace of such a mixture exists in their pedigrees unless it crept in with Anne Montolieu, his French grandmother.

Kinson's portrait gives this impression of foreignness particularly and in after years, with a black and curly beard and sidewhiskers, Charlie's aspect in armour was truly Saracenic. As a child, however, it made him in-

MARY LADY MONTGOMERIE & M? CHARLES LAMB.

7. Lady Montgomerie and Charlie Lamb (by Kinson, 1821) from an engraving in *The Memorials of the Montgomeries* by Sir Wm. Fraser

teresting and attractive. With his white gown-like smock touching his feet and his head of curls, he resembles the boy in the much loved picture of a later period who is seen in a desert in a nightie with various wild animals.* It illustrates the sixth verse of the 11th chapter of Isiah 'The wolf also shall dwell with the lamb, and the leopard shall lie down with the kid; and the calf and the young lion and the fatling together; and a little child shall lead them.' And certainly, if Charlie had modelled for this infant, he would have done so to perfection.

As often happens in such cases with children of radiantly angelic countenances, although Charlie had a way with animals and might easily have managed to make lions and leopards and lambs and kids lie down together by personal magnetism, he could not have done so by the assertion of holy innocence. For inside he was thoroughly wicked, or at least according to the opinion of the few adults who described him a quarter of a century later and who judged him then by the standards of orthodox Victorian morality. For no account of his childish character written at the time has come down to us.

While he was truly a born naturalist and loved shells, birds, insects and guinea-pigs, and much preferred to spend his time with them, even at that age, instead of with other children, he soon began to make seriously impious observations about them. It was not long before he decided that fundamentally there was little difference between beasts and men at all except, of course, that human beings could talk and were highly developed. Therefore, he concluded, the whole concept of the immortal soul was ridiculous.

In this, as in many other subjects, his ideas were ahead of his time; and if he reported his early life to his children

* By William Strutt, 1896, Brecon Cathedral.

accurately, and if they, in their turn, writing many years later still, recorded them correctly, he reached them all entirely by himself at a very early age.

He became an agnostic, a socialist, opposed to capital punishment and in favour of homeopathy and birth control, not knowing the predelictions of Sir Charles and the temptations he was likely to inherit in connection with this last doctrine.

The fact that upset his descendants the most was the early age at which he adopted all these practices. For, according to his first and practically illegitimate daughter who became the well known authoress 'Violet Fane' and who recorded these details about him in a biographical novel called *Sophy* in 1881, he was still only a child when he did so. He was hardly ten when he first began to think about them and in two years time had come round to them all, including an absolute refusal to pray and an open denouncement of religion. She could not refrain from adding in the novel that a judgment fell upon him because of it and that, like Saul, he lost his eyesight—which in actual fact he did before he was middle-aged.

At this point, it was generally felt by the family afterwards, his mother ought to have taken a firm line with him and led him back to the meadows of virtue. But as it happened, Lady Montgomerie herself had long since given up any idea of praying to God or supposing He took any interest in her although she was born, presumably, with His benevolence, into a coveted *milieu* and one of the richest heiresses in Scotland.

But when her first father-in-law, the 12th Earl of Eglinton, had assumed the custody of her sons against her will at the time when she married Lamb, and when she had prayed to be given them back and only suffered the death of her eldest child instead, she had quite lost faith in

God's justice or prayer's efficacy. If religion opened the gates of Paradise in after life, she was glad to hear it and she hoped her little Hugh was there already, but she herself decided to worry about this at a later date and for the time being to enjoy the world as she knew it. Naturally enough, she permitted Charlie to do the same thing.

In this respect, as well as in every other, Lady Montgomerie was a complacent mother and the perfect wife to Charlie's father who thought, too, that the only thing to do was to live in the present and to drink, travel and amuse himself so long as he had the inclination. If God existed at all, He clearly favoured the aristocracy, and as they were both born in the highest social scale—Lady Montgomerie especially—there was obviously nothing to worry about.

This particular aspect of both their philosophies—their aristocratic outlook and their belief that only Kings, Princes, Dukes (and not many of them, either) were better than the Earls of Eglinton—was one of Lady Montgomerie's dominant characteristics, and for her the world was divided simply into two social strata, the upper— containing Sir Charles Lamb, herself and their families, known privately as 'Ourselves'—and the other—embracing everybody else who were vaguely called 'The Others'.

She was two years younger than her husband, being born in 1787, and was thus twenty-nine at the time of Charlie's birth. How she met Lamb has not been established, but she seems to have known him well before the death of Lord Montgomerie for she planned to marry him only eight months afterwards and would have done so but for illness. Possibly she met him in Sicily, for the secretary to Lord William Bentinck was called Lamb and he may have been a connection of the Henry Lamb who bequeathed the fortune to the Burges family, and he may have brought them together. If this happened, and if she met Sir Charles at Palermo, she might well in such a restricted community have got to know him intimately. Otherwise, in spite of his Arabian good looks, of the Knight Marshalship and the family baronetcy, she might, in a larger city, have classed him as one of 'The Others'.

She herself was not particularly handsome, having a rather heavy face in her portrait photograph, with a low forehead overhung by coils of dark hair, lidded eyes, full nose and lips and the same pointed chin that is seen in Charlie. She was not considered beautiful by the Lamb family and, in fact, to speak the truth, she looks rather goat-like. But in the lithograph she is depicted much more delicately, and perhaps the lithographer drew from Kinson's original while the photographer worked from Brooke's copy. As both are missing it is now impossible to say. Her presence and carriage made up for her looks, however, for she was above middle height and had an imposing and gentle manner which, in the best sense of the word, was thoroughly aristocratic.

By temperament she was yielding, lazy and affectionate, loving animals like her son, Charlie, proud of her wealth and the comforts it brought her family but too lethargic ever to attend to its management or even to dictate its succession after her death. So she died intestate and caused an appalling struggle between the Lambs and the Montgomeries for, although her estates were entailed and went to Lord Eglinton, her marriage settlement, drawn up by the old 12th Earl, was, in the view of both parties concerned, such a 'triumph of Scottish Law' that no one from that day to this has ever been able to untangle it.

She had much money, plate, furniture and many family pictures and jewels which had not been left in tail male by her grandfather, the 9th Earl, in his new Will in 1729, but left in tail general and had therefore descended to her absolutely. Nevertheless, the Montgomeries claimed them as family heirlooms and the Lambs held on to them and said they were nothing of the sort.

So it was that if anyone asked her to see about anything, to make a Will or come to a decision about the future, she nodded and promised to do so but never got round to it.

The same process occurred over Charlie's atheism. She meant to tell him to try to be a Christian but she quite forgot and only smiled when she said good night to him, and constantly omitted to insist that he said his prayers.

Probably the last time that he went on his knees for any purpose except for a maiden's love was when he attended mattins on his last morning at Eton in the autumn of 1828. There, where daily worship was compulsory, he must have knelt on the hard floor beside Lord Eglinton, secretly raced mice and beetles up and down the long bench seats of the hard stalls beneath their faces or sat and admired the chapel's Gothic sublimity while he listened to the Scriptures.

A year or two before that he had probably worshipped beside Lord Eglinton at Mitcham, for although it is not certain that he went with him to the academy there, it is likely that he did so. There, in terms of early Gothic experience, he was lucky, too, for Mitcham's ancient parish church had just tumbled down and been rebuilt in a style that was 'strictly Gothic'. It was one of the earliest examples of the more 'correct' Gothic work which preceded the Gothic Revival in church architecture and it was, according to Pigot's Directory of 1824, 'perhaps as beautiful a structure as is to be met with in any village in the Kingdom.'

Whether he went to Mitcham or not, it is certain that he stayed with Aunt Jane at Wimbledon at times between

1825-1827, for several letters written from there to his mother are among those that she treasured. They reveal him, in these last years of his childhood, as a very normal, genial little fellow, except for his special interest in shells, butterflies and insects. Every letter contains references to them, either pleas to his mother to be sure to collect some from where she happened to be staying, or else reports of having written to those family friends who were going abroad to do the same thing, or else details—already too technical for normal understanding—of those he had found locally. They are often sketched, too, for Charlie knew how to draw charmingly.

It is clear that he ought to have been a naturalist and in this respect he took after his grandfather's sister, Mary Anne Burges, who was born in 1763 and was known in the family as Maria. In her circle she was recognised as a woman of outstanding intelligence and ability, reading Latin, Greek, German and Swedish, speaking French, Italian and Spanish, drawing and painting excellently and being also a keen botanist and leaving among her MS a beautifully illustrated account of the lepidoptera of the British Isles.

She was also, it would seem inevitably, an absorbed student and composer of Gothic literature and, although she never published in this field, she left to the family a MS novel in twenty-four books entitled *Aracynthus*. It is faultlessly written in a clear hand, and superbly illustrated in water colours with almost as many pictures of knights in combat, maidens and bleeding dragons as there were of dragonflies and moths in her catalogues of lepidoptera.

It is evident from Charlie's letters that he loved staying at Wimbledon with Aunt Jane and his half-brother and was much happier there than he was at Eton. He was not miserable at school but all forms of work beyond his specialised interests bored him. He seems to have suffered from cold and chills frequently which he welcomed in a way for they forced him to stay indoors out of class. They allowed him, in writing to his mother, to enjoy the contradiction in terms of being 'out' because he was 'in' and enabled him also to stop wasting his time with scripture or mathematics and to concentrate on insects and medieval history. He often wrote to his mother for books on these subjects and she sent them to him conscientiously, including Mawe's *Conchology*, Nicholson's *Encyclopaedia*, *The Cunynghame Tales* and *Melmoth*. This last, a grisly Gothik Tale, he enjoyed particularly.

There is an account of him in his half-brother's diary during this time, written many years afterwards but still probably describing him as he appeared to many people at that age as his personality developed.

I have seldom met with a more extraordinary character than his (Lord Eglinton wrote). He was gifted with talents of a very high order, a wonderful memory, and a power of argument that I have never seen surpassed, but there was no discretion, no judgment, no system, and I do not believe that under any circumstances he would ever have made a practical or brilliant use of his advantages. As he was, he was utterly thrown away. He was spoilt by both parents, by kindness on the one side and indifference or worse, on the other. He left school at the early age of 12 and had no teaching, except what he picked up for himself afterwards. Biassed at first by the base and irreligeous principles of his father, under the influence of a bad course of reading and an unfortunate choice of friends, he became I fear almost an infidel, he never went into society, and spent his time entirely in the country among his shells, insects and guinea pigs, of which latter collection he had several hundred. Of his unfortunate marriage and miserable end* I shall speak afterwards. With all his faults he was a fine, honourable, warmhearted fellow, and I was very fond of him.

There is an account of Charlie's departure from Eton in one of his letters, or rather a prayer that he may be allowed to leave at the same time as Lord Eglinton which, in fact, he did. It is the last of the series, the last indeed of any of his letters which have survived, and parts of it are worth quoting for they give a picture of the cheerful, whimsical, likeable characteristics which Lord Eglinton attributed to him. He begs his mother to be allowed to leave, if only because of the cold to his toes in the coming winter, especially during the lessons before breakfast under the terrifying Dr Keate whose very shadow could chill the bones of anybody.

Money is scarce, what beautiful things there are at Eton to desire! We have scarcely got as much as we might want, even with next allowance.

I hope the guinea pigs are all well, you should put them into some warm place, now the cold weather has come on, or they will all die! every man jack of them; would not that be a pity?     Yours     C. Lamb

Now lastly! if you have any humanity or natural affection you will make us leave, or you will have your son's toes drop off one by one and the apalling sight would [word missing] terribly I know!!!

This fearful prospect obviously weakened Lady Montgomerie's resolution for she gave in to him and he left in

* Disowned by his father and deserted by his wife he died blind and alone at the age of forty in a cottage near Eglinton Castle.

the Christmas holidays of 1828, having only just passed his twelfth birthday. He had hardly been at Eton for three halves and by the standards of the day he ought to have stayed there for another two or three years at least. But his mother and father both agreed that scholastic education was unnecessary. So he made his *vale* and returned to Beauport, saving his toes and ensuring also the precious lives of his guinea pigs.

There is absolutely no record of his life and activities during the next few years but, according to his half-brother's diary, his mother, father and Lord Eglinton himself spent the next few years travelling about Europe, and presumably he did also. Until Lord Eglinton reached his majority in 1833 and took up residence at Eglinton Castle on his own, which caused the family to split to some extent and to live more independently of each other, they all seem to have followed the same pleasant circuit together, spending the summers in Geneva, the winters in Nice and the intervening months at Eglinton or Beauport.

The boating portrait of Sir Charles Lamb was done at this time, in 1831 at Geneva, and since Sir Charles failed to attend the coronation of William IV, which took place that September, perhaps his interests or family in Switzerland prevented him. It was the first of the new, economical coronations without the banquet in Westminster Hall and the ceremony of the Champion in which, as the wits said, the Government half crowned a half-wit for half-a-crown— and perhaps Sir Charles was so disgusted by this parsimony that he refused to take part in it. At all events, he was absent and his place was filled by the Deputy Knight Marshal, his cousin George Head.

Lord Eglinton speaks of these four years between leaving Eton and gaining his majority as being the happiest in his life, and the same was probably true for Charlie.

On one occasion, however, they—or, at least, Lord Eglinton—nearly found himself in prison. They began playing cricket on the Plaine de Plainpalais, then an open space outside the city walls, when one of the Genevans walked into the middle of the pitch and asked them to stop. The park was a public place, he said, and the game was a nuisance. Lord Eglinton refused to listen to him and one of the batsmen drove a ball at the citizen's head with such force that it almost cracked his skull. The police arrived, Lord Eglinton had to appear in Court and only escaped a term of imprisonment by paying a large fine.

It must have been during this period that Charlie came to know Sir Egerton Brydges, for one fact is certain about his interests and development after he left Eton—that once he escaped from the chains of scholasticism and was left to himself to study as he liked, he spent more and more time working on heraldry, genealogy and medieval history. His next manuscript proves this conclusively. After the completion of the History of Winnipeg, he set about a full scale family history and autobiography, the same history of his life and adventures which he had promised his mother to write in his first letter to her from Beauport, now so many years ago.

This work, entitled *The Red Book of Beauport, by C. Burges*, 1832, is of no interest as a book in itself for it is not finished and, unlike the history of the guinea pigs which stands on its own as an enthralling childish work, is also very dull. But as a guide to the way in which Charlie was growing up, it is truly fascinating. For it shows him ripening into an exceptional product of romantic gothicism and more and more living in what he imagined to be the atmosphere of the 12th century, if not yet as a knight errant rescuing captive maidens, then at least as a monkish chronicler, recording dynasties and wars.

It is not revealed why he chose this particular title but perhaps he possessed and enjoyed a collection of stories about King Arthur and his knights entitled *The Red Book of Hergest*, a book that contained, as well, a group of tales from Welsh mythology known as the *Mabinogion*, meaning, appropriately enough, 'The instruction of young bards.'

And if the bardic profession included the ability to write Gothic script, to illuminate capital letters, to compose family histories and to illustrate them in the margins by colourful pictures of great events and coats of arms, then Charlie did not waste his apprenticeship.

For the Red Book, written naturally on parchment, had all these items in profusion, including the coat of arms of Ludovici de Burges suspended by a choleric cherub with scarlet wings; a dramatic representation of Colonel Burges snatching the standard of Bonnie Prince Charlie's bodyguard at the Battle of Culloden; and a superscription over the preface of two knights fighting on horseback, their lances just at the point of impact, one red and the other blue, chased by a tiny squire in a Roman legionnaire's skirt waving a miniature sword.

I, Charles James Saville Montgomerie Burges of Beauport in the year of our Lord one thousand eight hundred and thirty three, in the second year of the reign of our most gracious sovereign William, and the sixteenth year of my age have begun this writing, meaning it to contain an account of the period I live in, adding thereunto anecdotes of individuals of my acquaintance such as may prove interesting to those living hereafter, perhaps two or three hundred years, as illustrating the more minute particulars of the manner of life of their ancestors.

To this I shall add all I know concerning my family

estate, &c., and other things which might prove curious to my immediate descendants (if I should have any). And should this book not be brought to light till some far distant far distant period when British men and laws and manners may have passed away, it may still be looked into with curiosity by those who have heard that such a nation was. Great events too may happen in my days which may lend it a double interest. Affairs seem to be taking serious aspects which may end in wars, rebellions and what not—there is only one who knows.

Now, more than one hundred years later, when we, too, beside the God that Charlie refused to believe in, are blessed with the knowledge that the Reform Riots to which he referred never developed seriously, that the British nation still survives, and that his Red Book has certainly proved curious to his immediate descendants, are burdened also with the depressing knowledge that he never managed to finish it.

The Gothic script which begins so boldly with the words '𝕳e 𝔉amilia' at the head of the first chapter, recording the lives of remote ancestors in the early Middle Ages, dwindles away by the time it reaches Charlie himself to a spidery running hand and finally, after unexplained blanks and missing paragraphs, peters out in wispy pencil memoranda. The illuminations suffer the same decline. At the beginning, as in the case of Charlie's own complete armorial achievement, they cover entire pages. But after this the or, argent, sable and azure tints give way to bare outlines of ink and at last, as the MS comes to an end, they are only sketched in pencil.

It is clear that the whole effort became a bit of a bore and, seeing the work that must have gone into it, for a boy of sixteen, this is not surprising. For it is one thing to dream of the leisure and tranquillity of a medieval scribe but quite another, given the chance of trying it out, to sustain the purpose and inner composure to enjoy it.

Perhaps he came back to Beauport from the Continent one day in the early spring, sensed the primeval urge of rising sap, once again looked at his MS and suddenly felt that there was no point in going on with it and that he had been a monk long enough. At any rate, he gave it up and turned his thoughts to chivalry. If he had lived in the Middle Ages he would then have been a Squire or shield bearer; so he bought a razor, stroked his chin and began to think of ways of proving his manhood.

It is well known that no knight is worth the smallest rivet in his harness unless and until he can find an exquisite, young and virginal maiden in the clutches of a dragon and carry her off with perfect chivalry far away to his own impregnable demesne. It is well known, too, that no manly indignation at lascivious conduct can equal that of a Casanova who has sinned like a dragon himself, and if the next recorded step in Charlie's medieval apprenticeship is any guide to the way in which he passed the next few years, it is safe to assume that he spent them in practising seduction.

He could hardly have failed to do anything else, given a father like Sir Charles Lamb whose only pleasure in life was wenching and whose only paternal instruction—so far as Lord Eglinton was concerned, according to the diary, and presumably so far as Charlie was concerned, too—was the practical step of handing down to his children a series of cast off mistresses. But a gap exists in the history of Charlie's life after 1833, and every detail of his day to day occupations, his education, travel, hunting, shooting and fishing, breeding of guinea pigs and chasing butterflies and women must all remain surmised.

Being only the son of a baronet, having only an allowance of £500 per year which, by contemporary standards was small, not bothering to race or hunt beyond his own county of Sussex or his half-brother's of Ayrshire, he left no public record of any of his doings in the *Court Journal* or any of the national or even local newspapers. The family archives, such as they are, have left this period undocumented.

But after five years his life suddenly comes back into focus again with authenticity. And what appears fully makes up for the blank in the missing years.

At the end of July, directly after the coronation of Queen Victoria, he went over to West Sussex for a week's racing at Goodwood. On the whole, this pastime bored him, but he thought of Goodwood as his local course and always went there, and he liked it particularly because of the sublime new Gothic grandstand which had just been built in the Perpendicular manner. He rented lodgings at Bersted, near Bognor, a few miles east of Chichester, an area which at that time was just becoming a fashionable seaside resort and which liked to describe itself as the 'Montpellier of England'; and in all likelihood he shared them with his half-brother although it was still some years before the latter raced at Goodwood. He did not bring a damsel with him hoping, as usual, to find one near the course.

One morning, as he went for an early ride along the shore, he found instead, to his perfect astonishment, a young maiden, alive but wilting, quite alone and clearly in terrible distress. She was weeping bitterly and wading into the waves towards the Witterings. She was so upset that for half an hour she could hardly bring herself to speak.

At length, as Charlie sprang from his horse and led her to dry sand by a breakwater, she explained her predicament which, to a man of Charlie's experience, was perfectly familiar. She worked as a maid in one of the villas at Bersted and during the previous night the owner had tried to seduce her. She was only fourteen and even Charlie could see that she spoke the truth when she said she was inexperienced. The man had sworn at her through her bedroom keyhole and promised that the coming night he would make a woman of her. This in itself was frightening enough but the type of man that he was made it worse: he came from India, said he was a Raja, appeared to be an infidel and certainly was black.

It is quite unnecessary, knowing Charlie's obsession with knights and chivalry and also his amorous temperament, to recount what happened next. Research has failed to authenticate a great deal of what became a family legend but a few facts exist to confirm it sufficiently. The girl, who was called Charlotte Gray, was aged fourteen, the eldest daughter of a draper, Arthur Gray, who conducted his business in North Street, Chichester. The date of her birth is not recorded but she was baptised on the 14th of March, 1824, in the parish church of St Andrew, her mother's name being Maria, according to the Baptismal Register, and her father describing himself as a mercer. She was the second child of several brothers and sisters.

The Raja, if this part of the story is true at all, may possibly have been Raja Ram Roy, the son of the late Ram Mohun Roy, the distinguished religious reformer, for he was the only eminent and educated Indian who moved in English social circles at that time and a friend of Lord William Bentinck, Lord Eglinton's god-father. This is mere speculation, however. In spite of her youth, Charlotte was a strapping girl, as Charlie found out later to his disadvantage.

At this moment he did not waste time testing her

biceps, identifying her enemies or meeting her family. Incensed at the idea of such a young and beautiful girl—as indeed she was—being placed in such circumstances, he swore by the bones of Sir Walter Scott that he would rescue her.

She had hardly dried her tears, put up her hair—which was raven black and literally reached to her feet, according to Little Gilmour, the Black Knight at the Tournament, who met her afterwards—before Charlie had made a plan and explained it to her. She was to go home and watch for a series of daring, romantic and complicated signals, which were quite unnecessary, and come back that evening to the same barnacle-encrusted breakwater and wait for him.

Twelve hours later, cloaked and hooded, with all her possessions in a small black hair trunk which survived to become a sacred family relic, she returned to the *rendezvous*. And before the last beams of the day's sun had set on the Bognor briny, Charlie had met her with a darkened coach, lifted her into it and carried her away.

As time went by and the news of his knightly deed leaked out amongst his friends, it was thought by some, including Lord Eglinton, that he had behaved rather foolishly. But it only seemed to Charlie himself that under the circumstances no gentleman with a grain of chivalry could have acted otherwise and that, so long as he wished to be true to them, all the principles on which he had based his life in the last eighteen years absolutely demanded this course of action.

For now he had become, at the age of twenty-two, an exceptional product of the 19th century romantic gothicism. Byronic, artistic, intelligent, sensitive, claiming to be born with almost as many coats of arms as Lady Clara Vere de Vere and ready, too, to protect and admire the flower of a simple maiden.

He was not a snob but all the same he preferred people to be noble if they could be, and as he and Charlotte arrived in sight of the new portcullis of Arundel Castle, shining in the moonlight, he whispered in her ear that he proposed to give her the courtesy title of 'Lady'.

When it came to dialectics of this kind, Charlotte was no fool herself and she whispered back that it was hardly necessary for, as it happened, her maternal grandmother had been sired by the Duke of Norfolk.

Only one thing was now missing in Charlie's imaginary world and that was the actual experience of wearing mail, tying his paramour's favour to the point of his lance, and challenging other fearful opponents to mortal combat in the lists. For this purpose he began to collect armour and to build a tilt yard in the garden at Beauport, the existence of which is still remembered by many of the older inhabitants.

In a few weeks all these preparations became unnecessary. For unexpectedly, the half dozen casual words by his half-brother about having a Champion at the next race meeting at Eglinton Park flashed up and down the country with the speed of the newly developed electric telegraph and became in a week the germ and promise of a genuine medieval tournament.

The latent Gothic emotions of half the people in the Kingdom were set alight, and the romantic longing to see a joust which had stirred so many for a hundred years and had grown so great since the publication of *Ivanhoe* were brought to the point of dramatic hysteria.

Thus, with veritably magic speed and unexpectedness, in the summer of 1838, in the twenty-third year of his age, Charlie Lamb found himself summoned to a tourney.

Every knightly ambition seemed to be coming true and every youthful dream of chivalry brought to the point of fulfilment.

I

## PART TWO

## The Event

A gentle Knight was pricking on the plaine,
Ycladd in mightie armes and silver shielde,
Wherein old dints of deepe woundes did remaine,
The cruel markes of many 'a bloody fielde;
Yet armes till that time did he never wield:
His angry steede did chide his foming bitt,
As much disdayning to the curbe to yield:
Full iolly knight he seemd, and faire did sitt,
As one for knightly giusts and fierce encounters fitt.

Spenser
*The Faerie Queen*
(Canto I. 1589)

Now Eglinton, let minstrels praise
Who, spurning cold formality,
Restores 'the light of other days'
And, eke, their hospitality.

*Bell's New Weekly Messenger**
21st July, 1839

* Later, the *News of the World* 1855

# Chapter Seven

DURING THE year which began in the summer of 1837, the first in the reign of Queen Victoria, many events took place throughout the realm of exceptional interest to everybody.

A number of these, like the maiden speech in Parliament of Benjamin Disraeli, the legendary heroism of Grace Darling, the publication of the *Pickwick Papers* or the tragic decease of Lady Flora Hastings, are still remembered today.

Many others, now forgotten, enthralled everyone at the time, too, and none more so than a handful of items which were symptomatic of the prevailing Gothicism.

On the 8th of July, 1837, two weeks after the Queen's accession, the *Court Journal*, a gossipy newspaper of no official standing, revealed the news that the Queen was planning a tournament. The heralds were setting off to all parts of Europe to announce it, after the fashion of the Middle Ages, and one hundred Knights of England, picked from the ranks of the nobility, would be called to defend her name against the challengers. It would be held in the autumn at Windsor and run for four days on the lines of a knock-out competition. On the final day the last six combatants would fight to a finish with sharp lances. The Queen herself would crown the victor and shortly afterwards make him her Prince.

Such was the state of public opinion at that time, so great the pleasure of having a young and virgin queen and so wide the enthusiasm for medieval life that many people believed it.

'We already behold the "Mad Marquess" biting the dust . . .' continued the *Journal* in the next issue, referring to Lord Waterford who was well known as a dashing blade and spirited practical joker. Warming to his task as letters poured in asking for confirmation, the editor wound up by saying that Lady Seymour and other fashionable beauties planned to attend in medieval costumes and that, to conform to the habit of pledging a quaint vow to enhance a feat of chivalry, Lord William Beresford, Lord Waterford's brother, had sworn to ride night and day through the streets of London until he had captured the glazed hats of one hundred policemen with which to adorn his tent.

The *Court Journal's* rival, the *Court Gazette*, poured scorn on all these fairy tales and said they were ridiculous. But the author proved himself a gifted journalist with this piece of nonsense, for two years afterwards the Eglinton Tournament brought his fantasy to life. He had sensed the spirit of his times perfectly and had even predicted the behaviour of individuals. Lord Waterford did tumble off his steed and bite the dust, and Lady Seymour and the rest of society's beauty did come to the lists in medieval dresses.

He had only failed to mention Lord Eglinton, and for this he must have kicked himself. But the moment he heard the rumour of the Tournament, he seized his chance to make up for it. In one, short, unchivalrous article, he squashed the *Court Gazette* with the obvious claim, if not the truth, that the whole idea had been his. This was simply not the case, in spite of the coincidence, and there is no evidence of any kind that Lord Eglinton had ever heard of the Windsor tournament, or ever perused the *Court Journal*. When he announced his own Tournament, however, it must have helped him. Then everyone must have remembered it, and transferred to him their frustrated enthusiasm.

Another item of a similar nature which beguiled the fashionable world in the first year of Victoria's sovereignty was an opera written by Lord Burghersh, the eldest son of the 10th Earl of Westmorland. To the joy of the editor of the *Court Journal* and of all the other addicts of medieval life, it was called 'THE TOURNAMENT'. Lord Burghersh, a professional soldier and diplomatist, the founder of the Royal Academy of Music and an excellent amateur musician, had written it twelve years earlier in Italy but for some reason had never produced it in England. He did so now, in the summer of 1838, and the whole *ton* of London's society flocked to the St James's Theatre to listen to it.

The scene was set in the 12th century, and the plot hinged on the love of Helen and Albert, two members of the court of the King of England. Their hopes of marriage were crushed when Albert's father was found dead and Helen's father was thought to have murdered him.

In the second act, Helen's father was thrown to the ground by an unknown knight at a tournament. This knight proved to be Albert, and Helen, who was the Queen of Beauty, was caught between honour, love and duty. For when the victor approached her throne she ought to have crowned him Lord of the Lists.

Suddenly Albert's father was found to have died by accident, so all came well in the end. The two lovers plighted their troth, and the curtain fell on a note of happy revelry.

The *Court Journal* and other fashionable newspapers received this opera well, but the *Musical World* did not think quite so much of it. Mrs Bishop, the wife of the immortal composer of 'Home Sweet Home', and Miss Windham, a star member of the Italian Opera Buffa Company, who took the parts of Helen and Albert respectively, were in excellent voice. But the man who played Helen's father—Ivanoff, the 'Nightingale of Russia'— was hoarse and Mr Stretton, the bass, who assumed the role of the king, growled at the audience 'most vilely' and was asked by the critics never to appear again.

It is not recorded whether Lord Burghersh was satisfied with this performance or whether he tried to have it improved at another production with other artistes, but he never appears to have done so. Lord Eglinton did not go to it and nor did he subscribe to its publication which took place a year afterwards. But he knew Lord Burghersh well and asked him to his Tournament, and perhaps then he was given a copy of it. Possibly, too, as several other people were staying at Eglinton Castle at the same moment whose names appear in the list of subscribers—notably Lord Saltoun, another well known musical enthusiast who was at the Tournament as Judge of Peace—he was also favoured with some of its arias and melodies.

For those people who failed to hear this opera and perhaps, also, missed the joke of the Windsor Tournament in the *Court Journal*, there was much to be seen of Gothic interest at the exhibition in the Royal Academy which had just moved from Somerset House to the present National Gallery in Trafalgar Square.

As had been the case for many seasons, narrative compositions of medieval life had drawn the crowds increasingly, and they were now, without argument, acclaimed the cream of the exhibits.

There was a great triumph for Daniel Maclise, the R.A. who had passed the previous winter in composing a huge tableau, 'Merry Christmas in the Baron's Hall'. During these months the Thames had frozen throughout its length, the snow had lain in drifts fifty feet deep, the poor had perished in the workhouses in flocks, and Charles Dickens, torn by their condition, had written *Oliver Twist*. 'This is an admirable work,' reported the editor of the *Brighton Guardian*, one of the many provincial papers that kept abreast of art. 'The various groups offer enough for half a dozen pictures.'*

There were, also, many illustrations from the books of Sir Walter Scott. For of all the sources of inspiration available to artists of that period, from history itself to Shakespeare and Byron, none charmed the painters so much as the 'Great Enchanter's' romantic masterpieces.

It is hardly possible to realise today the immense influence of this author on contemporary drama, literature and art. His early poems like the *Lay of the Last Minstrel* and *Marmion*, which were first published in 1805 and 1808 respectively, and his great series of tales in prose which began with *Waverley* in 1814 and reached its peak, according to many critics, with *Ivanhoe* in 1819, the year Lord Eglinton succeeded his grandfather, truly hypnotised all who read them.

The proof of this may be seen at a glance in the catalogues of the major exhibitions throughout the country. In the twenty-five years between the first appearance of the Waverley Novels in 1814 and the Eglinton Tournament in 1839, two hundred and sixty-six different pictures inspired by the pen of the 'Wizard of the North' appeared in public galleries; every summer without a break, a scene from *Ivanhoe* was the subject of two of them.

This year they were shown in the Royal Academy. The first, which depicted the knight 'Ivanhoe' himself, was painted by 'I.S.B.'; the other, 'The Tournament at Ashby de la Zouch' was presented by Thomas Allom.

Many other canvasses besides these delighted all who came to see them. There was 'Marmion' by J. Waylen;

* July 25th, 1838

119

'Tales of the Crusaders' by G. P. Jenner; two illustrations for *Talisman* by Charles Landseer; and two by his famous brother, Edwin, not perhaps inspired by Scott but at least tainted with genuine medievalism. Their titles were as follows: 'The life's in the old dog yet' and 'None but the brave deserve the fair'. The first depicted a hound in a crevasse and the other two stags preparing for a tournament.

There were, finally, three others of particular interest to Lord Eglinton: a portrait by J. Wood of John Fairlie, a friend and neighbour in Ayrshire whose son, James, was the Knight of the Golden Lion at the Tournament; 'Earl Percy and Earl Douglas meeting at the battle of Chevy Chase' by G. Morley, the famous encounter of 1388 at which Lord Eglinton's ancestor, Sir Hugh Montgomerie, had smitten Lord Percy with a spear which had gone through his body and come out the other side 'A long cloth yard and more'; a fine composition by Joseph Severn, the well known artist and friend of Keats, who had married Lord Eglinton's natural, paternal, half-sister, Elizabeth, the ward of Lady Westmorland, step-mother to Lord Burghersh.

Severn had won the Royal Academy Gold Medal in 1819 with his 'Una and the Red Cross Knight in the Cave of Despair' and he now exhibited an inspiring work, 'The first Crusaders in sight of Jerusalem'. Here, in truth, was a subject to uplift the imagination: Godfrey of Bouillon, Raymund of Provence, Tancred, nephew of Bohemund of Otranto, and ten thousand knights standing before the walls of the Holy City on the 15th of July, 1099; then, 'sobbing for excess of joy' as, after an appalling combat, they reached the Sepulchre through rivers of blood.

Any members of the public who were bored by art and never went to the Royal Academy had another way to uplift their imagination during the first year of the reign of Queen Victoria. They could go to Astley's Amphitheatre at Westminster Bridge, opposite the Houses of Parliament, and reserve a seat at one of its fabulous tournaments.

Astley's Royal National Amphitheatre of the Arts, as it was called in full, the Mecca of circus lovers throughout the world, had been founded seventy years earlier by Philip Astley, the modern father of this form of entertainment, a retired sergeant major in General Elliott's Light Horse. It had started life as a riding school and, having been burnt down and rebuilt several times, it was now the finest covered arena in London, one hundred and forty feet in length and sixty-five in width, and owned by Andrew Ducrow, the foremost ringmaster in Europe.

As well as being a circus it was used as a glorified music hall and from time to time it transfixed its audiences with *Love, Jealousy and Revenge—a Day of Strife*, or with *Jack o' Lantern in the Dismal Swamp with an Extensive Frozen Landscape*. As a real people's theatre in the classic tradition, reflecting the taste of the times, it also presented dramatic historical pageants. Many of these were set in the Middle Ages and their dazzling panoplies of medieval life were superb examples of popular romantic Gothicism.

These stupendous peeps at the past were just as famous as Ducrow's feats of dressage and acrobatics. Vast, glittering, equestrian spectacles, they were one of the rare treats of the metropolis, with emperors, queens, knights, princesses, ferocious bands of antagonists who frequently lost their tempers and had to be torn apart at the end of the performances, and colossal fortresses which were actually burnt to the ground in front of the audience.

Their titles still read excitingly on the old playbills, now to be seen in the Victoria and Albert Museum. *The*

*Storming of Seringapatam and the death of Tippoo Saib*;
*The Conflagration of Moscow*; *The Victory of Waterloo*; *The
Seige of Jerusalem*; *The last days of Napoleon*; *The Conquest
of Mexico*; *The Battle of Agincourt and the Field of the Cloth
of Gold*.

One of the best was Byron's *Mazeppa* in which, at the
end of a terrific battle, the hero, Ivan Stephanovich, Polish
nobleman and Hetman of the Dnieper Cossaks, was
strapped naked to a wild horse which was lashed round and
round the arena until it was nearly demented. Many others
were based on popular mythology. Others, again, were
drawn from the works of Scott. For here, once more, at
Astley's Amphitheatre, almost as many romantic tours de
force were inspired by the 'Great Northern Bard' as they
were in the Royal Academy.

Andrew Ducrow was completely uneducated and can
never have read a word of the Waverley Novels or anything
else, but their fame was such, even amongst his illiterate
colleagues, that he knew their plots and dramatised many
of them.

He staged the magnificent revels in *Kenilworth*; the
dramatic elopement of Lochinvar in *Marmion*; the savage
battle in *Rob Roy* in which he galloped about the ring on
tip-toe, clad in a kilt and sporran; and, best of all, the
prodigious tournament in *Ivanhoe*.

But as time went by and the Gothic mania increased and
spread downwards, even to simple audiences, the success
of the tale of the Disinherited Knight completely eclipsed
the rest.

This same triumph was repeated on many other stages
besides Ducrow's. For when *Ivanhoe* first came out as a
play in 1820, having been published the year before, it
created a record. It carried London by storm in five
different interpretations running concurrently in separate

theatres, while before the end of the year it appeared in a sixth.

Ever since it has kept ahead of all the other dramas based on the books of the same author. Several fresh texts have been written in every decade, and nearly fifty original scripts in many languages for stage, screen, ballet, opera, radio and television are now recorded on the shelves of the world's libraries.

In spite of the moves which were going on at this time in the House of Commons to extend the laws of copyright and preserve an example of everything published— sponsored by Thomas Talfourd, the famous Sergeant at Law to whom Dickens inscribed *Pickwick Papers*— Ducrow's *Ivanhoe* has vanished. There were probably never many copies at all, for nobody spoke much at these performances, according to the theatrical chat of the day, and if they did so they soon shut up.

'Cut the cackle and come to the 'osses', Ducrow used to bellow at them, helping them up with a smart flick from his long ringmaster's whip which often surprised them frightfully.

This year, at least, they could not be touched, for all were clad in armour from head to foot.

The scarlet words on the bills which proclaimed *Ivanhoe* in huge dimensions throughout the city promised a thrill that was hardly exaggerated—a Jew, a Prince and a Queen of Beauty; a maiden carried away on a Spanish steed by a black Saracen; a raving Saxon hag and a burning fortress; four divisions of champing cavalry; twenty armed knights in a fearsome tournament.

The show ran throughout the summer to packed houses for more than fifty performances; and after this it remained a standard part of the repertory for the next fifty years until, at last, in 1895, many old buildings south of Westminster Bridge were taken down to widen the road and Astley's, too, was demolished.

Lord Eglinton never visited Astley's Amphitheatre, or if he did so he never left any record of it. Although he loved horses, he disliked circuses and was thoroughly bored by theatricals.

It was often said that if he had watched a Ducrow tournament he might never have held his own, seeing the obvious cost and immense difficulties of such a production.

Yet these things never troubled him at all and, on the contrary, the sight of so many knights—possibly even a representation of his own ancestor, Sir Hugh Montgomerie, in *The Battle of Chevy Chase*, or Ducrow as the King's Champion in *The Coronation*, actually casting a glove—would more than likely have made him keener than ever.

For one of the deepest yearnings of all people with romantic temperaments in the 19th century was the urge to experience every emotion personally; and the great ambition of every Gothic revivalist was to taste the drama of medieval life in as many ways as possible—in hawking, archery, in a Merry Xmas in the Baron's Hall with a yule log, malmsey wine and a boar's head; and also, naturally enough if given the opportunity, in wearing armour and taking part in a tournament.

Another spectacle of great interest to which Lord Eglinton never went in this first year of the reign of Queen Victoria but to which the public swarmed excitedly was Queen Elizabeth's Armoury. This was a splendid hoard of suits of armour, long preserved as works of art, that had once been used at various royal tournaments. Since it was housed in the Tower of London and guarded by Yeomen in antique dress, it was, to any Gothic enthusiast, trebly worth the cost of a special visit.

The person to whom it owed its gleaming state and magnificent presentation at this particular moment was the leading expert on medieval weapons, Sir Samuel Rush Meyrick. Born in 1783, the son of Hannah and John Meyrick—the former an heiress, *née* Rush, the latter an agent who worked in Westminster—he began his life as an attorney. But finding himself more and more absorbed in the Middle Ages, he decided to leave the Courts and become an antiquary.

At the age of twenty he married against his family's advice and was disinherited although in some unexplained way when his father died he managed to gain control of the money which legally passed to his son. Using his son's name, he formed a collection of arms and armour for which he became famous and which, by a twist of fate, in spite of his parents' wishes, he finally came to possess. For his son, dying as a young man without children, he became the next to succeed to it.

Long before this, however—which only happened in 1837—he found, as many other collectors had done before him, that he needed a house equipped with a proper armoury. For his own in London at 20 Upper Cadogan Place had become like a medieval battlefield. The whole area was strewn with weapons, and every approach was barred by knights who fell upon his guests with frightening suddenness.

So, having for many years coveted Goodrich Castle—a perfect ruin near Tintern Abbey where Wordsworth had met the child of *We are seven*—he approached the owner, hoping to buy and restore it.

When she refused—luckily enough for us since the castle is one of the finest in Herefordshire—he bought the hill on the other side of the river which overlooked it across a deep dingle. Retaining Edward Blore, Sir Walter Scott's architect at Abbotsford, he constructed a house in the style of Edward II.

Approached by a drawbridge, through a groined gateway, between two round towers which led to a Gothic porch above which were turrets, pinnacles and battlements, it was put together with hunks of local red masonry and embraced a Grand Armoury eighty-six feet in length and twenty-five in width. Here he installed his collection—forty-six figures in full armour, ten of which were mounted on barbed stallions; many others from India, Asia and the Pacific and, in a special 'hastilude chamber' an enormous tableau of a tournament.

As the house completely wrecked the prospect from Goodrich Castle, Wordsworth, to whom the whole district was sacred because of its many poetic associations, wanted to 'blow away Sir Samuel's impertinent structure and all the possessions it contained.'* So, too, did the person to whom the ruins belonged, a Miss Catherine Griffin. Now, perhaps, their ghosts may smile for, like many buildings of the same period, good of their kind but extremely large, it has recently been demolished.

Meyrick, however, who looked in the other direction, was naturally very pleased with the view while Blore, the architect, was perfectly delighted with it and capped his triumph by having his plans hung up at the Royal Academy.

At about the same time as he started to build his house, Meyrick was asked to report on Queen Elizabeth's Armoury because he had written a book in which he criticised it. Much of the contents needed repair and, after a series of talks with the Master General of Ordnance in charge of military stores which still, technically, included suits of armour, he recommended a number of changes

* Quoted by Arthur Mee in *The King's England—Herefordshire*. p. 76.

including a different form of display, and offered to do the work at his own expense.

As a result, a new museum was built at the Tower of London, shaped like a capital 'E' of a typical Tudor manor, lit by eight sash windows of Georgian type and topped by a fringe of battlements.

Inside it was a beautiful Gothic cloister, one hundred and forty-nine feet in length, which framed the figures of twenty gleaming knights arranged historically from Henry VI in 1450 to James II in 1685, interspersed by dashing noblemen like the Duke of Suffolk in 1520 and the Earl of Strafford in 1635. Each sat on an armed horse beneath an arch from the point of which hung a crimson banner on which was written his name and the date of his armour in golden Gothic lettering. All around them were shining weapons and dazzling suits of armour of different types.

This had been finished in 1828 but because, under an ancient precedent, the price of admission had been kept at three shillings, one of which went to the Beefeater who showed the visitor round and the other two to the principal storekeeper's pocket—large sums in those days—it had not been often or easily seen by the ordinary members of the public.

By the year of the coronation of Queen Victoria, however, under the vexatious pressure of Joseph Hume, a champion of public rights for thirty years who, according to the Dictionary of National Biography, 'spoke longer, oftener and probably worse' than any other private member of the House of Commons but who usually got what he wanted in the end, the fee was lowered to one shilling.

As soon as this reduction was announced the place was literally beseiged. A special contingent of eighteen extra Beefeaters had to be massed to protect the ticket office

K

which happened to be in a former lion's den of the old menagerie, and more than one of them lost their tempers and compared the mob to a pride of wild beasts, all of them being perfectly enraged at having their perquisites diminished.

The files record that one, Thomas Kinnak, called a tourist a 'drunken vagabond' twice—right in front of a figure of Henry VIII.*

Forty-two thousand people entered the armoury during the following months, and twice as many did so again when the fee was cut to sixpence.

All fell into a Gothic trance as, pushed along by sullen Beefeaters, they gazed at the treasures within it.

There was, finally, in this first year of the Queen's reign, another vision of medieval life which entranced the coronation visitors as well and inspired Lord Eglinton personally. This was a display of arms and armour staged by Samuel Luke Pratt, a young but already well known dealer in Bond Street. Although it did not compare in size or quality with Queen Elizabeth's Armoury, it possessed a glorious advantage: that, apart from being easy to reach, its entire contents was actually for sale; so that any schoolboy wanting a battle-axe, any artist seeking a model or any antiquary forming a collection had only to go there and buy whatever he required.

Many great and rich families collected armour during the early part of the 19th century, and more and more as the years passed and the Gothic mania attacked them. Involved, naturally enough, in other Gothic endeavours as well, nearly all of them dabbled in architecture and quite a number in the struggle for ancient peerages. One family enthused another and often enough they were either married or related.

* Public Record Office—WO/44/304.

An interesting case is that of the Russells of Brancepeth
Castle in Co. Durham, and the famous family of Tennyson.
Matthew Russell, the richest commoner in England,
married Elizabeth Tennyson, the poet laureate's aunt.
His collection of arms and armour was renowned and he
lived in fabulous baronial state in a palace restored for
£120,000 by John Paterson, the architect of Eglinton
Castle.

Elizabeth's brother, George, who was head of the
family, changed his name to Tennyson d'Eyncourt to
enjoy the Gothic particle. He amassed enough arms and
armour to equip a small crusade and so fortified his home,
Bayons Manor in Lincolnshire, with moats, walls, draw-
bridges and keeps that even his sister could hardly hack
her way into it.

Two of the others who were not related were Lord
Brougham and Vaux, the extraordinary Lord Chancellor
who incorrectly claimed descent from the Barons of Vaulx
and the ancient Lords of Brougham Castle in Westmorland, and Lord Zouch, better known as Robert Curzon
the distinguished author and traveller whose title, recently
prized from abeyance, dated from 1308. Both these
accumulated splendid collections.

All four, and everyone else, visited Samuel Pratt. So,
too, did Charlie Lamb whose great collection, when it was
sold, comprised, according to a note by an expert* 'all
varieties of arms and armour of the choicest and rarest
kinds.'

In spite of the fact that Pratt traded at the same premises
in Bond Street for forty years—No. 47, on the corner of
Maddox Street—practically nothing is known about him.
Any record, if there ever was one, of his looks, character or
private life, whether written in a diary by himself or by

* Cripps-Day, *Armour Sales*, p. 249.

anyone else who ever dealt with him, seems to have vanished completely. Apart from the armour he bought and sold, much of which is still recorded, nothing else has survived. He died in 1878 at the age of seventy three; his Will may be seen in Somerset House*; but any descendants have proved impossible to find.

One thing is certain about him, however, that arms and armour were the whole passion of his life. And at least in 1838, as well as providing a comfortable income, their direct contact with the Middle Ages, their authentic connection with famous princes and their very damage in forgotten combats really appealed to him personally.

One of his claims to fame today is the valuable manner in which he compiled his catalogues, being the first in the Gothic Revival of arms and armour to describe the various pieces properly and also the first to illustrate them. This has enabled collectors to trace them since.

The way he wrote also revealed his enthusiasm.

'To gaze on the plumed casque of the Mailed Knight equipped for the Tournament, and to grasp the ponderous mace, yet encrusted with the accumulated rust of centuries, cannot fail to inspire admiration for the chivalrous deeds of our ancestors,' he declared in the preface of his first catalogue, the one for the year 1838.

As the Tower Armouries were inconveniently far away, he continued, he hoped his galleries would please the public generally, while since the exhibits might also be bought he aspired as well to help collectors revive 'the splendour of our ancient Baronial Halls.'†

This, indeed, he certainly did; and not, as experts discovered afterwards, entirely with genuine pieces.

But in this first year of the reign of Queen Victoria, his

* No. 808 of 1878. Personal estate under £10,000.
† V & A Library, Fine Art Pamphlets, 1838, H.8.

own opening year in Bond Street, probably few of his wares were fakes and most of his efforts were put to showing them off.

'This splendid pile of steel . . .' he proclaimed of one particularly massive suit of knight's *cap-à-pie* armour, 'is replete with all the additional defences worn at the JOUST, consisting of *Passegardes and Garde de bras of grand character*.' 'THE GEM OF THE COLLECTION' he pronounced of the costly, engraved and inlaid harness of Alphonso II, the last reigning Duke of Ferrara, the home of the finest swords in the world, which was shown complete on a stuffed horse, itself encased in armour of violet and gold; 'A noble Suit of *Cap-à-pie* Tilting Fluted Armour . . . of collossal size'; 'A suit of Engraved and Gilt German Armour for a Knight . . . of peculiar grandeur and beauty'; 'A Massive Polished Steel Shield, 60 lbs in weight'; so on and so forth, throughout the catalogue which had six hundred and seventy items, many of which referred to knights who were shown on horseback, locked in combat, as though engaged at tournaments. There was even 'A very singular suit of bright steel armour evidently made for a *Female* . . .' Although its history was actually unknown, he could not resist the obvious temptation of alluding to Joan of Arc to whom, he said, it might have belonged and whom he quaintly termed the 'Virgin Combatant'.

His own shop being too small to contain such a huge collection, he leased another across the road in 3 Lower Grosvenor Street and fitted it up with the help of the architect Lewis Nockalls Cottingham who had worked for Lord Brougham and Vaux at Brougham Castle and had won a reputation for medieval work by restoring Magdalen College Chapel at Oxford and for building Snelston Hall in Derbyshire in a style that was 'richly Gothic'.

He designed for Pratt 'a truly Gothic Apartment'*; and the *Gentleman's Magazine*, which both had led and reflected aristocratic taste for more than a hundred years, thought the exhibition was 'one of the most brilliant and interesting ever seen in London.'†

So, too, did Charlie Lamb who rushed Lord Eglinton to see it.

And when, towards the end of the summer, the latter decided to hold a tournament, he naturally turned to Pratt for help and advice.

So that Pratt, as well as Charlie Lamb, was given the chance of a lifetime. For never, in all his grandest dreams, can he possibly have thought of selling armour to the very cream of Britain's nobility for the very purpose for which it had once been made.

In the same dramatic and unlooked for manner, by the same strange assembly of events, all his hopes of wealth and success and every conceivable romantic ambition were suddenly placed on the brink of reality and brought within his grasp.

* *The Times*, Apr. 16th 3.b.
† May, p. 532.

# Chapter Eight

TOWARDS THE end of the autumn of 1838 when, after the usual summer holidays, the fashionable world had returned to London, Lord Eglinton compiled a roll of competing knights and called a meeting to discuss the preliminary arrangements. According to Grantley F. Berkeley whose *Recollections* have been quoted earlier— one of the many dashing youths whose pulse had surged at the news of the Tournament—this took place at Pratt's showroom in Bond Street. One hundred and fifty competitors came to it and, by a strange and ominous coincidence, this was just the number of knights that once met at King Arthur's Court and swore to honour the vows of the Round Table.

To stage a pageant of any past event, let alone to attempt to revive it, requires a knowledge of all the basic facts. Before Lord Eglinton held the conference he ought to have tried to master them, either by reading Strutt's *Sports and Pastimes of the People of England* or Samuel Meyrick's *Antient Armour*, both of which are known to have been in his library. But being in no sense an antiquary and accustomed to leave the details of life to somebody else, he never bothered to do so; and he soon discovered that Pratt's specialised knowledge of arms and armour did not wholly cover the running of tournaments.

All sorts of problems quickly presented themselves. How were tourneys proclaimed, for example; ought one to ask the Queen's permission; should the College of Heralds be approached; what were the proper dimensions for the lists?

Each of these and many others about costs, scoring, forfeits, challenges, *gages d'amour* and the Queen of Beauty were all debated interminably, every knight having his own ideas, right or wrong, sensible or otherwise, according to his strength, wealth and temperament, and each insisting that he alone was right. Towards the evening, most of them lost their tempers and, but for Pratt's agonised entreaties, the Eglinton Tournament might have begun that night.

Before any question could be answered, a decision had to be taken on styles and dates, for during the time that tournaments were held—a period of more than six hundred years—they changed their form completely. What kind did Lord Eglinton want—a simple, brutal, medieval struggle; a colourful, chivalrous passage of arms; or a mere parade with dainty jousts of the time of Charles I?

Invented, so it is said, by a French seigneur, Geoffroi de Preulli, who died tourneying in 1066, they started out as baronial gang fights or private battles. Groups of knights met by arrangement in an open space, armed with swords, lances or battle axes, and fought either on foot or horseback, trying, in certain types of combat, to cut off the crests of each other's helmets.

Hence the use of the word 'crestfallen', for the ones who lost forfeited their horses and armour although they could always buy them back. By such ransoms many tough knights like the famous 1st Earl of Pembroke in the 12th century, who is said to have conquered five hundred opponents, earned a cheerful living, while those who paid them, by going from one tourney to another, often lost their whole family's inheritance.

They were likely, too, to suffer terrific casualties, for only men of huge strength and in perfect training had any chance of ending the day on their feet.

'A youth must have seen his blood flow and felt his teeth crack under the blow of his adversary and been thrown to the ground twenty times . . .'* before he could hope to be worthy of manhood, wrote the old chronicler, Roger de Hoveden, one of Pembroke's contemporaries.

Sir William Montague, a knight founder of the Order of the Garter, killed his own son in a tournament in 1383 and his father, the 1st Earl of Salisbury, died of wounds in another. History is filled with tales of similar losses; in one simple engagement at Cologne in 1240, more than sixty knights are said to have perished.

Of these, many died of asphixia, for lack of air and excessive heat were always hazards to a man in armour, and how the Crusaders, dressed in thick quilted tunics under their mail shirts and similar garments under their helmets—much of which they never took off for months—survived the burning sun of Palestine remains an historical mystery.

At tournaments, too, there was always a danger of dust, for the ground was strewn with sand or other soft material to break the falls of the combatants which, although usually watered beforehand, often rose in choking clouds; while any knight who unstrapped his helmet to take a breather literally chanced his neck.

Those who survived had to eat, drink and dance all night and be ready at dawn for a final test of prowess. For although the ladies whose favours they wore in the lists were always supposedly virgins or married women of perfect virtue—known as paramours because, according to the rules of chivalry, the champions fought for them *par amour*—the knights also frequently became their lovers.

Those who did not and were self-controlled had to be beware of prostitutes. These rampaging professional

* *The Tournament*, p. 2. F. H. Cripps-Day.

paramours came to the tournaments in hordes; and fierce groups led by Amazons who were sometimes clad in suits of armour challenged the knights as they clanked homewards and, with threats or taunts of weakness, dared them to come to bed.

Understandably, the Church tried to prevent these pointless struggles, saying that all who fought would be excommunicated, and by making clear that the ones who fell, being denied a Christian burial, would be carried away by the Devil.

But most of the knights decided to take pot luck and in the end, as in the case of actual warfare, the Popes were forced to capitulate.

William the Conqueror forbade tournaments in Britain altogether—it is thought to avoid unnecessary incidents between the French and Saxons; for, like any form of thrilling public contest, as for example football matches today, they brought together large numbers of supporters who frequently stormed the field and took part in the fight.

And so, although tournaments may have been held earlier, they are not recorded in England before the 1130's. They did not receive official sanction until Richard Coeur de Lion signed an edict at Lewes in 1195 allowing them at five specified places—Salisbury, Warwick, Stamford, Brackley and Tickhill—to which, by custom, was added Smithfield in London. The Archbishop of Canterbury was obliged to supervise them, and the knights were taxed according to their wealth and status.

Clearly this species of tournament—a free-for-all by teams of knights, called a *mêlée* by those who invented it and a pelly melly by the Saxon underdogs who could never master the Norman language and were much laughed at by the French in consequence—was not the kind for Lord Eglinton.

His idea was for individual knights to fight on horse-back with lances, watched by the others—a form of combat only used in the early days to settle a private feud or limber up before the actual *mêlée*. This kind of engage-ment, known as a Joust of War or Joust of Peace, de-pending on whether the weapons were sharp or blunted, superseded the *mêlée* as time went by and attained its greatest vogue in the 14th century.

If the jousts were held for fun between small gatherings of knights to pass the time, then the meeting was known as a Round Table—what, in fact, was actually given by Lord Eglinton; and if they were staged before the King with all the trappings and procedure of chivalry, then the occasion merited the title of a tournament.

This was the time, now thought of as the legendary age of chivalry, when knights were given peacock pie at fabulous banquets and issued poetic vows to prove their valour, sometimes adding strange conditions to make their tasks more difficult.

An authentic case is that of Michel d'Oris, an esquire from Arragon who sent a challenge to the English knights at Calais in 1400, swearing to wear a piece of leg armour until he had jousted twenty times and earned the right to remove it. He must have hobbled about for life since the tournament never came off.

Such engagements, when they were met, were full of excitement and pageantry. At one such in London in 1386 before King Richard II, the proceedings began with 'three score Ladyes of honour mounted on fayre palfreys, ryding on the one syde, richely apparelled; and every ladye ledde a knight with a cheyne of sylver, which knights were apparelled to just.'*

Not so hard as the earlier *mêlées*, these colourful battles

* *The Tournament*, p. 60. F. H. Cripps-Day.

were still ferocious; and as time passed and the fire of chivalry began to wane, a fence was installed in the middle of the lists, five or six feet high, running lengthwise half-way down, to prevent the risk of collision.

The knights charged on either side of it, keeping it on their left and not the other way round as one might expect, and since, under the rules, they had to hold the lance in the right hand, they could only aim at an angle of 30° over their horse's necks and merely strike the hardest blow obliquely.

This restriction lessened the perils enormously and, although there were sometimes serious accidents—the King of France, Henry II, was actually killed by one of Lord Eglinton's forebears, a Count Montgomery, in 1559, jousting across a barrier—the use of a fence or 'tilt', first mentioned in 1429, brought an end to the days of excessive casualties.

It also altered the whole tenor of the joust which became a trial of skill instead of force. Those men who were born bullies and who, in the past, had challenged others just for exercise and often killed them, were forced to look for other forms of amusement. For if the knights were using 'arms of courtesy'—blunted lances with spiked iron rings on their tips, known as coronels, or wooden discs, known as rochets—and if they were wearing the enormous helmets and huge shields that were made specially for such contests, they were half blind, half deaf, half stifled and half cooked, and if they struck their opponents at all, they only gave them a buffet.

Doomed to be drawn like this for ever afterwards by caricaturists, by the end of the reign of Queen Elizabeth they were nearly as helpless as tortoises; they could hardly mount their steeds without assistance and they fell as heavily as ripe coconuts the moment they lost their balance.

Such encounters were known as 'triumphs'; and in these twilight years of chivalry, interminable complaints by hoary knights of the abominable decadence of modern youth compared to the strength and prowess of their grandfathers were heard in every country in Europe.

They inspired the story of Don Quixote which was published in Spain in 1605 and translated into English seven years afterwards. As Byron said: 'Cervantes smiled Spain's chivalry away.'*

It is interesting to compare an authentic challenge of the 14th century with another from a triumph of 1612, the one an invitation in clear, cordial terms to a trial of manly skill and courage, the other a perfect example, almost meaningless, of the rhetoric of decadent chivalry.

In 1389, three famous French knights, de Boucicaut, de Sampi and de Roye, wishing to avenge a technical insult to one of their friends and also to impress some 'frisky ladies', obtained the royal consent to the following announcement:†

From the great desire we have to become acquainted with the nobles, gentlemen, knights and squires bordering on the kingdom of France, as well as with those in the more distant countries, we propose being at St Ingelvere‡ the twentieth day of May next ensuing, and to remain there for thirty days complete; and on each of these thirty days, excepting the Fridays, we will deliver from their vows all knights, squires and gentlemen, from whatever countries they may come, with five courses with a sharp or blunt lance, according to their pleasure, or with both lances if more agreeable.

* *Don Juan* xxxvi.
† Froissart, Johnes Edn. Vol. 4, p. 99.
‡ A village in Picardy near Calais.

On the outside of our tents will be hung our shields, blazoned with our arms; that is to say, with our targets of war and our shields of peace. Whoever may choose to tilt with us has only to come, or send any one, the preceding day, to touch with a rod either of these shields, according to his courage. If he touch the target, he shall find an opponent ready on the morrow to engage him in a mortal combat with three courses with a lance: if the shield, he shall be tilted with a blunted lance; and if both shields are touched, he shall be accommodated with both sorts of combat. Every one who may come, or send to touch our shields, must give his name to the persons who shall be appointed to the care of them. And all such foreign knights and squires as shall be desirous of tilting with us, shall bring with them some noble friend, and we will do the same on our parts, who will order what may be proper to be done on either side. We particularly entreat, such noble knights or squires as may accept our challenge, to believe that we do not make it through presumption, pride or any ill will, but solely with a view of having their honourable company, and making acquaintance with them, which we desire from the bottom of our hearts. None of our targets shall be covered with steel or iron, any more than those who may tilt with us; nor shall there be any fraud, deceit or trick made use of, but what shall be deemed honourable by the judges of the tournament. And that all gentlemen, knights, and squires, to whom these presents shall come, may depend on their authenticity, we have set to them our seals, with our arms, this twentieth day of November, at Montpellier, in the year of grace 1389.

Three hundred years later in England, the Duke of

Lenox and the Earls of Southampton, Pembroke and Montgomery* issued the annexed terms for a joust, the MS of which may be read in the British Museum.†

To all honourable men at Arms and Knight adventurers of hereditary note and exemplary nobless that for most memorable actions do wield either sword or lance in quest of glory:

Right brave and Chivalrous wheresoever through the world we four knights errant denominated of the fortunate Island, servants of the destinies awaking your sleeping courages with Martial greetings.

Know ye our sovereign lady and Mistress, mother of the fates, Empress of high achievements, revolving of late the Adamantine leaves of her eternal volumes, and finding that the triumphal times were now at hand, wherein the marvellous adventures of the Lucent Pillar should now be revealed to the wonder of time and men (As Merlin, secretary to her most inward design did long time since prophesy) hath therefore most deeply weighing with herself how necessary it is that some opinion should prepare the way to worthy celebration of so unheard of matter, been pleased to command us, her voluntary but ever most humble votaries, solemnly to publish and maintain by all allowed ways of knightly arguing these undisputable propositions following:

1. That in service of ladies knights have no free will.
2. That it is Beauty maintains the world in valour.
3. That no fair lady was ever false.
4. That none can be perfectly wise but lovers.

The St Inglevere tournament, held on the 21st of the

---

* No relation to the Eglinton family.
† Harl. MS. 4888.

141

'charming month of May' in a place that was 'smooth and green with grass', was a great success, and more than sixty English knights and squires sent their armour to Calais and jousted there for a week.

The challenge of 1612, if it ever was met, was probably held on the Whitehall tiltyard, the present Horseguards Parade, part of a triumph that was organised annually to mark the King's accession.

It is strange to reflect, when thinking about these latter-day attempts at knightly endeavour, so often inspired by the myths of King Arthur's Court, that none of the great legendary heroes of the British Isles—like Lancelot or Tristram—ever took part in tournaments at all or ever consciously observed the canons of chivalry.

King Arthur was probably a Welsh chieftain, lightly armed with a mail shirt and a bronze shield and helmet, who rode a pony and, if he ever lived—which has never been proved—he did so during the 5th or 6th centuries, hundreds of years before the age of the joust.

He became a knight in the Middle Ages when scribes, living in a feudal society, wrote about him as one of themselves in terms of their own environment. The invention of printing caused their texts to be fixed, the standard version in the English language, published by Caxton in 1485, being Sir Thomas Malory's. But for this, the tales might have gone on changing, each generation portraying Arthur in the form they admired the most and, if such a thing were possible, in two or three millennia to come, he might have been said to have been a knight of space.

The fact, however, that the sagas became settled in the Middle Ages had this important consequence. That the deeds described, the jousts and tournaments, and the way the knights prepared and fought in them, allowing only for poetic exaggeration, are quite correct and perfectly feasible in terms of the age of chivalry; for Sir Thomas Malory, a knight himself, wrote from his own experience. This gives the tales an authenticity and accounts for their great appeal to Gothic revivalists.

*So when King Arthur was come they blew unto the field; and then there began a great party, then was there hurling and rushing. Then Sir Tristram came in and began so roughly and so bigly that there was none might withstand him, and thus Sir Tristram dured long. And then Sir Tristram saw . . . forty knights together . . . and he fared among those knights like a greyhound among conies; and at every stroke Sir Tristram well-nigh smote down a knight. Then King Arthur with a great eager heart he gat a spear in his hand, and there upon the one side he smote Sir Tristram over his horse. Then foot-hot Sir Palomides came upon Sir Tristram, as he was upon foot, to have over-ridden him. Then Sir Tristram was ware of him, and there he stooped aside, and with great ire he gat him by the arm, and pulled him down from his horse.

Then Sir Palomides lightly arose, and then they dashed together mightily with their swords; and many kings, queens, and lords stood and beheld them. And at the last Sir Tristram smote Sir Palomides upon the helm three mighty strokes, and at every stroke that he gave he said, Have this for Sir Tristram's sake. With that Sir Palomides fell to the earth grovelling. And then Sir Tristram . . . rode to an old knight's place to lodge them. And that old knight had five sons at the tournament, for whom he prayed God heartily for their coming home. And so, as the French book saith, they came home all five well beaten. And to make short tale

_____
* Book Nine—the tournament at the Castle of Maidens.

143

L

in conclusion . . . by cause Sir Launcelot abode and was
the last in the field the prize was given him. But Sir
Launcelot would neither for king, queen, nor knight
have the prize, but where the cry was cried through the
field, Sir Launcelot, Sir Launcelot hath won the field
this day, Sir Launcelot let make another cry contrary,
Sir Tristram hath won the field, for he began first, and
last he hath endured, and so hath he done the first day,
the second, and the third day.'

To what extent, if any, all these various facts were
finally unearthed by the Eglinton knights before they left
the meeting at Pratt's workshop is not precisely recorded.
But when they parted, one point at least was clear to
everyone—that if they were going to fight at all they would
have to do so over a tilt, and the very most they could hope
to revive was something after the style of the 16th century.
Anything else in modern times, any form of open joust, or
any attempt at a general *mêlée* would be obviously quite
impossible. So in the end they decided to settle for a
'Triumph'.

At this more than half of them resigned, especially
those who were young and tough, who had looked forward
to a rollicking fight with the hope of winning a ransom.
For only a few were as rich as Lord Eglinton, and none of
the others could agree to the rule that, if they lost a joust,
they would forfeit their equipment.

About forty determined to go on, for the more they
talked of the deeds of old—even the tilts of Henry VIII—
the more they longed to attempt them.

So it was decided to meet again; and those who had not
got armour at home and had no friends from whom they
could borrow it, gave provisional orders for suits to Pratt.

During the months that followed, the winter of 1838,

nothing special occurred of any interest. Lord Eglinton spent the season hunting, taking a lodge at Melton Mowbray to follow Lord Suffield's hounds; the Lamb family went to Nice; Pratt visited Portugal, Spain, Italy and Germany and purchased quantities of armour.

Little happened either in the country generally. The various sources of contemporary history, like the *Annual Register* and the *British Almanack*, merely record a number of petty events which were strange then because they were new, are quaint now because they are old, but had no intrinsic significance.

The famous astronaut, John Hampton, ascended 9,000 feet in a balloon, jumped out of it over Cheltenham and floated safely back to earth by parachute. A man who was aptly surnamed Hopper ran half a mile in less than two minutes. He actually did it in one hundred and twelve seconds by leaping down a hill, but at the bottom he nearly died of exhaustion. An equinoctial gale of amazing velocity blew a pair of locked, empty railway carriages $24\frac{1}{2}$ miles in the middle of the night on a new unopened line from London to Maidenhead.

It was, if anything, a winter of plans and projects and, although many of them are seen now as important bricks in the constitutional fabric, they were unappreciated at the time and completed later. This was true of the scheme for a penny postage. The idea of a flat rate, paid in advance by way of a sticky stamp for all letters up to half an ounce to be carried to any place in the British Isles embraced a new principle. It was then in the hands of a Select Committee of the House of Commons and quite inevitably many people, especially all the officials of the Post Office, swore it would never work.

Another important change was urged by the Chartists. Called thus because they supported a 'People's Charter', recently devised by the famous Feargus O'Connor, they demanded the following reforms: annual parliaments, manhood suffrage, votes by ballot, and payment of Members of Parliament who should not be required to be owners of property. Drawn from the new industrial working classes whose already pitiful state was doomed to be worse as sodden harvests raised the price of bread and old restrictive laws forbade its import, they stole weapons, drilled secretly and went at night to wild heaths for mysterious torchlight meetings. As yet they were only a nuisance to local authorities although, before the end of the coming decade, they forced the Government to prepare for a civil war.

In the late spring the Whig Government, which had lost ground steadily for several years, failed to get a majority and the Prime Minister tendered his resignation. Queen Victoria sent for Sir Robert Peel, the leader of the Tories, but when, contrary to normal practice, she refused to dismiss her Ladies in Waiting and appoint others with different sympathies, Sir Robert declined to co-operate. This was a stroke of luck for the Ladies in Waiting, as well as a tactical triumph for the Whigs. So Lord Melbourne had to be asked to return, and as the Queen particularly liked him—to such an extent, in fact, that people had started to comment—she, too, felt in luck and there was, to use an Arthurian expression, 'great joy and great nobley' in the hearts of all who lived at Buckingham Palace.

For one of these ladies, however, there was only misery and death and on her account the first stain fell on the record of the Court. Lady Flora, the daughter of the Marquess of Hastings, who attended the Duchess of Kent, the Queen's mother, and had held her train at the coronation, was a quiet woman of thirty-three who had never chosen to get married. Quite suddenly, she appeared to be having a baby. And because she held such a prominent position it was felt that she ought to be questioned. When accused she proclaimed her innocence and, in the end, to quell the rumours, permitted a doctor to make an examination. A few months later she died of cancer of the liver. So there was a scandal of another sort and some unjustly blamed the Queen for ever allowing such doubts on a lady's honour.

As the months passed and the summer approached, the Eglinton Tournament came more and more into prominence. What had been planned as a private garden party had developed into a rout for practically everybody. Each week in all the newspapers there were more notes about the arrangements, more gossip about the knights, more details about their armour and more stories about Lord Eglinton himself. For the Tournament, now, had made him a national figure and, within the limits of those days when important people still had privacy, everything he said and did was published in the press.

When the hunting season was over, he went to Ayrshire for his annual spring race meeting and Easter house party. At this time, when he had first thought of it, he had hoped to hold the Tournament but, even after the opening meeting at Pratt's in the previous autumn, he had seen clearly that, with so many difficult matters to organise, such an early date would prove impossible. So he had put it off to the end of the summer.

Among his guests at Eglinton Castle were both the Londonderrys, the Marquess soon to be King of the Tournament and his wife, so the papers hinted, the one for whom the jousts were really to be given. For no one could believe that there was not a woman in the background. In fact, nothing was further from the truth for, although Lord Eglinton and she were friends and a generation younger than her husband, there was never the slightest trace of an affair between them.

When news is scarce trifles are recorded. The *Glasgow Courrier* announced that his guests had presented £30 as an Easter offering to his local kirk at Fullarton; *The Times* confirmed his arrival in London; the *Court Journal* revealed that he went to a ball at Buckingham Palace; the *Morning Post* reported his presence at a dinner at Holderness House.

This banquet, held by the Londonderry's, was given in honour of the official visit of the eldest son of the Emperor of Russia, traditionally known as the Czarevitch. He was making his first tour of Europe on coming of age and, to mark the occasion, he founded the famous Czarevitch stakes at Newmarket. He had been at Turin during the previous February and there his host, the King of Sardinia, a noted collector of arms and armour, had welcomed his presence with a tournament. Although it had not really been anything more than a military review with knights in groups, every detail, if he spoke about it, must have interested Lord Eglinton.

For now, at the height of the summer season, the latter's own attempt was drawing close. And because, like any budding knight he and his horse required experience, he decided the moment had come to arrange some practices. So after the races at Ascot, at which the unfortunate Queen was hissed because of the demise of Lady Flora, he and the rest of the Eglinton knights—now reduced to thirty-five—agreed to arm and stage a series of rehearsals.

Pratt having been badgered almost beyond his wits by the press in the previous months—being a mere tradesman in a shop without the protection of class or money—knew the public would like to watch and managed to persuade the champing knights to agree to it.

So the dates of the rehearsals were announced and, in the words of a contemporary journalist, 'all persons of good taste and rank and fashion were on the *qui vive*.'*

* Richardson, p. 1. intro. to *The Eglinton Tournament*.

# Chapter Nine

To WALK about in a suit of armour is a strange and interesting experience.

When the knights went round to Pratt's and saw their harness hanging in lifeless shapes on dummies—the correct term for which is a dobble—they must have expected like everyone else who has ever tried one on in present times that, apart from the apparently obvious limitation on ordinary movement, the weight alone would be crippling.

But that all suits of armour weighed an enormous amount is a modern popular fallacy. The average field suit for wear in battle during the 15th century, when armour was still in normal use, tipped the scales at five or six stones or eighty pounds, and this included the clothes that were worn underneath it. (see plate 8.)

These garments certainly—the stiff, quilted, sleeved bodice of leather or fustian, known as the arming doublet, and the heavy iron shirt of mail, the hauberk, reaching almost down to the knees to protect the fork—constricted the wearer seriously—but the armour itself, so long as it fitted—and this was a matter of the greatest consequence— felt extraordinarily light.

The reason for this was the distribution of its weight which, as all soldiers knew, was achieved best when the cut of the suit was correct. Every wealthy knight kept his own armourer and dobble and, if he commissioned a suit from abroad, from one of the great smiths in Germany or Italy, he had to send his precise measurements, very often a suit of clothes, and sometimes even a wax model of his legs.

For these limbs had to be fitted perfectly. The shoe, naturally, had to snug the foot; it was called a sabaton and was really a sole-less overshoe. The gaiter above it was properly called the greave. Here, both the length and diameter were critical; it had to be fashioned to enclose the calf and it had to bridge the exact distance between the heel and the kneecap. Over the knee was a 'U' shaped piece called the poleyn and connected to it, over the thigh, a wide, flattish, curved plate, the cuisse. The length was the point to watch with this. If it was too short, it exposed the groin and, if it was too long, it fouled the tasset, the overlapping plate which hung down from the cuirass.

The cuirass itself, which comprised the back and breastplates together and enclosed the trunk, weighed about a third of the whole and was also particularly important. It had, of course, to box the chest comfortably and it had to rest on the hips and shoulders exactly. If it did not it could cause the greatest discomfort, either by hanging too much on the neck or by bearing down too hard on the pelvis. It might even choke the wearer to death, the collar, or gorget, pressing against his Adam's apple and the chin guard, or bevor, supposedly called thus from the French 'to dribble', grinding against his jawbone. He would then not be able to open his mouth, draw a breath or even gulp to his squire that he wanted his help.

The need for the right pieces for the hands, the correct size in gloves or gauntlets, and the proper sheaths for the shoulders and the arms—called respectively the pauldrons and the vambraces—is basically the same as that for the feet and legs and is clear and perfectly obvious.

With the helmet, the requirements were rather more complicated. Weighing six pounds at least, which is three times more than the modern military equivalent, it had to sit on the head correctly because of the level of the sight.

This was the slot through which the knight peeped and, with the type of helmet known as the sallet which swept away at the back and was used for ordinary fighting, this line had to be even with the eyes.

As a result, apart from having to fit, it had to be firmly fixed for, although it provided excellent forward vision when it was adjusted, it blinded the wearer at once the moment it slipped. Lined with leather and worn on a specially padded cap, it was held in place by a sometimes painful chinstrap.

Most of the armour supplied by Pratt was sold afterwards and has since vanished, but the suit worn by the 3rd Marquess of Waterford was bought at a sale the following year by the Tower of London for exhibition in Queen Elizabeth's Armoury. It can be seen now at Windsor Castle and, although in fact a fake, it is such a good one that Pratt himself undoubtedly thought it genuine.

Of a type generally described as 'Gothic'—that is to say, of the 15th century—of thin, light hard steel that even now refuses to be welded, it was probably made in Germany. With long detachable points to the toes, shapely sabatons, elegant greaves, winged poleyns, fluted cuisses, laminated vambraces, massive pauldrons, pouting breastplate and sweeping sallet, all shining with a grey light like old, smooth, burnished silver, it is indeed a work of beauty and craftsmanship. To stride about in such a suit is to sip the cup of vanity. No wonder that a 'shining knight' has remained a popular image!

Lord Waterford certainly looked superb in it and, once the others had joined him at Pratt's and assumed their own as well, they were all suddenly touched by a medieval spell. They strode about, couched lances, admired their figures like a group of actors and banged each other cheerfully on the head.

Pratt was completely enchanted, too; and thus, in June, 1839, the final steps were taken to launch the Tournament.

The place at which the knights decided to rehearse was a large garden behind the Eyre Arms, a popular tavern close to Regent's Park. Now a block of flats called Eyre Court, on the Finchley Road, it stood on a hill on the route to Golders Green, a traditional, spacious, comfortable, Georgian hostelry. Its roof, from which the view was magnificent, was furnished with tables and chairs for the summer evenings, and its green and shady grounds were used for sports like cricket and archery, as well as for launching balloonists. It contained, too, a small theatre and ballroom in which there were cheerful plays and other amusements; for St John's Wood was the haunt of many charmers. One of the sweetest, Elizabeth Howard, was soon to become the mistress of Louis Napoleon. Known earlier by the name of Haryett, and then protected by a Major Martin, she is said to have first seen the Prince during the Tournament rehearsals.

If the knights supposed, like the crowds who came to see them, that having to practise wearing armour and generally limbering up for a tournament was a shameful necessity, enforced by modern conditions, they were very greatly mistaken. The only cause they had for shame, in terms of genuine knightly habit, was the age at which they were doing it.

In the days of chivalry, a potential knight, having left his mother to become a page or varlet at the age of seven, advanced to the state of esquire at the time of puberty and from that moment rode in armour and embarked on a course of the strictest military training.

If he were tough he might have started earlier like the great French knight, de Boucicaut, one of the three challengers of the tournament at Calais in 1389, who beat his tiny friends to jelly almost before he could talk and in later youth, according to the *Livre des faits de Boucicaut*, hardened himself by wearing armour for every conceivable exercise—for running, jumping, turning somersaults and even for swimming and dancing.

Most of the Eglinton knights were tough, some even had left their homes at the age of seven but none, naturally, had ever done anything like this.

The ground on which they assembled behind the Eyre Arms was railed off against the public to prevent accidents, just as it would have been during the Middle Ages, and contained a tilt or barrier down the centre as well as a piece of equipment known as a quintain. This gadget for training mounted spearmen—one of the oldest methods there is and still employed by cavalry today—resembles a man's torso with arms outstretched and was so fixed to an upright pole that it twirled freely like a weathervane. If it was struck on the chest exactly square by the charging knight, it caused his lance to shiver; if it was hit on the right or left breast it spun about and whacked his head as he passed it.

As well as this there was a dummy knight perched on a wooden horse on wheels which rocketed down a pair of grooves towards the barrier and which, therefore, might be used as an opponent. Everyone called it the Railway Knight and thought it a real piece of contemporary ingenuity; in fact, they were three hundred years behind the times, for just such rolling dummies were used in the 16th century.

If the knights discovered that nothing new could be said about learning to joust, so when they tried it they encountered all the difficulties known to their medieval ancestors. The greatest of these was teaching the horses to gallop close to the barrier, not so near that the rider's leg was crushed, and not so far that a blow became impossible. Some of the mettled hunters on which they were mounted simply refused to do it while others only finally complied after weeks and weeks of exhausting and tedious training.

Eventually most of them managed to succeed, including Lord Waterford, riding, according to the *Morning Post*, 'a handsome bay horse with a plain smooth bit in his mouth, with which no other man could possibly control him.'* But this was only after repeated tumbles, made the worse in Lord Waterford's case on one occasion by being locked in his armour, face downwards on a heap of dung and sawdust for twenty minutes while his baffled squires struggled to wrench him out of it.

Even this was an old experience. Jousting armour was held together with nuts and bolts which required a spanner to take them apart and if they were damaged they often jammed. In Arthurian legend, the young Sir Percivale who, like the Eglinton knights, had never been trained as a page or esquire and had reached manhood without a knight's experience, having killed the Red Knight in his first joust, could not unfasten the latter's suit of armour. So he decided to build a bonfire and consume the body inside it; but, as he began, Sir Owain arrived and showed him the proper way to take it to pieces.

A knight who failed to school his horse completely was the Hon. Edward Jerningham, 2nd son of Lord Stafford of Costessy Hall in Norfolk, an old house recently modernised in the latest Gothic manner. He appeared as the Knight of the Swan, his family emblem, and so perfectly copied the flight of this marvellous bird that, darting down the lists at the Railway Knight, he lost his balance and flew

* July 8th 3.c.

into the sunshine while his horse, suddenly relieved of his control, trampled over an innocent nearby varlet.

Everyone laughed but, had they known it, many an ancestor had done the same before him. One is even specifically recorded doing so—Henry Jerningham, the first of Costessy, who fell off his horse outside Calais in 1547 as he, too, rehearsed for a coming tournament.*

Oddly enough, however, apart from a few sprains and bruises, there were no serious accidents except in the case of one Scottish laird, John Campbell of Saddell, who allowed himself to be charged at the first rehearsal to test the force of the impact. Sitting motionless on his horse and wearing only a breastplate, he received a direct hit from a lance which slipped to the side, pierced his elbow and snapped off, dragging him out of the saddle. This could never have happened had he been properly armed. He was said by a wit—reputedly Theodore Hook—to have lost his family seat; and many weeks passed before he recovered.

From other points of view beside his own, it was just as well that he survived since, when the news of his accident reached the Sheriff of Ayr in whose shrievalty Eglinton Castle stood, it caused the latter, very sensibly, to threaten to ban the jousting altogether. For according to 'No Tilter' in a letter to *The Times* on the 11th of July, who quoted Blackstone, any knight who caused the death of another would be guilty of manslaughter, while anyone present, even, for example, the Queen of Beauty, could be charged with aiding and abetting him.

This was assuming, quite correctly, that Lord Eglinton held the tournament without the Queen's permission; at least no trace of an application has survived in the Royal

---

* *The Encyclopaedia of Sport*, V. II.—article on tournaments by Viscount Dillon.

Archives; for which, under the edicts of Henry III, he ought to have lost his honours and been disinherited.

If, however, he failed in this respect, in all others he took the greatest precautions. He assured the Sheriff that no knight would engage in combat without being wholly and properly equipped and that all the spears would be arms of courtesy which, to make them snap cleanly and not splinter, would be cut from light pine on the cross grain. As the ground would be deep with sawdust and as the knights would be clad in armour, they would suffer far less danger in a fall than they would if they fell out hunting.

Furthermore, at the rest of the rehearsals, he issued the following instruction:

> It is expressly ordered by the Earl of Eglinton, and must be distinctly understood by each knight upon engaging to run a course, that he is to strike his opponent on no other part than the shield; and that an atteint made elsewhere will be adjudged foul, and the match forfeited.
>
> Particular attention is most earnestly requested to be paid to this injunction for the general good and credit of the proposed tournament, as any untoward accident might throw discredit upon it, or even prevent its ever taking place, by force of law or public opinion.*

All these efforts had their effect; no further accidents occurred and after a while the Sheriff withdrew his objections.

One of the points about which the press wrote much and everyone talked for hours was the probable cost which was obviously going to be stupendous.

* *The Standard*, July 15th, 4.b.

When the knights had met at Pratt's showroom the previous autumn, they had worked out, with the latter's help, that they ought to have managed for £40 each—perhaps £150 in the 1960's.

But before the summer, the figure per head had risen to £400 while even this, for any knight who wished to make a display with a fine retinue of men at arms and tents, banners and heraldic trappings, was clearly going to be inadequate.

One of the knights for whom this was the case was Lord Glenlyon, aged 25, nephew and heir of the 5th Duke of Atholl. Both Pratt's estimate before the rehearsals and the receipted final account, which was settled two years afterwards, as well as the very armour itself, are still to be seen at the family's ancestral home, Blair Castle in Perthshire; and so, from them, we can note the actual facts.

Although Lord Glenlyon bought his armour, the printed estimate, headed 'THE EGLINTON TOURNAMENT' in Gothic letters, for the 'ARMOUR, HORSE CAPARISONS, &c., of a KNIGHT, with the COSTUME, &c., for the ESQUIRE and PAGES,' reveals that he might have hired it.

'A plain Suit of KNIGHT'S *Cap-à-pie* Armour, fitted and lined with leather, &c., &c., with Tilting pieces complete', could be bought for 150 gns or hired for 60 gns, the 'Modelled Crest and emblazoned Banner' which went with it being for purchase only at 8 gns. The '*richest emblazoned* Housings, Saddle, Bridle, and Horse Armour, as equipped for the Tilt to the Plain Suit,' could be bought or hired for 50 gns or 20 gns respectively; a 'KNIGHT'S Encampment, two Pavilions, Camp Bed, &c.,' could be borrowed for 40 gns.

If this was a lot, it was only the beginning. Lord Glenlyon's account came out as follows:

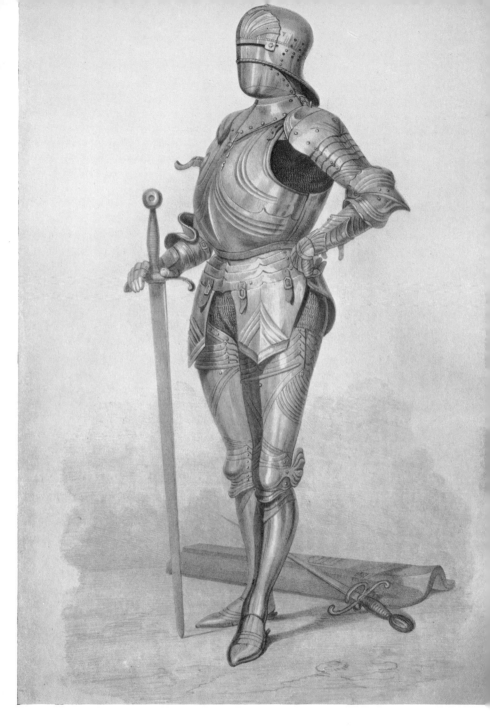

8. A suit of armour, in the Musée de Tsarskoye-Selo, similar to the
one worn by the Marquess of Waterford (a lithograph by Asselineau
of a drawing by A. Rockstuhl)

| | | | |
|---|---|---|---|
| A suit of Knight's polished steel *Cap-à-pie* Tilting Armour with steel Manteau d'arme and Mentonière, &c. | £105 | o | o |
| A Modelled Crest and emblazoned Banner | 8 | 8 | o |
| A set of Horse caparisons with tilting saddle and Horse Armour complete | 42 | o | o |
| Loan of encampment consisting of large tent & two pavilions in own colours with Bed, &c. | 42 | 10 | o |
| A buff Leather Dress to wear under Armour | 5 | 5 | o |
| Extra, for a finely fluted and engraved helmet instead of plainer one for suit | 7 | 7 | o |
| Emblazonments of armorial bearings on Horse caparison—extra | 4 | 4 | o |
| An Emblazoned Shield with Armorial bearings highly finished* A rich silk Gonfalon Banner edged with rich fringe with Armorial bearings & staff complete | 11 | 11 | o |
| Additional crests made from mould and finished in proper colours | 2 | 18 | o |
| Emblazoning Manteau d'arme with Armorial bearings—at the point of attaint | 1 | 11 | 6 |
| Expense of cleaning and repairs of Armour after practice at St John's Wood, cartage to ground and attendance, &c., Gauntlets, &c. | 12 | 14 | o |
| A rich velvet Mortière cap for practice | 1 | 12 | o |
| A rich silk velvet hood for procession | 2 | 12 | 6 |
| A chain mail hauberk shirt, to order | 12 | 12 | o |

* The cost of a shield like this in 1278, made specially for a tournament at Windsor, was 5d. R. C. Clephan *Armour* p. 81.

M

| | | | |
|---|---|---|---|
| A strong mêlée sword made after ancient model with Buff Belt, Mêlée scarf, etc. | 4 | 4 | 0 |
| Loan of a coronet for Helmet | 1 | 5 | 0 |
| Making up a rich evening costume out of tartan velvet supplied by Lord G. with cap & plume and a pair of superior scarlet silk hose pantaloons | 17 | 0 | 0 |
| An extra pair of elastic silk hose pantaloons | 3 | 3 | 0 |
| A rich velvet mantle made to order lined with satin edged with rich lace, &c. | 8 | 8 | 0 |
| Embroidering Ancle Boots | | 15 | 6 |
| A short silk shirt | | 16 | 6 |
| A polished steel demi suit of Armour for practice in Scotland, with buff coat, gloves, &c. | 9 | 9 | 0 |
| Case for ditto and packing | | 3 | 6 |
| Loan of 15 additional lances painted in own colours (3 splintered) | 10 | 10 | 0 |
| A pair of gilt Knight's spurs | 3 | 3 | 0 |
| Case for Armour and packing up ditto, & encampment costume &c., & expense of carriage of ditto to Eglinton Castle and part back | 14 | 15 | 0 |
| A beautiful model of *cap-à-pie* suit of armour on jointed figure | 12 | 12 | 0 |

£346 9 6

In addition to this, Lord Glenlyon spent £1,000 in equipping, clothing and feeding a grand retinue of 78 officers and men from the private regiment, raised in 1777, which is still maintained by the Dukes of Atholl today, known as the Atholl Highlanders.

No final total is available but, including the usual,

unforseen expenses which are paid in cash and never recorded, it must have been little short of £1,500.

For the other knights who had not inherited feudal, ancestral retainers in highland garb, Pratt ordered four hundred authentic uniforms from Messrs Haigh, Theatrical Costumers, of Covent Garden, every one of which was exactly copied from a portrait or medieval manuscript.

Such a desire to have everything perfect, characteristic of the whole tournament as well as the Gothic Revival itself, was a real proof of Pratt's enthusiasm and also, perhaps, of the folly of those who paid him; for the work and time involved in this alone must have been quite prodigious. At least he was praised as well as being remunerated. Every reporter from every newspaper proclaimed that what he had done was truly marvellous.

The particular day about which the press wrote with such enthusiasm was Saturday afternoon, July 13th, the last and dress rehearsal. The first really huge crowd, 2,690 of 'the very *élite* of the most *élite*,' in the words of the *Court Journal*, drove out to see it in brilliant sunshine, each bearing a personal card of admission, specially printed and signed by Pratt, the mere labour of doing which must again have been enormous. Every road and street within half a mile of the Eyre Arms was jammed with carriages three and four abreast and by 2.30 the block was complete, in spite of the efforts of a strong contingent of Division 'S' of the Marylebone Police under Inspector Furlong. Late arrivals had to walk, and some very peculiar medieval words were said to have passed between them.

Inside the grounds things were better. The lists, a long rectangle of four acres, had tiered benches along the sides with plenty of room for everybody, and groups of tents at either end, some for use of the competing knights and others for distinguished visitors.

The guest of honour was the Duchess of Cambridge, Princess Augusta Wilhelmina Louise of Hesse-Cassel, the wife of the 7th son of George III, to whom Lord Burghersh had dedicated his opera *The Tournament*. His absorbing work, now a year old but still remembered, had just appeared in print and, according to current rumour, was soon to be followed by another. This was more than some could bear and Barnard Gregory who, as editor of the *Satirist*, was always in trouble for spreading impertinent scandals about the aristocracy, implored his Lordship to have the courage to destroy it.

The knights, first 150 strong, then diminished to 35 and now reduced to 19, were announced in the papers as follows: The Duke of Beaufort; the Earls of Eglinton, Cassillis, Craven; The Marquess of Waterford; the Viscounts Alford, Glenlyon; the Lord Cranstoun; the Hon. E. Jerningham; the Baronets F. Bathurst, F. Johnstone, F. Hopkins; the Captains Gage, Maynard, Beresford, Fairlie; the Esquires J. Campbell, C. Boothby, and Charlie Lamb.

The Marshal of the Lists who acted as umpire was not, for some reason that is not explained, the official already appointed, Charlie's father, Sir Charles Lamb, but Lord Gage, his neighbour, of Firle near Lewes.

Apart from the fact that the jousts did not begin until nearly four o'clock—although they were due to start at three—everything went off perfectly. All the knights were bright with armour, all their steeds were gay with caparisons, all their tents were adorned with banners, all the heralds were tricked in tabards, while men at arms in appropriate costumes kept the crowds at bay with gleaming halberds. The combatants charged the Railway Knight, attacked the quintain, and then, after a pause to adjust their harness, bowed to the Duchess of Cambridge and ran their courses.

No scores were kept but although several knights, notably Lord Glenlyon and Captain Gage, were still unable to control their horses which swerved away from the barrier, most of the others, including Lord Eglinton, struck each other's shields with a bang and broke their lances splendidly. Captain Maynard—a knight who did not appear at the real Tournament a month later, perhaps through illness—performed various modern lance exercises on a 'very beautiful charger' and leapt back and forward over the barrier in full armour. Throughout the day the weather was hot and brilliant; not a cloud crossed the sky and not a breeze stirred a hair or ruffled the hem of a petticoat.

Even those who, up until then, had condemned the affair as silly were forced to admit that, after all, perhaps it was fairly effective and, setting aside the already much debated social question of whether or not a man might do what he liked with his own, agreed that the Tournament looked like being a success.

For in every respect the knights were jousting properly; and no amount of reading *Ivanhoe*, staring at pictures in the Royal Academy or watching a fight at Astley's Amphitheatre could give so good an idea as the actual thing.

Nothing remained now but the Tournament itself which the papers announced for the 28th of August. All the knights went off to the races at Goodwood—Lord Eglinton staying with the Duke of Richmond and running St Bennett, one of the best horses he ever possessed—while most of the others reposed at Bersted, the very place from which Charlie Lamb had ridden forth the year before to meet his fate in Charlotte. After the meeting, on Saturday

August 3rd, they went to Firle Place. Here, the Gage family home since the 15th century, where Captain Gage's Eglinton Tournament armour may still be seen, his father, Lord Gage, whose very title derived from the glove that was flung by knights for a challenge, gave them a farewell banquet. Then, in a state of gay excitement, they galloped away to their own ancestral homes.

'My dear Rush,' Lord Eglinton wrote at the last minute to his personal chaplain, Henry John Rush—possibly a cousin to Sir Samuel Meyrick and the local vicar at Beauport—the only invitation in his own hand that research has brought to light.

> If you have any idea of ever coming so far north, and you think a Tournament a sufficient temptation to undertake so long a journey, I hope my Chaplain will give me the pleasure of his company on that occasion. Pray excuse the lateness of this invitation, and believe me,
>
> very sincerely yours,
>
> Eglinton
>
> Newcastle, Tuesday.
>
> I am so far on my way to Eglinton.

For those intent on every development and not blessed with intimate notes like Henry Rush, the newspapers kept them posted.

Every day every editor released a revealing titbit. Even the sober readers of *The Times* were kept informed to the minute. They were told that everything was going splendidly; the final work at Eglinton Castle was progressing with 'railway speed'.

# Chapter Ten

THE COUNTY of Ayrshire, towards which so many people began to turn their thoughts as the month of August progressed, lies on the west coast of Scotland to the south of Glasgow and forms the eastern shore of the Firth of Clyde.

Although it is in the Lowlands and only fifty miles from the English border, its moors and hills, if not so grand, are as wild and beautiful as any to be found in the north, while towards the sea, towards the capital of Ayr itself and towards Lord Eglinton's castle and estates its farms and meadows are rich and lush and justly cause its cheese and cattle to be famous.

The air is sweet in this part of the country, soft, enchanting and filled with the promise of the sea. Gulls mew in the wake of the plough, the sparkling bays are splashed with tumbling gannetts and the grey cliffs and beaten rocks echo the piping cry of the paddling oyster-catchers. After rain on a sunny morning, the view of the mountains over the shining white rippling sands and green water— the isles of Bute and Arran and the Mull of Kintyre— casts a spell on the heart and memory of all who have ever seen it.

The only great snag is the changeable weather. The prevailing, warm, Atlantic wind causes persistent rainfall. If the hills can be seen clearly, then it is likely to be wet soon and if they cannot be seen at all, then it is certain to be raining already. The sun shines, the sea evaporates, clouds form and are wafted to Ayrshire. There they begin to lift and precipitate, finally to burst with the force of a Biblical deluge.

By a stroke of exciting luck for all who wished to go there from the south—those who wanted to attend the Tournament and the usual sportsmen who were after grouse—a large part of the journey could be made in a train. A new railway stretched as far as Liverpool and, although the fare was double that by coach—roughly 3d per mile instead of 1½d—the time taken was exactly half and the extra comfort and convenience almost incalculable.

A first class, single, day ticket for one of the four places in a 'car' cost fifty-three shillings. This was a beautiful black and Post-Office red carriage which bore the mails, the seats upholstered in drab cloth with a silk fringe and a padded headrest, facing each other in pairs as they did in a stage-coach. Second class carriages were roofed but open at the sides and third class were simply uncovered trucks. Ten trains left Euston daily; the 8.45 in the morning, for example, permitted time for refreshments in Birmingham and reached Liverpool at 6.15 that night.

By a second stroke of exciting luck, the rest of the journey could then be made by steamer. The Glasgow and Liverpool Royal Steam Packet Co. had just purchased two splendid and powerful ships, the *Royal Sovereign* and the *Royal George*, the first iron steamers to be taken into service.

Both had about the same displacement of 290 tons; carried sails, fore and aft, and one tall black and white funnel between the paddles. The promenade deck of the *Royal George* was two hundred feet in length and her engines at 21 r.p.m., at full pressure, developed 'the muscular strength of two hundred and fifty horses.'* A passenger could travel inside or out at a fare, respectively, of twenty or seven shillings.

* *Liverpool Courier*, 7th August, 1839, 255, e.

Both these steamers made connections with some of the trains from London and, as the end of the month approached and huge crowds began to travel, the owners scheduled an extra call at Ardrossan. Anyone sailing from Liverpool in the evening sighted Ayrshire as the sun rose and stepped ashore in time for a Scottish breakfast.

After this, if no train or carriage were available, a man could easily finish the journey on foot. It was only eight more miles to Eglinton Castle; and already the visitor stood on Eglinton property; already he cast his eyes on heroic ground.

During the course of the month the press had announced that, while the knights would be seen perfectly from the rising, wooded slopes which enclosed the lists, admission to which would be free to all, the best view would be had from the open, tiered stands on either side of the Queen of Beauty's Pavilion, tickets for which could be had from the Eglinton Office. One of the factors, Stewart Blair, had been seconded from his normal duties and given the special appointment of 'Clerk to the Tournament'; and these tickets could be had gratis by all who chose to apply for them.

It was only after this announcement that most of the staff on the Eglinton Estate and even, perhaps, Lord Eglinton himself had any idea of the scale of coming events.

Of course they had reckoned on a large turnout; all the people from round about, probably a sizeable contingent from Glasgow, and possibly one or two coaches with parties from Edinburgh; and in preparation for a crowd like this, such as they got at the Eglinton race meeting of a thousand or fifteen hundred at the most, they had made arrangements for all to be comfortably seated.

For although they had thought to hear from the well-to-do who subscribed to *The Times*, the *Morning Post*, the

*Court Gazette* and the other important or popular journals in which the offer of tickets had appeared, they had never expected that thousands of others who only perused the local newspapers like the *Bath Figaro*, the *Cornish Guardian*, the *Sheffield Iris* or the *Wisbech Star in the East* would also immediately write to them. But such papers took their national news from the national press and, as well as having relayed an account of the rehearsals, they had also, later, repeated the offer of tickets.

These readers wrote to Lord Eglinton in scores. From every county in the British Isles, ten thousand visitors, at least, seemed to be heading for Ardrossan. Their letters spoke in terms of numbers—parties of twenty, fifty and a hundred—which left his staff aghast.

Nearly a thousand of these epistles—nine hundred and forty, to be exact—are still to be read in the family archives, bound with leather into hefty books, the largest quantity of surviving Tournament documents.

They reveal in many charming ways how terribly badly people wanted to be present.

Since the word had spread about that Lord Eglinton hoped that as many people as possible would come in costume, uniform or fancy dress, a large number of aspirants promised to do so.

'We would be happy to appear in our Knight Templars dresses,' wrote J. W. Dunlop of himself and three friends from Edinburgh. 'I intend to appear in a Red Hunting Coat,' announced James Edington from Glasgow. 'I beg to solicit the information whether I will be admitted in the Walking Summer Costume de Campagne of a French Gent. of La Manche, Normandy, viz: a large straw hat and Blous of Checked Cotton' enquired Jas. Tertius Momsen who lived in Avranches. 'I will appear with the Livery of His Majesty of Sweden whose Consular Representative in this city I have the honour to be,' undertook Mr J. Brook, a Director of the Ayrshire Railway. 'As to fancy costume, I doubt not every gentleman will comply as far as possible,' assured James Dalglish who proposed to make up a party of fifty and charter a steamer from Glasgow.

I find on a hurried enquiry today that some of my friends have such dresses as they wore at Fancy Dress Balls at different festivals in England—these can be used if wished and upon receipt of a reply I can call a meeting of all our party who are here and request that those who have no such dresses may appear in sailors dresses with Tartan Scarves.

'If costume be necessary, I for one, will come in that of the Royal Archers of Scotland,' promised Robert Monteith. 'Two of us will appear in full Highland Costume, and the other in the dress of an old Farmer in ancient times,' engaged a Mr Wish. 'Being a Proprietor in the Highlands and as Member of Direction of the Celtic Society it is my intention to wear the Garb of the Celt,' said a Mr Patrick Forbes.

Will you be kind enough to secure a ticket for myself and wife—she expresses so great an inclination to be present that I cannot refrain from troubling you in this matter (wrote Andrew Maclure who was printing the tickets—founder of the firm of Maclure and Macdonald which is still in business in Glasgow today).

I sent a variety of Costumes to Mr Moffat—male and female—of the 14th and 15th centuries—for him to choose upon—he seems divided between a plain Citizenie garb and that of a Scottish Peasant (early) which will become him much, and be easily got up. If like I will send you a few sketches of costumes I have them from good authority.

I shall send a proof of the admission ticket, I expect, tomorrow evening.

A letter from Messrs Dale and Lockhart in Glasgow bears the following endorsement by Lady Montgomerie:

Mr Dale is of Ayrshire and much interested— Mr Lockhart is the brother of John Gibson Lockhart* and with his partner is likely to appear in some peculiarly fanciful and becoming garb for which Mr L has a great taste and fancy.

Many others based their claims on feudal connections, a common ancestry or a mutual love of the past. They confessed that, like Lord Eglinton himself, (or rather, if they had known it, Charlie Lamb), they had always dreamed of the days of chivalry, had always doted on the tales of Froissart, had always admired the works of Scott and had always, more than anything else, longed to witness a tournament. Amongst these was Lieutenant Sydney Gore of the U.S. Navy, a Dr W. F. Montgomerie from Dublin, and a Mr Douglas of Glasgow who described himself with a Gothic touch 'as one of loyal vassalage.' Another stated, 'I am a vassal of the Earl of Eglinton and Lady Mary Montgomerie—I served under the late Earl as an officer in the Ayrshire Volunteers 35 years ago, and was repeatedly employed by his Lordship on business.'

Others, again, presented their requests politically. Lord Eglinton was known to detest the Whigs and so dozens of applicants played on this and affirmed or implied they supported him.

'I have the honour to be
      A staunch Conservative—and
            Your Lordship's
                  Most obedient Servant,'

* The biographer of Scott.

wrote a Mr W. B. Coates in a strange, backward sloping hand, in bright blue Tory ink.

'Give a ticket' minuted Lord Eglinton.

'The *only Conservative* in Stevenstone,' Lady Montgomerie scribbled at the foot of a letter from a Mr Allen.

Other tacticians were not so lucky. A Mr Paxton, writing from Kilmarnock, was just about to be sent a ticket when somebody checked him up. His letter bears the following evidence:

'Granted' (heavily scratched out)
'Enquire if a Conservative'
'NO'
'Refused' (fiercely underlined)

Robert Owen, the 'Founder of Socialism' also wrote to Lord Eglinton. In a curious document entitled *A Challenge—To the most learned and experienced in all countries . . .* he outlined his co-operative theories in twelve paragraphs and sent it off with the annexed personal note:

It may be added that it is the highest interest of each guest at your Tournament to promote the fair and full examination of these subjects, not only in the British Empire but over the World.

In consequence the Queen of Beauty and the Hero of the Tournament are requested to recommend to all Foreign Knights and their Esquires to urge the learned and most experienced in their several nations to accept this *Challenge* which is given solely to promote the happiness of all the human race.'*

Owen did not receive a ticket.

'Sir,' wrote a Mr W. F. Blair in a covering note to his namesake, the Clerk to the Tournament,

* The Eglinton papers, No. 2841. Register House, Edinburgh.

I am afraid I am taxing you too much, but as this application comes from one whom we are very anxious to be friendly too Mr MacDonald who has taken our Iron Works and who is to make us all rich, of course I am anxious to favour him.

Sir (wrote a Mr William Aitcheson) I have taken the liberty of soliciting the favour of three tickets for the Tournament to my wife, my daughter and myself. I intended to have made this application in person but could not get away. If political conduct is any inducement to grant such a great favour, it is well known that my wife with a Candlestick and I with my sword as a Leve Lieut of the Sharpshooters nearly killed a Radical at the rising in 1819 and on that occasion it was the public opinion my wife ought to have had a pension. I have suffered unendurably by adhering to the Tory party for fifty years. My daughter will be in costume and my wife very well and for myself I shall wear my cocked hat as Town Clerk of Anderston (the western suburb of the city) the most steady adherents of the Conservatives.

Glasgow, 23 Aug. 1839

By the 21st of August, however, two days before Mr Aitcheson wrote, all hope of getting a ticket had gone; for a letter of that date from a Mr Murdoch who acknowledged a couple and asked for others is minuted, 'To be written to that no more could be procured, and that it was with difficulty that these two were.'

So unless the Town Clerk was given a special seat in Lord Eglinton's private enclosure which, from his record, he certainly deserved, he must have been disappointed.

In certain cases letters were exchanged which combine to form a series:

S. F. Blair, Esq. Redburn, Irvine.

Dear Sir: Observing in the Glasgow paper of this morning a notice that application for seats at the Tournament at Eglinton Castle is to be made to you, and being anxious with a few lady friends from the United States to witness the sports, I will feel much indebted, if agreeable to the Right Honourable Earl of Eglinton and yourself if you will reserve and forward me by mail four tickets.

Being myself from the United States, and somewhat a stranger, I beg you will excuse me if my application be ill timed; and with many apologies for troubling you,

Believe me, Your very obdt Servt

B. F. Babcock

Glasgow, Aug 13, 1839
My address is Care of W. B. Huggins and Co. Glasgow.

*Paid* Glasgow 21 Aug 1839

Dear Sir: I have the pleasure to acknowledge your esteemed favor of yesterday, and am very much indebted for your kindness and politeness in proferring your services to procure lodgings etc for myself, Mr Ricards, and the two ladies. I accept with much pleasure and many thanks your good offices so courteously tendered, and will feel obliged by your engaging for me two bedrooms with parlour if practicable and Co. from the afternoon of the 27th to the morning of the 30th. I shall be quite satisfied with neat plain accommodation, and not disposed to grumble at some inconveniences on such an occasion. The names of the Ladies who are much indebted to you for your attention are

173

Miss Maria E. Babcock  }
Miss Harriet P. Swan    } of New York

who with Mr Ricards and myself make up the proposed party.

Again acknowledging my obligation for your courteous attention, with many wishes that I could reciprocate the favor, and many thanks,

I am Your mo. obd. Servt.

B. F. Babcock

S. F. Blair, Esq
Irvine

Glasgow, 19th Aug 1839

Sir: I am favored with your note of yesterday. Since I had the pleasure of writing to you soliciting tickets for the Tournament for myself and ladies from the United States, the difficulty or rather impossibility of securing accommodation at or near Irvine has compelled the ladies with much reluctance to abandon their intention of accompanying me. I will feel much obliged if tickets be granted to myself and my friend Mr Jms R. Ricards of Baltimore, U.S.

With many thanks for your attention

I am Sir

Your obd. Servt.

etc., etc., etc.

B. F. Babcock

S. F. Blair, Esq.
Redburn
by Irvine

Glasgow, 22nd Aug., 1839

Dear Sir: It is with a sad heart I address you today. The Physicians have pronounced my dear and only child, now very ill, past hope of recovery. Myself and

9. Charlotte Lamb
(by Grant, c. 1843)

10. Charlie Lamb
(by Grant, c. 1843)

11. The Marquess of Waterford
(by Thorburn)

12. Louisa Waterford
(by W. Ross, R.A.)

sisters therefore on whose behalf I addressed you yesterday will not visit the Tournament.

I cannot, my dear Sir, express my thanks for your kindness and consideration, nor sufficiently deplore the sad cause which blasts many, very many, of my hopes and plans.

I hope you will hand me note of any expenses incurred on my acct. through disappointment in lodgings you may have engaged for me or otherwise which I will cheerfully repay you—and believe me
Your much obligd and humble Svt
In haste
B. F. Babcock

S. F. Blair, Esq.
Irvine

This last group of letters which, by their sudden, pitiful climax, wring the heart for the unknown Babcock and, by the answers they obviously received, throw such a warm light on Blair, reveal, too, one of the latter's almost insuperable difficulties. This was the finding of places for people to sleep.

In those days even the humblest professional and business people travelled with servants—every woman, at least, took a personal maid—and this factor doubled the problem for a start. More than two weeks before the event every single available space had already been bespoken and yet, by then, only half the potential visitors had so much as asked for tickets.

When they did so in all innocence, with no idea of the struggle ahead and never dreaming that others were doing the same, they were even quite peremptory.

'Dear Sir,' wrote one to a friend, the proprietor of the

175

N

Head Inn, close to Blair's office, marking the letter 'Deliver Instantly';

> By return of coach I will thank you to procure and send to me three tickets of admission to the Tournament agreeable to the enclosed note and the cash what ever it is shall be immediately returned. Do not forget this and say if you have any spare beds if good and their price. No Wines Rum, Brandy, or Ginger Cordial required on the present occasion (but?) Champaigne or claret. I am in haste
>
> Yrs truly
>
> James Alexander Jr

This friend lived in Irvine, the nearest so-called town, 2½ miles from Eglinton Castle, a typical, ancient, Lowland burgh with one long wide street, 'Not only beautiful but very salubrious',* and five thousand inhabitants. Its only decent hotel was the Eglinton Arms, and here in normal times he might, if his own house had been full, have arranged the accommodation. But on this occasion its every room from attic to cellar had been booked in advance by Lord Waterford.

There was nothing else but the homes of the local inhabitants. Rooms which were let casually sometimes during the summer at four or five shillings for bed and breakfast were offered and seized at a pound and, as more and more people poured into the vicinity, every house and cottage became crammed, and even the Presbyterian Minister thanked God for a heaven-sent opportunity to practise Christian hospitality and rented his manse to a party for 30 guineas.

A similar boom in accommodation was soon enjoyed in all the towns and villages round about, and especially so

* *The New Statistical Account of Scotland*, Parish of Irvine, 1841, p. 624.

at Ardrossan. An American author, Nathaniel Parker Willis, 'a fine, tall, handsome man with an intellectual face and refined manners,' an essayist now entirely forgotten but one whose works, after his death were said to have 'floated triumphantly down the literary Ganges with their burning lamps rendering the air bright and odorous to their many admirers,'* described the scene in his *Loiterings of Travel.*

He boarded the *Royal Sovereign* at Liverpool on the 26th and disembarked at Ardrossan the following morning after a very rough passage of seventeen hours. On the trip he had shared a cabin with an English businessman who was also bound for the Tournament and, having been told that the best hotel in the place—in fact the only one—was the Eglinton Arms, they got hold of a porter together to carry their bags and trudged after him towards it down the slipway.

This hotel, like everything else in the town, had been built by the 12th Earl and was a fine, commodious Georgian edifice with eighteen bedrooms, well equipped for a normal volume of traffic which, as the harbour had never been finished, was yet extremely small. Twice a day for the last few days, however, the *Royal Sovereign* and the *Royal George* had landed people by the hundred. The weakest members of the previous contingent were still fighting at the front portico as Willis and his friend arrived.

One hundred and fifty years ago, before the Americans were rich, they were hardy travellers and Willis, who seems to have stood the uncomfortable journey better than most of the two hundred others who staggered after him down the quay, punched his way through the entrance and called for the landlord. He asked for a place in which to wash and shave, and when he was told that this was out

* *Poems of N.P.W.* with a Memoir, Routledge and Sons, 1891.

177

of the question and that even rooms reserved for weeks had all been stormed and occupied by others, he went upstairs to take a look for himself.

Finding an open door on an attic landing through which he observed a number of beds and wash stands, he pushed into it, took some water and made a start to his ablutions. From time to time some youthful maids whose room he supposed it to be, rushed in, squeaked and rushed out again; but he took no notice of them. He washed thoroughly in the largest basin and, since he lacked a towel, he used their sheets.

After a meagre breakfast of tea and toast—all there was to be had for love or money—he went out to look for a billet. For most people at this time—only a day before the Tournament—the task would have proved impossible, but Willis had not, at the age of thirty-two, travelled across the Atlantic and about Europe without discovering how to look after himself, and by nine o'clock he had fixed his arrangements perfectly. He and his Liverpudlian friend had cajoled a cottar, at what price can only be guessed, to provide them with bunk or 'press' beds, let into the wall, each with clean linen and a copy of the Bible. They were in a garret whose skylight overlooked the horsedrawn railway which led to Irvine and, seeing a carriage about to start, they ran downstairs, determined to take a ride in it.

Within an hour they arrived at Eglinton Castle. 'The day was heavenly;' Willis wrote with excitement, 'the sun-flecks lay bright as 'patines of gold' on the close shaven grass beneath the trees.'

He spent the morning lounging happily around the Park admiring the Lists and then, as nobody seemed to object and the doors were open, he even went into the Castle. Here all was frantic hustle and bustle. The great octagonal hall—which was hung with weapons and trophies of the chase and furnished with a frightening antique chair, made from the rafters of 'Alloways' auld haunted kirk', the work of a tiresome local antiquary—was bright with the blazoned banners of the visiting knights. Beyond, in what was normally the library, were crates of pink costumes for the servants, embroidered with a huge 'E' and a coronet, and staggering quantities of halberds and armour for the men-at-arms and retainers. The place was packed with members of the staff waiting to be given appropriate suits and Pratt himself with thirty assistants was busy taking their measurements.

As well as various people like Willis who were merely idle and curious spectators, another group who were not so innocent passed the day before the event in apparently casual reconnaissance.

Ever since the first announcement, all stratas of the kingdom's underworld had looked forward to attending the Tournament with the keenest professional enthusiasm. Now they descended on Eglinton like locusts; the Swell Mob, the aristocracy, terrifying characters like Elephant Smith who travelled north in their own carriages; gangs of others who came by rail; and a huge rabble who made the journey on foot.

Hardly able to believe their luck, they found, in the guise of harmless tourists, they could ask as many questions as they chose and go wherever they pleased to recon- noitre.

As nobody at Eglinton had given security a thought, they had every reason to expect a perfect field-day. There were no police in Ayrshire at all and the nearest regular corps was in Glasgow, thirty miles away to the north, with no prerogative to act beyond the metropolis. Apart from two sleuths from the latter force who wore plain clothes and could be hired privately who were sensibly retained by the

Irvine authorities and two of the famous Bow Street Runners, urgently engaged in London by Pratt, there was no one to prevent them stealing whatever they liked. Two hundred special constables had been sworn for the occasion by the local authorities but these were merely ordinary civilians who had never even so much as arrested a tramp.

The only experienced detective present, the Chief Criminal Officer for Stirlingshire, was solely there, as his letter shows, because he proposed himself.

Lennoxtown, 17th Augt, 1839

My Lord

May the Subscriber who has been a Criminal Officer in the west of Scotland for a number of years and has a knowledge of the greater part of notorious Bad Characters that are in the habit of frequenting Public Places of Resort state to your lordship that he intends to be Present at the grand Tournament to be held under your lordship's Special Patronage. I therefore Most Respectfully solecites that your lordship will give such instructions as your lordship deem proper, to furnish me with a *Ticket of Admission* to the said Tournament that I in my official Capacity may have a Sharp Look out after Bad Characters who invariably attend all places of Public amusement, and of which at this Place and time there is every Reason to Expect a great number.

I have the honour
to be your lordship's Most
Obedient Servant
James McDougall

It is strange to record that Captain Miller, the Superintendent of the Glasgow Police, by far the nearest and most important official, who ought to have been consulted first, was only approached at the last minute when he wrote to Blair for a ticket.

He was naturally rather piqued by this.

> Police Chambers
> Glasgow 26th August 1839

Sir:

I received your favour this morning and feel obliged for your kind offer to keep a couple of tickets for the approaching Tournament.

I have already complied with the Town Clerk's request to send two of our Criminal Officers to Irvine tomorrow or on Wednesday at farthest, and am still willing to send a few additional men, if necessary.

With reference, however, to your request that I should myself go to Irvine by the Coach on *Tuesday night* and that I should 'superintend on Wednesday and Thursday', I beg to say that this being the first notice I have received of a wish that I should attend, and being in total ignorance of the arrangements made, it is impossible that I could, with any degree of satisfaction to myself, undertake such Superintendence in a matter of so much difficulty and responsability. I would have most cheerfully, tendered to the Noble Earl the benefit of the experience I have acquired in Police matters, if an opportunity had been afforded me of previously inspecting the ground and making myself acquainted with the intended arrangements on this great occasion. But, while I am not even yet aware of these, or of the regulations to be observed by the spectators, I do not see, I could now render available and creditable assistance in the way of Superintendence.

At the same time, I shall be happy to offer any suggestions that may occur to me in reference to the arrangements, on hearing from you, and of a proper conveyance by which I can travel—the stage coaches being all already engaged.

If Elephant Smith and his friends had been able to read and if they had managed to see this letter, they would surely have laughed like anything. For well before the time it arrived, the penultimate day before the event, they could all have briefed the Superintendent perfectly.

Another, smaller, professional group who spent the day before the event in getting to know the lie of the land were the people who had to report it.

From all over the British Isles they arrived at the Castle in scores, for although Lord Eglinton seemed a reactionary —he could hardly pretend to be anything else considering what he was doing—he had, with a curious, incongruous and modern touch, promised the newspapers a special stand with two places for each of their representatives.

In the ordinary way newspaper correspondents remain anonymous, especially those who relate the doings of Society, and this is particularly so of another age; so, for a change, it is nice to salute their ghosts and turn the tables; for, since they had to write for tickets, they left a record of their names.

Glasgow Herald Office
19 Aug 1839

Sir: The bearer is Mr Pagan, our Reporter, for whom Mr Johnstone, Redburn, was kind enough on being applied to, before your name appeared officially to promise every necessary accommodation at the Lists at the approaching Essay of Arms.

Well aware of the annoyance, both yourself and Mr Johnstone are likely to encounter in applications for Tickets, we should be sorry to add thereto, but as

The Queen of Beauty, Lady Seymour, surrounded by her escor
James Henry Nix

s-of-honour and Atholl Highlanders (an engraving of a drawing by
shed 1843)

the 'Press' is usually privileged to claim somewhat of a preference in such exhibitions, on *public* grounds, we hope you will so far extend your indulgence as to allow one or two tickets in addition to Mr Pagan's one, as Mr Dun, at least, one of the acting partners of the *Herald* is very desirous of witnessing the assault of the Knights.

John Richardson corresponded for *The Times*, James Hedderwick wrote for the *Scotsman*, Charles Mackay for the *Morning Chronicle*, James Paterson for the *Ayr Observer*, all of whom were successful literary figures; for the editors took the Tournament seriously, and either sent their ablest journalists or, like W. P. Brynem of the *Morning Post*, actually reported it themselves. Some of them wondered what to wear and *The Times* advised the *Ayr Observer* to accoutre its scribes in foolscap.

As remains the case in Society today, newspaper men were considered dangerous and were hardly classified as gentlemen. They were, therefore, placed in a stand by themselves as far away from the nobility and gentry as possible. In the Castle they were offered refreshments but told to eat them in the servants' hall and, although they were reasonably democratic, they felt that such treatment was unnecessary.

John Richardson who, perhaps because he represented *The Times* or because he was in the Church and a Doctor of Literature, seems to have been the doyen of the corps, was deputed to make a complaint. He sent a message to the Majordomo that unless they were treated with greater respect not one word about the Tournament would appear in a single newspaper. As a result they were given a room to themselves.

A fourth group which arrived on Tuesday, the 27th of

August, and spent the day reconnoitring the grounds was a company of the Atholl Highlanders.

During the summer, Lord Glenlyon, who was due to appear as the Knight of the Gael, had called for volunteers from amongst his clansmen to form his official bodyguard or, as they say in Scotland, to make his tail; and having returned to his home in Perthshire after the rehearsals, he had chosen seventy-three of the fiercest applicants.

These men—four officers, three sergeants, four corporals, four pipers, two orderlies and fifty-six privates—whose names, addresses, occupations and heights may now be read in the published family *Chronicles** were led by his brother, James Plantagenet Murray.

Each was equipped in a new and specially made uniform of a blue jacket with short tails without facings, green kilt and plaid of hard Athole tartan, red and white diced stockings, black brogues and blue Glengarry bonnet with a silver badge, and each carried his kit in a knapsack lettered ATHOLE and defended himself with a light target and a broadsword.

They had left Perth the previous Thursday, floated down the river to Dundee, shipped around the coast to Edinburgh, barged along the canal to Glasgow and, finally, on Tuesday morning, had arrived by steamer at Ardrossan.

There Lord Glenlyon had inspected them and, to the noble measure of the pipes, had marched them up to the Castle.

The kilt is never worn in Ayrshire and the sight of so many hairy mountaineers from the heathery north made the hearts of the natives hesitate; and, in a picture painted two years afterwards, they certainly looked extremely grand and ferocious.

* *The Atholl Chronicles*, by the 7th Duke of Atholl. Printed privately, Edinburgh, 1908.

In the evening after dinner they entertained Lord Eglinton's guests with a stirring exhibition of piping and reels.

Lord Glenlyon was the last of the Knights to arrive and if there was little hope of a bed in the district for all who were merely casual spectators, the same, by now, was equally true in the Castle. Lord Glenlyon himself had shelter for, as one of the Knights, he was naturally given a suite, but his brother had to put up with a tent, while a host of minor relatives and friends had to make do in the stables.

A list of the Castle guests would be tedious—of which, according to Dr Richardson, there were all together ninety-one—but the Knights must be enumerated. In alphabetical order they were:

Viscount Alford, aged 27
    Knight of the Black Lion.
Capt. Beresford, aged 32
    Knight of the Stag's Head.
Earl of Cassillis, aged 23
    Knight of the Dolphin.
Earl of Craven, aged 30
    Knight of the Griffin.
Capt. Fairlie, aged 30
    Knight of the Golden Lion.
The Hon. H. Gage, aged 25
    Knight of the Ram.
Viscount Glenlyon, aged 25
    Knight of the Gael.
Sir F. Hopkins, aged 26
    Knight of the Burning Tower.
The Hon. E. Jerningham, aged 35
    Knight of the Swan.

C. Lamb, Esq, aged 23

> Knight of the White Rose.

R. Lechmere, Esq, aged 40

> Knight of the Red Rose.

W. Little Gilmour, Esq, aged 32

> The Black Knight.

Marquess of Waterford, aged 28

> Knight of the Dragon.

In all, in spite of hopes to the contrary, and not including Lord Eglinton himself, there were, in the end, only thirteen combatants.

But such by then was the final excitement that nobody thought to lament their absent friends, and what with pages, esquires, varlets, a troup of 'pilgrims' who followed Lord Waterford, an escort of archers for Charlie Lamb, to say nothing of Lord Glenlyon's highlanders, the scarcity of actual knights was hardly noticed.

There were, too, the other noble participants: Lord Eglinton himself, the Lord of the Tournament; the Marquess of Londonderry, the King of the Tournament; Lord Saltoun, the Judge of Peace; Sir Charles Lamb, the Knight Marshal; each of whom had a corps of attendants; also their wives with ladies in waiting; Lady Seymour, the Queen of Beauty, with sixteen graceful handmaidens; and the principal, official guest of honour, Louis Napoleon, the Knight Visitor, with a suitable retinue headed by the faithful Persigny.

When at last they sat down to dinner, all was laughter and gaiety. The knights were obliged to call each other by their crests, so that Waterford, for example, could only be addressed as Dragon. This gave rise to a certain amount of nonsense. Burning Tower went out into the garden because, he said, he was overheated; Swan began to talk too much and was told that he ought to be mute; and White Rose, deeply flushed with goblets of claret, was warned that unless he drank some water he would soon be taken for a hybrid.

There was, naturally, talk of an all-night medieval vigil to prepare the spirit for the morrow's struggles, but this idea was defeated. They all felt they had done enough as it was and by twelve o'clock they were more than ready for bed. In spite of the usual, inevitable rush at the last minute and the times when it had seemed that nothing would be ready, all, in fact, appeared to have been completed. Even the weather had remained perfect; and now, in the warm summer night, a huge, golden moon hung over the trees.

It is hard to guess what they may have thought as they climbed the great wrought iron staircase which encircled the central hall to the height of the upper turrets and took their candles to bed. No record of the night survives and although they must, in a way, have felt a certain natural anxiety, they probably hardly gave the morning a thought. Too many days had been spent preparing for it, too many nights had been passed discussing it.

Charlie Lamb possibly dreamed of his guinea pigs; for at last his childish dreams were about to be consummated. Lord Eglinton probably dreamed of nothing at all, slipping away into fathomless sleep, content, amused and tired.

# Chapter Eleven

As all could see who arrived the following morning and bought the special 'Guide to the Tournament' with 'MAP, (see front endpapers) shewing Eglinton Castle, Grounds, & Tilt Yard, with the approaches thereto', on sale by touts at every entrance and produced by Messrs Maclure and Macdonald who printed the tickets, the Castle stood to the east of a road that is now the A78, between the little towns of Irvine and Kilwinning.

For many years it has been demolished although the ruins can still be seen, but it rose then on a small bluff, built of blocks of brown freestone, a vast, rambling, impregnable pile, if not exactly hoar with age, at least impressively Gothic.

It was only Gothic in the literary sense, however, for in actual fact it was really a square Georgian mansion with a great embattled, octagonal central tower and four smaller embrasured turrets at the corners in a style that is known as castellated.

Yet, with the ancient family name, it had somehow acquired a medieval air and, as the home of the Lord of the Tournament, it suitably inspired the spirits of all who saw it.

At the foot of the bluff ran a small river, the Lugton, which flowed through the park in a wide horse-shoe loop, in the 'U' of which, a quarter of a mile to the east, was the field assigned to the Lists. The land rose on all sides, making a shallow amphitheatre, and the river was spanned by a newly constructed cast-iron Gothic bridge. Now the

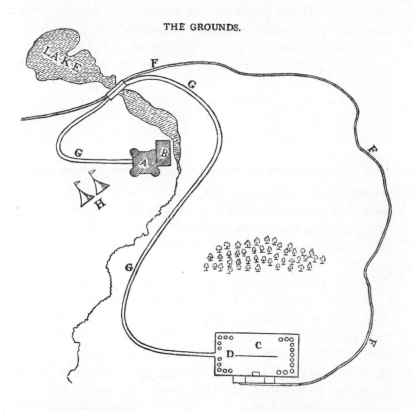

| | |
|---|---|
| A. Eglinton Castle | G. Enclosed space by which the Knights, etc., approached the Lists |
| B. Temporary Banqueting Hall | |
| C. The Lists | |
| D. The Barrier | H. Purple Pavilion |
| F. Route taken by the company on their way to the Stands | |

A drawing in *Tait's Edinburgh Magazine*
November 1839

site is nothing but a marsh, but it was then, especially in summer, a beautiful, springy meadow. On the rising slopes there were marvellous groups of old umbrageous trees, and deer and sheep had nibbled the grass to a nap as fine as velvet.

To erect the spectators' stands at the Lists required a competent team of men and, as well as several hundred joiners from the Eglinton estates, Pratt had mustered eighty carpenters from London.

All the stands except the one for the press were along the east side which faced the Castle, the tower of which, with banner waving, could be seen beyond the trees and, extending for nearly six hundred feet—almost the whole length of the Lists—seats were provided for four thousand people.

In the middle, soaring up to a height of fifty feet, was a covered grandstand in the Gothic manner—fretted, pinnacled, arched and castellated—which might, indeed, have come from the desk of Sir Walter Scott although it was probably conceived by the architect Cottingham. A royal box for the Queen of Beauty, approached by stairs on either side, jutted forward under a canopy and the columns, sides and even the roof were hung with cloth of gold and crimson damask.

The Lists themselves were a long rectangle, six hundred and fifty feet in length and two hundred and fifty feet across, running approximately north and south which was not, in fact, the medieval practice because the sun would have dazzled the eyes of the knight who stood at the northern end. Down the centre ran the barrier, three hundred feet in length and five and a half feet in height, with a deep layer of sawdust strewn beside it to break the falls of the combatants. Round the edge was a double post and rail fence to keep off the crowd, while at both the ends were

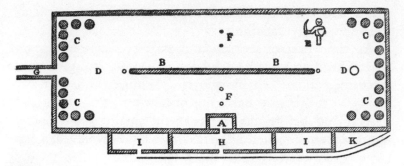

A. Loge of the Queen of Beauty
B. The Barrier
*C. Knights' Pavilions
D. Piles of Lances
E. The Quintain
F. Ring Posts

†G. Enclosed space by which the Knights entered the Lists
H. The Queen's Gallery
I. Open Galleries
K. Route taken by the company on their way to the Stands

gates to admit the knights whose martial tents were pitched on either side of them. In the south-west corner nearest the river was a small uncomfortable pen for artists and the press.

At an early hour people began to converge from all directions and those like Willis who had come in advance and had managed to find some form of accommodation were soon repaid for their efforts. Once again he mounted the horse-drawn railway and arrived at the Castle by nine o'clock, but even by then the roads were packed, both by a huge company on foot and a vast number in various types of vehicles.

It is usually not realised today that the complex problem of controlling transport did not begin with the motor car. Long before the 20th century, in the narrow thoroughfares of many cities, the queues of traffic were often streets in

* In actual fact these were outside the Lists.

† There were in fact two entrances — one at either end.

o

length and at any public event like a race meeting the jams were frequently appalling.

As time passed and noon drew near, everything on wheels heading for the Park became completely stationary. According to one reliable witness, the thirty mile highway from Ayr to Glasgow had a line of coaches almost from end to end and before the Tournament finally began every approach was blocked by carriages whose owners had left them where they stood to finish the journey on foot.

People who came by sea were hardly luckier, for although they reached Ardrossan in comfort and prepared for the day with a piping nautical breakfast, they had still, somehow, to cover the remaining distance. Many had hoped for a seat on the railway but a party of eighty Campbells from Dunoon, with the canny foresight for which that clan is famous, had chartered a special steamer of their own and skillfully managed to reach the quay and get to the station before them.

Camouflaged in tartan from head to foot, they captured all the available trucks and trundled off towards the Lists, led by a band of fearsome pipers playing 'The Campbells are coming.'

This was all very fine for them but, as the journey took over an hour and as there was only a single track, it was not so stirring for everyone else who had nothing to do but wait for the wagons to return.

In the interval, vessels berthed from as far away as Dublin and ships from the Royal Northern Yacht Club tacked their way across the Clyde and docked in a perfect flotilla.

It was fully eight miles to the Lists and the thought of hiking there and back daunted the spirits of many of the passengers, half of whom decided to stay in Ardrossan.

But the Royal Yachtsmen had been given tickets and

had promised Lord Eglinton to parade in uniform; so they determined to step it out; and they marched off to the cheers of the natives, forming up behind their Commodore, James Smith, Esq., of Jordanhill.

The people who really fared the best were those who travelled in a proper train to Irvine. A new line had just been finished from Ayr, and as it had only been opened a week, they were almost the first members of the general public to use it. Traffic figures for the day are not available but the company, the Glasgow and Ayrshire Railway, must have enjoyed a splendid profit for, as well as the eight scheduled services—four one way and four the other, the line having only a single track—four Tournament Specials were announced, and the price of the tickets was trebled.

Even so, the passengers fought to buy them for at least they knew they would arrive safely and then have only a couple of miles to walk. To go to a medieval tournament by train was thought an amusing anomaly, and especially when, as was actually the case, the engine's name was MARMION.

To compute the size of a crowd in an open field is difficult enough, but to do so at Eglinton Park was almost impossible. Even the press, who were used to multitudes, could hardly so much as guess its proportions or think of an adequate phrase with which to describe it; in the end they could only report that nothing comparable had been seen in Scotland since the coronation of George IV when, in 1822, he had driven in state through Edinburgh.

There were swarms of boys in every tree, countless parties staring at the Castle, innumerable groups on the roofs of carriages, four thousand people in the stands and possibly seventy thousand on the banks of the river.

A total of one hundred thousand was thought a conservative estimate. Guesses like these are often exaggerated, but, from its universal adoption, such a figure was probably fairly accurate.

As all could read who had bought a programme (see pp. 249-259), the cost of which was half a crown, and which, in suitable Gothic lettering, revealed the names and titles of the knights, the Tournament was due to start with a procession which was timed to leave the Castle at twelve o'clock. When noon passed and nobody appeared, the crowd began to get restless; after a while a Castle minion, a halberdier in the Eglinton colours with a blue and yellow soup-plate hat, announced that the knights would be late.

The cause of the delay was lamentably obvious to those who were close to the Castle. All who have ever been in the army or any similar professional body will know the problems involved in arranging a parade, and the task was twice as hard at Eglinton because, instead of being experienced, all the participants were amateurs.

The procession consisted of forty different groups and all of them had to march to the Castle, collect an officer, knight or damsel and retrace their steps to halt at a pre-arranged point.

This manoeuvre was difficult enough, easy though it is to describe, but the site of the Castle made it much more complicated. For, being built at the end of a promontory, instead of having a pair of entrances—one for IN and one for OUT—it had only a single drive for all the traffic; and so all the troops who were marching up had to make their way through those who were marching down.

According to Willis—once again at the centre of excitement, the knights were mounted with difficulty. The first, the Earl of Craven, the Knight of the Griffin, was forced in the end to call for a chair, being quite unable in the weight of his armour to manage alone with the stirrup. The next,

Lord Waterford, ascended nobly, although he got up with such a vault that he nearly broke his charger's back. Lord Eglinton proved the best of them all, nimbly climbing into his seat with the skilled address of a "parfit gentil knight."

When finally everyone was ready—the Eglinton Herald in a massive tabard, the Judge of Peace in crimson velvet, the Knight Marshal in steel and surcoat on an armed, plumed, caparisoned horse, the Ladies Visitors in minivered jackets, the Ballochmyle Archeresses ' a band of nymphs in Lincoln green', the King of the Tournament in cape and coronet, Lord Eglinton himself in a suit of gold, and all the Knights complete in armour, with pages, esquires, retainers, musicians—more than a hundred of whom were mounted and more than a hundred of whom were armed—the procession was half a mile in length and more than three hours late.

Last to be called to her place was the Queen of Beauty and, as her horse was led to the porch, as it was announced by a blast from a trumpeter, as her name was cried by a chamberlain, as her train was lifted by her pages, as her ladies brought her to the door, the Park was shaken by a fearful clap of thunder. In a sudden hush and a strange darkness, a single flash of lightning parted the sky.

Now a storm of rain began which destroyed the hopes of everybody. During the morning the sun had shone but those who had known the Ayrshire weather had looked across at the mountains of Arran and had seen them much too clearly. By ten o'clock the warm, moist air from the Gulf of Florida had once again begun to gather in ominous condensations; and the first drenching squall struck just as the procession started.

In the 'good old days' the knights could have called the Tournament off—no records of jousts in the rain exist—but a cancellation in Lord Eglinton's case was felt to be inadmissable; for what had begun as a private fête had become a public festival.

So, in a pelting, icy torrent, the cavalcade without the ladies who, on Lord Eglinton's personal command had been told to shelter and wait for carriages, at last set off for the Lists.

The immediate consequence of this arrangement was that none of the crowd could see the Queen of Beauty, many of whom had waited hours to do so.

Jane Georgiana, Lady Seymour, was the youngest daughter of Tom Sheridan, son of the famous Richard Brinsley, who had married a celebrated beauty, Henrietta Callendar. One of three radiant sisters who were called, inevitably, the Three Graces—the eldest of whom became Lady Dufferin and the second the well known Caroline Norton—she was twenty-nine at the time of the Tournament, the wife of Adolphus, Baron Seymour, the son and heir of the 11th Duke of Somerset.

It tends to be axiomatic in Society that all who are rich or grand are beautiful, but Lady Seymour had, in truth, a rare and appealing loveliness. Willis who, in writing afterwards, had no incentive or desire to flatter and was only concerned with reporting the facts—which was not the case with all the journalists, some of whom were inclined to toady—watched as she crossed the hall of the Castle and was wholly, instantly enchanted.

She was dressed in a long, full, violet velvet skirt which reached to her feet and was covered in golden heraldic wings, 'two wings, conjoined in lure, the tips downwards, or, for SEYMOUR,' to quote their technical description. Above she wore an ermine and miniver jacket, and over her shoulders a superb, voluminous, crimson velvet mantle; round her throat were chains of diamonds and on her head was a crown encrusted with pearls.

She was not tall but she walked with a graceful upright carriage which revealed her figure charmingly; and all agreed on the beauty of her face which, framed by raven hair, had the lily skin and roseate cheek of traditional Celtic colouring. Her manner, too, was all that is said to be Irish—fanciful, gay, spontaneous, witty and amusing.

Why she was given the honour is not recorded. The expected choice had been Lady Londonderry whose puffy features were always said to be fine because she was an heiress, being, the gossips said, Lord Eglinton's mistress; but when her husband agreed to be King of the Tournament she was forced, against her will, to be Queen beside him.

By common consent, Louisa Stuart, the second daughter of Lord Stuart de Rothsay who, at the age of twenty-four married Lord Waterford three years afterwards, was the loveliest woman present; but perhaps for reasons of Victorian etiquette and also possibly to prevent Lord Eglinton having to make an invidious choice, the Knights decided only to offer the post to a married woman.

Whatever the reason, it fell to Lady Seymour, who performed the duties with a sweet and pleasing gaiety. Some thought that Lady Londonderry might have acted with greater fire and theatrical grandeur, having a more imperious temperament, but all concurred that none, in looks, could have equalled Lady Seymour.

There was, however, one fact about her which, in spite of all her virtues, ought to have made her ineligible; at least, that is, to Charlie Lamb and any of the knights who loved him: one of her favourite hobbies was cooking and some of her choicest dishes were made with guinea pigs.*

This taste, had he known about it, would surely have

* *Leaves from the Note-Books of Lady Dorothy Nevill;* p. 15. Macmillan, 1907.

turned him against her, for Charlie was one of those whimsical people—sometimes lovable and often tiresome—who carry a childish streak into adult life and only the week before at Beauport, as though to seek a guinea pig blessing, he had paid a visit to the cemetery of Winnipeg and sat by the graves of two of the original Knights of the White Rose: Sir Heliodorus, Prince of Rarribun, and Turkwine, the Earl of Newton.

Happily enough, no one at Eglinton ever knew anything about it and all the knights, and Charlie, too, were dead before, in the next century, anyone beyond her immediate family learned of her predeliction.

The rain cascaded down Charlie's neck as, superb in a Gothic armour, on a white charger, barded and caparisoned, he made his way to the Lists. Only aware of the dream in which he lived, he ignored completely the actual conditions —the cakes of mud on all the trappings, the scowling clouds that obscured the sky, the sheets of water that drummed like thunder on the crouching knots of miserable spectators who lined the procession's route beneath umbrellas.

In his third and last illuminated MS, in a colourful if rather primitive miniature, he depicted himself riding to the contest cheered by groups of tartaned peasants under the lea of Eglinton Castle beneath a cloudless sky.

Now he was clad in a goodly suit of polished steel. Hys surcote covered over with white roses which were also embroidered upon hys belt, whereon was the legend of *une seule*, and one white rose in hys cap, all in token of his Lady love. Hys shield emblazoned with the arms of Burges, hys father's house. The crest of the same upon his helmet, with plumes of his tinctures and a mightie sword in hys hand readye to do battaille with

There were two stages to the Tournament. In the first, two kni
him with his lance. In the second, which is shown above, all
Lord Waterford lost his temper; he is shown here, left, in con
(an engraving of a drawing by Ja

down the Lists and each tried to unhorse the other by striking
 its taking part engaged in hand-to-hand fighting. In this *mêlée*
st Lord Alford. Sir Charles Lamb is on the left with his baton.
y Nixon, published 1843)

all comer, and how he and others sped thereat will be seen in the sequence of thys historie.

For it has seemed as must be known to everyone that a great Tournament was proclaimed to take place on the day I have mentioned at Eglinton Castle. It was talked for a year and a half previous over all England, Scotland and France. That and nothing else. It was now two centuries since such a thing had been seen in Europe. Passages of arms had indeed been attempted on a few occasions in these times such as the one in the United States of America*, where Earl Cathcart presided, also at Malta by some officers of the garrison† where the armour of the Knights of St John was used. An annual joust took place until very lately on the Bridge at Pisa‡ in which all the combatants wore armour but all these were on a trifling scale to present one from the pomp and splendour in which it was held. No one indeed believed that it would take place. Howsoever many gallant young gentlemen prepared to appear in the lists. Those who did appear, for many failed at the appointed time, were Henry Marquess of Waterford, that reckless and gay young nobleman who from a street brawl to daring the lion on ye plain of Africa was ready at home or abroad for all that promised novelty or adventure. He came handsomely equipped with a splendid retinue. He wore a suit of German armour fluted, his horse with caparisons of black and white. He was attended by Lord John his brother, Sir Charles Kent, baronet, Lord Maidstone, Richard Lumley, Mark White-Kerr and Lewis Ricardo Esquires, all mounted wearing his tinctures of black and white with back

* At Philadelphia in 1778. See the *Annual Register* for that year, p. 265.
† On the 19th of February, 1828, at the Palace Square, Valetta.
‡ The last of these was held in 1808.

breast and head pieces of polished steel. With him also were Lord Ingestrie, habited as a Turkish dervise and one in the garb of a friar. These with grooms and foot-men armed with pikes completed his train. He himself was tall and handsome and so were his followers. He was known by the name of the Knight of the Dragon, from his crest. The Earl of Craven came next. He was equipped in a very handsome inlaid suit of Milan armour which became him admirably. His colours were red and gold. His brother Frederick and James Mac-donald (ye Lord's brother) were his Esquires. Then came Lord Alford, his colours blue and white, followed by his brother Charles and Richard Gascoigne Esquire. He was called the Knight of the Black Lion from his crest. There were with him several men on foot armed with halberds. The Lord Glenlyon came from the highlands to this tournament. Sir David Dundas and Balfour of Balbirnie were his Esquires. He was accom-panied by seventy men of Atholl. There were several gentlemen among them and they were all picked men equipped and armed with swords targets after the manner of their country. They marched up the castle with their pipes playing, having a gallant appearance, he at the head of them on foot, having come so thro' the low countries. Mr Edward Stafford Jerningham, son of Lord Stafford, was called the Knight of the White Swan, from his crest. Mr Stevenson was his Esquire who was related to the Laird of Macleod. His colours were white and gold. James Fairlie of the Lion came to break a lance for the honour of the Shire of Ayr. He was a handsome gentleman, skilled at all manly exercises. His appearance when armed and mounted was excelled by none. He wore a suit of gilded armour and over that a surcoat of cloth of gold with a red lion embroidered

before and behind. The trappings of his horse were blue
and crimson. His banner was borne by Mr Charles
Cox, his Esquires John Purvis and Thomas Pettat of
Gloucestershire. Fifteen chosen yeomen armed with
halberds formed his train. Mr Lechmere, a gentleman
of good birth from the West of England, came next.
He wore for his cognisance a red rose in memory of the
part taken by his ancestors in the Wars of York and
Lancaster. He was a big strong man and wore a massive
suit of fluted armour with a very handsome plume of
crimson feathers and mounted upon a fine grey stallion.
Two gentlemen named Smith and Cory were with him.
I do not think he had any more. After him came Walter
Gilmour who was called the Black Knight. He was a
tall and handsome man. His Esquires were Lord
Drumlanerig and James Hunter Blair. They were
habited as well as the serving men in black attire and the
Knight himself wore a suit of black armour. The horses
and the trappings were also black, such being the
humour of Mr Campbell of Saddel who had intended to
have come but at the time he was taken very ill and
requested Mr Gilmour to go in his place. Mr Gage,
second son of the Lord Viscount Gage, called the
Knight of the Ram. His Esquires were Robert
Fergusson of the Kilkerran family, and a gentleman
named Murray. The Earl of Cassilis appeared also.
He was known by his cognisance of the dolphin. He
had no retainers but accompanied Mr Gage. He was
a sorry representative of his ancient race in appearance,
but did not want for gallantry. Sir Francis Hopkins an
Irish gentleman of fortune was called from his crest of
the burning tower. He had no retinue but I must [word
missing] his charger was far more beautifully accoutred
than that of any other knight. His trappings were of

black velvet, such being the field of his arms, and reaching to the ground, his charges embroidered upon it from the neck downwards. He was a most excellent sitter and a powerful horseman.

All these noble knights and also all the superb officials, similarly described in Charlie's MS., trotted towards the Lists in perfect weather. The shivering multitude which actually watched them only beheld a bedraggled crocodile; and Lord Londonderry riding in the centre of it holding aloft a tremendous green umbrella.

As often happened in genuine tournaments, the King and Queen and other notables were expected to parade round the Lists before they took their places on the throne but—as it was almost four o'clock, as all were soaked and chilled to the bone, and as the crowds were becoming restless—having at last arrived at the gates, they decided to cancel all the preliminaries and go at once to their seats.

As a result, the Knights were denied the romantic ceremony of riding up to the grandstand to choose their paramours and of being given scarves or handkerchiefs to tie to their lances or helmets; the Eglinton Herald was denied the privilege of standing alone in the hushed arena while reading out the rules; and the crowd, too, most unhappily, was denied a glimpse of Lady Seymour, who would have ridden round in state and allowed the expectant world to admire her beauty.

As it was, she arrived in a carriage and entered the dais from the back, and was hardly noticed amongst the others —Lady Londonderry, Lady Montgomerie, Aunt Jane and Louisa Stuart—until her brother, Charles Sheridan, clad in an exquisite suit of plate, took his stance behind her throne and unfurled a crimson parasol over her head.

For now another calamity had happened. The planks of wood which formed the grandstand roof, instead of being tongued and grooved, had only been laid together edge to edge, being merely required temporarily and being, anyway, covered with scarlet cloth. By the time the Queen of Beauty arrived, the rain had begun to filter through them, and long before the jousts began the entire royal box was flooded, as well, naturally, as every corner of the grandstand.

For those who were there as Lord Eglinton's guests this was an absolute disaster. Having been told that their seats would be covered, only a few had brought their overcoats and, as a final touch to their misery, many had come in expensive fancy costumes. The women, especially, suffered agonies. All had planned their hair and dresses for months and, as jets of water fell on their shoulders and gusts of wind removed their hats, young and old were filled with grim despair.

When at length everyone was seated, the only person left in the Lists was the Jester. He was an actor called Robert M'Ian who had made a name for himself portraying Robin Oig M'Combich in *The Two Drovers* and other plays that were drawn from Sir Walter Scott. Riding a donkey, and dressed in cap and bells, he jogged about and made some feeble jokes. But, like many people of the same profession, without a script he was just a bore, and nobody thought him amusing. 'His repartees were like a series of slight electric shocks', wrote one of the journalists, trying hard to be nice about him.

In the end he lost his temper and handed his wand to the Eglinton Herald who had sent the crowd into fits of laughter, striding about in a streaming tabard, trying, in spite of orders to the contrary, to declaim the rules of the joust.

'You take it,' M'Ian snapped at him, 'One fool in the Lists is enough for me.'

All eyes were turned now on the various Knights' pavilions. These, in keeping with everything else, were exact replicas of military tents such as are seen in the illustrations of Froissart—striped according to the owner's colours, a shield of arms above the entrance, and lit by a series of tiny dormer windows on the tops of which were little flags, held open stiff like the tails of weathervanes. Each encampment consisted of three—a marquee and two bell-tents, joined together in a suite; and all were furnished with tables, chairs, wash-stands, carpets and beds.

Pitched at either end of the Lists outside the railings, even under sheets of rain they managed to provide a busy and romantic spectacle. Banners lapped the wind before them, horses pranced and shook their trappings, men at arms bustled in and out, esquires collected and tested lances, poursuivants hurried from one to another and, from time to time, a knight emerged to observe the state of the weather.

All who watched were tense and hushed for the first great climactic moment: the flinging down of the champion's glove and the crying out of the noble terms of the challenge.

For some reason that is not recorded, perhaps simply because of the storm, which had now increased to an absolute tempest, the noise of which would have drowned a megaphone, the first opponents suddenly appeared without the smallest ceremony.

In the good old days, at a friendly Round Table such an event would have mattered hardly at all for, except in the case of an Unknown Knight who would, of course, have concealed his identity, the crowd would have known who the combatants were by their shields.

In the present case the situation was different. Apart

from the fact that to make a challenge had been Lord Eglinton's greatest ambition—the omission of which at the coronation had actually caused him to hold the Tournament—and apart from the fact that the crowd, too, after waiting so long in the rain, had expected to see a complete performance, the whole value of such a ceremony in the changed conditions of the 19th century would have been to announce the names of the competing knights.

Now, as they rode to their places in the Lists, locked inside their suits of steel, their faces hidden by their crested helmets and unproclaimed by any of the heralds, only two or three specialised antiquaries were able to say with any certainty which two of the Knights were about to fight.

For only one per cent of the public had any practical knowledge of heraldry in spite of the wide popular enthusiasm for everything connected with the Middle Ages and, in the case of the people at Eglinton, few, if any, had learnt the arms by heart.

The press who, more than anyone, ought to have known the combatants' names, found themselves completely foxed, their stand being so positioned—far away at the end of the Lists—that even a scribe from the College of Arms could have told them little without the aid of a telescope.

Some had actually brought these instruments; but the wind blew them round and round and they never managed to hold them still enough even to get them focussed.

If, as the crowd watched the Knights who rode slowly to the ends of the barrier, couched their lances under their armpits, and waited for the Marshal to signal the charge, all were sorry to have missed the challenge, almost as many regretted the omission, equally inevitable because of the weather, of another picturesque ceremony.

After the procession had circled the Lists, the King and

Queen had ascended their thrones, and all the officers had taken their positions, the heralds ought to have addressed the contestants and given them a number of instructions.

This spectacle, if not so thrilling would at least have been traditional and would, also, have given the spectators a chance to hear the rules.

These ancient regulations—specially printed copies of which had already been given to all the Knights—were based on a set of 1602, written by Norroy King at Arms for the last jousts held in the reign of Elizabeth. They were, however, drawn from others which had been composed for Edward IV by the Earl of Worcester, in 1465; and they were, therefore, quite as authentic as the words and procedure of the challenge.

The Ordinances, Statutes & Rules, made by John, Lord Tiptofte, Erle of Worcester, Constable of England, by the King's commaundement, at Windsore 29 Day of May, *Anno Sexto Edwardi Quarti;* and commanded in Eliz. 4; to bee observed or kept in all manner of Justes of Peaces Royall, within this realme of England. Reservinge alwaies to the Queen, and to the Ladyes present, the attribution and gifte of the prize, after the manner and forme accustomed: to be attributed for their demeritts according to the Articles ensueinge.*
How many waies the prize is woone.
1. Who so breaketh most speares as they ought to bee broken, shall have the prize.
2. Who so hitteth three times, in the sight of the healme, shall have the prize.
3. Who so meeteth too times, cournall to cournall, shall have the prize.

* *The Triumph holden at Shakespeare's England* by F. W. Cripps-Day, 1912, p. 7.

4. Who so beareth a man downe with stroke of a speare, shall have the prize.

How many waies the prize shall be lost.

1. Who so striketh a horse shall have no prize.

2. Who so striketh a man, his back turned, or disgarnished of his speare, shall have no prize.

3. Who so hitteth the foile (or tilt) 3 times shall have no prize.

4. Who so unhealmeth himself two times shall have no prize, unlesse his horse doe faile him.

How broken speares shall be allowed.

1. Who so breaketh a speare, between the saddle and the charnell of the healme, shall be allowed for one.

2. Who so breaketh a speare, from the cournall upwards, shall be allowed for two.

3. Who so breaketh a speare, so as hee strike his adversary downe, or put him out of his saddle, or disarmeth him in such wise as hee may not runne the next course after, or breaketh his speare cournall to cournall, shall be allowed three speares.

How speares shall be disallowed.

1. Who so breaketh on the saddle shall be disallowed for one speare-breakinge.

2. Who so hitteth the toyle once, shall be disallowed for two.

3. Who so hitteth the toyle twice, shall, for the second time, be abated three.

4. Who so breaketh a speare, within a foot to the cournall, shall be adjudged as no speare broken, but a fayre attaynt.

For the prize to be given and who shall be preferred.

1. Who so beareth a man downe out of the saddle, or putteth him to the earth, horse and man, shall have

P

the prize before him that striketh cournall to cournall 2 times.

2. Hee that striketh cournall to cournall two times, shall have the prize before him that striketh the sight three times.

3. Hee that striketh the sight three times, shall have the prize before him that breaketh most speares.

Item, if there be any man that fortuneth in this wise, which shall be deemed to have abiden longest in the field healmed, and to have runne the fayrest course, and to have given the greatest strokes, and to have holpen himself best with his speare, he shall have the prize.

(subscrybed)
John Worcestre

Although enumerated rather differently and described as 'Actions worthy of Honour', these five paragraphs of rules formed the basis of those for the Eglinton Knights. They were only modified in one respect: because of the warning from the Sheriff of Ayr that anyone causing a fatal accident might be charged with manslaughter, or even murder, the Knights were not allowed to aim at the helmet; the point of attack for the highest score was made the coat of arms emblazoned in the centre of the shield.

The method of marking down the score, to be seen today in the great tournament rolls in the College of Arms, was simple, neat and interesting.

A jousting tally was called a 'Cheque', and this was merely a piece of paper on which was drawn a long rectangle marked in half by a line lengthways projecting beyond one end. On the three parallel lines thus formed, a vertical tick, or sometimes a pinprick was made to note a result: on the top for an 'atteint' or satisfactory hit; on the middle for a spear correctly broken; on the bottom for a fall or penalty. In the middle line beyond the box a tick was put to denote the number of courses.

It is sad to record, when so many medieval cheques exist, that none of the Eglinton ones survive if, that is, they were ever written. The Knights' scores are therefore lost and, because of the awkward seating of the press and because, also, of the poor visibility, the tallies given in the newspapers do not agree.

And by now, when at last the Knights were poised, more than four hours later than scheduled, many of the reporters had fallen asleep, having been up since the peep of dawn, having eaten nothing since breakfast and having swallowed pints of whisky to allay the effects of the weather.

As the Knight Marshal raised his baton, as the heralds shouted '*Laissez les aller*', as the Eglinton Trumpeters blew the charge, as the Knights dropped their lances in the rests, as the dripping horses skidded forward, a few of the journalists snored and moved uneasily. But all the designated courses were run before they roused themselves enough to see them.

They only opened their eyes in the end because of a roar of laughter. For the two Knights who had started jousting —who proved to be Swan and Golden Lion, Edward Jerningham and James Fairlie—had thundered down the squelching Lists and merely galloped past each other. Their second course had fared no better and their third had gone even worse. Fairlie again had poked thin air while Jerningham, trying to reach his opponent in a last, frantic exasperated effort, had almost repeated his flight at the rehearsals and, in a fearful struggle to stay on, had dropped his spear, tied to which was his wife's cambric handkerchief.

From this moment, if not before—if not from the very day it was thought of—the Eglinton Tournament was doomed to certain failure.

Nothing in the world is worse than ridicule and the more a pageant aspires to grandeur the more, if it fails, it will sink to bathos. Once the spectators have started to smile, it is almost impossible to stop them.

So now, as the other Knights appeared, as the Knight of the Dragon challenged Lord Eglinton; as Sir Francis Hopkins jousted Mr Lechmere; as Lord Glenlyon ran at Lord Alford; and as, in the last combat of the day, the two lords—Waterford and Alford—clumped together and tried to impale each other, the crowd watched with impatience and contempt or, once in a while, with a rueful grimace of sympathy.

It was far worse than the most boring point-to-point or race meeting. There were long gaps between the courses while the Knights rested and adjusted their armour and when at length they ran again, each time, with few exceptions, they either botched their strokes or missed completely.

The only combat of any reality was between Lords Eglinton and Waterford. Both were exceptionally able horsemen, both had taken their training seriously, both had comfortably fitting armour, both were out to prove their skill and, in spite of increasingly difficult conditions—for every hoofmark had become a puddle and the Lists had become extremely slippery—both dashed at each other as hard as they could. Although on the second course they missed, on the first and last Lord Eglinton engaged, striking the centre of the Dragon's shield and breaking his spear on it perfectly.

He remembered, too, as soon as he had done so to throw away the butt. Such an act was most important for the long splinters of a broken shaft easily penetrate the opponent's visor, the very thing that had actually happened to his own forbear, Count Montgomerie, when he killed the King of France.

There was, finally, by way of a diversion, a fight between two gigantic swordsmen. One was a soldier entitled Redbury and the other an actor called Mackay, the latter having, like the Jester, made his name on the Scottish stage in plays from Sir Walter Scott. Their two-handed swords were formidable and they whacked away at each other like Roman gladiators. But the crowd, now, had seen enough and when the combat came to an end, one of them actually breaking his weapon, no applause greeted the victor and no sound broke the stillness except the patter of the rain.

In the long, depressing pause that followed Lord Eglinton suddenly appeared in the Lists and galloped up to the barrier. It was clear that he wanted to make an announcement and once more the multitude stirred as people dried their ears with handkerchiefs and peered from under their umbrellas.

He began by saying how sorry he was that everyone had got so wet, especially those who had come from a long way off. Speaking as one who lived in Ayrshire, who had known its weather all his life, he wanted to say that he, at least, had never seen anything to equal the present deluge. Not that he wished to make excuses but he felt that the fact might like to be known. Should conditions improve, he would try again, if not tomorrow, then the next day, or else the following week. In the meantime he bade them farewell and wished them all a successful journey homeward.

He then rode closer to the Grandstand and addressed his personal friends and guests, the two thousand people with special tickets. They, he said, through his own carelessness, for which he feared they would never forgive him, were doomed to bear another and final disappointment. The much advertised medieval banquet as well as the costume ball to follow had both, now, at this last minute, been unavoidably cancelled. The magnificent tent behind the Castle in which these functions would have been held had, in the same manner as the Grandstand, having a weakly constructed roof, become the victim of the weather. He had no alternative but to offer his apologies and hope that they, too, would get safely home.

Almost five minutes had elapsed and Lord Eglinton had ridden back to his pavilion before, in the first shock of disappointment, the full portent of what he had said was realised.

Many of his guests lived far away—quite a few on the other side of the county—and most of them had planned, after the Tournament, to rest and change with friends who lived in the district. They had, therefore, sent their carriages away and told them not to come back until after midnight. How, then, could they get in touch with them to explain the change of plan?

As they sat in the waterlogged grandstand and turned this problem over in their minds, the friends with whom they were going to stay became aware of another one. How were they, these lucky locals, to get to their homes themselves? They, naturally, had ordered their carriages to return in the course of the afternoon at such time, whenever it might be, as the jousts were expected to finish. But when they went to the exits to look for them they only observed a single conveyance, one of Lord Eglinton's personal coaches slowly vanishing towards the Castle, bearing away the Queen of Beauty and her suite.

Not another vehicle was to be seen, for, as in all rainy districts, the rivers in Ayrshire rise swiftly, almost as soon as a storm begins, and the Lugton, winding round the Lists, in drought a dancing, shallow burn, had become a raging torrent.

As a result, the Lists had flooded, being really lush water meadows, hardly above the level of the river even during the summer; and the fact was that since lunch time nothing less than a chariot and four, of which Lord Eglinton's was the only one, had been able to return to the Grandstand.

Then began a confused exodus which truly defied description. As one hundred thousand spectators began to make their way from the Lists, forced to head for home on foot, the rain pouring, the wind howling and the mud pulling their shoes from their feet, young and old, rich and poor, jostled together like cattle at a fair and behaved with as little civility.

On the high road beyond the policies the walking should have been easier but instead the slough got worse and worse, for the lucky few who got to the front deposited a trail of slimy mire which had to be traversed by those behind and which, as a result, was carried farther and farther. Any carriages which happened to appear were seized by force by the nearest pedestrians, quite regardless of the person to whom they belonged, and the one train that departed from Irvine had such an extra load of passengers clinging to the coaches, trucks, wagons and even astride the engine itself that some of them had to push it to make it start.

As often seems to happen in life, only the wicked reached their firesides in comfort. Elephant Smith, Bill Caughty and other bigwigs of the Swell Mob had come to the Tournament in suits of armour which, it is fairly safe to assume, they had hired from Samuel Pratt. With helmets on and visors down they had entered the Park with hilarity thinking that, in this disguise, they were safe from all detection.

But a man in armour is like a horse with blinkers, only able to see what is straight in front of him, and so, as they strolled among the crowd, they failed to notice that someone had started following them.

For although Pratt had made mistakes, he had not forgotten to deal with the problem of burglars and after the rehearsals he had been to Bow Street and retained the services of Goddard and Ballard, two of the country's sharpest police detectives.

Also equipped in medieval style, although in the handier costume of Franklins, they spotted the mobsters in half an hour and long before the jousting started ordered them on to the horse-drawn railway and packed them off to Ardrossan.

Warm and dry but much annoyed, the Mulberry Hawks and Bill Sykes's threw their armour into the harbour and sat in the saloon of the *Royal Sovereign* until, as the sun began to set, they were joined by other parties of spectators, most of whom had been forced to walk from the Lists.

This was the chance for which they had all been waiting. Mingling among them and offering them drinks, they helped themselves to their money and watches and, when they berthed the following morning, legged it down the gangway and vanished in Liverpool.

Many people who lived at a distance—particularly women in fancy dress, and especially those of humble birth—never, never forgot the night that followed. By nine-thirty it was pitch dark, the rain continued to fall in sheets, the roads were still chaotic in all directions. In desperation they sheltered in cowsheds, they burrowed caves in the sides of haystacks, they crouched in the boles

After the disappointment of the actual tournament, the medi-
temporary banqueting hall, proved a moderate success. All gu
seated on the dais. (An engraving of a drawing by James He

quet and ball that were held two days later in the specially built
e in medieval dress; Lady Seymour and Lord Eglinton are shown
on, published 1843)

of hollow trees, even returned and huddled beneath the grandstand.

When at last morning came they reached places like Ayr and Kilmarnock, only to find that others had got there before them. There was no food, no drink, no accommodation, no transport, not even a change of clothing for those who could pay for it. In the great rush of the evening before every single thing had been sold and, to the shame of honest citizens, at more than eight times the normal profit. One woman who had come from Edinburgh, a Mrs Stott of Gayfield House, had, it is still recollected in the family, been compelled to give eighty shillings for a single pair of stockings.

At Eglinton itself the Knights had not been happier. No record has come to light, if ever one was made at all, of how they got away from the Lists or what they said or did when they reached the Castle. If, at least, they had warm bedrooms with bright fires stoked high with the finest coal from the Eglinton collieries, attentive servants to bring them hot water, diligent maids to dry their clothing, silent footmen to bring them wine and a company of chefs to cook their dinner, they must have felt they deserved these comforts and must, still, have had to struggle to keep aside their depression.

And when early the following morning they cantered down to inspect the Lists, still lashed by occasional squalls, they must have caught their breaths and gasped with misery.

The scene in the once gay amphitheatre was fit for a troubadour's lament. Although the grandstand had withstood the storm, very little else had managed to survive it. Harness and equipment were strewn about, broken lances eddied in the burn, here and there a piece of armour lay in the mud, already rusting, only heaps of sodden canvas marked the sites of their once magnificent pavilions.

If no quantity of time and money had been able to bring to life a tournament, no amount of study and expense, neither by artists at the Royal Academy, nor by Meyrick at the Tower of London, nor by Cottingham at Pratt's showroom, nor by Ducrow at Astley's Arena could have managed to reproduce a scene that was anything like this.

Here was a field of battle and of rout, at one sweep, fulfilling perfectly all the mixed demands of romantic gothicism. Owned by a peer of noble lineage, it was ancient, desolate, inspiring, chivalrous: and for those who had taken part—the most difficult of all conditions—its picturesque and medieval air had been felt and known as something real in their own personal, costly and bitter experience.

# Chapter Twelve

In this way the Eglinton Tournament, held on Wednesday, the 28th of August, in the third year of the reign of Queen Victoria, really came to an end. Failure always requires a scapegoat and so, as the weakest person available was easily the wretched Samuel Pratt, everyone made him the butt of their disappointment.

'I must write you a line of thanks for remembering me at such a moment,' Lady Londonderry scribbled to Disraeli who had just got married to Mary Anne, heading her letter 'From Eglinton Castle, Thursday, August 29th, 1839'

and I beg you will accept my sincere congratulations and very best wishes for your happiness.

You tell me to send you accounts of the Tournament which, alas! has been spoiled by the weather. Nothing could have been more perfect than all the arrangements. The lists all beautiful and most picturesque with all the tents and encampments. The procession was gorgeous and the whole reception splendid, 300 feet of temporary room having been erected, thousands and thousands flocking from everywhere, even from America when as usual in our horrible climate down came that sort of vicious, spiteful pour that never visits other countries except in the rainy season when people know what to expect and make their arrangements accordingly.

My 1st feeling was to sit down and cry—my 2nd to tear Mr Pratt into small pieces, not that he could help the rain, but for putting up tents that would not resist a shower, much less a deluge. The weather however today shows signs of repentance and amendment and tomorrow we hope for better things.

*Adieu*, you should hear again before I leave England, but I would not delay writing one line to assure you of the interest I take in your happiness which I hope is now fixed.

Believe me yours very truly

F. A. Vane Londonderry*

Lady Londonderry, as a woman of fashion and possibly the country's richest heiress, might easily have added her tears to the rain, tears of rage at not being seen for, having failed to be Queen of Beauty, she had hoped, at least, to outshine the latter in appearance. She had, therefore, worn a gown so encrusted with gold and jewels that she might, according to one of the observers, have exchanged the pearls on the headdress alone for two or three German Principalities.

Lewis Mark Mackenzie of Findon, a young officer sitting close to her and one of the few who managed to admire it, wrote to his mother the following week and did his masculine best to convey its effect.

The tilting commenced at ½ past 3 but perhaps before I proceed to give you an account of the tilting you would like to hear a little of the dresses of the ladies who were present and I will first tell you of Lady Londonderry's dress which was by far the most magnificent of all. The headdress was a velvet cap coming down to the shoulders, but as to its further description I cannot tell you but will shew you in your book of costumes, it was covered with pearls and diamonds and presented a most

* Disraeli MS at Hughenden.

splendid appearance. The dress was also of velvet (crimson I think) and across the breast were bands of solid gold about an inch and a half in breadth, set with precious stones, Emeralds, carbuncles and amethysts of a very large size. I should think there must have been about three of these bands besides quantities of diamonds all the way down the front of her dress, hers was certainly the most remarkable of all the ladies dresses, but all the others were very splendid and costly, altho' no one had so great a profusion of jewels about them as her.*

It was not, of course, only Lady Londonderry who wanted to collapse and give way to grief, for apart from all the other women who had spent months and considerable sums planning and perfecting their various dresses, and apart from many of the opposite sex who, like the local Irvine Archers—a band of Ayrshire Robin Hoods—had taken pains to equip themselves suitably, the unhappy host, poor Lord Eglinton, had longed to weep most bitterly.

For as well as the failure of the whole project and aside from the waste of a minor fortune, he, too, had worn an outfit, a superb suit of gilded armour fit, indeed, for a dashing German princling; and without a gleam of sun, let alone in the pouring rain, only a few of his friends had been able to see it.

Like nearly all relics of the Tournament, especially those belonging to the family, later generations of which have failed to realise its social interest and only thought it a monstrous folly, this suit was put to auction and now cannot be traced. Beautifully engraved with leafy scrolls, the breastplate decorated with a pair of wyverns, above which, from the Eglinton crest, was a 'lady dressed in

* The Mackenzie papers, Vol. 19, British Museum 39,200. f. 98.

ancient apparel', every part of it was richly gilt and, in the sun, its effect would have been magnificent. (See plate 16).

That only a handful of people close to him had actually seen how marvellous he looked was a fact that really depressed him. Not without a manly vanity, this was a little pinch of fate he was often heard to bemoan.

Apart from this he bore the fiasco wonderfully. He alone of all the Knights, even including Charlie Lamb, had behaved as though the sun had shone, had bowed and smiled to all the crowd and calmly rearranged the programme as though the curtailments had really been improvements. As befitted a noble leader, he had ridden first among the Knights and been the last to return to the comfort of the castle. And, as behoved the owner of the park, once he had taken off his armour and seen to the comfort of all his guests, he galloped back to the public stands and did what he could to help and cheer the spectators.

The admirable manner in which he behaved, his genuine anxiety and sorrow for others, his absolute lack of pity for himself, his perfect calm and natural cheerfulness were, according to all observers, hardly human or credible; from this moment justly earning him a reputation for invariable sportsmanship which he held for the rest of his life.

When after breakfast on Thursday, having returned from inspecting the Lists he called a conference of all the Knights and suggested they jousted again tomorrow, everyone's spirits rallied and began to rise. Every joiner on the Eglinton estate was employed in sealing the roof of the ballroom, every one of their wives and sisters was put to cleaning and drying the interior, the Lists were drained, the tents put up and as many repairs as possible made to the Grandstand.

Within the castle the activity was just as great. Maids washed and mended frantically, for most of the costumes had shrunk and were stained; armourers hammered and scoured like demons for much of the armour had been dented and was rusty; and after lunch, to keep their hands in, the Knights assembled in the drying ballroom, much to the annoyance of those who were cleaning it, and fought with staves and broomsticks. One of the combats even had to be stopped, Sir Charles Lamb restraining Charlie who, becoming completely involved, lost his sense of what was proper and almost got the better of Louis Napoleon.

The next day, Friday, dawned with a sky that was bright and cloudless. The procession set off in brilliant sunshine, great crowds assembled to watch it, the jousts were held with moderate success, the Knight of the Swan was winged in the arm and had to be attended by a Dr Guthrie, one of the several medical practitioners who, the Tournament letters reveal, had come to the event with their lancets and bone-setters; and although, according to the rules, Fairlie gained the highest score, Lord Eglinton was led to the Queen of Beauty and given the golden circlet reserved for the victor. There was even a form of medieval *mêlée* at which the Knights, divided into teams, charged one another in front of the Grandstand and tried, with a single blow of their swords, to cut off the crests from each other's helmets. They were meant to swipe and gallop on but Lord Waterford, failing to keep his temper, perhaps because he had lost his dragon, suddenly wheeled and pounded after Lord Alford. The two began to fight in earnest, providing the finest combat of the day, and the Knight Marshal, at extreme risk, was forced to rush between them waving his baton.

Then in the evening, in fancy dress, the disappointed guests of Wednesday arrived at last at the Castle. Regaled at first by a medieval banquet with every imaginable ancient dish—they had flagons of malmsey, bowls of syllabub, quarts of hippocras, pints of ping, boars' heads, pots of swan, lamprey pies, prymrose tarts and eight hundred pounds of turtle, escorted personally from London by a chef on the steamer *Sir William Wallace*. The meats were eaten from dishes of silver and the puddings consumed from others of gold, all of which had been specially commissioned from a firm of London goldsmiths. No accounts for the banquet exist but, as four hundred people were invited, the plate alone must have cost a sum that was fabulous.

Quite inevitably, many of the victuals were thought to be totally disgusting. William the Conqueror's favourite dilligrout smelled and tasted like a bran mash and the peacock pie had such a crust that Lady Londonderry was heard to remark that it must have been made of armour and supplied by Pratt. But the Pope's posset and flummery caudle were palatable and more sustaining; and after the usual toasts and speeches, and after the ladies had gone to the saloon, the Knights were able to stretch their legs and wassail.

Last, to the strains of Thompson's orchestra and the band of the 2nd Dragoon Guards, all of whom were dressed like minstrels at, one presumes, Lord Eglinton's expense, two thousand guests and friends danced in Pratt's marquee. Banked with vast quantities of flowers, hung with tapestries, carpeted with velvet and lit by thousands and thousands of candles in coloured lanterns and chandeliers, it moved the prosaic Dr Richardson—perhaps elated by draughts of drangollie—to liken its effect to Fairyland.

Certainly many of the company's dresses were of hardly mortal description. Aunt Jane was in dahlia satin with an Indian veil embroidered with gold; Lady Montgomerie, in

16. The Queen of Beauty, Lady Seymour, standing beside Lord Eglinton's helmet and breastplate. (an oleograph of a miniature by W. J. Newton)

rich cerise, had a headdress 'tastefully adorned with cameos'; Lady Graham, a popular beauty, her jewelled bosom swathed in green, had a string of pearls about her waist which might have been used for a skipping rope; a Mrs Campbell was 'trimmed with bullion'; Lady Charleville, a friend of the Lambs', was 'festooned with bouquets of precious stones'; many an aristocratic waist—like the Duchess of Montrose's in ruby velvet, was hidden beneath a diamond stomacher, fastened with emeralds, amethysts and sapphires in place of hooks or buttons.

Most of the men, too, were dressed magnificently. Lord Chelsea was suited in emerald velvet, Lord Maidstone mantled in golden lace, Lord Saltoun robed in crimson satin, Sir Charles Lamb in sky blue silk—all might have come from Oberon's Court to awaken Sleeping Beauty. In this respect Charlie Lamb was already ahead of the others for, having hidden Charlotte in Edinburgh at 105 Princes Street, he was able to wake her with a kiss whenever he liked. Still romantically and deeply in love with her, he was dressed as a knight of the 15th century in buckskin boots, violet hose, a long black velvet tunic held at the waist by a crimson belt on which was embroidered his chosen motto '*Une Seule*' and a single silver rose.

Friday, in fact, was quite a success although it was only a poor reflection of what Lord Eglinton had dreamed. For although the jousts had taken place, the Lists had been covered with a foot of mud; although the roof of the Grandstand had been mended, all the hangings had been torn to ribbons; and although the spectators had arrived and enjoyed it, many had come in ordinary clothes for their fancy dresses had been ruined.

As for the ball, splendid though it was, it was nothing better than a hundred others to which the people who had supped and danced were already thoroughly accustomed.

'The banquet took place in an immense temporary room', Louisa Stuart wrote in a letter to her friend, Lady Jane Bouverie,

> each knight having his banner held by a page behind him. Then followed a ball in an equally large temporary room. Some of the dresses were most absurd, others beautiful. Lord Fitzharris had a magnificent dress of green velvet and fur, which would have made a good drawing. I did a number of studies, from which I must try to give some idea of the beauty of the sight. The ball and banquet one could easily have dispensed with, being the same as such like in London, but the procession into the Lists, and the tilting, the *mêlée*, were such beautiful sights as one can never expect to see again.*

And Louisa's view of the Knights and the jousts was charmed by awakening love. Strange though it seemed to many of her contemporaries, she became enamoured of the 'Mad Wag Knight',† the dashing, rich but slightly insane Lord Waterford. Seeing him first as he rode to the Lists and from that moment falling in love with him, until she

---

\* *The Story of Two Noble Lives*—Augustus Hare, Vol. I. p. 207.

† 'His "eccentricities" as a young man, for which he was notorious, are thus described by Ralph Neville (*Sporting Days and Sporting Ways*, pp. 7-8). 'He painted the Melton toll-bar a bright red, put aniseed on the hoofs of a parson's horse and hunted the terrified divine with bloodhounds. On another occasion he put a donkey into the bed of a stranger at an inn. He took a hunting box in the shires, and amused himself with shooting out the eyes of the family portraits with a pistol. He smashed a very valuable French clock on the staircase at Crockfords with a blow of his fist, and solemnly proposed to one of the first railway companies in Ireland to start two wagons in opposite directions on the same line in order that he might witness the smash, for which he proposed to pay.'

The above quote is from a footnote to Lord Waterford's entry in the *Complete Peerage*.

married him three years afterwards—and, indeed, for the rest of her life—she cared for no one else.

As the moon set on Saturday morning the rain began to fall again with the same tropical ferocity. Vague plans, weather permitting, had been made to joust in the afternoon, but the high wind and thunderous clouds made such hopes impossible. And the fact was that most of the Knights, nearly all the Castle guests and certainly Pratt and the members of the press were frankly extremely thankful.

By Tuesday morning everyone had left and, so far as conditions permitted or were ever likely to do so for months, Lord Eglinton resumed a normal life and the Castle began to revert to its usual appearance.

In the great octagonal hall, however, where the Knights had assembled before the procession and where they had gathered, three days later, to say farewell to their generous host, a change was made in the decoration which was never afterwards altered.

Before they left, in the medieval manner, they presented their banners and shields to Lord Eglinton who hung them up on the walls with his own, their names and titles, in Gothic lettering, suitably painted beneath.

There these knightly trophies hung until in the early 1920's they were sold at auction as curiosities when the Castle was partially demolished.

Today the hall is open to the sky and all that remains of the Eglinton Knights is a faint, fading trace of some of their names.

As Coleridge wrote of Sir Arthur O'Kellyn:

> 'The knight's bones are dust,
> And his good sword rust;—
> His soul is with the saints, I trust.'*

* *The Knight's Tomb*, 1817 (?).

Their names were:

Alford
Beresford
Cassillis
Craven
Eglinton
Fairlie
Gage
Glenlyon
Hopkins
Jerningham
Lamb
Lechmere
Little Gilmour
Waterford

# Chapter Thirteen

## EPILOGUE

Any event which makes a splash which involves the lives of many people invariably affects others, too, by a simple form of chain reaction; and of this sequence of cause and effect the Eglinton Tournament provided an excellent example.

Apart, normally, from newspapers and journals, the most sensitive national sounding board is always the popular theatre; and of those in London, Astley's Amphitheatre was usually far the best. With *The DEAD SEA and The Crocodile's Grot*, which brought to a close *The SEIGE OF JERUSALEM*, even before the Tournament took place Ducrow published the following thrilling announcement. In the only copy which seems to be available, some of the lines at the end are missing but the treat in store for all who read it is clear.

Mr Ducrow is happy to inform the Nobility, Gentry and Visitors of the Amphitheatre, from the great sensation caused by the forthcoming chivalrous pageant of the TOURNAMENT at Eglinton Castle! Has induced him to form arrangements for the veritable Real Armour, and other decorations used on the occasion with complete suits for a Troop of Foot and Mounted Cuirassed men, constructed in Paris by that unequalled Manufacturer Mons. D. Baranger, who executed those so admired in the Jewess. The Theatre is undergoing extensive alterations for the above purpose (when those Ladies and Gentlemen who may not have an opportunity of witnessing the Representation . . . (words missing) . . . of the most extraordinary, faithful and Gorgeous Delineations ever produced in the . . . (rest of the words missing)*

Ducrow's version was a great success and 'attracted immense audiences.'† In a letter to a friend, Wilson in Edinburgh, Sir Walter Scott's biographer, Lockhart, who had been to the rehearsals in St John's Wood and had also seen Ducrow's announcement, wrote what he thought of the one and predicted of the other.

Astley's, to be serious, is a better thing by far than, from witnessing the rehearsals, I expect the performance to prove.‡

Most of the people who went to both agreed that his prophesy came true.

Other take-offs on the subject were equally effective. At Covent Garden the whole Tournament starred in the Christmas pantomime. With all the trimmings of Mother Goose, Puss in Boots, etc., etc., the last and most spectacular scene was a 'Grand Moving Panorama of the Clyde from Glasgow to Eglinton.' With a 'short knight and a long day', a 'short RAIN' for the Queen of Beauty, and heaps of spears which became umbrellas, the lovers at last, luckily for them, were transported to the 'Realms of Sunshine.' On the whole, the critics liked it but, as one of

---

* Astley's playbills, the Enthoven Collection, Victoria and Albert Museum.

† *The New Monthly Belle Assemblée*, October, 1839.

‡ *Life and Letters of John Gibson Lockhart* by Andrew Lang, Vol. II. p. 211. Lockhart to John Wilson, Professor of Moral Philosophy at Edinburgh University, August 26th, 1839.

them wrote laconically, 'At the fall of the curtain there was much applause, mingled with something that was not applause.' The panorama, however, was 'very beautiful.'

At the Adelphi, the celebrated Yates produced a full length drama.* Based on Ainsworth's novel *Crichton* with Yates himself as Henri de Valois, the knights appeared on actual horses, the armour and costumes were supplied by Pratt and the stage was lit, in the final scene, by the very turquoise chandeliers that Starr and Mortimer, the London silversmiths, had supplied for the banquet at Eglinton. Entitled *The Knight of the Dragon and the Queen of Beauty*, Lady Seymour's husband went to see it.

India Board
November 20, 1839.

I had no time to write you yesterday, for I went to see some lunatics, and, happy to say, I found a few returned to their senses, and fit to be let out; examining these people took the whole afternoon. In the evening I went with M. Stanley and Byng to the Adelphi, where we saw the latter part of *Jack Sheppard*, and then a piece called the *Tournament*, or, as the actors pronounce it, 'Tournamong'; they also called 'joust' 'a juice'. It was the stupidest thing ever seen; the queen of beauty entangled her hair in the long flowing wig of one of the knights, and they were held fast together, which made us laugh; and Yates, fearful that such laughter might injure the performance, turned to our private box, and begged us not to laugh—rather an impudent request! However, we had no more chance of laughing; it was too dull.'†

---

* On Monday, Nov. 18th, 1839.
† *Letters of Edward Adolphus Seymour*, p. 90. Bentley and Son, 1893.

Thus, at last, some of the participants, Knights and Squires, peers and gentlemen, who had taken part in the actual affair, had a chance to see what the world thought of them, and to laugh at themselves as well.

One such who had been to the rehearsals but had not, for an unrecorded reason, taken part in the final event was a Member of Parliament, Colonel Fane, as the papers put it 'yclept the Honest', who lived in Oxfordshire at Wormsley Park. A second cousin of Lord Burghersh whose opera, *The Tournament*, he had much enjoyed, he was very amused at the show at the Adelphi and decided to hold a minor tournament himself.

Less in sympathy with the deeds of old than he was with the struggles of Sancho Panza, he determined to mount his knights on donkeys and make the affair a burlesque. On the 6th of August the following year, almost the Tournament anniversary, he and his friends assembled at his home, armed themselves with kitchen hardware, and, before an immense gathering jousted in front of his house.

For this tournament the weather was cloudless, and five thousand local inhabitants watched it. The Thame band provided the music, led by guardsmen in crimson lace and nine children with penny trumpets; the procession began with a Wormsley Herald; the Knight Marshal was a Colonel Drake; the Lord of the Tournament was Colonel Fane; his son, John, was Knight of the Gridiron; other knights were teapots or kettles; and the Queen of Beauty in Elizabethan costume, although apparently of feminine shape, displayed, the crowd were surprised to observe, above an extremely *décolleté* bodice, a beard and black moustaches.

Then, in the evening, in a nearby barn, three hundred friends and neighbours sat down to a sumptuous banquet. One of the knights had composed a song to the tune of

'The King of the Cannibal Islands' which, as the port went round and round, they began to sing uproariously.

> Oh! have you heard the news of late
> About a very famous fête,
> For if you've not, it's in my pate,
> The Tournament at Wormsley:
> Where knights did meet their arms to pass,
> And each was mounted on an ass,
> And Eglintoun it did surpass,
> For *that* to this was quite a farce:

*Chorus:*

> Houst'em, joust'em, tilt away,
> Donkeys gallop, and kick and bray,
> I never saw so funny a day
> As the Tournament at Wormsley.*

The following day when the knights departed they gave their host a presentation—a pewter inkstand, two feet high, of twelve gallons capacity. The symbolic meaning of this is lost, if, that is, there was any at all, although the article itself survives, almost impossible, indeed, to get rid of, embedded now in the hall at Wormsley, usually filled with umbrellas. Perhaps it stood for nothing at all and was just a final schoolboy dig at the other Knights in Ayrshire; for they, when their own Tournament had ended, had given Lord Eglinton, as a mark of gratitude, a handsome silver trophy.

The Eglinton Trophy, which survives too, was made by Garrard, the London silversmiths, designed by the artist, Edmund Cotterill, whose special bent was creating silver ornaments. Nearly five feet in height, it rose from a wide crenellated base round the sides of which were the shields of the Knights to form an ornate Gothic pulpit beneath a pinnacled canopy. Here stood the Queen of Beauty,

* Family papers, Wormsley.

placing a wreath on the brow of the Lord of the Tournament. Beside him rode the Knight Marshal with squires and halbardiers.

Much praised at the time of its construction, much ridiculed, inevitably, afterwards as a gross piece of Victorian materialism, it is once again widely approved as a fine example of the type of work of the period. Certainly no one who likes the Gothic and enjoys a display of Victorian skill can fail to admire its robust romantic magnificence.

Two hundred and thirty-nine of Lord Eglinton's friends subscribed to it, the maximum amount allowed being twenty guineas.

'You hear, I suppose that we have entered into a subscription to present Eglinton with a piece of plate, to commemorate the revival of the days of chivalry!' wrote Jerningham's Esquire, W. Stephenson, to Lady Shelley of Michelgrove.*

I don't know if our ancestors were equally pugnacious, but we cannot even carry this through without quarelling! A committee had been formed to carry this into effect; at the head of it was Lord Londonderry (not to promote the pugnacity, but the subscription), and till he left the Castle all went smoothly. But, after his departure the names of Burghersh and Lord Chelsea were added, which was no sooner made known to the King of the Lists than he wrote a most frantic letter, declaring they ought to have nothing to do with it, and withdrawing his own name. I have not heard since if the matter has been set right, but I believe the first intention was to take him at his word!

* *The Diary of Frances Lady Shelley*. Ed. Richard Edgcumbe. 1913. Vol. II, p. 261.

Four years were needed to complete the trophy which now stands, for all to admire, in the County Hall at Ayr.

No one can read of an item like this, let alone of the Tournament itself, without considering the cost; and although the bill for the Trophy survives—£1,775:0:7d— all the principal accounts for the Tournament are missing. Nothing remains in the family archives, now safe in the Edinburgh Register House, except the following sundry and minimal items:

Expenses in connexion with the Tournament, 1839:—

| | | | |
|---|---|---|---|
| Sawing Timber | £98 | 8 | 5½ |
| Carriage of do. | 42 | 11 | 0 |
| Timber bought | 11 | 5 | 4½ |
| Sundries | 20 | 3 | 8 |
| Constables and Others | 184 | 7 | 6 |
| Joiners and other workmen and labourers paid by Gardener per separate Account Book | 486 | 2 | 0 |
| | £842 | 18 | 0 |
| Value of Timber from Estates | 666 | 9 | 0 |
| | £1,509 | 7 | 0 |

Expenses in connexion with the Tournament, 1840:—

| | | | |
|---|---|---|---|
| Timber | £942 | 16 | 6 |
| Joiners | 90 | 3 | 11 |
| Carriage of Timber | 33 | 6 | 3 |
| Sundries | 149 | 4 | 3 |
| Constables Expenses of distributing tickets, etc. | 35 | 12 | 6 |
| | £1,251 | 3 | 5 |

Beyond these trivial details one has to fall back on the estimates given by the press. The average figure is £40,000 and taking everything into account such a sum is reasonable. With this amount, at that period, Lord Eglinton might have built a church—like, for example, St Luke's in Chelsea—or, like Lord Acland before the Reform Act, he might have spent it in rotten boroughs, virtually buying a couple of seats in Parliament. In either case, had he done so, history now might have said he had spent it better.

For except for the silver testimonial, the Knights' shields and banners at the Castle and a couple of suits of armour and dresses retained by one or two of the Knights, everything else went back to Pratt and after twelve months had passed nothing remained of the Eglinton Tournament at all.

Pratt decided to hold a sale which gave him another excuse for an exhibition. Everything left was put on view; the suits of nearly all the Knights, their esquires' armour, their retainers' costumes, their lances, gonfalons, crests, caparisons; even Little Gilmour's sword still bearing the stains of Jerningham's blood.

Then in June all was sold, Lord Waterford's equipment fetching the most—£240 with £20 in addition for its plaster horse.

As *entrepreneur* of the Tournament itself, Pratt undoubtedly made a profit, nearly all at Lord Eglinton's expense, for many of the others were slow in paying him and a few, even, never did so at all; Lord Eglinton, being the man he was, eventually settled their accounts. But the sale afterwards was not a success and most of the items, especially the dresses, went for sums that were trifling.

A knight's black velvet costume, slashed with white and bound with silver, including a cloak that was lined with satin—the bill for which had been £100—made only

234

ten guineas; an even finer geranium robe, actually worn
by Louis Napoleon, fell to Ducrow, the only bidder, for
a mere seventy shillings.

Many of the clothes, of course, had been spoiled by the
weather and in this connection it is worth considering
whether, knowing the climate in Ayrshire, such a party in
the open air should ever have been considered. The average
rainfall in August at Eglinton for the first quarter of the
present century was one inch every week and although
Lord Eglinton was bored by statistics and did not, in fact,
record the rain, he knew, naturally, as well as anybody, the
extreme likelihood of at least some heavy showers. A few
miles away at Rothesay the rainfall in August, 1839, was
more than five inches; compare this with the fall in Edinburgh which, during the same period, was rather less than
two. It was bad luck, nevertheless, that nearly the whole
of the monthly average seems to have fallen on the very
day that was scheduled for the opening of the Tournament.

If he should not be considered rash to have chanced so
much on his native climate, he must, at least, be severely
criticised for having shown such extravagance. This, with
a certain natural vanity, was the one really serious weakness
he displayed throughout his life. And of this span, after the
Tournament, he had more years than his present descendants—still trying to recoup his losses—might perhaps
have wished. Not that he lived long, however, for he died
suddenly when forty-nine, but in these last twenty-two
years he spent money at such a rate that any sums defrayed
on the Tournament were entirely insignificant. But he
never paused to consider finance, leaving that to factors
and solicitors, and even the locked pages of his diary
reveal not a single worry about his debts.

What they disclose, in a way, is infinitely worse. At the

time of the Tournament he was still a bachelor but shortly afterwards, in 1841, with needless haste and reckless obstinacy, against every caution of sense and judgement, he became engaged to the widow of a naval officer.

One of eight natural children of the second and last Viscount Newcomen, and perhaps because of this unhappy status—non-existent in the legal sense so that, on paper, her father was childless—she was so determined to maintain her position as the wife of a normal, legitimate nobleman that she made his life a pilgrimage of misery and Eglinton Castle a gaol.

'It was the great, the most important, error of my life,' he wrote of his marriage to Theresa Cockerell.

Hardly in one respect did we suit. She had many good qualities. She was good hearted, conscientious, resolute, truthful to the highest degree, devoted to me throughout, but she was irritable and domineering, she was of a most suspicious disposition and her jealousy amounted to absolute madness. There was not a servant whom she did not suspect of cheating her, there was not a woman under 70 who she did not fancy was making love to me. At church I was accused of ogling someone, in a Country house I was sometimes goaded to desperation by her jealousy, when I could not guess which of the party was the object of her suspicions, if I was absent for a few hours I found her generally in tears and pacing about the room in a species of frenzy, and I was called on to give an account of how I had spent my time, if I was detained later than usual at the House of Lords, I was forthwith accused of the worst conduct. I have had to carry her upstairs to her room in hysterics, because she was jealous of an ugly woman of 50, I have had to run out of the room to prevent a scene which would have disgraced us both. The greater portion of our nights used to be spent in fierce altercation; I have known her dash herself against the wall and beat her head on the floor, I snatched my razor away when it was at her throat, I struck a bottle of laudanum out of her hands when it was at her mouth. All this too went on without the shadow of a cause for it. I never during the 13 years we lived together was faithless to her in thought, word, or deed.

His avowal of chastity is almost certainly honest for although in his teens and early manhood he had lived as promiscuously as anybody else, he changed entirely after his marriage, gave up hunting almost at once, sold his stud within the decade and, whenever he managed to escape from home, devoted himself to politics. For this, in the end, he received his reward, twice serving as Viceroy of Ireland under Conservative governments.

There were plenty of sneers at this selection and all the obvious jibes were quickly made about him. The year was 1852, the Gothic Revival was still in force—indeed more so than ever before—and the front cover of *Punch* for January showed the British Lion as King of a tournament, Britannia as Queen of Beauty beside him, and Mr Punch, the triumphant victor, receiving a wreath for defeating Humbug and Folly.

With great pleasure the DIRECTOR of the NEW PALACE THEATRE, WESTMINSTER respectfully announces to the Nobility, Gentry and Clergy that the Performances at this establishment have recommenced under new management. The Company has been completely reorganised. The comic entertainment of *Dublin Castle* will be revived for Mr.

EGLINTOUN, and the splendid real armour will be introduced, as worn at the Scottish Tournament.*

Thus, with jokes of a similar caste, *Punch* and others announced Lord Eglinton's appointment. Everyone lived to eat their words for he proved to be the best Viceroy there had been for a generation.

'Sociable, jovial, frank, open,' he was always ready to talk to the humblest, perfectly impartial on the question of religion, entirely fair in domestic politics, and grandly hospitable to all.

He even managed, on certain occasions, to score a point on his wife. Whenever he gave an official Drawing Room he had, in accordance with established protocol, to bow gravely to all the gentlemen and to greet their wives and daughters with a gentle kiss. He once, according to a note in his diary, embraced nine hundred and thirty in a single evening. It was almost more than Theresa could bear and if he approached them rather warmly, as he sometimes did, at the end of the evening she used to hiss nervously behind him and once was heard to mutter, 'It is too much.'

She died unexpectedly the following year, meeting a sudden and painful death courageously. Of middle height, handsome figure, dark hair which fell in ringlets and, in repose, an agreeable face, she was well aware of her destructive weakness and had always managed, at least, to control herself in public. She bore Lord Eglinton four children, one daughter and three sons, from the second of whom, George Arnulph, the present male line of the family descends.

With such an unfortunate marriage behind him, endured with gentleness for thirteen years, Lord Eglinton swore he would never attach himself again but when in Ireland in

* Feb. p. 123.

17. Cartoons in *The Tournament* by Richard Doyle

| Pratt arming Jerningham | Marquess of Londonderry and Jester. M'Ian | Mackay and Redbury |
| Heralds | Lord Glenlyon and the Railway Knight | Jerningham and Esquire |

18. 'The Eglinton Tomfooleryment'
(cartoon from *Cleave's Penny Gazette*)

1858 on his second tour of duty as Viceroy he fell in love with Adela Capel, the eldest daughter of the 6th Lord Essex and married her within the year. With her, sixteen years his junior, he was instantly intensely happy; and her death in childbirth two years later caused him a greater depth of anguish than any he had known before.

He, too, though unaware of it, had only months to live. On the 1st of October, 1861, he was having dinner with a friend at St Andrew's, Whyte-Melville, the father of the novelist, when he suffered a fit of apoplexy. During the day he had played some golf and had seemed in excellent health although for some months before he had been complaining of minor hallucinations. He never regained consciousness again and died on October the fourth.

He was so widely known in Scotland, so popular with every class, even amongst his political opponents, such a grand and familiar figure at every public and sporting event, always fit, cheerful and vigorous, that when the news of his death was published people could hardly believe it; and the warmth and sincerity of all his obituaries moved many who had hardly known him to feel a personal bereavement.

'What a loss Lord Eglinton was!' exclaimed the editor of *Blackwood's Magazine* in a conversation recorded later.

Of him it may emphatically be said that honour was his polar star, and no consideration whatever could induce him to swerve one step, to the right or the left, from what he believed to be the path of duty.*

To his large circle of personal friends the loss was infinitely greater. His finest quality was generosity; many people whom he hardly knew often stayed at Eglinton for weeks, and those whom he loved—like his natural sister

* *Blackwood's Magazine,* Nov. 1861.

R

and the three daughters of his wife's first marriage, each of whom he dowered nobly—missed him bitterly with all their hearts and were never again, in the head of the family, to find such a sympathetic patron.

'I remember as a little boy my father's poignant regret at the death, at the age of fifty, of the thirteenth Earl of Eglinton,' wrote Abbot Hunter Blair.*

The Abbot's father was the son of Sir David, then approaching his eightieth birthday, who, thirty years before, had refused to allow Lord Eglinton a horse at Eton. It is pleasant to observe such a happy ending to what must have been a strained neighbourly relationship, and pleasant, too, to record how it came about.

On the 10th of March, 1856, five years before his death, Lord Eglinton wrote to Sir David the following letter:

> St James's Sq.
> March 10, 1856
>
> Dear Sir David,
>
> I have this morning been informed by Messrs Hunter, Blair and Cowan that the Trust created by my grandfather has been closed, and that you are at last released from the duties imposed on you by it.
>
> While I congratulate you on this escape from a business which must have caused you so much trouble and anxiety during the many years it has endured, I beg that you will receive my very sincere thanks for the kindness and assiduity which have distinguished you in the performance of your duties.
>
> May I trust that you have long since forgiven any hastiness, and even rudeness, of which I may have been guilty during the earlier portion of our connection, and

---

* *A Medley of Memories.* Sir D. Hunter Blair, 1919, p. 113.

that you have had little cause to complain of me since I have attained to years of discretion.*

With best regards to Lady Hunter Blair, believe me,
Very sincerely yours,
Eglinton & Winton.

Sir David answered him three days afterwards:

My Dear Lord,

I don't think I ever in my life received a more gratifying and pleasing letter than your's of the 10th of March just received. I shall keep it as a treasure to my dying day.

I assure you I have long since entirely forgotten any little *contretemps* that may have formerly happened in the management of the Trust in its early days. The uniform kindness & friendship you have constantly evinced to me & my whole family since you became your own master have been a source of great delight to me, and I shall ever deeply feel that the cordial expressions of regard you bestow upon me deserve my best gratitude.†

Thus, with characteristic sincerity, Lord Eglinton achieved the Trustees' blessing and, so far as they were concerned, atoned for the sins of his youth.

No one reading the Eglinton history and learning the appalling cost of the Tournament can fail to wonder what, if anything, the Trustees did to prevent it. Dealing as they were with a headstrong nobleman, the answer is that whatever they attempted was bound to come to nothing; for as a result of the Act of Parliament, all Lord Eglinton's money was his own and their only legal responsibility was to clear the debts at Ardrossan.

* Family Papers, Blair.
† Family Papers, Blair.

And during the first half of his life, that is to say until he got married, he always behaved exactly as he chose and absolutely refused to listen to criticism. Such an attitude was almost inevitable, given his upbringing by his aunt' and mother, both of whom spoilt him hopelessly, given the fact that he held a peerage—a tremendous asset in the 19th century—and given his enormous wealth. Having decided to hold a tournament, and having all the means to do so—the place, the money and the organisation—nothing in the world except the law or, of course, an act of nature, certainly not a former Trustee, could have made him agree to stop it. Remaining cheerful, polite, hospitable, even inviting Sir David to attend it which, in fact he actually did, his son squiring Little Gilmour, dressed in the style of Henry VIII, Lord Eglinton brushed aside his advisers and refused to be warned of its cost. For this he must take the full responsibility; only his step-father and his brother Charlie can reasonably be said to share a little of the blame.

Apart from failings in this direction and apart from a certain lack of ambition which, at least in early manhood, enabled him to live without a care—only hunting, shooting and racing, all of which were harmless enough but hardly worth his exclusive attention—his character was sociable, open, manly and immediately attractive to all who came to know it. He was never heard to show his temper, never seen to be rude or unkind, always ready to help his friends, just as gay when he lost a game as he was when he usually won it. For, from his very earliest manhood, he had been extremely athletic; and few could manage better on a horse, run so tirelessly behind a hare, master him at tennis, squash or racquets or beat him at fives or billiards.

The happiest part of his life was spent on the turf and here he made a genuine contribution. Apart from winning all the classics, and apart from owning a magnificent stable which, with typical impetuosity, he sold suddenly for 2,500 guineas, hardly a fifth of what it was worth, his personal example of sportsmanship and honour at a time when doping and swindling were rife, helped to achieve that standard of honesty of which the racing world is proud today.

After his marriage he changed, naturally, but far from being embittered by unhappiness he merely lost a little of his gaiety and turned his mind to those duties for which by birth he was placed. Not endowed with outstanding intellect but full of judgement and common sense which made him an invaluable chairman of committees, he was by conviction a profound Conservative and was one of the Whips of his party in the House of Lords. At home in Ayrshire he was Lord Lieutenant, patron of innumerable sporting events and Lord Rector of Glasgow University; always proud of his family history, he engaged Sir William Fraser, the antiquary, to write the *Montgomerie Memorials*.

But, in the hearts of his family today, all these excellent qualities are blurred by his terrible extravagance. This weakness was perhaps inherited for many of his ancestors had led the way; but they at least had died with something to show for it. At least his grandfather had built a harbour and at least all his other forbears—from 'Greysteel' to Mundegumbri—had either actually increased their wealth or left a promise of substantial capital improvement.

But Archibald William, Earl of Eglinton, Earl of Winton, Lord Montgomerie, Lord Seton and Tranent in Scotland, Baron Ardrossan in the United Kingdom, Hereditary Sheriff of the County of Renfrew, Knight of the Thistle and Doctor of Laws only left an honoured name, substantial debts as Viceroy of Ireland, many others for racing and hunting and one of £40,000 for the whim, at the age of twenty-seven, of holding a friendly tournament.

When, in 1872, Disraeli was planning to write *Endymion*, an historical novel of the 1830's, he decided to include an account of the Tournament and wrote to the former Lady Seymour to ask for anecdotes and souvenirs.

'My Dear Mr Disraeli,' she answered from 30 Grosvenor Gardens on October 31st:

> I am very unwell or I would have answered before your letter of Oct. 26th. I do not know what I can find of the Eglinton Tournament, except a colored print which I will send you—I had all sorts of relics, points of splintered spears with the colours of the Knights but a stupid old house-maid considered them as 'rubbish' as she said, and burnt them together with a Blessed Palm that I had caught in mid air from the Pope's own hands, but I will certainly look out whatever I can find.
> Ever most truly yours
> Jane G. Somerset.*

Such a reply must have struck Disraeli as symbolic, and although the book was a fair success and is still useful to students today it had only a short and inaccurate account of the Tournament.

Yet, in regard to the event itself, what indeed can be said about it? Genuine tournaments must have been thrilling when the knights were tough and used to jousting and were able to ride and fight with skill and ferocity. But the Eglinton Tournament, for all its cost, for all the care that was taken to arrange it, for all the practice put in by the Knights, never really came to life and was never more than an aristocratic pageant.

Viewed now in the telescope of history, it throws an interesting light on the period and the way in which the Gothic image, like Rebecca's charms in the Lists at Ashby,

* Disraeli MSS, Hughenden, E/VI/T.1.

drove frantic the wisest men that lived. But as an attempt to revive the past it was plainly a total failure.

During the reign of Charles VII in the first half of the 15th century when jousts were still extremely savage, a Turkish ambassador at the Court of France is said, when watching a certain tournament, to have made the following comment: that if it was in earnest it was not enough, and if it was a game it was too much.*

This remark was remembered and quoted when, in 1559, Lord Eglinton's kinsman, Count Montgomerie, fatally wounded the King of France.

Three hundred years later it was used, too, for the Eglinton Tournament. For naturally, after a little while— especially when the costs were known—as the sun rose on the Age of Steam while the Gothic spirit blossomed in architecture and reached sublime heights in poetry, some harsh facts had to be faced by all who actually wished to be shining knights.

For those who had tried it, the *preux chevaliers* who had left their shields and banners in Ayrshire, had found out from their own experience that the Turk's verdict was only too correct.

---

* 'Si c'etait tout de bon, ce n'etait pas assez, et que si c'etait un jeu, c'etait trop.' (Leber - *Coll. des Dissertations* XI, 363).

# APPENDIX I

The following is a list of some 18th and 19th century tournaments:

| Date | Place | Remarks |
|---|---|---|
| 1750 | Berlin | Held by Frederick the Great. See Carlyle Vol. V. p. 262. |
| 1769 | Parma | In honour of the marriage of Ferdinand, Duke of Parma, to Maria Amelia, Archduchess of Austria. A splendid affair, magnificently recorded in a book by Bodoni. B.M. Pressmark 650:c:6. |
| 1777 | Sweden | Given by Gustavus III who wrote that he wished to revive tournaments of the age of chivalry in order to counteract the present day effeminacy. Journal of the Royal Armoury of Stockholm, V. iv:4. |
| 1778 | Philadelphia | In honour of the retirement of General Sir William Howe. Known as the 'Mischanzia', it was organised by Lord Cathcart, a young officer. His family seat was in Ayrshire, and he lived to see his grandchildren take part in the Eglinton Tournament 61 years later. It is well described in the *Annual Register* for 1778. |

| Date | Place | Remarks |
|------|-------|---------|
| 1781 | Sweden | |
| 1785 | Sweden | |
| 1788 | Sweden | |
| 1791 | Copenhagen | |
| 1791 | Dresden | |
| 1799 | Sweden | |
| 1800 | Sweden | This was the last of these tournaments in Sweden (until 1894) because they were felt to be unlucky. Many spectators were injured on this occasion. Some were shot by two excited knights; others were squashed when the Grandstand collapsed; the rest were laid out by an epidemic of measles. |
| 1800 | Vienna | At about this time the Emperor Francis I built a special Gothic Tilt Yard at Laxenburg and held tournaments there. |
| 1814 | Vienna | On the 20th November in honour of the Allied Sovereigns. A MS account of this is possessed by the Duke of Atholl. |
| 1827 | Firle Place | A tilting party by Viscount Gage. |
| 1828 | Malta | Held by the officers of the Garrison in the Palace Square, Valetta. |
| 1833 | Barcelona | Held in honour of the accession of Isobel as Queen of Spain. |
| 1839 | Turin | Held by the King of Sardinia in honour of a visit by the Hereditary Grand Duke Alexander of Russia. |

| Date | Place | Remarks |
|------|-------|---------|
| 1839 (June) | New Orleans | This and many other tournaments were held in the southern states of America during the 1840's and 1850's. They were inspired by the same Gothic fever that was over-running Europe. See R. G. Osterweis, *Romanticism and Nationalism in the Old South*, Yale Historical Publications, Vol. XLIX, 1949. |
| 1839 (August) | Ayrshire | The Eglinton Tournament. |

[APPENDIX II — A FACSIMILE]

# Programme

OF

# THE PROCESSION

FROM THE CASTLE TO THE LISTS,

AT

# The Tournament,

AT

# Eglinton Castle,

AUGUST 28th and 29th, 1839.

LONDON: PRINTED BY J. DAVY, QUEEN STREET,
KING STREET, NEAR LONG ACRE.

# Programme.

---

---

## MEN AT ARMS,

In demi Suits of Armour and Costumes.

## MUSICIANS,

In rich costumes of Silk—their Horses trapped and caparisoned.

## TRUMPETERS,

In full costume—the Trumpet and Banners emblazoned with the Arms
of the Lord of the Tournament.

BANNER BEARERS of the LORD of the TOURNAMENT.

## TWO DEPUTY MARSHALS,

In costumes, on Horses caparisoned.
Attendants on foot.

## The Eglinton Herald,

In a Tabard, richly embroidered.

TWO POURSUIVANTS,

In emblazoned Surcoats.

## The Judge of Peace,

### (LORD SALTOUN.)

In his Robes, and bearing a Wand, on a Horse richly caparisoned.

RETAINERS,

On foot, in costumes, carrying heavy Steel Battle Axes.

## Officer of the Halberdiers,

On horseback, in a Suit of demi Armour, with a Gilt Partizan.

HALBERDIERS,

On foot, in Liveries of the Lord, carrying their Halberds.

MEN AT ARMS,

In demi Suits of Armour.

## The Herald of the Tournament,

In his Tabard, richly emblazoned with emblematical devices.

---

## The Knight Marshal of the Lists,

### (SIR CHARLES LAMB, BART.)

GROOM.  In a rich embroidered Surcoat, and embossed  GROOM.
and gilt Suit of Armour—his Horse richly
caparisoned, &c.

Esquire,                                               Esquire,

LORD CHELSEA.                          MAJOR McDOWAL.

ATTENDANTS OF THE KNIGHT MARSHAL,
In Costumes of his Colours, Blue, White and Gold.

HALBERDIERS OF THE KNIGHT MARSHAL,
In Liveries of his Colours, with their Halberds.

## Ladies Visitors,

LADY MONTGOMERY,         LADY JANE MONTGOMERY,

MISS MACDONALD,

On Horses, caparisoned with blue and white Silk, embroidered with Gold
and Silver, each led by a GROOM in costume of their colours.

---

## The King of the Tournament,
### (MARQUIS OF LONDONDERRY,)

HALBERDIER.     In his Robes of Velvet and Ermine,     HALBERDIER.
and wearing his Coronet—his Horse
richly caparisoned.

Esquire,                                    Esquire,

COLONEL WOOD.                        H. IRVINE, Esq.

HALBERDIERS,
In Liveries, as before.

---

# The Queen of Beauty,

GROOM.       (LADY SEYMOUR.)       GROOM.

In a rich Costume, on a Horse richly caparisoned—a Silk Canopy borne
over her by Attendants in costumes.

### LADIES ATTENDANTS ON THE QUEEN,

In rich costumes.

### PAGES OF THE QUEEN,

In costumes of her colours.

Esquire,                 Esquire,

F. CHARTERIS, Esq.

---

# The Jester,

In a characteristic costume, bearing his sceptre, on a Mule, caparisoned
and trapped, with bells, &c.

### RETAINERS,

On foot, in Liveries of the colours of the Lord of the Tournament.

---

## The Irbine Archers,

In costumes of Lincoln Green, black Velvet Baldric, Rondelle, &c.

### CLAUDE ALEXANDER, Esq.

| | |
|---|---|
| LORD KILBORN | A. CUNNINGHAM, Esq. |
| SIR ROBERT DALLAS | C. S. BUCHANAN, Esq. |
| CAPTAIN BLAIR | SIR A. HAMILTON, Bart. |
| STUART HAY, Esq. | CAPT. MONTGOMERIE |
| J. BROWNLOW, Esq. | J. BURNETT, Esq, |
| — HAMILTON, Esq. | HONBLE. J. STRANGWAYS |
| CAPTAIN BLANE | GEORGE RANKIN, Esq. |

RETAINERS of the LORD OF THE TOURNAMENT.

HALBERDIERS of the Lord, in Liveries of his colours.

MAN AT ARMS,        THE GONFALON,        MAN AT ARMS,
in Half-Armour.          Borne by a Man at Arms.          in Half-Armour.

## The Lord of the Tournament,

### (EARL OF EGLINTON.)

GROOM.        In a Suit of Gilt Armour, richly chased;        GROOM.
on a barded Charger—caparisons, &c.
of Blue and Gold.

#### The Banner

Borne by LORD A. SEYMOUR.

Esquire,                Esquire,                Esquire,

G. DUNDAS, Esq.        F. CAVENDISH, Esq.        G. McDOUAL, Esq.

RETAINERS of the LORD, as before.

S

HALBERDIERS OF THE KNIGHT OF THE GRIFFIN,
In Liveries of his Colours.

MAN AT ARMS,     THE GONFALON,     MAN AT ARMS,
in Half-Armour.     Borne by a Man at Arms.     in Half-Armour.

## The Knight of the Griffin,

### (THE EARL OF CRAVEN.)

GROOM.     In a Suit of engraved Milanese Armour, inlaid     GROOM.
with Gold; on a barded Charger—caparisons
&c. of Scarlet, White and Gold,

Esquire,     The Banner     Esquire,
THE HON.     Borne by a     THE HON.
F. CRAVEN.     Man at Arms,     F. MACDONALD.
    in Half-Armour.

RETAINERS.

————————

HALBERDIERS OF THE KNIGHT OF THE DRAGON.
In Liveries of his Colours.

MAN AT ARMS,     THE GONFALON,     MAN AT ARMS,
in Half-Armour.     Borne by a Man at Arms.     in Half-Armour.

## The Knight of the Dragon,

### (MARQUIS OF WATERFORD.)

GROOM.     In a Suit of polished Steel Fluted German     GROOM,
Armour; on barded Charger—caparisons, &c.
of Blue and White.

Page,
LORD JOHN BERESFORD.

Page,
MARK WHYTE, Esq.

Esquire,
Sir CHARLES KENT.

The Banner
Borne by a
Man at Arms.

Esquire,
L. RICARDO, Esq.

RETAINERS.

---

## HALBERDIERS OF THE KNIGHT OF THE BLACK LION.

MAN AT ARMS,
in Half-Armour,

THE GONFALON,
Borne by a Man at Arms.

MAN AT ARMS,
in Half-Armour.

## The Knight of the Black Lion,
### (VISCOUNT ALFORD.)

GROOM.

In a Suit of polished Steel Armour, on a
Charger—caparisons of Blue and White.

GROOM.

Esquire,
THE HON. MR. CUST

The Banner
Borne by a Man
at Arms.

Esquire.
T. O. GASCOIGNE, Esq.

RETAINERS.

---

## HALBERDIERS OF THE KNIGHT OF GAEL.

MAN AT ARMS.
in Half-Armour.

THE GONFALON,
Borne by a Man at Arms.

MAN AT ARMS.
in Half-Armour.

## The Knight of Gael,
### (VISCOUNT GLENLYON.)

GROOM.

In a Suit of polished Steel Armour, on a
barded Charger—caparisons, &c. of Green,
Blue, and Crimson.

GROOM.

| Esquire, | The Banner | Esquire, |
|---|---|---|
| Sir David Dundas. | Borne by a Man at Arms. | John Balfour, Esq. |

RETAINERS.

---

## RETAINERS OF THE KNIGHT OF THE DOLPHIN.

| Man at Arms, in Half-Armour. | THE GONFALON, Borne by a Man at Arms. | Man at Arms, in Half-Armour. |
|---|---|---|

# The Knight of the Dolphin,

### (EARL OF CASSILLIS.)

Groom.    In a Suit of engraved Steel Armour, inlaid    Groom.
with Gold, on a barded Charger—caparisons,
&c. of Scarlet, Black and White.

Esquire,                                                        Esquire,

---

# The Knight of the Crane,

### (LORD CRANSTOUN.)

In a Suit of polished Steel Armour, on a
barded Charger—caparisons, &c. of Red
and White.

Esquire,                    The Banner                    Esquire,
Borne by a Man
at Arms.

---

## RETAINERS OF THE KNIGHT OF THE RAM.

## THE GONFALON,
Borne by a Man at Arms.

# The Knight of the Ram, _×_ *Swan—*

## (THE HON. CAPT. GAGE.)

GROOM.    In a Suit of polished Steel Armour, on    GROOM.
a barded Charger — caparisons, &c. of
Blue, White and Crimson.

Esquire,                 The Banner                 Esquire,
R. MURRAY, Esq.       Borne by a Man         J. FERGUSON, Esq.
at Arms.

---

## HALBERDIERS OF THE BLACK KNIGHT.

MAN AT ARMS,      THE GONFALON,      MAN AT ARMS,
in Half-Armour.      Borne by a Man at Arms.      in Half-Armour.

# The Black Knight,

*Mr. Glover*
## (JOHN CAMPBELL, ESQ. OF SADDELL.)

GROOM.    In a Suit of Black Armour, on a barded    GROOM.
Charger—caparisons, &c. of Black.

Page,                                              Page,
MASTER J. FLETCHER.                    MASTER FLETCHER.

Esquire,                 The Banner                 Esquire,
CAPT. BLAIR.          Borne by a Man          CLANRANALD.
at Arms.

### RETAINERS.

---

## RETAINERS OF THE KNIGHT OF THE SWAN.

MAN AT ARMS,      THE GONFALON,      MAN AT ARMS,
in Half-Armour.      Borne by a Man at Arms.      in Half-Armour.

*[the programme continues for another five pages]*

# BIBLIOGRAPHY

*PART ONE*

1. The Eglinton family papers, the Scottish Record Office, Edinburgh.
2. *The Memorials of the Montgomeries*, by Sir Wm Fraser, Edinburgh, 1859.
3. *Historical Memoir of the House of Eglinton and Winton*, by John Fullarton, 1864.
4. *Origin and History of the Montgomerys*, by Count Bo Gabriel de Montgomery, 1948.
5. *History of the House of Seton*, by Viscount Kingston, 1829.
6. *Kay's Edinburgh Portraits*, by James Paterson, 1885.
7. *Chapters from family chests*, by Edward Walford, 1887.
8. *Ayrshire families*, by G. Robertson, 1823.
9. *History of the County of Ayr*, by James Paterson, 1847.
10. *Survey of Ayrshire*, by W. Aiton, 1811.


*PART TWO*

1. *The Eglinton Tournament*, text by 'B', Drawings by Edward Courbould. Published by Hodgson & Graves, London, 1840.
2. *The Eglinton Tournament*, text by the Rev. John Richardson, LL.B. Drawings by James Henry Nixon. Published by Colnaghi & Puckle, London, 1843.
3. *The Tournament*. Drawings by Richard Doyle. Published, London, 1840. The related text is in his *Journal for* 1840, published by Smith, Elder & Co. London, 1885.

4. *The Passage of Arms at Eglinton*. Anon. Published by Stewart and Murray, London, n.d.

5. *The Field of the Cloth of Gold of Eglinton*, by H. Curling. Published by Sampson Low, London, 1839.

6. *The Grand Tourney*, by James Bulkeley. Published by Saunders and Otley, London, 1840.

7. *The Eglinton Tournament*, by Peter Buchan. Published by Simpkin, Marshall & Co. London, 1840.

8. *An Account of the Tournament at Eglinton*, sketches by W. Gordon. Text by James Aikman. Published by Hugh Paton, Edinburgh, 1839.

9. *Grand Tournament at Eglinton Castle*. A Broadsheet sold for one penny in Edinburgh by N. Bowack, 46 Leith St. J. Neilson, Printer.

10. *Guide to the Tournament*. Published by Maxwell Dick, Irvine, 1839.

11. *The Tournament*. A mock heroic ballad with eight illustrations by Alfred Crowquill. Published by Thomas M'Lean, Haymarket, London, 1839.

12. *Backward Glances*, by James Hedderwick, LL.D. Wm. Blackwood & Sons, Edinburgh, 1891.

13. *Autobiographical Reminiscences*, by James Paterson. Maurice Ogle & Co. Glasgow, 1871.

14. *Kilwinning*, by Wm. Lee Ker, M.A. Published by A. W. Cross, Kilwinning, 1900.

15. *Through the Long Day*, by Charles Mackay; W. H. Allen & Co. London, 1887.

16. *Recollections*, by John Richardson, Published 1856, by C. Mitchell, London.

17. *Memoirs of a Bow Street Runner*, by Henry Goddard, Ed. Patrick Pringle, Museum Press, London, 1956.

The files of the following newspapers for 1838/39 at the following places:

| | |
|---|---|
| *The Aberdeen Journal* | Aberdeen University Library |
| *The Ayr Advertiser* | Ayr Public Library |
| *The Ayr Observer* | Glasgow Mitchell Library |
| *The Dumfries and Galloway Courier* | Glasgow Mitchell Library |
| *The Glasgow Argus* | Glasgow Mitchell Library |
| *The Glasgow Chronicle* | Glasgow Mitchell Library |
| *The Glasgow Courier* | Glasgow Mitchell Library |
| *The Glasgow Herald* | Glasgow Mitchell Library |
| *The Perthshire Courrier* | Perth Public Library |
| *The Paisley Advertiser* | Paisley Public Library |
| *The Stirling Journal* | Stirling Public Library |
| *The Scotsman* | National Library of Scotland, Edinburgh |

At the British Museum Newspaper Library, Colindale:
*The Age*
    *Bell's Life in London*
    *Bell's New Weekly Messenger*
    *Bell's Weekly Messenger*
    *Cleave's Penny Gazette*
*The Court Journal*
*The Court Gazette*
*The Evening Chronicle*
*The Evening Mail*
    *Franklin's Miscellany*
    *John Bull*
*The Morning Chronicle*
*The Morning Herald*
*The Morning Post*
*The Observer*
*The Penny Satirist*

*The Social Gazette*
*The Spectator*
*The Times*
*The Weekly Despatch*

American papers at the above library:
    *Daily National Intelligencer*, Washington
    *New York American*
    *National Gazette*, Philadelphia

# Select Index

265